THE NOVELS OF
STEVE MARTINI

THE LIST

"ABSOLUTELY IRRESISTIBLE . . . [A] wild and wooly tale."   —*Kirkus Reviews*

"INTRIGUING ANTAGONISTS: the man of action versus the woman of thought. Their dueling turns *The List* into a fast, and often funny, offering."   —*Chicago Tribune*

"GREAT GOOD FUN . . . the final paragraph is worth the price of admission."   —*Cleveland Plain Dealer*

"THE PLOT BARRELS RIGHT ALONG, Abby is a strong and sympathetic character, and the climax is nicely twisty. Along the way, Martini gets in some sharp asides on the nature of fame."   —*The Seattle Times*

"AN EXCITING, SURPRISING ENDING . . . Martini deftly conceals the killer until the last flaming finale."
—*Booklist*

"SWIFT PACING AND MULTIPLE PLOT TWISTS."
—*People*

THE JUDGE

"RIVETING . . . a suspenseful tale, right up to the satisfying climax . . . legal thrillers don't get much better than this."   —*Publishers Weekly*

"A COMMANDING VOICE . . . the author answers just about every question you've ever had about the games lawyers play."   —*The New York Times Book Review*

"MARTINI, a former trial attorney, is fascinating on legal strategy."   —*People*

continued . . .

W9-AZT-331

PRIME WITNESS

"RIVETING, YOU-ARE-THERE IMMEDIACY . . . ingenious . . . nail-biting . . . fascinating . . . first-rate . . . Prime is indeed the word for this involving read!"
—*Publishers Weekly*

"THE TRIAL BEGINS and Martini rolls up his sleeves to do what he does best . . . packs a satisfying punch."
—*Kirkus Reviews*

THE SIMEON CHAMBER

"CHILLING . . . PROVOCATIVE . . . STUNNING."
—*Publishers Weekly*

"A FINE FOOT-TO-THE-FLOOR THRILLER!"
—*New York Daily News*

"INTRIGUING TWISTS AND TURNS."
—*The Orlando Sentinel*

"THRILLING . . . a winner . . . Martini demonstrates a confident and deft control of literary suspense . . . excellent, top-quality adventure."
—*The Sacramento Bee*

CRITICAL MASS

STEVE MARTINI

JOVE BOOKS, NEW YORK

CRITICAL MASS

A Jove Book / published by arrangement
with the author

PRINTING HISTORY
G. P. Putnam's Sons edition / September 1998
Published simultaneously in Canada
Jove international edition / April 1999

ISBN: 0-515-12583-0

A JOVE BOOK®
Jove Books are published by The Berkley Publishing Group,
a member of Penguin Putnam Inc.,
375 Hudson Street, New York, New York 10014.
JOVE and the "J" design
are trademarks belonging to Jove Publications, Inc.

PRINTED IN THE UNITED STATES OF AMERICA

This book is dedicated to the selfless men and women of science who work to combat the dangers of nuclear proliferation, and in particular the people of the Russian Republic who have managed against impossible odds to keep the deadly genie in its bottle.

There were people in Hiroshima whose shadows were printed by the blast on the concrete walls of buildings and pavement. These shadows can still be seen. Some of the bodies that made them were never found. It was as if they never existed. There are those who have seen these shadows scorched on the hard ground, to whom they are mere curiosities of history—images of a time that has passed. If that is all they have come to be, then they are indeed the angels of apathy.

CRITICAL MASS

PROLOGUE

The *Dancing Lady* was not a thing of beauty. She was sixty-three feet of welded steel, much of it dripping rust down her sides like dried blood.

Her raised forecastle deck and flaring prow were plowing the dark waters west of Vancouver Island at seven knots. She climbed the swells and plunged into the deepening troughs, straining to make headway in weather that was quickly turning foul. Her usual crew of five was down to three—the skipper, Nordquist; his son; and one other crewman who was like family, and like the family was now working for nothing.

The boat was a durable stern trawler with twin diesels designed for deep water. On her aft deck was a massive reel, and wrapped around it was a half mile of open mesh netting, window dressing for this cruise.

The *Lady* was a bottom fisher, a work boat as common as ten-penny nails in these waters. It was the reason they used her. She wouldn't be noticed even by overhead surveillance.

She rolled in the swells and wallowed in the troughs. Hydraulic fluid seeped from the hoses that drove her massive boom, and one of her engines was a thousand hours past a needed overhaul, but Nordquist didn't have the money for the repairs. Working eighteen-hour days in bone-numbing cold water and ice-covered riggings, Nordquist was going broke.

His wife was doing her shopping at the food bank, and loans were overdue on the boat. And still, the federal government did nothing to stop the Canadians from overfishing the areas west of Vancouver Island. They had killed the northwest salmon runs and were now busy taking everything they could find off the bottom. Nordquist and his compatriots couldn't afford the campaign contributions necessary to bribe their own government into action.

He looked out over the prow from the raised wheelhouse. She kept losing RPM on the starboard engine. Nordquist had to fight to hold her steady in the increasing swells. They rose up in front of him like ominous mountains, there one instant, and gone the next. The *Lady* was starting to pound. The weather was getting worse.

His son was straining to find a horizon through the fifty-power binoculars, eyes fixed to the west.

"Oh, shit." The boy didn't have to say more.

Nordquist looked over his shoulder and saw it: a thirty-foot wall of water rushing down on them, on their starboard beam. He spun the wheel to the right, and thirty years of hands-on experience brought the bow of his boat like a knife toward the mountainous wall of water. It cascaded around the wheelhouse and shuddered the *Lady*'s steel to her keel. She plowed through and came out, plunging down the back side of the wave.

The wave had knocked the kid to the deck. He sat there in amazement, looking at his old man and marveling at his power to focus, even in the face of death.

THE ISVANIA WAS a rusted-out hulk, a remnant of the once powerful Soviet fishing fleet. She'd been condemned for scrap the year before, but like everything else in the new Russia, even this was behind schedule. Heading for the boneyard, she was on her last voyage. She crossed the Bering Sea, threading her way through the Aleutians and the Gulf of Alaska, then down the Canadian coast. Her holds, fore and aft, were empty except for a light load of scrap metal. In the captain's safe were papers transferring the ship's title to a scrap yard outside of Bangkok. She ran with a skeleton crew of seven and made only one brief stop at Prince Rupert on the Canadian coast to pick up a small load of lumber, which now rested, stacked on her decks. This was a cover in case she was stopped and boarded by coastal authorities, her justification for crossing the Bering Sea and hugging the American coast. Bills of lading showed the lumber to be delivered to Oakland, California, though her captain had no intention of going there. The lumber would be thrown overboard once *Isvania* dropped its real cargo. Then the ship would head west and south, toward the Indian Ocean and its final resting place.

The helmsman brought her five degrees to port as her captain, Yuri Valentok, strained his eyes through binoculars for anything on the horizon. The *Isvania* was taking on water in the forward hold and getting sluggish in the deepening troughs. The bilge pumps were handling it for now, but Valentok wasn't sure how long they would hold up. He couldn't see a damn thing through the binoculars. Drops of rain, driven by the wind, pelted the windows on the bridge like bullets. Only one of the wipers was working, and that was useless. The wind-whipped mist and froth from the waves created an impenetrable haze. Valentok could scarcely see the prow of his own ship. To make things worse, his radar was out. It hadn't worked since the ship left Vladivostok. Twice they'd had to come to a dead stop in shipping lanes for fear of hitting other vessels. They laid on their foghorn and hoped the other ships could see them on their own radar. *Isvania* was like everything else in their crumbling country: coming apart with no money for repairs.

Valentok carried onboard one other waybill for an additional piece of cargo, but it was only to be used in the event of an extreme emergency, if his ship was forced into port. This particular waybill was forged. If the item was discovered, the captain would argue that he didn't know the nature of the cargo. Whether it would work with the American authorities he doubted, especially given the nature of what he was carrying. He would spend a long time answering questions, perhaps a long time in jail. He wondered if American jails were better than those in Russia.

He went to his charts on the table and braced himself against one of its metal legs. He checked the ship's position one more time. If his calculations were correct, they were precisely 112 nautical miles due west of the Strait of Juan de

Fuca, the passage to Puget Sound, and the U.S. city of Seattle beyond.

Isvania's captain had never been to the U.S., though he had friends who sailed there recently, in a ship not unlike his own, a rusted-out scow ready for scrapping. It was becoming a common practice for Russian fishing vessels. They would clear customs and immigration, and as soon as the American officials left the ship, the entire crew, including her captain, would go over the side to start a new life, in a new land. They let the Americans deal with the scrap metal. Valentok thought he would like to go there himself one day, perhaps to Seattle when this was over.

————————

FOUR MILES TO the east in driving rain and surging seas, Jon Nordquist gripped the wheel of the *Dancing Lady* with a firm hand. He used the leverage of his body to fight off the force of a giant rolling comber as it slid under the hull and slammed against the rudder. The boat listed heavily to port. For an instant he thought perhaps she might not come back. Then she responded to the helm, slowly.

"It's turning to shit out there. Can't see a damn thing." Ben had his face pressed tightly into the covered scope of the ancient Furuno radar screen. "How the hell are we supposed to find it?"

"Keep looking." Nordquist cast a quick glance at his son and then back out to the mountainous wave that loomed before them, dwarfing the sixty-foot vessel. Their boat was like a matchstick in a flood.

The towering waves created vaporous green images on the radar screen like islands thrust up from the bottom of the sea. On the next sweep of the radar beam they were gone.

"She could run over us, and we'd never see her." Ben was scared, and it showed. He'd sailed in heavy seas, but nothing like this.

The thought of collision had entered Nordquist's mind, but it remained for his son to say it. For the moment he was more worried about broaching, or pitchpoling down the face of one of the waves, nosing in, never to come up again. There were a million ways to die at sea.

"Nothing." Ben pressed his head closer to the radar screen

until the pressure against his forehead actually hurt. "Besides, even if we find 'em, how the hell are we supposed to bring the thing on board in this?"

"One crisis at a time," said his father. He checked his watch. From his pocket he took a small black plastic object, not much larger than a calculator. With his teeth he pulled out the three-inch antenna and pressed a couple of buttons, then waited, one eye on the sea, the other on the portable global positioning satellite (GPS) unit in his hand. Two sets of numbers appeared, one over the other for longitude and latitude. The pocket GPS unit was not as reliable or accurate as its larger cousins that ran from fixed computers on bigger ships, but still it was not likely to be off by more than a few hundred feet. At this location the Russian ship should be no more than a quarter mile off their starboard beam, that is, if it was on time and hadn't gotten lost.

There was no way to communicate by radio. Other ships were certain to pick up the signal, perhaps the Coast Guard. They patrolled the waters, even at two hundred miles out, the limits of their jurisdiction. They had satellites and planes and used both to interdict drugs and track vessels carrying human cargo, seeking to deposit their huddled masses on American soil. Two vessels meeting in open sea were not likely to go unnoticed. For this reason a careful procedure for drop and recovery had been worked out. But would it work in this weather? Nordquist didn't know. No one had anticipated the fucking storm of the century.

HE TURNED HIS ship into the weather.

"All ahead slow." Valentok couldn't wait. Besides, the cargo he was carrying was not something he wanted onboard an instant longer than was necessary. *Let the Americans find it*, he thought. He had been paid handsomely to carry it, but it was their problem now.

He gave orders to raise the cover on the aft hold and swing the crane over the opening. He sent his first mate aft to supervise and watched from the outside starboard wing of the bridge as the cargo hook slipped into the hold and disappeared. He waited two anxious minutes. It seemed an eternity. The hook rose on its steel cable. Valentok saw it. It was attached to a heavy metal ring. Connected to the ring was a net, ringed with three large floating buoys. The entire package looked like a pouch closed by a drawstring at the top. Inside the net was an object wrapped in a canvas tarp. It wasn't large, about the size of a washing machine, and heavy for its size, though it was no problem for the massive cargo crane of the factory ship. It was lifted easily over the deck and swung toward the stern of the *Isvania*. Slowly it slipped into the water, the cable descending.

Valentok had his back to the bow of his own vessel, watching the action, when he heard a scream from the wheelhouse. He turned, and in a flash of lightning from the darkening sky, he saw it. Barreling down the face of an oncoming wave was a sixty-foot stern fisher, the glass on its forecastle windows gleaming in the flash of lightning.

"Hard to port." Without thinking Valentok gave the order to turn. His ship was still in the trough of the wave.

The helmsman didn't question, but spun the wheel.

Isvania began to heel to starboard. She listed as the luminous green and white wall of water hit her on the curve of her prow like a tidal wave. It washed over the forward deck and slammed into the windows of the bridge twenty feet up, blowing out glass like an artillery shell.

A thirty-foot wall of water swept down the companionway on the port side, slamming men and machinery into the bulkhead and washing them over the side. Like Niagara it swept toward the yawning uncovered hatch of the open aft hold. Thousands of tons of green water cascaded over the edge, down into the ship's belly.

Valentok's grip on the rail was the only thing that kept him from being ripped over the side by the onrushing water. Like steel, his fingers bit into the railing as he found himself contemplating the strange sensation of being totally submerged in the sea while standing on the deck of his own ship. He was waiting for the wave to pass, waiting for an eternity. He held his breath until his lungs felt like fire, until he realized that neither he nor his ship was coming up.

SHE TURTLED IN front of his eyes. There was a flash of barnacled keel and two mammoth bronze propellers still turning as the ship rolled over. Then, before Nordquist could blink, the Russian ship was swallowed by the sea.

He stood motionless at the wheel, stunned, his knees locked as cold sweat ran down his face.

He was quickly jarred back to reality by the pounding of the *Lady* as she plunged to the bottom of the wave's trough. He held his breath, wondering if the wall of water rising in front of him held a deadly surprise: a hundred tons of twisted Russian steel tumbling just under the surface.

He gripped the wheel, white-knuckled, and waited for the screech of metal ripping metal. The diesel engines lugged down as the *Lady* climbed the face of the wave and seemed to pass harmlessly up and over.

It shot from the depths directly in front of him, and Nordquist caught only a glimpse before he felt it slam against the hull, a stack of lumber still bound by its metal bands. It rolled under the hull of the *Lady* like a giant square log. Nordquist threw the engines into neutral, trying desperately to save the props. He felt the lumber bounce along the bottom and watched as it drifted to the surface behind them.

He had his back turned, so he got only a fleeting glimpse when he turned. There in the white-tipped froth on the crest of the next wave were three large orange buoys.

They slid from view down the back side of the wave.

"Did you see them?" Nordquist pointed for the kid to look.

His son's attention was focused toward the stern, to the place in the sea where the Russian had been swallowed.

"Shouldn't we go back?" He was looking now at his father.

"What for?"

"Maybe some of them are alive."

"None of them are alive," said Nordquist.

"How can you be sure?"

"Could you survive that?"

The answer was obvious to them both. Still the kid wanted to do the right thing.

"We could look," he said.

"For what? To make ourselves feel good?"

"If it was us . . ."

"It wasn't us. They knew the risks." Nordquist had no love for the Russians. His boat had been nudged twice in the last year by larger Russian trawlers seeking an edge in the good fishing grounds. They brought their huge factory ships in and took what they wanted. They would slice you in half if you got in their way.

"Don't argue with me. Turn that thing on." The old man gestured with his head toward a drab green metal box mounted on the boat's console as he struggled with the wheel.

In the mounting seas, the kid had to fight his way back across the wheelhouse to the radarscope and the metal box mounted next to it. He flipped the switch, and the screaming signal nearly pierced his eardrums. He reached for a knob on the side and squelched the noise. The subsonic transceiver was Russian military surplus, part of the deal. It could pick up a signal a hundred miles away. This one was coming from a transmitter very close. It could not be heard on normal marine radio bands. The transceiver was a backup in case the two vessels missed each other in the open ocean. The buoys were designed to float for four days, then to sink with their cargo if no one picked it up. The subsonic transmitter would beam its signal for the entire period until it went down. Then the pressure of the deep sea would crush it.

The signal was confirmation. Somehow they'd delivered before they went down.

"How . . . ?" The kid looked at his father.

Nordquist shook his head. He wasn't sure.

The *Lady* mounted the next wave and Nordquist saw them again. He was drawing up on the orange buoys quickly. If he wasn't careful, he would run over them, foul his prop in their lines or net. Without power, in heavy seas, they would quickly join the Russian at the bottom.

"Get to the winch. Tell Carlos to come up."

"What about the pumps?"

"Forget the pumps. Right now we got to get it onboard."

Nordquist's son headed out the cabin door toward the open aft deck.

The old man brought the bow of the *Lady* into the wind and reduced power just enough to hold her in the heavy seas. It gave him lateral maneuvering with little or no headway. He would wait for the sea to bring the buoys to him.

They would have only one chance to pick them up. If they missed, by the time he came about in these seas, they would lose visual contact. Then they would have to track the package using the subsonic signal. Nordquist had been warned to get it onboard as quickly as possible and to turn off or disable the device. While the Coast Guard might not pick it up, American submarines, the so-called "killer subs" that hunted their Russian counterparts, listened on these frequencies. If they got curious, they might take a look.

Nordquist saw them on the crest of the wave, bobbing like orange barrels. Tethered beneath them in the depths probably fifteen feet down was the cargo, wrapped in a net. He had no idea of its weight or size. The fact that the Russian had rolled made him wonder if the load was heavy. Maybe that and the fact that a wave had hit them on the beam with so much weight over the side had caused them to capsize. If the Russian couldn't handle it, how could he?

Nordquist maneuvered using the wheel, as well as the throttle controls for the two engines. He guided the *Lady* so that the package would pass on her starboard side. Nordquist alerted the two men aft using the boat's bullhorn, then looked over his right shoulder and saw his son leaning over the side straining for a view. The men swung the boom over the side and with a long gaff guided its cargo hook toward the buoys as the current carried them along the side of the boat. Nordquist could hear the cable of the net's line scraping the hull as the load passed beneath them.

Suddenly he felt the *Lady* heel over heavily to starboard. The hook had snagged the buoys. The drag caused the *Lady* to make a slow, lingering turn in the trough, a ten-degree list, fifteen. This was what the old man was worried about: getting caught in the trough of one wave and hit from behind by another. The classic broach. She would roll and capsize.

He goosed the controls for the starboard engine, giving her more thrust on that side, then brought the wheel to port a few degrees. This brought the *Lady*'s bow into the wave at a forty-five-degree angle. The engines strained as she climbed the wall of water, dragging her cargo alongside.

The two crewmen struggled with the winch controls and finally swung the boom around the stern. They kept the cargo amidships and in the water, neutralizing its weight until they could get a break between seas to try to lift it onboard.

Nordquist tried to steady the boat as he looked out one of

the stern portholes from the wheelhouse. He saw smoke and
steam rising from the winch drum. The load was too heavy.
Even over the howl of the wind, he could hear the screeching
of the winch's clutch as it struggled to catch and pull the cargo
up out of the water. He could see the tethered cables below
the buoys as they rose slowly from the depths.

Another wave, and Nordquist had his hands full. He could
only hope that the weight of the load wasn't out of the water
yet. His eyes to the front, he deftly handled the engine throttles
and wheel to keep the boat balanced. The cargo dragging in
the water acted like a sea anchor and actually helped him. For
now, it was a friend. The moment they got it out of the water,
it would be another matter. If a wave struck, the load would
begin to swing like a pendulum. Its weight could bring them
over.

The boat seemed to settle in the water. The winch was
cranking again, smoke rising from the drum as it turned
slowly. Nordquist got the first glimpse of the tethered net. It
rose slowly, dripping seawater over the stern. The canvas
wrapping around the cargo had opened and filled with water,
adding to the weight.

Slowly it came up until it cleared the transom and hovered
over the stern. Another wave hit the prow of the *Lady*, and
the load began to sway with the motion of the sea. The kid
didn't wait. He panicked, pushed the winch lever forward and
the entire weight crashed down on the afterdeck. There was a
thunderous roar as the weight buckled one of the deck plates.
Splintered wood and tons of seawater spilled out of the canvas
cover as it ripped along one side. A small silvery sphere the
size of a grapefruit rolled out of the smashed container and
across the steel deck. It hit the gunwale with a deadening thud
and began to roll back the other way with the motion of the
ship.

Stunned, the two crewmen were frozen in place, their gaze
glued to the object now loose on the *Lady*'s deck.

From the wheelhouse, Nordquist could see it.

The men moved, trying to corral it, but they were too slow.
The *Lady* heaved forward over the crest of a wave, and the
heavy metal sphere rolled along the passageway, beneath the
forecastle deck and out onto the prow. Over the steel deck, it
sounded like a bowling ball. Nordquist could hear it slamming

against equipment and metal bulkheads. The only thing keeping it onboard was the boat's high gunwales. It careened around the boat like a pinball, slamming into a hatch cover. Nordquist could tell that it was dense and very heavy. He didn't know precisely what it was, but he had a good guess. The guys from Deming and Sedro-Woolley hadn't told him everything, but they'd given him hints, enough to put him on guard. He tried to warn his son with frantic hand signals. Finally he got to the microphone and pushed the button for the bullhorn.

"Stay away from it. Get clear." His words echoed from the loudspeaker mounted atop the wheelhouse.

The boy looked up at him, anxiety written in his eyes. They'd ridden heavy seas for days, survived a near collision with the Russian, and managed to snatch the buoys from the teeth of the storm. He wasn't going to lose it now.

The boy dove onto the deck trying to trap it between the steel gunwale and his outstretched hands. He got his fingers on it and held on, as Carlos came in on top of him.

"No!" Nordquist screamed into the bullhorn.

They managed to subdue it, trap it against the gunwale. With their bare fingers underneath, rubbing and chafing at the sphere, it seemed to coat their hands with something like shimmering chalk. The powdery substance filled the air and drifted against the steel bulkhead beneath the wheelhouse window. The sphere was like a magical substance, and very heavy. Neither of them had ever seen anything like it before.

From the wheelhouse above, Nordquist looked on, slack-jawed, from under dark, furrowed brows. For some strange reason, he didn't have to be told. He knew that his son was as good as dead.

ONE

FRIDAY HARBOR, WA

Burned out at thirty-two, she'd had enough.

They knock L.A., but it isn't the place. It's the people. Too many of them. Lincoln talked about the better angels of our nature, but even angels have limits. Put them in a congested maze, pump in heat and foul air, and you can watch while they rip off one another's wings. Joselyn Cole's were long gone.

Two years ago she pitched it in, sold her furniture, listed the condo at Marina Del Rey, and started looking for a life. She headed north, up the coast, and kept driving, reading population signs as she went. In three weeks traversing back roads and taking her time, she found she had gone about as far as she could without leaving the country. So she left the road and took a ferry. At her first port of call, she stopped, looked around, and decided she was home.

Friday Harbor in the San Juan Islands was a ninety-minute boat ride from Anacortes in Washington State. It may as well have been the back side of the moon. The island was small and the town was smaller. Some say it is like a scaled-down version of Martha's Vineyard. Joselyn would have to take their word for it, never having seen that other place. What she discovered was that it was quiet, and the people, for the most part, were friendly, while they minded their own business. Once the islanders realized that she was there to stay, she became a local. Acceptance was automatic. Within a week, the clerks at the little grocery store were all calling her by her first name.

It took a few months to hurdle the Washington State bar exam. Once she did, she hung out her shingle.

JOSELYN COLE
ATTORNEY AT LAW

Those who knew her for more than a week called her "Joss." Business was slow. There were some drug cases, mostly marijuana grows, nurseries in houses and old barns run from generators big enough to light a small city. The Feds could detect them with thermal-imaging devices that picked up heat from the Gro-Lites through a six-inch wall.

There are more than four hundred islands in the San Juan chain. Some of these are nothing more than a few rocks that disappear at high tide.

But with an international border only a few miles across open water, Victoria to the west, Vancouver to the northeast, the islands were a smuggler's paradise. Joss thanked God for small favors. With the small-time drug cases, the occasional DUI (driving under the influence), and a few divorces, it kept the wolf from her door, even if her door wasn't much.

She learned that it was possible to survive without a VCR or, for that matter, a television. On Friday nights she found her feet tapping the floor to the strains of Jimmy Buffet off a hi-fi she had bought when she was a kid. She was slowly reading her way through volumes from the local library. Occasionally, she would lose all sense of economic perspective and buy a new paperback.

In winter it was dark by four in the afternoon, and the streets of Friday Harbor were usually empty. Most of the summer businesses shut down for the season. Like bears, the fishermen and blue-collar types would hole up in any cave they could find, mostly the few dimly lit bars that form hangouts for the locals. The winter was when you found out who was hard-core.

Joss stared across her desk into the face of one of these hard-core types. Weathered like leather, its only soft aspect were two brown, basset-hound eyes looking back at her.

"There oughta be something you can do. I mean at least get 'em to pay the doctor bills." George Hummel was smiling at her, but she could tell that he was scared. George was not exactly a picture of health. He had some signs of bleeding at the gum line. His hair was falling out like dry straw. Hummel was a fisherman, or at least that was what he did for a living when he wasn't too sick to take to the water. He was a client, one of five sport fishers trying to get the state to pay disability benefits for what they claimed was an industrial-related illness. All five men had the same symptoms: red blotches on the skin, loss of appetite, bleeding gums, hair loss. George had become their spokesman.

"I know damn well it's industrial," he said.

"You don't have to convince me, George."

"Fine, then do something. I'm running out of money." His savings were nearly gone. His wife and kids had to eat.

From his lawyer's expression, he could tell that the prospects were not good.

"What are the doctors saying?" She took notes on a legal pad at her desk, George's file spread out in front of her. Its contents were meager except for her own unanswered correspondence, mostly to doctors and state agencies that were not much help.

"The doctors. They don't know from nothing. They want to send me for tests to Seattle."

"Do it," she told him.

"It costs money. My health insurance won't pay. They say it's to pursue litigation, not for treatment."

The great insurance circle jerk. What the politicians, for a hefty campaign contribution, called "managed care": a panel of physicians under the insurance company's thumb saying "no" to anything that costs money. They had now managed to drive the system down the public's throat.

George told her that the insurance company was stalling, waiting for him to die. "Then it won't cost 'em anything."

"I need medical records," said Joss. "I can't do anything without a diagnosis."

For the state to pay disability, she had to show some industrial connection, some job-related cause for George's condition. For this, she required a medical expert to go out on a limb, to tell her in medical terms the probable cause of George's illness, exactly what he had.

"We all know what it is. It's the damn cheese-heads." This was George's unflattering term for his neighbors across the border to the north.

"They been pumping raw sewage into the sound at Victoria forever. They take our fish; now what's left all has three eyes. I got one the other day," he told her, "was startin' to grow front legs like a dog."

The fight over diminishing salmon runs had taken on the specter of a war. Ferries stopping at Friday Harbor and headed for Sidney on Vancouver Island had been blockaded by fleets of commercial fishing boats in protest and held for hours at the docks. The Canadians had retaliated by blocking the Alaskan ferry up north. Indian nations had gone to court to uphold fishing rights granted in treaties with a term that was supposed to last "as long as the grass grows and the winds blow." Unfortunately, the salmon couldn't breed fast enough to cooperate. There were too many fishing boats chasing too few fish.

"It's a good theory, George." She was talking about the charge of Canadian pollution. "But I need evidence, medical records I can take to the state."

"I'll bring 'em the fucking fish," said George. "The one with the two front legs."

They'd had this conversation before. It was becoming circular. His hands were trembling. He was scared. He had slipped markedly since their last meeting two weeks earlier.

"They gave me a transfusion. Did you know that?"

"No, I didn't."

"Well, they did. Last Thursday. They told me I'm anemic. Red blood count is low."

There might be something new in his medical records. Joselyn made a note. "They didn't say anything about what might have caused this anemia?"

"Not to me," he said. "They asked me if I'd been around any chemicals."

"That's a start."

"You would think they would suspect something."

Doctors didn't usually like litigation, even if it wasn't aimed at them. Their suspicions don't often end up in their notes. She didn't tell George this. It would only make him feel more forlorn. She made a note to get the latest medical records.

"I gotta leave something for the family," he told her.

When she looked up from her pad, she could tell by his expression that George was thinking cancer. He had crossed the great divide. He knew he was dying. Joselyn knew he was right.

She told him not to give up hope, tried to cheer him up. "It may not be as serious as you think." They both knew she was lying.

"I'll talk to the doctors. Try to get them to pressure the insurance company to cover the tests. Rattle their cage with threats of a bad-faith claim for withholding coverage. It might get their attention."

"Might?" said George.

"There are no easy answers."

"I don't know how long I can last."

She told him to hang in, to come back in a week. "I may have something by then." Their meeting was over.

"You will call me?" He looked at her with that hopeful basset-like gaze.

"As soon as I know something."

"You'll call the doctors?" He moved reluctantly toward the door.

She was up from behind the desk, moving with him now. "This afternoon. I'll follow it with a letter." She took one of his hands. It was shaking, like palsy.

George's wife was waiting in the outer room. He refused to allow her to attend these sessions, afraid she would only become more depressed.

There was another guy sitting in the reception area eyeing George as he stepped through the door. The man tried to be discreet, but he couldn't help looking. George was one of those sights that no matter how hard you tried, you just couldn't divert your eyes—like the man without legs propped against a building wall selling pencils from a cup. He made you feel uncomfortable, but you had to look.

The other man was well dressed: cashmere sweater and Boston loafers. He had a lean face, sandy-colored hair, and deep-set eyes. There was that serious business look about him, something that said no nonsense. He wore an expensive wristwatch and a tan with that glow of humidity that screams the tropics. Just sitting in the chair, he looked like money. Not one of her usual clients.

She could feel the man's eyes move over her as his gaze left George.

George tried to put a brave face on bleak circumstances for his wife. "Ms. Cole's gonna help us with the doctors. Gonna get insurance coverage for the tests."

He was making promises Joselyn might not be able to keep.

George's wife smiled. "I knew she could help us."

"You will call me?" said George.

"Don't worry, George. I said I'd call, and I will."

"Good." George shook her hand. His wife slipped an arm under his, more to help him than to be escorted, and they were gone, through the door and out to the parking lot.

When Joss turned, the man in the chair was now on his feet, blocking her path back to the office.

"Joselyn Cole?"

"Yes."

"Dean Belden," he said, extending a hand as if she was supposed to know who he was.

"Have we met?"

"I was referred by Dick Norman down at the bank."

She searched her memory. Then she remembered. She'd met Norman once at a Chamber of Commerce meeting.

"Well, if he's sending me business maybe I owe him a lunch."

"I'm sure he'd enjoy it. Your office is pretty new." The guy was looking around, appraising the empty walls and the reception cubicle with its frosted glass window, closed and dark.

"I haven't had time to get a receptionist yet."

"Good help is hard to find." He looked at her and smiled.

Belden was a quick study. He knew instinctively it was not time but money that was the problem.

"Your client there looks pretty sick." He gestured toward the door through which Hummel had just disappeared.

"Yes."

"You gonna be able to help him?"

"I hope so."

"Is it serious?"

She gave him a shrug.

"Sorry, I shouldn't pry. Too nosy sometimes. Suppose you couldn't say even if you knew. Wouldn't be kosher."

"No, it wouldn't."

"Still, I hope it's nothing contagious."

The thought of catching whatever George had never entered Joss's mind, not until that moment.

"I think we're safe. What did you say your name was?"

"Belden. Dean Belden. You can call me Dean."

"Well, Dean, what can I do for you?"

"Handle a little business," he said.

"Let's step into my office." She moved around him in that direction, and he followed her.

"I'm trying to set up a small plant on the island." He talked while they walked, not one to waste time.

"What kind of plant?"

"Assembly."

"Have a seat."

"High-end items." He sat in one of the client chairs as if he intended to all along, never missing a beat. "Electronics. Mostly switches used in industrial computers. It's not high volume, so transportation is not a major consideration. You might be wondering why I picked the islands?"

"Not really," said Joss. "Would you like some coffee?"

"No, thanks. We have a contract to supply another company up in Canada, so the location works well. I need to incorporate in Washington State. Get a business license. Comply with the taxing authorities. Employer I.D. number. The usual stuff," he said.

Joss was getting coffee for herself from the machine in the corner and wondering if maybe the guy at the bank had her confused with somebody else in town. Business law was not her usual fare, and as she turned back to her desk she ended up wearing the thought on her face.

"You can do this kind of thing, can't you? I'd be willing to pay a sizable retainer."

For the first time, he had her undivided attention. The sound of money.

"Oh, I could do it. I mean, incorporate a small business, pretty straightforward. It's just that I'm . . ." She was thinking of ways to cover the blank expression on her face. "I'm pretty busy right now. But I could probably squeeze it in." She picked up her calendar book from the desk and opened it, shielding the empty pages from his view. "I could move this around, and cancel here until next week." She looked up at him. "I could fit it in."

This could cut into reading time at the library and the parrot-head music hour at night.

He smiled like maybe he knew B.S. when he heard it. "And what's your usual fee?"

Before she could say a word, he said: "I'm assuming a hefty retainer against an hourly fee."

Belden must be flush. What Joselyn knew about business law she could write longhand on the cuticle of one fingernail. But it would include the fact that corporate documents were usually done for a flat fee. A few thousand dollars at most, depending on the complexity. In some places it could be done mail order.

"I guess I'm just curious. Don't get me wrong," she said. "It's not that I don't want the business. But why didn't you just hire one of the big business firms down in Seattle?"

"It'd cost me more," he said.

"Maybe," said Joss.

"Besides if I'm going to live and do business in the islands, I thought it would be best to have somebody here. I'm going to need somebody local on a regular basis for other matters."

Joselyn didn't want to press the issue and lose a client.

"What kind of matters?"

He offered a thoughtful expression. "Foreign licenses. Mostly to do business across the border. Pretty easy stuff. You've never done it?"

"No." She wasn't going to lie to him.

"I'm sure you're a fast learner. It's pretty simple. Like piloting a plane, once you've done it."

"I don't fly," she told him.

"I do."

"Why am I not surprised?"

He looked at her and they both laughed, like breaking the ice.

Belden was not unattractive. Closely cropped hair graying at the temples. He was over six feet and athletic in build. He wore a polo shirt, and stretched it in all the right places.

"Are you interested?" he asked.

Definitely, thought Joselyn. "I think I can put the documents together for you."

"No. No," said Belden. "I'd want to give you a retainer to serve as counsel to the company." He smiled and bared even white teeth that could be an ad for the dental association. There was a twinkle in his eyes, which were a shade of green she had never seen before.

"We could end up buying a substantial amount of your time," he told her.

"My professional time is for sale."

"But you are not." The way he said it was more of a statement than a question. She answered it anyway.

"I enjoy working for myself."

"Good. An independent woman. I understand. Of course it could cut into the time available for your other business." He looked at her and smiled a little as if perhaps he knew this was not a problem.

"I'll worry about that."

"Good. Then it's agreed." He reached into a pocket and came up with a checkbook and pen. "What kind of a retainer do you usually take?"

"On the island I don't usually see a retainer."

He looked up from his checkbook.

"Most of my clients are local," she explained. "I bill them, and they pay. When they can."

"How about ten thousand?" he said.

It was a good thing her chair didn't recline any further. She would have been on the floor.

"And for an hourly fee?" He looked up again.

She was having a little trouble catching her breath, but thought quickly: "How about two hundred an hour?" It was more than she charged her other clients, but it looked like Belden could afford it.

"How about three?" he said.

"You should be my business manager," she told him.

"I always like to think my lawyer will take my phone calls when I have a problem."

He had a light leather folder that he'd placed on the floor next to his chair. Now he reached into it and pulled out a manila letter-sized envelope, then started to write the check.

"I think all the information you'll need is in here." He nodded toward the envelope. "If you have any questions, my business card is there as well. Just give me a call."

"In the interests of full disclosure," she said, "I think there's something you should know."

He didn't look up. He was too busy putting all the zeros in the right places on the check.

"I know," he said. "You don't have an extensive practice in business law."

"Is it that obvious?"

"No."

"Then how did you guess?"

"The banker told me." Now he was looking at her across the desk, a piercing green gaze over an in-your-face smile.

"But you said he recommended me?"

"Oh, he did. Very highly. I asked him if there were any good-looking women lawyers in town." He was stone serious with only that little smirk. "It was a short list," said Belden. He said it shamelessly, so that she couldn't help but laugh.

She was still laughing when he passed the check across the desk, along with the file of information on his corporation.

She stared at it for awhile.

"Like I say, it would cost me at least as much down in Seattle."

From all appearances, Belden was a man who was used to getting his own way. There was something military about him, like he was used to giving orders and having them followed. She wasn't sure she liked it, but she liked the money. Maybe that's what bothered her, the feeling that she was selling out, trading her independence for a check.

"You've got the retainer, all the information. Then we're agreed."

She looked at the check again. "I suppose."

"Don't look so sad," he told her. "Having money should not make you depressed."

"Oh. It doesn't." She put a face on and smiled.

"That's good. Now tell me. What brought you to the islands?" He made it sound like business was over, pesky stuff out of the way. He knew what he wanted and was almost a little too focused and fast.

"What makes you think I wasn't born here?" she asked.

"You don't have the look."

"There's an island look?"

"A slight gathering of moss on the northern exposure," he told her. "You look . . ." He considered for a moment. "Like California."

"It's that obvious? I suppose the moss hasn't had time to form."

"That and the license on your wall." He nodded toward the certificate from the California Bar framed next to the one from Washington State.

"You have sharp eyes."

"Wait 'til you get to my teeth," he said.

That's what she was afraid of.

"What are you doing for dinner?" he asked.

"Sorry. I've got plans." Once she cashed his check, a nice steak and Jimmy Buffet, thought Joselyn. He was moving much too fast. She wanted to do some checking around town. See if anybody knew him.

"Maybe some other time."

"Perhaps. When do you want this done?" She tried to get back to business, tapped the envelope on her desk.

"Oh. I don't know. How long do you think it will take—without rushing?"

"A week, maybe ten days, if I don't run into any problems."

"Then I'll see you in a week."

He was up out of his chair. "No need to show me to the door. I can find my way. Next week, then."

"Next week."

TWO

SANTA CRISTA, CA

Gideon van Ry rocked lazily back in the old office swivel chair. It was ungainly and undersized for his tall, lanky body. In front of him the government surplus desk was stacked high with papers: three weeks of unread correspondence and reports. Van Ry was part of a U.N. arms inspection team and had just returned from the Middle East.

He was a product of the Cold War. Gideon had been born in Holland but raised in later years in the Soviet Union. His mother was Russian, his father Dutch. They had met in the university after the War, but the marriage was not to last.

Gideon learned his English, as every Dutch schoolchild does, in the public-school system, and his Russian during summer vacations living with his mother in Moscow. His university education came there, where he showed a flair for the sciences, and he was climbing through the hierarchy in the academic world of physics when the old Soviet Empire collapsed.

His specialty was nuclear magnetic resonance. He had spent two years in Southern California at Cal Tech, where he did not take a degree but learned everything there was to know about nuclear weapons design.

He had always been mechanically inclined, even as a child. He had taken his family's grandfather clock apart when he was eight. It had never maintained accurate time since. But his parents didn't have it repaired. His mother considered it a remembrance of his childhood.

Anyone watching might have feared that Gideon's slouching six-foot-five-inch frame would go over backward in the chair, except that his long legs served as a counterbalance. He turned a little to face the window as he studied the document in hand and ran long fingers through his long, wavy blond hair. He had blue eyes, dimpled cheeks, and fair skin.

"You have read this?" He spoke with a slight British accent. He was talking to the woman standing in the doorway to his office.

"Yes." Caroline Clark was a graduate student from Britain via Princeton University, where she had taken her undergraduate degree in physics. She was one of four interns assigned to work with van Ry on analysis and reporting.

There was a veritable stream of young interns who passed through the institute, remaining for anywhere from six months to two years. When they returned home, many of them, in time, went on to play prominent roles in the weapons control programs and policies of their own countries. It was one of the principal goals of the institute: to plant that seed in fertile multinational ground.

"Have you shown this to anyone else?" asked Gideon.

"Not yet. I was going to if you didn't get back today. I didn't think it should wait."

"You're right."

The notes were cryptic, typed quickly on an old typewriter. It was a note from an old friend of Gideon's, a fellow student from his days in Moscow. Gideon had maintained correspondence with him for several years during his studies at Cal Tech, but had not heard from him in more than a year.

Yuri Valentok worked deep in the bureaucracy of Russia's nuclear industry, one of the many bureaus that issued statistics and records on what was becoming a burgeoning business behind the old Iron Curtain: the dismantlement of nuclear armaments.

The Institute Against Mass Destruction (IAMAD) had gone to great lengths to maintain contacts with people who worked in this field. It fostered communication across national boundaries, all with a common purpose: the dismantlement of weapons of mass destruction, the science of nonproliferation.

IAMAD had gone to great lengths to avoid being accused of fronting for any government. Its information was available to the world. Anyone with the price could log on to its database, one of the most extensive lists of nuclear, biological, and chemical weapons in the world. Its purpose was to shine light into a dangerous crevice, the deadly and growing commerce in weapons of mass destruction.

Founded in the late 1980s, the institute had sprouted like a field of wild mushrooms until it now occupied a sizable Spanish colonial bungalow in the historic area of old Santa Crista. It was a deceptively tranquil location for activities that took its resident scholars and graduate students to some of the hottest spots on earth: the Middle East, the volatile republics of the former Soviet Union, and the fractured former Yugoslavia, ethnic hotbed of the Balkans.

"What do you make of it?" he asked her.

She shrugged, a sign that she couldn't be sure. "It's possible it's just a case of poor record-keeping." It sounded a lot like wishful thinking.

"You know the problems over there. Limited staff, no money. Items get misplaced all the time."

"True." Still Gideon knew it had to be checked out.

"Could they have been dismantled?" he asked.

She shook her head. "If so the Pu-239 from them would have shown up in the stockpile of raw materials. It doesn't."

It was like the daily tally of cash drawers in a bank. If significant amounts of plutonium or highly enriched uranium showed up missing at the end of a month, alarms would sound off all over the institute and the information would be beamed around the world on its database.

Gideon checked his watch. There was an eleven-hour difference. "I don't think this can wait. If we have no one in place, I am going to have to call the director, get authorization for travel."

"You're going to Sverdlovsk?"

"I'm the only one who could gain access," said Gideon.

He was right. Sverdlovsk was one of four nuclear-dismantlement sites in Russia. Each was heavily guarded. None admitted observers from the West. But Gideon was Russian. He had been raised largely in Russia, at least in his later years, and had contacts in the Russian government, people who, if he approached them in the right manner, might allow one of the fellow countrymen access.

"It could be a mistake," said Caroline. "Someone could have transposed a number. You know how they're over-worked." She was talking about the Russian nuclear techni-cians, scientists, and military men, most of whom hadn't been paid in months.

"In which case we will not embarrass ourselves with an erroneous report to the international community."

She looked at him as if she was not sure what to do.

"What if it's not a mistake?" Gideon knew that as things grew more desperate in Russia, the risk of a guard being paid to look the other way, or a technician to smuggle a few kilos of uranium from a facility, grew with each passing month.

"When did you get it?" he asked.

"Two days ago."

"Then figure two weeks," said Gideon. The question was, if the items were taken, when was it done? Operating on the principle of the worst possible scenario, Gideon was already working backward to determine how long thieves may have had to transport the materials across national borders.

"As it stands we either have a mistake," said Gideon, "ad-mittedly a rather gross one . . ."

She agreed.

". . . or loose nuclear devices or dismantled devices with weapons-grade material on the loose. In any event, if we've caught it, the Russian authorities have had enough time to discover the same discrepancy. Check and see if there are any signs of an investigation."

Russian-language analysts, either at the institute or at the Defense Language Institute, would be scanning newspapers and radio news reports from the region. They would check to see if these were reporting anything unusual.

"Then you don't want me to check directly with Russian authorities?"

"Not yet." Yuri Valentok had written to him in confidence. If the institute checked with Russian authorities directly, they would want to know the source of the institute's information. It was important for Gideon to protect his source. He would have to make discreet inquiries, use what contacts he had to gain access without causing alarm in the Russian nuclear community. If he wasn't careful, all the doors would slam in his face and an internal investigation would be conducted. He was half Russian, but he had lived for years in the West. It would require some diplomatic skills.

She made a note. Caroline had met some of the Russian scientists and technicians on a tour the year before. They were dedicated people, and she found it difficult to believe that any of them would sell nuclear materials on the black market.

Gideon scratched his chin. "What troubles me is that two items are missing. Why would they take two?" He looked at her.

"In for a penny, in for a pound? That is, if there is a theft."

He shook his head. "Yes, but it increases the risk of detection."

There had already been several documented cases of black marketeering, mostly low-grade fissile materials being smuggled from former satellite countries into Afghanistan and peddled with indiscretion so that the perpetrators were quickly caught. The usual pattern of theft was in the nature of pilfering: a few grams of low-grade uranium, probably not weapons grade, taken over an extended period until the thieves possessed a kilogram or so. It was stuff that might be used for a "dirty bomb," something that would never reach critical mass for a chain reaction but that might produce a toxic effect and could, with enough high explosives, contaminate a considerable area.

But the information Gideon had before him was something different—two intact nuclear weapons with detonators. This was on a scale so bold as to be unbelievable. It was the reason Caroline did not buy it, and Gideon knew he would need more information to convince others, if it was something more than a mistake.

"What do we know about the items?"

She had the file in her hand, working notes that included information that was not usually entered on the institute's base. This was stuff not generally for public consumption. For reasons of security, IAMAD did not usually identify the precise location of weapons storage facilities or the items contained in them, even if they knew. This would only serve to mark them as targets for terrorists or the Russian mob.

Caroline fingered quickly through handwritten notes in the file.

"The missing items are from Sverdlovsk-45. The facility was renamed about a year ago. It's now called Lesnoy, a principal location for dismantling warheads in the southern central part of the country." She pulled a printout of a map from the file, walked over, and set it on the desk in front of Gideon.

"Here." She pointed to the location on the map.

"It stores both plutonium and weapons-grade uranium. According to our information, it's one of Russia's largest weapons-dismantling sites. About fifteen hundred a year."

"Sounds like a good place," said Gideon, "if the plan were to lose something. They are no doubt backed up with business."

She agreed.

"Inadequate storage facilities. It might take them a while to discover that something was missing. Do we know their security status?"

Caroline looked down the sheets clipped into the file. The International Atomic Energy Agency rated all facilities in the world where fissile materials were processed or stored.

She sighed. "It's unsafeguarded."

"I could have guessed." The Russians didn't have the money to meet international standards for security. In some places, there were holes in chain-link fences through which children routinely climbed to play, where only meters away were earthen bunkers of plutonium-filled canisters behind rusting iron doors. It was a prescription for disaster, one that was getting worse, not better.

"According to information from Valentok, it looks like the two items in question were scheduled for dismantling," she said.

"Do we know what they were?"

"It looks like they were relatively small, core assemblies complete with detonating devices for two field tactical nuclear artillery shells. One hundred fifty-three millimeter. Assembled in the sixties."

"So no PALS?"

She shook her head. "No."

PALS were shorthand in the trade for "permissive action links," the security mechanisms for nuclear devices that would prevent their detonation without approval from multiple levels of government control. Many of the devices made in the early 1960s, in both the U.S. and the Soviet Union, lacked such controls. This made them prime targets for terrorists. The weapon of choice if they could get their hands on them.

The look on Gideon's face said it all. Devices that could be hidden anywhere and detonated without much difficulty. A terrorist's dream. The question was whether they would work.

"Do we know the yield?"

She shrugged, shook her head. "According to the book, eight-tenths of a kiloton. Of course the book is notoriously understated." During the Cold War, both sides lied regularly regarding the potency of their weapons in order to gain an edge in arms treaties.

"If they're similar to comparable U.S. weapons," said Gideon, "they are probably somewhere on the order of between two and five kilotons."

This would make them small, easily transportable, and nearly as powerful as the devices that devastated Hiroshima and Nagasaki. Alone, either device could take out the downtown section of a sizable city. Detonated together, they could destroy Manhattan and kill a half million people instantly, leaving another half million to die of agonizing radiation poisoning.

He picked up the receiver from his phone and punched a two-digit number on the com-line. "Sally." It was his secretary. "See if you can get a meeting with the director for me early this afternoon. Tell him it is very important. Cancel my afternoon appointments. If you need to reach me, I will be at home." Gideon would have to pack. He didn't know how long he would be on the road.

He put the phone in its cradle, picked up his briefcase, and made sure his passport was still inside.

"Get me a flight, as direct as possible," he told Caroline, "from San Francisco to Moscow." He knew he would have to wait until he got to Moscow to make connections over the Urals into Siberia. He had never been to that forbidding place, and the thought sent a chill through his bones.

THREE

DEER HARBOR, ORCAS ISLAND

The 1979 Ford pickup crabbed its way up the dusty road, its ass-end off to one side like a dog whose hind quarters had been run over. It was splattered with so much off-road mud that dirt would no longer stick. In the rear window was a placard the size of a license plate:

HOW'S MY DRIVING
CALL 1-800-EAT-SHIT

The truck skidded to a dusty stop in front of the lead-gray metal building. Oscar Chaney got out and slammed the door.

Another man stood in front of the building next to a pile of stomped-out cigarettes.

"You're late."

Chaney shot him a look. "Send me a bill for your time."

"Why all the games with these redneck idiots? I don't get it. Why's the colonel using code names. It's like we're dealing with a legit government."

"Exactly for the reason that they are idiots," said Chaney. "Sooner or later, they will make mistakes. He doesn't want those mistakes to take us down. It's the reason you're to have no contact with them. Understand?"

The guy nodded. "Fine by me. Where did you get the truck?" Chaney's colleague looked at it, unimpressed, taking in all the dents and dirt, something from a destruction derby.

"My contribution to local color," said Chaney. "It makes me look like one of them, don't you think?"

"Fuck local color. I just want to get this over with and get home."

"Patience, Henry. With the money we're getting for this job, you can take a nice, long vacation."

They had worked together for nearly five years. The colonel had kept them together ever since their time in the Caucasus under U.N. auspices, where they'd met as part of a peace-keeping force. Peacekeeping. It was a joke! They were professional soldiers, and they weren't even allowed bullets for their weapons for fear they might create an international incident. The four of them had mustered out, Fritz from Germany, Oscar from the U.S., Henry from the U.K., and the colonel who'd taken his training in South Africa but packed a British passport. Now they were on their own. In the last two years, they'd made a small fortune hiring out their services.

"What's it like inside?" Chaney gestured toward the building.

"Four walls and a roof."

Chaney took a few steps and pushed his way past and through the half-open door. He took a quick survey of the building.

Inside was an empty concrete floor heavily stained in places by oil and grease. There were a few pieces of scrap metal in one corner and a workbench against the far wall. On it was an electric grinding wheel, bolted down, and a vise. There were a few soiled rags lying about on the bench and a handful of discarded hand tools, assorted wrenches, and a pair of pliers.

A spray of light flickered through the metal roof where somebody had missed a few screw holes and the sun had blistered away the caulking.

"Has it got sufficient power for the arc welder? I'll need a big welder."

"Yes. Plus running water and lights. There's a latrine out back."

Against one wall of the building was a large sliding door,

suspended from a metal runner. Chaney walked over, grabbed the door, and gave it a hefty push. It rattled open, sliding along the outside of the building, and stopped with a thud. The opening was about twelve feet wide and ten feet high, more than enough for the job he had in mind.

"Who owns the place?"

"A woman in a place called Kirkland. Over on the mainland. Her husband used to use it to do what he called 'parting out' cars, taking the parts from stolen vehicles and selling them separately."

"Ah."

" 'Til one of cars fell off a jack," said Henry. "Crushed his leg."

"Bad luck," said Chaney. "It will do nicely. Secluded. Out of the way. This car-parting business. Were the police involved?"

"No. I checked. The man was taken to another location before the ambulance was called. They dumped a car off a jack out on the highway and called them. Then they took their time and got rid of what was here. The police have never seen the place."

"Good. That is good."

"What do you know about the people who own it?"

"The guy walks with a gimp. The woman has money."

"Are they likely to come over here looking around?"

Henry shook his head. "No. I did what the colonel said. Told them we would pay cash every month. It's twice what they could get in rent from anybody else. I told them that we needed lots of electricity. He has to be thinking drugs," said Henry. "That we are putting in lights for a marijuana grow. A sizable nursery. They didn't ask too many questions after that. I think the old man figures the less he knows, the better. So that if the government comes calling he can say he didn't know. That way they can't confiscate his property."

"Good. We chain off the road out there. Post some big 'no trespassing' signs, and get a couple of mean dogs. I am talking something that will rip the ass out of anything that moves. Chain them to the outside of the building and make sure they can reach both doors. And somebody's got to be here all the time. Sleep here at night."

Henry nodded, taking it all in. "How much time do we have?"

"Enough," said Chaney. "But just barely. The colonel told me this morning that the government is poking around, issuing subpoenas. They're looking for organization." He laughed a little. "Fortunately for us, they are sniffing up a road which is about to become a dead end."

He took a final appraisal of the building. "I'd say to be safe we have ten days."

"Can we do it in that time?" asked Henry.

"I can do the truck. I've got the frame and bed already. There's an old fertilizer tank on a farm on the other side of the island. I found it last week, talked to the owner. I can buy it and use it to fabricate the container on the back. The problem is the technical stuff. Handling it, and making sure we don't end up glowing like fireflies."

"I know," said Henry. "I don't like dealing with that stuff."

"Let Thorn worry about that. Besides the Russian is supposed to handle all of that. He is well trained. Knows what he is doing."

"Yeah. So well trained he's sitting in some county jail as we speak."

"The Russian's my problem," said Oscar.

"Your problem?"

"Thorn has a plan to get him out."

"He'd better do it quickly. I'm not handling that bomb."

"You worry too much."

"That's what they said in Chernobyl. Now they're all producing children with four legs and a single eye in the middle of their forehead. It's just that I would like to have at least one more child," said Henry. "And not be shooting blanks into the wife."

"We'd be doing posterity a favor," said Oscar.

They both laughed. Henry would have laughed harder if he wasn't so concerned about the risks.

"In the meantime, as the good old boys say over in Deming, 'Get me two ass-chewin' dogs.' Got it?" Oscar mimicked the tough talk of the rednecks who believed they had hired him.

Henry nodded. The meeting was over. Oscar headed back toward his truck.

"Ah," he turned around. "I almost forgot. We are going to need some raw sewage. Get somebody to bring in one of those portable latrines. You know the kind? Set it up out front there and tell everybody in here to use it. Better yet, lock the latrine around back so they don't have a choice."

"What for?"

"Never mind. Just do it."

TUKWILA, WA

Oscar Chaney knew he was going to get it, one way or the other: either an exploding dye pack or the infamous electronic wafer.

After he'd gone fifteen blocks and nothing blew up inside his car, he figured it had to be the wafer.

There were a lot of stupid crimes but none quite as witless as bank robbery, and Chaney knew it. Still, he had no choice. It was the one sure way to get busted by the Feds. Bank robbery was a federal offense. They would lock him up at Kent. The federal government had a contract with the county to house its prisoners at the Kent jail pending trial. The Russian was there, and Chaney had to get him out before the FBI discovered who they had.

Chaney had warned Chenko to keep a low profile. Instead the Russian started visiting the red light district downtown. Three days ago, Chenko tried to use Russian rubles to pay a hooker for services rendered. He had gotten drunk and abusive. The woman had made a scene, and her pimp had gotten involved. Chenko got a cut lip. The pimp ended up looking down the business end of a Taurus .45 automatic. Fortunately only loud words were exchanged, no gunfire. But by then cops had shown up. Chenko and the pimp both had been taken into custody. A check with immigration had shown the Russian was in the country illegally. That and the weapons charge had landed him in the Kent jail.

Chaney kept looking at the brown paper bag on the front seat next to him. He had allowed the teller to pick and choose. He knew that she'd given him one of the "bait packs." They were usually stacks of hundreds, something a robber wouldn't turn down. The old technology was the dye pack: an exploding bundle of bills containing an indelible dye, usually a bright neon color, orange or green, with a little tear gas mixed in for good measure. If it exploded, it would be all over Chaney as well as the inside of his car. It was the kind of forensic evidence a prosecutor loved. Tell your lawyer to explain that to the jury.

The dye pack had one drawback. If it exploded early, inside the bank, an edgy robber with a gun could panic and take hostages or, worse, start shooting.

The newest rage among the law enforcement set was the electronic wafer. Pasted between two hundred-dollar bills, the credit-card-sized transmitter was triggered by the spring-loaded wheel of the cash drawer. As soon as the teller pulled it out, the transmitter started sending a silent signal that the cops could track.

Chaney figured they were already behind him, a train of unmarked cars following slowly in traffic. Why do a high-speed chase when you could beat the suspect and meet him at his house? The cops operated through a Violent Crimes Task Force, a mix of local, state, and federal agencies, a SWAT team packing automatic weapons. For this reason, Chaney didn't carry a gun. He figured the teller wouldn't ask to see it if he put his hand in his pocket and threatened her. The idea was to get busted and booked into the Kent jail, not to get shot.

He had only two days to find the Russian and get him out. Without Chenko, the entire plan would have to be called off. Only the Russian could assemble the device and make sure it would work.

Chaney turned the corner and saw the lights: blue, red, and white flashing from five patrol cars at the end of the street. They had it barricaded off. Shotguns and rifles pointed.

Three more cars screeched up behind him and blocked the intersection. With their doors open for cover, the cops took up positions with weapons drawn and the bullhorn came out.

"Step out of the car with your hands up. Where we can see 'em. Now."

Chaney had all ten fingers out through the open window of the car before they finished talking.

FOUR

FRIDAY HARBOR, WA

When Joselyn got to the law office in the morning, she noticed that Sam's car was already in the garage. Sam was early. Samantha Hawthorne was her landlady and her best friend on the island.

Sam was hard-core. She was immune to island fever, a survivor who could find a niche in hell if she had to. She had been in Friday Harbor for fifteen years and, therefore, was almost a native.

Samantha was forty-five, and looked thirty, buxom and brunette, too mean to be married, a person to be reckoned with. On her office door was a wooden placard, carved and painted. Under her name were the words:

COUNSELOR AND HYPNOTHERAPIST

When Joselyn headed down the corridor to her office, she saw Sam's door open. Sam was sitting inside behind her desk and a large pile of papers.

"Glad you could make it," said Sam. "Sleep in, did we?"

Joss looked at her watch. "It's only nine o'clock."

"Yes, and some of us have been working. Heavy date last night?"

"Right. With a corporate form book." Joselyn had spent

the evening until the wee hours working up the documentation on Belden's corporation.

"Your phone's been ringing off the hook all morning," said Sam.

They shared a telephone system that Sam had installed when she moved in. She was hopeful of picking up a few more tenants so that they could soon share the cost of a receptionist.

"I finally answered it in self-defense," she said. "Couldn't get any work done." She pushed a pink telephone slip across the top of her desk. Joselyn walked in and picked it up.

"Cup of coffee?" Sam asked.

The telephone message was from Dean Belden.

"No. I had some on the way in. Was it urgent?"

"Hmm?"

"The message?" Her week to get the job done not yet passed, and he was calling already.

"Not what I would call desperate," said Sam. "Just judging from the tone of voice, I would say he's not the type to panic."

Sam was a quick study, even with only a voice on the phone to work with. She poured herself a cup of coffee from the machine on the credenza behind her desk.

"Yeah. But did he say what he wanted?"

"We didn't get that intimate." She sipped her coffee and looked at Joselyn over the top of the mug. "He wants you to call him. What is he? Domestic? Criminal?"

"Nothing you'd be interested in."

"How do you know? He sounded pretty good on the phone."

"He's a business client. And he pays up front." Joss shot Sam a wicked grin.

"Then I'm definitely interested. Business is always filled with stress." Sam winked across the desk at her. "Perhaps he could use a little counseling."

"Don't get your hopes up. Dean Belden doesn't seem like the kinda guy who lets a little stress get in his way. What are you doing for lunch?"

"Give me a call," said Sam.

Joselyn headed to her office, opened the door, and dropped her purse and briefcase on the chair. She dialed Belden's number. On the first ring, he picked it up.

"Yeah." The tone was somewhat more harsh, less refined than at their last meeting.

"Mr. Belden. Joselyn Cole. You called."

"Ah. Ms. Cole." His voice turned softer, more polished. "I have a problem," he said. "I have to see you today." It was more like a command than a request. Belden seemed used to telling people what to do.

"As soon as possible," he said.

He wanted his money back. Joselyn could smell it. He'd found another lawyer.

"I've started work on the documents," she told him.

"That's good."

"Filed for corporate name identification already. I've reserved the name."

"Excellent," he said.

"I thought we were going to get together next week. Everything should be done by then."

"This has nothing to do with that. Something has come up."

"I see. Well, when do you want to meet?"

"Right now. I'll be in your office in twenty minutes."

Before she could say another word, he hung up.

Fifteen minutes later, Joselyn heard footsteps on the landing outside her office. The door to reception opened and closed.

"I'm in here." She yelled through the closed door to her office.

Belden poked his head through a couple of seconds later. "I hope I'm not interrupting your day too much. Thanks for meeting me on such short notice."

"It's all right. Come on in. What's the problem?"

"I don't know how to explain it," he said. "I'm a little embarrassed. I've never had anything like this happen to me before. Not even a traffic ticket in ten years."

"What is it?"

He sat down in one of the client chairs across from her desk.

"Yesterday I was in my office, finishing some paperwork. This man walks in. He was dressed in a blue suit and black cowboy boots. He had a big mustache. Anyway, he was somewhat disheveled. He asked me if I was Dean Belden. Looking at the guy, I wasn't sure if I should say yes or no. You understand?"

She nodded.

"He was big. Not very polite, pretty beefy, mostly around the middle. Like a potted-out policeman. I told him I was Belden. What else could I do?"

"And?"

"And he hands me this." Belden reached into his inside coat pocket and pulled out an envelope. "Then, just like that, the man turned and walked out of my office."

He reached across the desk and handed her the envelope. It was already slit open across the top by something sharp.

Joselyn pulled a single folded piece of paper from the inside, and spread it out on her desk.

It was wrinkled and folded and had several coffee stains with the round imprint of a mug where it was picked up and laid down on top of the paper. Some of the typed letters were smudged.

"What in the world happened to this?"

"I got a little coffee on it," said Belden.

"A little? I can't read the date of the appearance," said Joselyn.

"Wednesday," he told her. "I assume you're free?"

She looked at her calendar but didn't answer the question.

"So I guess the guy was a process server," said Belden. "How was I supposed to know?"

"Either that or a U.S. marshal." She tried to read between the lines of what was on the page, as well as what was on Belden's face, in his eyes. The paper was brief and his expression an enigma.

"What's it about?" she asked.

"Search me."

"I mean, you must have some idea why they want to talk to you?"

"I don't have a clue."

She was not sure she believed him.

He put two fingers up like some kind of scout. "I swear."

Typical of a federal grand jury, the subpoena compelling Belden to appear in Seattle disclosed nothing about the substance of the government's inquiry. In this country, a federal

United States District Court

Western_____ **District of** Washington

TO: Dean Richard Belden   **SUBPOENA TO TESTIFY**
Route 12, Box 32   **BEFORE GRAND JURY**
Friday Harbor, WA. 98250

SUBPOENA FOR:
X PERSON __ DOCUMENT(S) OR OBJECTS

YOU ARE HEREBY COMMANDED to appear and testify before the Grand Jury of
the United States District Court at the place, date, and time specified below:

PLACE	COURTROOM
U.S. Courthouse	Grand Jury Room 3rd Floor
Western District of Washington	
1010 Fifth Avenue	
Seattle, WA. 98104	

YOU ARE ALSO COMMANDED to bring with you the following documents or
Object(s):

None Specified

This subpoena shall remain in effect until you are granted leave to depart by the court or
by an officer acting on behalf of the court.

CLERK

Howard E. Davies

This subpoena is issued on application of the United States of America	**By: ASSISTANT U.S. ATTORNEY** Thomas McCally, AUSA
William P. Wainright United States Attorney	Western District of Washington P.O. Box B 135874 Seattle, WA. 98104

grand jury probe is the closest thing to Courts of Inquisition or a Star Chamber that exists. There are few rights, nothing that comes close to cross-examination, and no right to counsel inside the jury room. There are no real rules of evidence. The only thing they can't do is torture you, and on that you must take the government's word.

"Was there anything else inside the envelope?"

"Like what?"

"Like a letter? Any instructions?"

"No. Just what you see."

"That's probably good news," she told him.

"Why?"

"There's no target letter."

"What's that?"

"If you were the target of their investigation, they'd have to notify you, give you what is called a target letter. Informing you of your rights. Mostly the right to remain silent. The fact that you didn't get one probably means they're looking at somebody else. You're just a witness."

"What should I do?"

"First thing is not to discuss the subpoena with anybody else. You haven't, have you?"

"No."

"Good. If you were a target I would advise you to take the Fifth Amendment. Make an appearance so they can't hold you in contempt, but say nothing. You can still do that of course, and it might be prudent."

"Won't they think I'm guilty of something if I refuse to cooperate?"

"What they think can't hurt you. Only what they can prove."

The problem with a federal grand jury probe was its range. Irrelevance was a concept that did not exist. They could turn your life upside down, subpoena all of your neighbors and business associates, spend a year defaming you by inference, and produce nothing but a sizable grease spot on your good name.

"In searching for someone else's crime, they may find one of your own," she told him.

"I've never done anything wrong."

"Saint Belden," said Joselyn. "I see." She looked at him, her own dark eyes matching the emerald look that stared back from across the desk. "And your tax returns," she said. "I suppose all of those are up to snuff, too? Never claimed any deductions you can't justify?"

He looked up almost whimsically toward the ceiling. "Ah, now, let me see." He thought for a moment. Put a single forefinger to his lips. "I don't think so. No. I'm sure of it. My only offense is one of lust, and that unfortunately has been committed only in my heart."

Joss couldn't help herself. She fought back laughter.

"Please," she said. "This is serious."

"I know."

"If you want to cooperate with them, that's fine. But I would get something in return."

"I'm trying," he said.

"Please, Mr. Belden."

"Call me Dean," he told her.

"Dean. You could get in real trouble. A good lawyer would demand immunity, just to be safe."

"If that's what you think we should do."

"If you're not a target, the government shouldn't care about granting you immunity. Perhaps use immunity."

"What's that?"

"As opposed to transactional. What it means is that the government can't use anything you say before the grand jury to prosecute you, as long as you tell them the truth."

"The trouble you can get into just doing what the government says. What's it all about?" said Belden. "I mean what are they looking for?"

"You don't have any idea?"

He shook his head.

"They must think you have information they want."

"What information?"

"Think," she told him. "Anything to do with your business?"

He shook his head slowly, as if searching his memory for some clue.

"What kind of business were you in before you came to the islands?"

"Electronics. It's always been electronics. I've never done anything else. It's my business. All I know."

"Maybe someone you did business with?"

Suddenly there was a glimmer of light in those green eyes. He slapped his forehead with one hand. "Of course! Why didn't I think of it?"

"Think of what?"

"Max Sperling. That's it. It has to be."

"Who's Max Sperling?"

"I had some business dealings with him two years ago. Or was it three?" He thought for a second. "Yeah, probably closer to three. He was a supplier of electronic parts out of the Silicon Valley. I heard he had some trouble with the law about a year ago, dealing in some stolen microchips or something. I didn't pay much attention at the time. I wasn't doing business with him anymore."

"What did you buy from him?"

"Microchips."

Bells started going off in Joselyn's head.

"How many?"

"Oh, I don't know. Couple of hundred thousand dollars' worth. It was a small order. He was a small supplier among independents. Moved up and down the coast."

She had visions of this guy selling out of the trunk of his car, and she wondered what Belden really knew.

"He traveled. His warehouse was down in the Bay Area. At least that's what he told me. At the time chips were hard to come by, especially the items he had."

"What made these chips special?"

"They were for switches, specially designed stuff for certain kinds of electronics."

The next question she framed with extreme delicacy.

"At the time that you bought these chips from Mr. Sperling, you didn't have any reason to suspect that they were stolen?"

She led him with a wink and a nod. You never want to know with absolute certainty that your client committed a crime, especially one with as many avenues of escape as receiving stolen property.

He shook his head solemnly. "No. Never. Not the slightest hint."

"Let's talk about the price you paid for these chips," she told him. What Belden thought was one thing. What a jury might think was something else.

"Did you pay a normal price?"

"It was a good buy." He conceded this like a wily businessman. "I wouldn't call it extraordinary. As I remember, it was on the low side of competitive," he said.

"How far on the low side?"

"I mean it was within reason."

She sighed. A request for immunity may not be an idle act after all.

"Was Mr. Sperling selling chips to anybody else at the time?"

"Oh sure. Everybody in town."

"To your knowledge were you one of his major buyers?"

"I don't know. But I wouldn't think so. There were others."

"Who?"

"Off the top of my head, I don't know."

"So you might have been one of his major buyers?"

"Could have been," said Belden.

"But it's your position that you had no reason to suspect or believe that anything was wrong in these transactions? That they could have involved stolen merchandise?"

"Absolutely not. I was simply doing business. He was selling, and I was buying."

"That is usually the case with stolen property," she told him. "It's what you reasonably believed that's important."

"I reasonably believed that these were legitimate," he said.

"Do you have any records of these transactions? Receipts? Purchase orders?"

"I might. I'd have to look."

There was a moment of silence as she studied the subpoena once more.

"What's wrong? Is there something there?"

"No. It's what's missing that I'm worried about."

"What's that?"

"Well, you would think that if your dealings with this Sperling were the issue, the government would be asking for your business records. Any evidence of your dealings with him."

He looked at her and shrugged. "I suppose."

"But they didn't."

He shook his head. "I don't know. My dealings with Sperling are the only thing I can think of."

"Well, if that's what it is, I would say you probably don't have anything too much to worry about. I think they probably just want to know what you know. But to be safe, you should demand immunity."

There was a palpable sigh of relief from the other side of her desk.

"I would go, make the appearance, answer any questions truthfully, but only if they give you immunity, otherwise remain silent and take the Fifth."

"What do you mean? You're not going with me?"

"I don't know that it's necessary."

"Well, I do."

"It will cost you a good deal of money."

"I don't care. You're my lawyer."

"They're probably on a fishing expedition, and your name appeared on a document or was mentioned by another witness."

"That's probably it," he said. "Still, I want you to be there."

"If you insist."

"I do. Name your fee." He reached for his checkbook again.

"I'd have to charge you for travel time."

"That's all right." He started writing before she could say anything.

"Have you ever done this before?" he asked.

"Not before a federal grand jury. But I've had clients indicted by the state."

"I'm not sure that's a recommendation." He looked up at her, and they both laughed.

"There's no need to pay me now."

"Nonsense." He continued writing.

"I'll call the U.S. Attorney's Office. My guess is they won't tell me anything over the phone, but I can try."

"Sure. Try."

"Really, there's no need for another retainer. I'll bill you."

He smiled and kept writing. "You've been too good to me. I don't want to stiff you on the fee."

"You're not going to be stiffing me."

"Trust me," he said. He finished writing, tore out the check, and slid it across the desk.

She was looking at the $5,000 written in the "amount" space when he said, "You know where Roche Harbor is?"

On an island, you tend to know where everything is. She nodded. He was moving toward the door.

"I'll meet you there on the dock Wednesday morning, seven o'clock."

"Wait a second. Are you sure that'll give us enough time to get down to Seattle?"

"Not to worry," he said. "See you then," and he was out the door.

FIVE

YEKATERINBURG, EAST OF THE URALS

It was six hours by air from Moscow, and Gideon was having a hard time sleeping. The climb over the Urals was like riding a sled down a rock-strewn mountain. Aeroflot did not use its European airbuses on this route. Those were reserved for national face-saving to Paris and London or for overseas flights to America.

On the Siberian runs, they used their aging fleet of Tupelevs, heavy lumbering planes that looked as if they would defy the physics of flight. Sometimes they did. There were no oxygen masks overhead, and only the foolhardy wondered if the seat cushions would float.

Gideon was used to all of this. He had spent his early life bumping around Europe between his father in Amsterdam and his mother in Moscow.

But he had never been to the eastern part of the old Soviet Union, beyond the Urals. Here there were pine-covered slopes, millions of square miles of trackless forest, a region rich in mineral wealth where Stalin housed his gulags and subsequent Soviet leaders hid their nuclear arsenal. It was an area that could swallow Western Europe whole and never belch.

It had taken him three days trekking between various bureaus and departments in Moscow, using every chit and buttonholing old friend, to obtain the government clearances just to get through the gates at Sverdlovsk. He was to be met at the airport by a government car and driver.

As the plane began to descend through the clouds, Gideon could see a strange and surreal landscape, a green carpet of pine and birch, spreading east as far as the eye could see. Periodically, strands of paved road would appear like curving ribbons out of the trackless forest, only to disappear once more, into the verdant sea of pines. He could see no traffic, even where the roads were visible for long distances. It was as if the plane were descending onto some vast uninhabited planet.

Gideon knew better. Yekaterinburg was a city of two million people, one of the fastest growing and most prosperous regions in the Russian Federation. Named for Catherine the Great, it was a fur-trading town when Jefferson crafted the Declaration of Independence. Gideon had seen pictures of mansions built by the fur czars, massive Georgian structures that still dotted the central area of the city, though they were now dusted by the soot of industry.

During the Bolshevik period the city got a new name: Sverdlovsk, after Yakov Sverdlov, first secretary of the Communist Party's Central Committee. The Bolsheviks were anxious to wipe the name of Yekaterinburg from the map for a single reason: During the early morning hours of August 16, 1918, in the basement of one of its larger homes, an appalling act of murder was committed that stained Russian history. Nicholas and Alexandra, the czar and czarina, along with all of their children, the last of the Romanovs, were shot to death. Their bodies were trucked into the forest and buried outside of town.

As if continuing some thread of history, nearly seventy years later the city gave up another of its citizens to lead the country. Before becoming premier of the Russian Federation, Boris Yeltsin had been mayor of Yekaterinburg. One of his acts while in office was to demolish the house where the dynastic executions took place, an act that he later claimed to regret.

In the early 1990s, with the fall of Communism, the city reclaimed its heritage and once again became the City of Catherine.

So much of Russian history had played out here that Gideon

had an abiding interest to see the place. As the plane dropped lower, he could see a sprawl of dismal white buildings on the horizon, an industrial complex that he knew only from photographs taken by satellite. It had been numbered during its heyday, and known only as Sverdlovsk-45. The areas around it were highly secured and Soviet citizens were required to possess special passes to travel in the area around Sverdlovsk.

The plane dropped below the sea of pines, and its wheels skidded on the tarmac, the engines reversed, and the old Tupelev shuddered to a slow roll down the runway.

It took Gideon more than an hour to collect his luggage and find his driver and the government car in front of the terminal building. Fifty minutes later he was passing through the gates at Sverdlovsk-45.

It was an immense dingy complex of buildings, the kind you see in every developed nation where industrial decay starts to nibble at the fringes of a community. Here it was gnawing. Flat roofs and broken windows seemed to predominate, though there was none of the graffiti that marked similar sites in the West.

Everywhere there was activity: heavy vehicles pulling trailers, men in overalls wearing hard hats, guards with Kalashnikovs. The driver pulled to a stop in front of an austere building, just inside the gates. There were two Russian-built cars, Ladas with considerable wear, a lot of dust and a few dents in them. And next to them, a spanking new Mercedes SL convertible, a gleaming powder blue.

The parking lot was strewn with the remnants of rusted out seagoing containers too large to be carried away and steel bands that had probably encircled wooden crates long since transformed into ash in some enterprising worker's fireplace. Gideon assumed that the building adjoining this parking lot had to be the administrative center.

Gideon knew that the bunkers that lay buried in the incline of gently rolling hills beyond were the focus of his inquiry.

It was known that there were 30,000 nuclear devices in storage or on launch pads in the Russian Federation. In addition to these, there were more than a thousand tons of highly enriched uranium and in excess of a hundred tons of plutonium in the country. It was these raw materials for bomb making that had most worried nuclear experts, both those in the West and their Russian colleagues.

There had been several episodes of smuggling in Germany and Italy, as well as other places in Europe and the new eastern republics. In all, about fifty cases documented so far. Almost all of these involved low-grade materials, some of it approaching weapons grade, but in very small quantities.

It was not the first time that a nuclear device or raw materials had shown up missing on paper in one of the institute's reports. Almost invariably these turned out to be record-keeping errors. In this case, however, it was the nature of the missing items that caused concern. Two small devices that might be easily transported would be at or near the top of any terrorist shopping list.

Gideon was familiar with tactical field nuclear artillery. These had been items of discussion and negotiation in treaties.

The United States had developed an eight-inch nuclear artillery shell in the early 1950s. Over the years, they had perfected and increased its destructive capacity by reducing barrel length and tamper bulk and by adding beryllium reflectors and more powerful high explosives to trigger the chain reaction. In their final incarnation, these shells measured no more than three feet in length, eight inches around, and weighed less than 250 pounds. Yet in this compact package, they could unleash ten kilotons of destructive force.

These were meaningless statistics until applied to the real world. The Oklahoma City bombing, which took 162 lives, would have leveled three square miles of the central city if one of these shells had been detonated instead of fertilizer and diesel oil. The death toll would have been measured in hundreds of thousands instead of hundreds.

If a nuclear shell had been detonated at the World Trade Center instead of a conventional truck bomb, the lower part of Manhattan would have disappeared, everything from the Financial District to Gramercy Park would have been totally destroyed.

The Soviets had developed similar artillery shells. This was what Gideon was looking for, hoping and praying to find at Sverdlovsk, two small packages lost in a monumental accounting glitch.

Gideon showed his pass to a guard at the door, who passed

it to an officer inside. Two minutes later he was led into a small waiting room, where he took a seat on a hard wooden bench and waited.

He checked his watch. Ten minutes passed. Finally the door opened and a tall slender man, balding and with glasses, came out.

He was holding the pass in his hand and spoke in Russian. Gideon answered him.

"I am Mr. van Ry."

The Russian looked him up and down. "What is this about?"

Speaking perfect Russian, Gideon gave him a business card from the institute and watched to see if the man could read the English printed on it.

The Russian's eyes darted between the business card and Gideon's face. The next words he spoke were in halting but clearly discernable English. "What is this about?"

"I am authorized by authorities in Moscow to speak with your director. He is available?"

"He is very busy," said the Russian.

"I think he will see me. Please, tell him I am here."

The Russian looked once more at the business card, then the signature on the security pass from Moscow.

Gideon could read his mind. He was wondering what a Russian citizen was doing working in the United States for an institute that dealt with nuclear weapons.

"Wait here." The Russian turned and closed the door behind him.

Gideon looked at the clock on the wall, turned, took a seat, and waited. A few moments later the door opened again, and the Russian stepped out. "Follow me."

The Russian led the way down a long corridor and through a rabbit warren of small offices and cubicles, most of which were empty and looked as if they hadn't been cleaned in months. A uniform film of dust covered the floors.

Their feet left concrete, and suddenly Gideon found himself walking on carpet. A few steps farther on, they stopped in front of a set of double wooden doors. The Russian opened one of them and stepped to the side for Gideon.

As he entered the room, he saw another man, seated behind a massive mahogany desk. There were pictures on the walls and several pieces of African art, masks and carvings of some expense, which seemed out of place against the stained acoustic ceiling tiles and drab walls of the office.

The man behind the desk stood to greet Gideon. He was dressed in a suit and tie. Well-pleated sharkskin, not something from Russian clothiers.

"Dimitri tells me you are from the institute at Santa Crista." He was smiling and held Gideon's card in one hand.

"Yes. That's correct." Gideon planted his best smile, crossed the office, and extended a hand that was eagerly taken by the Russian.

"We are not used to visitors here," said the man. "Please have a seat. You must be tired. Dimitri tells me you have come all the way from Moscow."

Gideon nodded.

"How is the weather there?"

Gideon sat down and Dimitri closed the door, leaving the two men alone.

"The weather was pleasant," said Gideon.

"You see what we have here. Overcast. Always overcast," said the Russian. "You must have some beautiful weather in California?"

"It can be nice."

"You know, I've always wanted to visit your institute. You must tell me how you obtained a position there. It is on the central coast, correct?"

"Yes."

"Is it close to Hollywood?" The man spoke perfect English.

"No," said Gideon.

The Russian seemed disappointed. "You must excuse me," he said. "Where are my manners? I am Yuri Mirnov, director of Sverdlovsk. Or what is left of it." He rolled his eyes toward the ceiling. "You have already met twenty percent of my staff." He was referring to Dimitri. "But then you know the difficult times we are having here."

"I am very much aware," said Gideon. "It must be very hard."

"You have no idea," said Mirnov. "Dimitri hasn't been paid in two months. I myself have had to endure three salary reductions in the last year. And the work, it just keeps piling up.'' He gestured toward stacks of paper on the floor strewn around his office.

Gideon was wondering who, under such conditions of austerity, owned the Mercedes outside in the parking lot. But he possessed sufficient diplomacy not to ask.

The area around Sverdlovsk was like few others in Russia. Since the fall of Communism, there had been a crippling crime wave. Those who did not know Russia attributed this to political dislocations for a nation trying to find its way. The fact was that crime flourished under the Soviet regime, particularly from the 1960s on. Artificial shortages of everything from sugar to nuts were state-manufactured in order to establish a thriving black market, which in turn was controlled by bureaucrats and other high-level party functionaries. They mingled freely with an underworld that was inbred in the Russian culture. Three hundred years of oppression had made the children of Mother Russia adept at avoiding the strictures of the law. Beneath the statue of Lenin, under the banner of Socialism, they had created shadow capitalism to avoid the failures of their own planned economy and proceeded to line their pockets.

With the demise of Communism, they were now free to come out into the open, a new age of robber barons, applauded by the West. It was a free-for-all on the order of Tombstone in the 1880s. There were a dozen shootings a day in Moscow, ''businessmen'' assassinating their competition. The only place where things were rougher was Sverdlovsk.

Here was a land of wide open opportunity if you had a private army and were willing to look under your car with a mirror every morning before leaving for work. What made it even more dangerous was that the region possessed thousands of nuclear, chemical, and biological weapons, a veritable bazaar of mass destruction.

Mirnov swiveled around in his chair to a credenza behind him. ''Can I offer you some mineral water?'' he asked.

Gideon was thirsty and tired after the long flight. ''Yes. Thank you.''

The Russian lifted two clear plastic cups from a sizable stack on the credenza and reached down somewhere below, where Gideon couldn't see. He came up with a liter bottle, not the cheap stuff from a Russian bottling house but Monteforte from Italy with a fresh seal on the cap.

Gideon seemed surprised to see that the bottle was already chilled and frosted and that Mirnov had no trouble finding ice cubes where he found the bottle.

The Russian noticed his expression.

"We still have a few conveniences," said Mirnov with a smile.

Gideon grinned and took the glass.

The Russian lifted another bottle containing a clear fluid and merely held it up as if there was no need to identify its contents, offering some to Gideon.

"None for me. I'm fine."

Then Mirnov poured a little vodka into his own glass and stirred it into the charged water with a swizzle stick.

"Now, what can I do for you?" he asked.

"As you know," said Gideon, "the institute gathers data on nuclear materials. Civilian power plants. Military fissile materials when we can."

"I am familiar," said the Russian.

"It has come to our attention that there may be some materials missing from your facility."

Mirnov's look suddenly went dark, his expression dour.

"It may not be accurate information," said Gideon. "Still, because of the specific nature of this information, we thought it best to check it out as discreetly as possible."

"You have told authorities in Moscow this information?"

"No," said Gideon. "We did not want to cause undue concern or alarm until we had a chance to talk to people in charge on site. As I said, it is entirely possible that our information is wrong."

"What is the source of this information?"

"I would rather not say. If it is inaccurate, it does not matter. If, on the other hand . . ."

"I see." Mirnov sipped from his plastic glass.

"A quick look at some of your records should clarify the matter," said Gideon.

"We would be happy to comply," said Mirnov, "though I am a little shorthanded at the moment. Perhaps if you could give us a little more direction, narrow the area of your inquiry?" He was fishing for specifics.

"Two field tactical artillery shells, nuclear," said Gideon.

"I see." Mirnov sat up straight in his chair and put his glass down. "We wouldn't want such misinformation to be reported."

"That's what we were thinking," said Gideon.

"I appreciate your concern for accuracy," said Mirnov. "I assume this error has not spread too far." He arched an eyebrow. The Russian was clearly referring to outside intelligence agencies, particularly in the U.S.

"The information has been maintained in-house," said Gideon. "There is still time to correct it."

"Good." There was a sigh of relief from Mirnov. "Of course, we will be happy to cooperate in any way we can. Where would you like to start?"

"Your own inventory numbers should make it very easy to check," said Gideon.

"True," said Mirnov. He punched the intercom key on his phone and picked up the receiver. "Dimitri, would you come in here, please?"

A moment later, the assistant entered.

"Dimitri. I would like you to pull these files." Mirnov made a note, pointing to a circled item. The assistant dutifully took the sheets and left the office.

"It shouldn't take him long to find them."

"Good," said Gideon. "I have a plane to catch back to Moscow."

"When do you leave?"

"About three hours."

"We should have you back at the airport in plenty of time. I can have one of my people drive you," said Mirnov. "I'm sure Dimitri would love to do it. He has a large new Mercedes," said Mirnov.

Gideon looked at him, wondering how a man who hadn't been paid in two months could afford this.

Mirnov could read his mind. "Dimitri is also an entrepreneur. He has a small business on the side."

In Russia this has become a euphemism for many things. "What does he do?"

Mirnov shrugged like he wasn't sure. "There are many business opportunities in the new Russia. I myself will have to investigate them, when I have the time," said Mirnov.

Gideon smiled but felt a sick feeling in his stomach. "Thank you for your offer, but I have a car and a driver." He took a sip from his own glass.

"I trust that the people at the institute are not too concerned about this mistake. They do happen," said Mirnov. "I myself have found records from our own facility where overworked employees have entered incorrect numbers."

"I am sure the people at the institute will be relieved as soon as I can call them," said Gideon.

"If it is our mistake, it reflects poorly on us," said the Russian. "As the manager of this facility, I am responsible. We would not want the institute to have a bad impression of us. We do our best." He was now talking somewhat nervously. They both noticed that minutes were passing, and there was no sign of Dimitri or the files.

"Of course," said Gideon.

"Either way," said Mirnov. "The information will be quickly corrected. We completed a fresh inspection only yesterday. So our records are accurate, up to the minute."

They waited while the Russian tapped out a pattern of thumps on the surface of his desk and Gideon emptied his glass. Finally Mirnov got tired.

"Let me check and see." He picked up the phone and dialed a number on the intercom. There was no answer. He dialed another number. This time it was picked up, and Mirnov spoke in Russian.

"Is Dimitri there? . . . What do you mean he left? . . . I see . . . I see." Finally he put the receiver down.

"Excuse me for one moment," said Mirnov. He rose and left the office, closing the door behind him. Gideon listened. He couldn't make out words, but he could hear voices rising in volume outside the door.

A moment later, Mirnov reentered the room. His face was ashen. There were beads of perspiration on his forehead.

"You will have to excuse me," he said. "We seem to have a small problem."

"A problem?" said Gideon.

"Dimitri has left the building. My staff is looking for him now." He wiped his lip with a handkerchief and took a deep swallow of vodka and water from the glass on his desk.

"Have they found the files?" said Gideon.

"No. That is part of the problem. It seems the records for the two items in question . . . They are missing," said Mirnov.

"And Dimitri has left to look for them?"

There was a blank expression on the Russian's face, followed by a slight shrug of the shoulders.

Gideon got out of his chair and headed for the door. He retraced his steps back out to the long corridor, followed closely by Mirnov. The two started at a walk and then a slow jog until they were running headlong toward the parking lot outside.

Gideon threw open the door. The Mercedes was gone.

SIX

PADGET ISLAND, WA

He was short with dark brown hair, thinning on top, and soft brown eyes, the son of a Kansas banker. Scott Taggart had been many things in the space of his forty-two years. In his youth, after an argument with his father, he left home and drove a truck for a local freight company to put himself through college. He worked nights busing tables in a restaurant to finish graduate school.

Scott's field was American history, and he wanted to teach. Jobs were hard to find, but what he lacked in credentials he made up for in persistence. He found a job at a small college in western Washington State, first as a teaching assistant, then as a part-time faculty member. It was there that he met Kirsten.

She could have been the poster girl for Norwegian beauty. When she ended up in one of his lecture series, Scott couldn't keep his eyes off of her. The feeling seemed to be mutual. The college had strict rules against faculty dating undergraduates, and for nearly a year he fought off the urge to ask her out.

The school solved this problem for him in the early spring when it passed him over for a tenured position. It seemed they wanted someone with an Ivy League pedigree. Taggart was forced to move on. But in the summer, he struck up a relationship with Kirsten, and when he moved, he didn't go alone.

They lived together for five months and were married the following November. Together they started over, this time in eastern Washington, where Scott found another teaching assignment. It was a step down, only a community college, but he liked the work and enjoyed the students, though most of them were not as serious as he would have preferred.

To make ends meet, Kirsten started a small bookkeeping business. She had studied accounting in college, though she hadn't finished her degree. A year later, they had their first child, a boy they named Adam, after her father. Kirsten's business grew rapidly. She was affable and outgoing, as blessed with social skills as she was with numbers. In less than three years, her business had blossomed so that by then she employed two other people.

It was about this time that the trouble began. It came in the mail, with a return address to the Internal Revenue Service in Ogden, Utah. Kirsten and her business were being audited. She couldn't imagine why. She'd made money, but not that much. She looked at the notice and discovered that they'd made a mistake. The notice of audit contained her name and the name of her business all right, but the employer identification number was wrong. It seemed that they had mixed up her business tax records with someone else's.

She called the telephone number on the notice, but no one could help her. They told her to tell her story to the auditor when he arrived. She didn't know whether to gather receipts and ready her books for audit or not. She assumed that when they discovered their mistake they would go away, leave her alone. She was wrong.

A month later, her first meeting with the auditor did not go well. The revenue agent was a middle-aged woman worn down to a humorless nub by years of civil service. When Kirsten suggested that they'd made a mistake, she was informed that "the service does not make mistakes."

When she tried to show the woman the erroneous information on the notice, the auditor merely gobbled up the document, told Kirsten she would review it, then demanded to see Kirsten's business ledger and receipts.

The audit dragged on for months with an ever-increasing demand for more documents, more receipts. When Kirsten insisted that they had made a mistake and wanted to know why the notice listed someone else's identification number, the revenue agent lost her temper. She told Kirsten that if she wanted to be difficult, her business would not be audited for one year, but for two. Within days, a second formal notice of audit for an additional year had issued. That would teach her to question the authority of the auditor. A level of personal venom now seemed to be driving the audit.

Scott tried to console his wife. He told her not to worry. Sooner or later it would be straightened out. They would discover their mistake, and it would be taken care of.

But for Kirsten there was no peace. The IRS gave her thirty days to gather her records for the entire additional audit year. Meeting the quixotic and ever-changing demands of the auditor became a full-time job for Kirsten. She no longer had time for business or for her family. She was forced to let one of her employees go. Her business suffered, and her income dropped. For seven more months, it dragged on with no indication from the government that they were getting any closer to the end. Kirsten still did not know what the IRS was looking for, whether she owed back taxes, interest, or penalties. Whenever she met with the auditor, the woman was unpleasant. Nothing Kirsten seemed to say or do was ever the right thing. The auditor would tell her nothing. Whenever Kirsten asked a question, the auditor would take a note and tell her she would get back to her with the answer, but she never did. It was as if Kirsten's every inquiry either was met with open hostility or disappeared into the vast black hole of government bureaucracy. Whenever the auditor called, it was always the same thing, a constant and unceasing demand for more records.

Now the government's search had led the auditor into Scott and Kirsten's personal tax returns. To Kirsten it seemed that the failure to find anything amiss only fueled the auditor's hostility. The IRS agent now had to justify an audit that had dragged on for fifteen months.

The auditor demanded an extension of the statute of limitations so that she could go back farther into their records, beyond the three-year limit. When Kirsten objected, the auditor told her that if she didn't agree to the extension, the IRS would file a tax deficiency with the courts, and they would be required to hire a lawyer. At one point the auditor even hinted at criminal penalties. Kirsten wanted to know what she had done wrong. The auditor wouldn't tell her.

Kirsten was losing weight. It seemed a day didn't go by without the auditor calling and demanding something. Kirsten couldn't sleep at night. Scott was worried about her. He tried to intervene with the IRS. He called the auditor and tried to discuss it with her. The auditor took a dodge. She told Scott that since the original audit was for his wife's business, he was not the taxpayer. She could not discuss the matter with him and promptly hung up.

Every time the phone rang, Kirsten feared it was the auditor with demands for more documents or, worse, the addition of still another audit year. Life was becoming unbearable.

Now when Adam cried at night, Kirsten became irritable. Nothing Scott said or did seemed to reach her. There was no easing the constant anxiety.

Still, Scott made the best of it, trying to ease his wife's anxiety, until one Friday afternoon when he came home early from work and told Kirsten that his teaching contract had not been renewed for the following year. Without notice, the IRS had attached his wages for the failure to pay unspecified back taxes. The college received government grants, and its students applied for government-guaranteed loans. It couldn't afford for its faculty to have problems with the Internal Revenue Service. The federal government was crushing Scott and Kirsten Taggart's lives.

The agony of the audit dragged on for two more months with no word as to closure. Scott and Kirsten received a foreclosure notice on their home. Without Kirsten's income, they were now unable to meet their mortgage payment.

On a Saturday morning in June, shortly after the end of the school year, Scott took Adam to the park for a ride on the swings while Kirsten cleaned out her office. Word of her troubles with the IRS had seeped into the local accounting community. Her last client had departed two weeks earlier, fearful that Kirsten's problems might be contagious.

At two-thirty in the afternoon, Scott returned home and called his wife at the office. There was no answer. Thinking that she might need help carrying boxes to the car or comfort in a moment of emotional anxiety, he left Adam with neighbors and headed to Kirsten's office. Inside, he found her at her desk, head slumped on the blotter as if she were taking a nap. It wasn't until he saw the thin line of spittle, a milky froth running from the side of her mouth, that he realized something was wrong. Kirsten had taken an entire bottle of prescription sleeping pills.

She survived on a ventilator for sixteen days, until the doctors determined that there was no hope. Kirsten was brain-dead.

At her funeral, Scott wanted to crawl into the grave with her and pull the dirt in on top of both of them. He was racked by grief. With Kirsten he could bear anything, surmount any problem, deal with any questions the IRS could throw at him. He could have found another job, started over. Without her, he couldn't find the will or the strength to get out of bed in the morning. He didn't know what to do with Adam. He finally took the child to Kirsten's parents in Seattle while he re-grouped and tried to find a reason to live. Strangely enough, it was the IRS that gave him that reason.

Three months after Kirsten's death, Scott received a computer-generated letter. The IRS advised Kirsten Taggart that the agency had made a mistake. Somehow a keypunch operator had entered the wrong employer I.D. number on Kirsten's estimated quarterly tax payments, crediting them to another taxpayer's account. Kirsten showed up as delinquent in their computer. She owed no taxes, interest, or penalties. The government, rather than investigating Kirsten's information that it had made a mistake, assumed that she was lying, that she had received income, and that she had failed to make estimated quarterly tax payments. For this, Kirsten had been badgered and pursued until ultimately she took her own life. Scott had lost his family, his career, and his home, and his infant son had no mother.

Scott Taggart didn't bother to inform the government of the price that he and his family had to pay for bureaucratic arrogance. He would deliver the message in his own time—and in his own way.

KENT, WA

The Victor portable was a honey of a torch. Chaney had picked it up at a tool shop in Everett for five hundred bucks.

It came in its own handy carrying case, the size of a large attaché, with two spare tips. He had ordered an extra bottle of acetylene, fearful that he might run out.

The torch was specifically designed for working in small places where a full-sized cutting torch wouldn't reach. It could cut through inch-thick case-hardened steel in a matter of minutes.

He had spent two days with a team of hand-picked militiamen setting the mission up, finding out where the Russian national Grigori Chenko was housed at Kent, and sizing up the jail. It was a two-story brick structure in an area of light industry on the fringes of town. The building didn't look like a jail. The architects had done what they could to mask it in order to avoid public controversy in its placement. Fortunately for Chaney, they had also compromised its security.

There were no high chain-link fences surrounding the facility and topped by rolls of concertina wire. Instead, the unit where Chenko was housed backed up to a street used mostly by trucks during the day to make their deliveries to warehouses in the area. At night, the road was mostly deserted. The jail was pleasantly bordered by a ten-foot strip of well-manicured grass with shrubs planted against the exterior brick walls. From the outside, it was designed to blend in. It looked like most of the other commercial buildings in the industrial park.

It was only two years old, and on the inside it was like a country club. Those in custody were usually held here only a short time, pending trial. If convicted, they would be transferred to one of the permanent state or federal prisons to serve their time.

There was a large dayroom on the ground floor with a thirty-inch television set bolted to supports suspended from the second-tier balcony. A Ping-Pong table and six stainless steel tables with fixed benches all bolted to the floor did double duty for cards and meals. There was exercise equipment, a weight machine, and two-and-a-half-pound barbells for running in place.

Within minutes of being booked, strip-searched, and given orange jail togs and rubber thongs for his feet, Chaney was issued a blanket and marched through the dayroom to a cell up on the second tier.

The Russian saw him when he came in behind the guard. Chenko was playing Ping-Pong.

Chaney waltzed into the cell.

"You get the upper bunk." A grizzled loser with a gut like a canvas water bag was lying on the bottom bunk with his bare feet, toe jam and all, poking up toward Chaney.

"Not to worry, hotshot. I won't be here that long."

"Right. You're really with the Secret Service. They just put you in here for training."

Chaney ignored him. He threw his blanket onto the empty bunk up top and disappeared out the cell door. He headed down the stairs to the dayroom and caught Chenko's eye. The Russian immediately put the Ping-Pong paddle down and walked away. He and Chaney found a quiet corner.

"Who's in the room at the end of the corridor?" Chaney nodded with his head. "On the left. Down there." There was a short hallway with cells on both sides, each with a solid steel door and small observation window of wired plate glass for the guards to look through.

"That's Tattoo and Homer," said Chenko.

The Russian's cell was up top, on the second tier, just like Chaney's.

"Get 'em for me."

"Who?"

"Homer and Tattoo."

"What do you want them for?"

"Just do it."

The Russian hesitated. "Tattoo is very ugly guy."

"Fine. Tell him I want to kick his ass. He might see it as an opportunity for upward mobility."

The Russian looked at him, shrugged as if to say "your funeral," and did the jailhouse strut, cool and casual, over to two men working up a sweat on the exercise equipment. One of them was stripped to the waist, with more tattoos than the lady in the circus. The Russian said a few words in his ear, and the guy with tattoos started giving Chaney mean looks. He draped a towel around his neck and flexed his pecs like Rocky Balboa, then led the way over to Chaney, followed by another misfit who Chaney figured must be Homer.

"My man here says you wanna kick my ass."

"As soon as I figure out which end it's at," said Chaney.

It took the synapse in his brain a moment to make the connection. Then Tattoo's expression went lethal.

"No skin off my ass, you wanna die," he told Chaney. "But just so I understand. Why?"

"Ugliness offends me," said Chaney. "I like to stamp it out before it can breed."

The Russian was looking at him like he was out of his mind.

"Where ya wanna do it?" Tattoo got up close now, right up in his face, a show of prison manliness. Chaney's face didn't seem to flex a muscle as his knee shot up like a spring-fired catapult into the guy's groin. Tattoo's eyes dilated like two glass marbles as his testicles were pulverized. Chaney's right hand moved so quickly that the Russian wasn't sure he actually saw it. What he was sure of was that Tattoo couldn't speak any longer, and both of his hands were occupied feeling his Adam's apple, making certain it hadn't been forced up, and out through his mouth.

Tattoo slid to his knees, coughing as he went.

Homer stood transfixed, either terrified or fascinated. He'd never seen someone disabled so quickly, especially someone as fit as Tattoo.

Chaney slapped Tattoo on the back a few times as the other man coughed his guts out kneeling on the floor.

"What's goin' on over there?" One of the guards saw him down on the floor and started to come over to investigate.

"Something went down the wrong pipe," said Chaney. "He's all right." Chaney slapped him a few more times on the back, put his hands under Tattoo's armpits, and lifted him to his feet before the guard could cross the dayroom floor. As he did it, he whispered something in Tattoo's ear. Then pulled his lips away.

Tattoo's hand went up, and he waved the guard away.

Chaney was now back in his ear whispering again, then he pulled away. "Understand?"

Tattoo couldn't talk, but he could nod, and he did it eagerly.

"Good man." Chaney slapped him on the back again. "Do it now."

Tattoo's face was a shade of reddish purple. Tears ran down

both cheeks. His hands were now busy holding his groin. He turned and waddled away toward his cell at the end of the hall. Homer wasn't sure if he should follow him.

"You're moving out of your cell," said Chaney. "You got a problem with that?" Homer was a short-timer. He didn't know why they wanted the cell, and he didn't care. He was due to be released in ten days. He smiled and disappeared down the hall.

"You could have given him cigarettes? A few dollars?" said the Russian.

"Like feeding fish to seals," said Chaney. "He'd be knocking on the door all night for more."

"Now he may turn us over to the guards."

"By the times he lowers his balls back into place, we'll be gone. Get your stuff. Your blanket and whatever else. We'll be bunking at the end of the hall. Down there." Chaney pointed toward Tattoo's cell.

The guards didn't care. As long as there were two warm bodies in each cell when lights went out, prisoners could wheel and deal for accommodations. One of them had even worked a deal with the guards to sleep out in the dayroom at night, a solution the jail practiced when it was overbooked.

Five minutes later, Chaney and the Russian, each with a handful of possessions, toothbrush, soap, and blanket were setting up housekeeping in the ground floor cell at the end of the hall.

This was critical to their plan. Each cell had a window, not large, but big enough for a man, if he wasn't too fat, to slip through.

On the inside, the windows were covered by a half-inch screen of solid acrylic, bolted by six heavy screws to the masonry wall. The screw heads were fitted with a special slot that permitted them to be tightened, but not unscrewed.

Beyond the acrylic screen was a light shaft that ran at a slight upward angle, so that the prisoners couldn't actually see out to the street or get their behinds up high enough to moon the public as they drove by outside.

Eighteen inches beyond the acrylic barrier, set far enough inside the window shaft to be unnoticed from the outside, were four one-inch steel bars. These were made of case-hardened tool steel. They could probably be cut with a hacksaw, if you had a month to do it and an inexhaustible supply of blades.

For Chaney, time was essential, not only because they needed Chenko to assemble the device, but because the longer they took to engineer the escape, the greater the chance of discovery.

He set to work immediately. Chenko hung one of the blankets over the window on the cell door and cut a deal with another inmate for cigarettes to sit outside the door and tap out a warning if anyone headed down the corridor.

The most critical obstacle was the acrylic screen. Unless they could get that off, there was no way they could work on the bars.

Chaney had planned ahead. He spent ten minutes taking a dump in the single open commode and, on the fourth push, heard a splash in the stainless steel bowl.

He stood up halfway and looked down into the commode. Mission accomplished. Delicately he fished something out of the toilet. The rubber prophylactic was still smeared with KY Jelly and sealed at the open end with a rubber band. He unwrapped this and shook the package until a piece of metal about four inches long, the size of a fountain pen, dropped out onto the cement floor and bounced with a metallic clank.

The Russian caught it on the second bounce. Both men held their breath and looked nervously at the door for several seconds, until it was clear that no one had heard it.

In Chenko's hand was a small tungsten carbide chisel, flattened with a sharp hatchet-like edge at one end.

"You got a hammer up there, too?" said the Russian.

"I'm gonna use your fucking head," said Chaney. He was not happy that Chenko had put him through this. Right now Chaney should have been back on the island, putting the final touches on the truck, welding the steel tank onto the bed. As it was, he would be up for three nights running in order to finish the job. That was if they could get out.

Chaney told the Russian to sit tight. He left the cell for a minute, and when he returned he was carrying one of the iron two-and-a-half-pound molded barbells from the set in the exercise room. He wrapped it in a piece of Chenko's blanket off the bed and went to work with the chisel.

It made quick work of the six screw heads holding the acrylic screen in place. The heads popped off neatly and bounced on the floor. Using the sharp edge of the chisel, Chaney levered the acrylic screen until he could get his fingers under the thick panel. He lifted it off the broken screw shafts that were still sticking out of the concrete wall.

He reached up and grabbed hold of the iron bars in the window well. They were secured solidly in the concrete walls surrounding the window.

Carefully he then put the acrylic window back in place. He retrieved the screw heads from the floor and, using small amounts of chewing gum, stuck the heads back in place so that if the guards checked during the day, the acrylic would look as if it had never been removed.

"Now what?" said the Russian.

"Now we wait."

SEVEN

YEKATERINBURG

To Gideon there was a certain irony in all of it, as if this place with its soil poisoned by the bones of the murdered czar was now playing out one more fateful hand in the game of history.

He had spent three days in a dingy hotel room guarded by security police. They did not allow him to make phone calls or post E-mail to the institute in Santa Crista. If Caroline didn't hear from him soon, she would be calling the State Department. Like the surrounding landscape, his face took on the appearance of a sprouting forest, a two-day growth of stubble under eyes that were bloodshot pools clouded by sleep deprivation.

For someone who had worked in the vineyards of nuclear control as long as he had, it was a depressing scenario. Gideon felt like a prophet wailing in the desert. The Cold War was over. The precarious balance of power that governed the globe for fifty years had been swept away. The two sides were awash in awesome weapons that could, in a single ignition, take a million lives. And now, one of these powers lacked the means to secure these tools of death.

At eight o'clock in the morning Gideon had been roused from his hotel room by two stern-looking guards carrying Kalashnikov automatic rifles. For a while, in the backseat of a car with one of the guards, the thought actually crossed his mind that they might be taking him into the forest to be shot. The forest around Yekaterinburg held many dark secrets.

But ten minutes later they pulled into the parking lot outside of Mirnov's office and led him down the familiar long corridor. When he walked through the door of Mirnov's office, he could see that the Russian was himself a wreck.

Mirnov had been up all night. He had informed his supervisors in Moscow only that morning of the possibility that two nuclear devices were missing. He had waited as long as he could, hoping his staff would locate the two artillery shells. Instead what they found was more ominous.

Reports and allegations of missing devices had been made before but never by someone with Mirnov's position and access to information. The authorities took it seriously. Mirnov's boss was now on his way from the capital with a team of Russian experts, apparently to close the barn door after the horse had escaped. They would be looking for a scapegoat, someone to take the fall if the incident became international. Mirnov knew enough about the Russian bureaucracy and human politics to see himself being sized up for this role. He had begged them for more staff and better security. But the government in Moscow pleaded poverty.

"You look awful," said Mirnov.

"You should see yourself."

"Yes, well, I have a reason. I have been working. Around the clock."

"Yes. Well, I haven't been sleeping too well. I'd like to get to a phone. I have been asking for hours now to make a phone call," said Gideon.

"In time, my friend. Sit down, please." Mirnov gestured to one of the chairs in front of his desk, and Gideon sat down.

"It is ironic, is it not?" said Mirnov.

"What's that?"

"That for fifty years we were at each other's throats, that the only thing that kept us from destroying one another was the threat of mutual annihilation. What was it the Americans called it?" He touched a finger to his nose as if it would come to him through the alcohol haze. "The doctrine they called MAD?" said Mirnov.

"Mutually assured destruction," said Gideon. "Part of game theory."

"That it is," said Mirnov. "Leave it to the Americans to come up with some catchy letters, an acronym they call it. That is why their culture is dominant. They did not conquer the world with armies, but with words, with their motion pictures and movie stars, McDonald's, and Disneyland. But you are Russian."

"And Dutch," said Gideon.

"Ah, the Dutch. They are wonderful people. I have been to the Netherlands, you know. Oh, yes. The Hague."

"If you have traveled to The Hague then you know that we are noted for our diplomacy," said Gideon.

"Indeed," said the Russian.

"Then I would suggest that you allow me to make a phone call to my office."

"I cannot allow you to do that. At least for the moment."

"Am I a prisoner?"

"Of course not." Mirnov issued a broad, beefy smile. "You are our guest. My superiors will be here shortly, and I am sure they will be able to answer all of your questions."

Mirnov did not want to incur the wrath of Western nations. There might be an international incident that would only worsen the publicity when van Ry was freed. There would be more blame for Mirnov.

"Please," he said. "Relax. Bear with me just a few more moments. A few more questions."

Gideon settled back against his chair, having no other choice.

"This game theory—is there a strategy to retrieve devices if they fall into the wrong hands?"

"That depends."

"On what?"

"On what their goals are. The West might be able to purchase the devices off the underground market, that is, if the objective of whoever took them is purely economic, to obtain the highest possible price. If on the other hand, it is political . . ."

"The West would submit to this?" said Mirnov. "Purchasing the weapons even though they had no hand in losing them?"

"I do not speak for any government. But I believe they would do whatever is necessary to take them off the market. As I am sure your government would. The other side of mutually assured destruction," said Gideon, "is mutual self-interest."

"And what if whoever has them has no goal other than to use them? What does this game theory say about that?"

"We find them, before they can use them. We are no longer talking theories at that point."

Gideon's words seemed to sober the Russian, who looked at him across the desk as if they had perhaps reached some spoken watershed. There was a long period of silence as he studied the Dutchman.

"I can tell you a little," he said.

Gideon's ears perked up.

"We know that the devices do not show up on our current inventory. Your information is accurate," said Mirnov.

"I assumed that when I came here."

Mirnov's eyebrows arched a little. "Then your people in California, they have reason to believe that this was no error in paperwork?"

"If I don't contact them soon, you can be sure of it."

Mirnov was spurred on. "The two devices in question are not in the bunker where they were supposed to be stored." He took another sip of coffee as if this was needed to strengthen himself for what was to come.

"Can I have a piece of paper and a pen?" said Gideon.

Mirnov thought about it, then figured it was better not to have mistakes of memory made. He handed over a sheaf of paper and a pencil, and Gideon set up to take notes on a corner of the desk. At least for the moment he was not demanding to leave.

"It's possible, I suppose," said Gideon, "that they could simply have moved the two devices to another location inside the facility."

"I don't think that is likely," said Mirnov.

"Why not?"

"The movement in this case does not appear to be an inadvertent act."

"What do you mean?"

"First, there is the question of their disappearance from our inventory records," said Mirnov.

"Surely it could have been an error in counting." Gideon had learned by sorry experience that the Russians' system of accounting for these weapons was primitive. There were no computerized bar codes as on the U.S. inventory of weapons, so they could not be tracked with a master computer as in the West. Here they did it the old-fashioned way, by finger count, if they did it at all. For more than two years, national security experts in the U.S. had feared the worst. Nuclear accounting in Russia was abysmal. The Russians had no firm idea of the precise quantity of fissile materials in their possession. So how could they know if any was missing? What Gideon was coming to realize was that their accounting for tactical weapons was also flawed. From the perspective of terrorists, why get materials if you can have the bomb instead?

"If it were only the inventory records, you would be right," said Mirnov. "But there is the more troubling matter of the facsimile shells."

"What facsimile shells?"

"We found two dummy devices in the bunker, empty shells, made to look like the real thing. We do not know how long they were there. It would appear that this is the reason we did not pick up the error in the count of the bunker's weapons." The Russian gave a heavy sigh.

"I don't understand," said Gideon. "Why would anyone go to the trouble of replacing the real thing with dummies and then simply drop them from the count on the inventory sheets?"

"I can think of only one reason," said Mirnov. "There was no need to continue with the deception, because the devices had been removed and were beyond our reach."

The Russian's cold logic sent a chill up Gideon's spine.

"Then let's start with one assumption," said Gideon. "Someone took the trouble to maintain false inventory records at least until they didn't need to cover their tracks any longer."

"That appears to be the case," said Mirnov.

"Who had access to these records?"

"That is the problem. Only two people. Dimitri and myself."

"That's it?"

"Yes."

"Where's Dimitri?"

"We have been looking for him since he left the facility. His apartment. Places where he has been seen. We have not found him. But we are still looking. Unfortunately, it appears that Dimitri is involved," said Mirnov.

"Obviously," said Gideon.

"I have called my sister to see if she has seen him."

"Why your sister?"

"Dimitri is my brother-in-law." Mirnov said it like Gideon should have known. No wonder he was doubling up on the shots of vodka. One thing was clear; Gideon had to get whatever information he could from Mirnov before his superiors got there. Once they arrived, the Russian was likely to be removed, taken someplace for debriefing, and Gideon would not see him again.

"We don't have much time. You know that, don't you?"

"Yes." The Russian said it with soulful eyes.

"Then you've got to tell me everything you know."

Mirnov looked at him for a moment and thought. He had worked for nearly five years at a salary that barely provided a subsistence for himself and his family. For months he had not been paid at all. His family was not eating well, and his children had holes in their shoes. Mirnov had done it out of duty to his country and a belief that Russia alone was responsible for its weapons of war. It had built this arsenal, and national pride dictated that it should control it. He could have done as Dimitri had and taken money. There were many in Russian crime who would pay handsomely for nuclear and chemical materials smuggled from Sverdlovsk. But Mirnov had never taken a ruble.

He looked at Gideon and wondered if the governments of the West were any better than his own. He had heard about politics in Washington on CNN, about a government run by and for the people "inside the beltway," about endless scandals over money. Still, under the skin, he felt some kinship with this man. Gideon was not part of any government. He did not have to travel all the way from California to Moscow and Sverdlovsk to double-check on an error in paperwork. The people at the institute could have simply published the information and garnered international headlines, but they did not.

There was something in that act of caution, a respect for the truth that impressed the Russian.

"If I were to tell you what we know, it would remain confidential?" said Mirnov.

"I would have to tell my people at the institute," said Gideon.

"Of course. But would it go any farther?"

"That would depend. If there was a bona fide threat, authorities would have to be notified."

"I understand," said Mirnov. "But you would not go to the press? You would not identify me as being the source of this information?"

"No."

"There would be no public disclosure? The Western governments would treat it as confidential?"

"I believe I can assure you that the information would be treated as confidential as long as public safety could be protected. No one wants a needless panic. And in any event, you would not be named as the source." Gideon could not control what would happen if the information was disclosed to authorities. But he could protect his source.

"We have discovered two forged waybills," said Mirnov. "A man named Grigori Chenko, a technician who worked at Sverdlovsk, prepared both of the documents. The first about four weeks ago. The second about two weeks after that. Each document listed machine parts that were crated and shipped east to the port of Vladivostok."

"How do you know these were the bombs?"

"We don't," said Mirnov. "Not with certainty. However, before they were shipped, the two crates were weighed. Each time the weight was precisely the same, a little over one hundred four kilos. Accounting for the weight of the wooden crates themselves, it is almost precisely the weight of the two field artillery devices."

"You say the first one was shipped a month ago?"

"Yes," said Mirnov.

Gideon corrected a note and looked at the scrawl he had written quickly underneath it as Mirnov spilled out his information. "This man Chenko. Where is he?"

"That is what causes us concern. We don't know. Shortly

after this shipment was made, he disappeared. He simply stopped coming to work.''

''And you never checked?''

''We assumed he found a better job. It is not unusual,'' said Mirnov. ''I have lost more than half of my staff in the past year. If you don't pay people, they stop coming to work. If I stopped to check with each of them, I would never get anything done. Do you know that months now go by and the military isn't paid? Soldiers and sailors, who were once gods, are now treated like trash,'' said Mirnov. ''When a government starts doing that, they are asking for trouble.''

He was right. What's more, Gideon knew the Russians weren't alone in this. Both sides were guilty of the sin of denial. The danger lay in the fact that it had become politically unfashionable to worry about the bomb. Nuclear winters and atomic holocausts were the phobia of the 1960s and 1970s, no longer chic in the world of the Internet and the global economy. Why should politicians warn their citizens that nuclear annihilation was still a possibility? Why trouble them with such negative thoughts? After all, the Cold War was over. In the West, they were closing military bases, wallowing in the peace dividend, appraising with new capitalist vigor the expanding world markets. The president of the United States and the premier of Russia were friends. Why worry people with reports that their cities might be incinerated by an errant nuclear bomb? This, even as daily intelligence reports told world leaders that Russia was losing its grip on the atomic genie. And what if the unimaginable happened? Gideon had no doubts. The American president would declare a national emergency, call out FEMA, and tell the survivors that he felt their pain. It was what passed for statesmanship at the end of the millennium, a poor cry from Roosevelt and Churchill.

''What type of work did Mr. Chenko do?'' asked Gideon.

''As I said, he was a technician. He was employed in disassembling the devices.''

''The warheads themselves?''

''Yes.''

''So he would know how to assemble them as well?''

''Of course.'' The Russian answered without any hint as to the gravity, though he obviously had considered the significance of this himself. Someone with these skills would be sought after by governments outside of the nuclear club or by "subnationals," one of the euphemisms in the intelligence community for terrorists.

Gideon looked at his notes, underlined several items, and went over them again, committing the details to memory, then asked Mirnov for a match. In front of the Russian, he put the single sheet of paper with his notes in a large ashtray on Mirnov's desk, struck the match, and set an edge of the paper on fire, then watched it burn until there was nothing left but smoking cinders.

"One last question," he said. "What was the final point of destination for the two shipments?"

Mirnov swallowed hard. His superiors would draw and quarter him. "We have not had this conversation," he said.

"Agreed."

"We cannot be certain with regard to the second crate. We do know that it is no longer in the warehouse at the port in Vladivostok. But the first shipment," said Mirnov, "had what you call a paper trail. The documentation of marine transshipment was telefaxed to me this morning."

He reached into his shirt pocket and began to unfold a piece of paper, spreading it out flat on the desk.

"No one except myself and the port administrator in Vladivostok have seen this, and he does not know the significance."

"I understand," said Gideon.

The Russian turned the paper around on the desk so that Gideon could read it and commit its terms to memory. The shipment was marked, at least on paper, for a destination in the United States, a company called Belden Electronics.

EIGHT

Roche Harbor, WA

A thin vapor of fog rose like steam from the surface of the water so smooth and mottled it had the appearance of a pane of windowed bottle glass. Joselyn could see wisps of smoke winding from the chimneys of homes on Henry Island, a mile away.

She checked her watch. It was now five minutes to seven. She was hoping they would make it on time. Federal judges have a bad habit of issuing bench warrants for the arrest of witnesses who fail to appear, warrants that, from time to time, may embrace a lawyer or two. It was her signature, under her letterhead, faxed to the court that had assured Belden's appearance.

She looked back from the dock toward the parking lot. There was no sign of Belden and no cars on the road winding down from the hill above the resort.

The white facade of the Hotel de Haro, with its second-story balcony wrapped in vines, looked like a wedding cake. Dating from the 1800s, it had been built by a business baron who owned a limestone quarry. The quarry had been closed forty years ago, but the hotel had found another heyday. With its adjoining restaurant, it was one of the most charming spots in the islands. Far from the glitz of Saint-Tropez and the Costa del Sol, the rich and famous, the sultan of Brunei and the

Microsoft king Bill Gates, had been known to moor yachts in the harbor and to take meals at the restaurant.

She looked again at her watch as she heard the monotonous hum of an engine somewhere overhead. She feared her suspicion was correct. She turned to fix it low in the sky and approaching from the west. Perhaps it was the early morning seaplane from Victoria. It serviced the island twice daily.

The plane swooped down toward the channel, gliding just above the mist, between Henry Island and the harbor, then settled onto the water and skimmed across the glistening surface. It made a big circling turn and headed toward the dock, throwing up spray behind it from the prop wash.

As it approached, the roar of the big radial engine shattered the tranquility of the inner harbor. A small flock of Canada geese took flight, followed by three mallards.

Joselyn had never been this close to a float plane before—no more than a hundred feet away, when the pilot cut the engines. All she could see was the outline of a dark silhouette in the cockpit. The plane drifted in silence like some mythic bird of prey, its momentum carrying it toward the dock.

At the last instant, the door under the wing opened and the pilot gracefully lowered himself down, one hand on the wing strut, one foot on the pontoon. In a fluid motion, he stepped across onto the dock. As if by some magic of leverage, he brought the heavy plane to a stop without the pontoon even touching the dock.

Joselyn's fears were realized. It was Belden. She wasn't hot to fly, even in commercial planes. Now this. The man was full of surprises.

"You were expecting me?" He looked at her and smiled.

"And we're going to fly down in that?"

"Unless you have wings." He had that cocky grin, like Robert Redford in *The Great Waldo Pepper*.

She stood looking at him, her feet frozen to the dock.

"Come on. It's only about forty minutes by air to Seattle. Besides, you'll love it."

Inside of Joselyn that voice that speaks to each of us silently was now spitting expletives. Taking her own name in vain for lacking the sand to tell him no. "I don't get into small airplanes with men I don't know. In fact I don't get into small airplanes at all."

"You are afraid?"

"No." What made her say it, she wasn't sure.

"Good. Then hop in."

Holding onto the strut of the plane, he took her briefcase and put it down on the dock, then helped her step across onto the pontoon.

"Use the step up."

She placed her left foot onto a metal step built into the strut of the plane. She had visions of falling between the pontoon and the dock: FLASH! "Woman Killed Falling from Plane." Embarrassing details to follow.

Somehow in heels and a business suit with a tight skirt that ended up high around her thighs, she managed to pull herself up into the pilot's seat. When she looked down, Belden was checking out her legs, and from the expression on his face, enjoying the view.

"Let's change clothes and you can try it," she told him.

He laughed. "No. No. I'm sure it wouldn't be as fetching."

She got up out of the seat, straightened her skirt, and stepped around the controls in the center console. There were six seats in the rear of the plane, two on either side and a bench across the back.

"Take the copilot's seat on the other side up front," he told her.

"Are you sure?"

"Of course. That way you can see where we're going."

"I may not want to."

"You're going to love it." He didn't give her time to argue. Instead he threw Joselyn's briefcase up to her. She caught it in midair and stumbled into the seat up front.

He pushed off before she had a chance to change her mind, and they drifted quickly away from the dock. He climbed up into the pilot's seat and closed the door, flipped a couple of switches overhead while he fastened a headset with a microphone over his ears. He flipped several more switches and turned a dial. Suddenly the propeller kicked over and the engine started.

Belden looked out the side window, watching to be sure that his wing cleared any obstructions on the dock. "Have you flown in a seaplane before?"

"Never."

"But you have been up in small planes."

She shook her head as he watched her out of the corner of one eye, his hands continually messing with the controls overhead.

"Then it should be exciting." He looked down at her skirt. "Though you might want to buckle your seat belt so it doesn't get too exciting."

She buckled the single belt, low across her lap, fumbled with it until the ends snapped together, then pulled the strap until it was tightly pulling her down into the seat.

"There's nothing to worry about." He looked over at her. He could smell fear. "I've been flying planes for years."

"I'm not scared." She lied.

"Good. Then that makes one of us." He gave her a smile, more Redford. Before she could say another word, he pushed a lever forward and the engine literally ignited in a burst of power. The plane lurched forward and into a slow turn, away from the dock and out toward the open channel.

Her knuckles were white from gripping the front edge of her seat. She looked over at him and the smile finally left his face. He was now all business concentrating on the channel out in front of them.

The movement of the plane over the water picked up a rhythm, and she began to relax, to settle in. It glided smoothly, then hit a wake, probably its own from the trip in. The plane lurched a little.

Belden made a turn and lined up in a straight path down the channel between the harbor and Henry Island. Without hesitation, he reached for the handle on a control that rested on the console between them. He pushed it forward and the plane began to move faster through the water, lurching over mild undulations in the surface of the sea. The noise and vibration of the engine increased until Joselyn could hear nothing but the rattle of metal and the pounding of pontoons on the water. The plane picked up speed as his hand pushed the control farther forward, and the noise became a roar that filled her senses, the vibration chattering her teeth and penetrating to the core of her body.

Belden's concentration was intense, eyes straight down the channel as they bounded over the water, until in one smooth motion he pulled back slowly on the wheeled yoke, and like

Pegasus they broke contact with the shimmering surface of the
sea and lifted skyward.

This was a new sensation for Joselyn, since she had never
flown in a small plane. Unlike heavily powered passenger jets,
they were buffeted by air pockets and rocked by crosswinds.
The sensation of perpetual climbing was strange, as if any
instant gravity would reassert its power and pull them down
into the sea.

Joss looked down at the islands of the San Juan chain,
hundreds of them, spread out beneath them, verdant mountains
rising from a carpet of blue water, shimmering in the morning
sunlight. "It's beautiful!"

"It's one of the reasons I like to fly. You can't see this in
a jet. They get above the clouds too fast. Besides, I'm a control
freak. When I'm going somewhere, I like to have my hands
on the wheel."

She nodded like she understood.

They continued to climb for several minutes as they circled
over the islands then headed south, down the sound. The engine ceased its struggle as they leveled off and settled into a
steady monotone.

"Why don't you take it for a second?"

"What?"

"The controls," he said. His hands were off the wheel
before Joselyn could say anything else. She grabbed the controls in front of her, and the right wing started to dip.

"Put your feet on the rudder controls." He pointed to two
pedals on the floor. "Just keep them even. Keep the nose level
with the horizon, and you'll be fine."

Joselyn found herself flying the plane, unable to speak, a
cold chill running down her spine. It was like an out-of-body
sensation. Pebbles of perspiration broke out on her forehead.
Sheer fright.

"How do you like it?"

"Great. Take it back."

"You're doing fine." He started looking through some papers he pulled from a pocket in the door, totally ignoring what
she was doing at the controls.

"Aren't you afraid I'm going to fly us into a mountain?"

"Nope." He didn't look up. "The only mountain I have
to worry about is behind us."

"Good to know you have confidence in me."

"I might even take a nap."

"Don't you dare."

He was smiling again.

Her eyes were darting from the dials and switches on the panel in front of her to the horizon and back. Terror ebbed toward discomfort as she began to get the feel of the controls.

"You're on a perfect heading. Another twenty minutes, and we should be over North Seattle."

"This is no way to treat your lawyer," she told him.

"Aren't you having fun?"

She wouldn't admit it, but actually she was beginning to.

"It's just like riding a bicycle," he told her.

"Yes, but if I fall off a bicycle the ground is a lot closer."

"The object here is not to fall. You're diving a little."

"So what do I do?"

"See your airspeed?" He pointed to one of the gauges. "Very easily pull back on the wheel just a little. That's it. Bring the nose up just a little."

She stopped talking and concentrated on the controls. The horizon slowly leveled out across the bottom of the windshield and the airspeed indicator dropped thirty miles an hour.

"Good. Now let's talk about what I can expect at the courthouse today." He had some papers spread out on his lap, like he was going to take notes.

"You're not going to be getting my undivided attention unless you take this back."

He laughed and took the wheel, putting his feet on the control pedals. "Relax. I've got it."

Joselyn took a big sigh and stretched back in the chair, feeling knots release from the muscles in her arms and shoulders where she'd stiffened up over the controls. She took a couple of deep breaths and then reached for her briefcase and the pad inside on which she had made notes. She flipped through some pages, and when she looked over his hands were off the wheel.

"Who's flying?"

"Autopilot," he said. "I'll keep a look out for other planes. You tell me what I'm supposed to do when we get there."

"If you say so." She picked up her notes. "First thing. We may get an idea of what they're looking for if there are other witnesses waiting when we get to the courthouse. You may recognize some of them. If so, it may give us a clue as to what they're fishing for. You have to tell me if you recognize anybody. There's still time to take the Fifth, to refuse to testify, but only if we have good reason.''

''I understand.''

''Once you get inside, the jury foreperson will swear you in. The prosecuting attorney in charge of the investigation, probably a deputy U.S. attorney, will advise you of your rights. The right to counsel, the right to remain silent, so forth. They will probably warn you that because you are under oath, if you do not tell the truth, you can be prosecuted for perjury.''

''I understand.''

''At that point the prosecutor will probably tell you something about the nature of the investigation. This is a critical point. If there are any surprises, if in fact they are not investigating this guy Max Sperling, the one you told me about, take a break. Tell them you want to confer with your lawyer. They have to let you do it. Don't answer any questions until you come outside and we have a chance to talk. Do you understand?''

''Piece of cake,'' said Belden.

''Let's hope so.''

''What happens then?''

''Once we get the ground rules nailed down, the prosecutor will start asking you questions. Think before you answer. Just answer the questions he asks. Don't volunteer anything. If you start giving long answers and getting into items he hasn't raised, it's just going to make the whole thing go on longer. That only serves to create more jeopardy for you. To open areas of inquiry the prosecutor hasn't thought about. Keep it short and sweet.''

''Got it.''

''Once you start testifying, tell them the truth. Don't hide anything.''

''But you just said I wasn't supposed to volunteer.''

''What I mean is that you have to answer their specific question directly and completely. But don't go beyond the specific question. Don't open the door on other matters. That's their job. The less you say, the faster you're going to be out of there. If you can answer a question with a single yes or no, do it.''

"Got it. Just a second.'' He flipped a switch and a dial on something that looked like a radio overhead, then talked into the microphone fixed to his headset.

"I.L.S. control. This is J-N eight-two-four-six. Coming in on vector . . .'' He looked at his compass and gave them a heading.

The tower talked and Joselyn could hear static but none of the words.

"Lake Union.'' There was another pause.

"Thank you,'' said Belden, then turned a dial on the radio.

"Sorry, had to clear for approach.'' He flipped another switch and took the controls. She assumed he had turned off the autopilot.

"OK, so I don't give them anything they don't ask for.''

"Right.''

"I talk to you if there's any surprises.''

"Right.''

"What else?''

"I'm not precisely sure. Procedures vary from district to district. Some prosecutors allow members of the grand jury to question the witness directly once the prosecutor is finished. I don't know if that will be the procedure here or not. I'll try to find out before you go in. But if they do allow jurors to question you, be careful.''

"Why?''

"Because the jurors are going to look like ordinary folk. That's what they are. Most of them are going to be friendly and smiling. They're not going to be talking in legal-speak. They're going to sound like your neighbors. There is a tendency to let your guard down, to get into a conversation with them. Don't do it! The prosecutor's going to be listening to every word, and any door you open he's going to walk through. These are not your friends. They didn't invite you down for a social meeting.''

"I understand. The enemy,'' said Belden.

"Don't be hostile; just be guarded.''

"Good. Does that cover it?''

"Pretty much. If you don't understand a question, get clarification. Don't hesitate to ask them to restate the question.

And if you feel that you want to talk to me, tell them you want to take a break to confer with counsel.''

"OK.''

Joselyn could see houses spread out like a carpet on a field of green beneath them as they started to descend over the northern suburbs. The University District spread out along the western shore of Lake Washington.

"Tell me a little more about your business?'' she asked.

This came out of the blue and seemed to surprise Belden.

"What's to tell?''

"Exactly what is it you make?''

"Switches.''

"I know. But what kind of switches?''

"The kind that turn things on and off.''

She looked at him, like "give me a break.''

"Right now we're actually into designing computer chips for voice-recognition systems. Used in security,'' said Belden. "It's like a fingerprint, only in this case what we're checking is a voiceprint. Somebody speaks into a telephone, or microphone, and the computer compares the voice to the voiceprint on record. If it matches, the door opens or the lights go on or an alarm is set. You can turn on your sprinklers or your lights long-distance. If the voiceprint doesn't match, the person doesn't get access.''

"Fascinating,'' said Joselyn. "They can actually do that?''

"Accurate to more than ninety-nine percent. Almost impossible to fool.''

"And what if I have a tape recording of somebody's voice?''

"Even with a tape recording of the right voice, the chip will pick up background noise, the slightest grain from the microphone on the tape, and lock you out. The best systems use coded words. With the right words you could control the world.''

He swung the plane wide to the east and began his approach over the university, cutting power and dropping his wing flaps. He banked steeply to the right and dropped rapidly, so that Joselyn's stomach felt as if it were going to bounce off the ceiling. They picked up speed, with the engine almost at idle as they dove toward Lake Union, over the I-5 bridge with traffic backed up to a standstill.

As they approached Lake Union, Belden pulled back slowly on the controls and slid the throttle forward for a little more power. The engine lifted the nose momentarily.

Touchdown on the water was smooth and barely perceptible, but for the spray shooting up from the pontoons to the side and behind them and some shudder in the plane as they glided across the water.

"There. I got you here in one piece." He looked over at her.

"I never had a doubt."

"Right," he said.

He taxied the plane toward one of the docks. A large sign on a green building read "Seattle Seaplanes." There were flowers, a fusillade of color in wooden planter boxes all along the dock, and several small floatplanes tied up, one of them pulled up on a floating dock that was partially submerged under the load.

"I made special arrangements to tie up here. Just for a few hours. I don't come down that often to have a permanent berth. We can call a cab from inside."

Joselyn checked her watch. He was right. They had plenty of time.

Ten minutes later, they were in a cab cutting through the downtown, heading up the hill toward Madison and Sixth, the U.S. courthouse in Seattle.

NINE

It was an absolutely wild scam, better than knocking over a bank, or using a pickup truck with a chain around the axle to pull an ATM machine out of a wall and haul it away. Nobody was going to get shot doing this one, and most banks didn't have this kind of cash on hand.

Besides, the tight khaki shorts made Buck's behind look real sexy. The little receptionist was checking him out as he stood at the counter and waited for her to finish her phone call. If she knew that the view was going to cost her employer a thousand dollars or more, she might have looked a little longer.

Buck Thompson lived in the small town of Sedro-Woolley in the extreme northern part of western Washington State. He was a lumberman by vocation, but he hadn't worked at it for three years. There were no jobs. He and most of his friends did whatever they could to keep their families together. From time to time, Buck took odd jobs in other states to make a few dollars. It was how he had gotten in on this current thing.

He'd made a decent living for ten years until the last compromise between environmentalists and the White House on timber harvests for federal land closed all the mills. Since then, Thompson and most of his friends had been out of work. One of his boys had dropped out of school a year ago, at age fourteen, to get a job. His wife held down two, cleaning offices at night and answering phones in a small brake shop during the day.

What made him mad was the constant drumming on CNN, telling everybody that the economy was just fine. The news media, or whatever they were calling themselves these days, had become nothing but a mouthpiece for the federal government, parroting press releases from the White House. If the president took a crap in public, they'd report that he shit gold bricks.

If Buck and his friends wanted to know what was going on politically, the only place they could get the truth was on the Internet. At least there they could pick their own bias, rather than having the news moguls spin everything for them.

Buck searched the Web nightly when he was home, hitting all the familiar sites, Aryan Nations, the Brotherhood, a handful of tax protest sites, all the places where people with militia leanings hung out. They communicated on-line, using code words and aliases. The feds were always listening, watching all the chat rooms.

Buck knew that jobs were being shipped to other countries in droves. The American trucking industry all along the Mexican border had been decimated. Unemployed truckers were big-time on the Net. Companies that had flourished for generations went bankrupt within months of the U.S. entering into the North American Free Trade Agreement. It was an unholy alliance between the political parties, Democrats and Republicans, and big business to screw over working people. As far as Buck was concerned, all politicians were a pack of pimps, anxious to sell their country to anybody in return for a quick campaign contribution, half the time from foreigners or foreign governments.

Buck thought the Justice Department was a joke. It did nothing but cover it all up. The FBI was interested only in chasing people like Buck, people who didn't fit the definition of being politically correct. Anybody who resisted taxes, made a critical comment about the IRS, or criticized the president found that they were suddenly being investigated or audited.

It had gone full circle. America had destroyed the Soviet Union only to replace it as the world's biggest totalitarian government, run by crooked politicians, and their corporate friends in the media, and administered by corrupt bureaucrats. It was America's legacy for the millennium.

It was the reason Buck took so much pleasure in the latest scam, screwing over the phone company, dialing for dollars. It was certain to raise a lot of money in a very short time. Buck guessed that something big was up.

He wondered who thought it up. He'd been told it was a Russian, a mobster from Moscow who had immigrated to the U.S. The Russians didn't rob banks or knock over liquor stores. They believed in making money the modern way, by reaching out and touching somebody. Surviving in the shadow of the Kremlin for seventy years, the Russian mob was more than a match for American law enforcement. In five years, the federal government would be wishing the Iron Curtain was back, trying to rebuild the wall in Berlin. America wanted to free the people of Eastern Europe. Be careful what you ask for; you may get it.

The scheme was brilliant. There were fourteen of them, all militia members, working it this afternoon. Each one wore the uniform of a different delivery company. They all carried a package under one arm and a metal clipboard with phony shipping receipts under the other. Though all of the guys came from the Northwest, today they worked the area around Culver City in Southern California, mostly light industry, a few warehouses, and a couple of large retail outlets. They picked businesses that looked large, the kind of company that might not notice an extra thousand or two on their phone bill at the end of the month.

The little blond receptionist was kind of cute. She reminded Buck of one of his nieces. She wore a headset like an airplane pilot and punched buttons on the phone's keypad like a pro. He was glad the money wasn't coming out of her pocket. She punched one of the buttons on her phone, looked up at Buck, and smiled. ''Can I help you?''

''Got a package for Mr. Zinsky,'' he told her.

The girl looked at him quizzically, like she didn't recognize the name. There was no reason she should. Zinsky didn't exist.

''You sure you have the right address?'' she asked.

Buck read her the name of the company and the address from the shipping label inside its clear plastic holder on the package.

"Maybe he's new," she said. She rifled through the roster of employees on the counter in front of her. "Hmm." Nothing. "Why don't I take it," she said, "and I'll call your office if I can't find him."

"I can't do that," said Buck. "He has to sign for it."

"I can sign," said the girl.

"Special handling," said Buck. "Requires Mr. Zinsky's signature."

"Well." Now she wasn't sure what to do. "I could call my boss." She started paging through the printed roster one more time just in case she missed his name. Still nothing.

"It's a priority overnight," said Buck. "Must be something pretty important."

She offered a pained expression. She didn't want to get in trouble. But she didn't know what to do.

"Could you spell the name?"

"Harold Zinsky. Z-I-N-S-K-Y."

She looked some more. There was nobody by that name. By now the phones lines in front of her were all lighting up, bells ringing everywhere.

"Just a second." She answered one of the phones. "Can you hold." She went down the line. "Please hold." She did it six more times until all of the lines were flashing, but quiet.

"That's the right address, and our company," she said. "But there's no Mr. Zinsky here."

"Emm." Now it was Buck's turn to look troubled. "I wonder if I could use your phone. Check with the dispatcher. It's an eight-hundred number."

"Sure. There's one at the end of the counter there. Just press nine for an outside line." The girl went back to her phones, relieved that she didn't have to make a decision, at least for the moment.

This one was gonna be a cakewalk. Buck sidled down to the end of the counter five feet from where the girl was talking on the line. He picked up the phone, dialed nine, and then the number. Only it wasn't an eight-hundred number. He dialed nine-hundred and then the phone number. It was what is known as a "pay per call" service, one of those numbers used by some legitimate businesses but known mostly as the telephone equivalent of the red-light district. "Call me. My name is Sherie. I'll tickle your dingle-dangle long-distance with a feather for three dollars a minute."

What the average phone user didn't know was that some telephone companies allowed businesses to charge as much as $250 per call when someone dialed their nine-hundred number.

The service provider, usually one of the big telephone carriers, would take a small percentage, or a flat fee per call, and would forward the rest of the money earned during the month to the customer possessing that particular nine-hundred number. In Buck's case, this was the Western States Militia, a consortium of well-armed and organized patriots. Only they didn't use the militia name with the phone company. Instead they used something nice and respectable: "Rock Island Finance and Investment." They would change it next week when they moved to a different area of the country and did the scam again with a different number and corporate name.

Buck listened and waited for the taped message to end. It was very brief, something innocuous about financial planning, no more than ten words in length.

He hung up the phone without saying a word. The girl looked over at him. She was talking to somebody else on the switchboard.

"Busy." Buck whispered to her.

She read his lips, nodded, and smiled like she understood. She kept talking, forwarded a call, and picked up another.

Buck dialed again. Did the same routine. By the time he was finished, he had dialed the number five times: $1250 on the company's phone bill. The charges would be sent along to the receptionist's employer at the end of the month, and unless the company's bookkeeper was Ebenezer Scrooge, it would probably be paid without much question. The phone company in turn would send the money along to the militia under its corporate alias.

Buck could have done it four more times, but he took pity on them. Besides it didn't pay to be greedy with one pigeon. This was the land of opportunity. There were at least a dozen other good-sized businesses on this same street who wouldn't notice the charges on their phone bills for at least two or three months, if ever. He would hit them all within the next two hours. Then he would move a few miles away and start over again. Tomorrow they would pull up stakes and move out to

Orange County and from there down to San Diego. Welcome to the electronic superhighway.

Buck walked back over to the receptionist. She looked up at him, still dealing with a caller on the line.

"Can you hold a moment?" She pressed the hold button.

"The line's busy," said Buck. "I don't seem to be able to get through. Tell you what. I'll check the information with my office from the cell phone in my truck. Have 'em run a trace on it and call the party who sent it out. They probably either got the name or the address wrong. We'll straighten it out, and if it's supposed to be delivered here, I'll come back and drop it by this afternoon."

"That'd be great." The girl flashed big pearly whites at him like he'd just solved a huge problem for her.

Always willing to help, thought Buck. After all, he shouldn't be wearing their uniform unless he was willing to provide the service.

He turned and headed for the door. He could see her checking out his tight ass in the dark smoked glass of the front door just before he opened it.

He had done a quick calculation in his head before getting started that morning. If each one of the fourteen men working the scam that day averaged $1000 a hit, and they could do five businesses in an hour, they were pulling down $70,000 an hour. Times eight hours, was $560,000 for the day. The militia would take ninety percent. The other ten percent would be divided among the fourteen men working the scam. Buck wasn't asking any questions. No matter which way you cut it, it beat the shit out of climbing trees and whacking off limbs.

KENT, WA

Toothpaste and toilet paper did the job on the smoke detector in the cell. The smoke detectors were there so the guests wouldn't light up at night and burn the jail down.

Chaney molded a flat baffle out of a dozen pieces of the toilet paper and held it together with toothpaste and water. He fit it precisely over the smoke detector, then used more toothpaste to seal it off.

Quickly Chaney moved to the window, removed the screw

heads, and lifted the acrylic screen off, setting it gently on the floor against the wall. Taking a single match he held it up as high as his arms could reach into the well of the window and allowed the match to burn like a candle for several seconds.

"What are you doing?" said Chenko.

"Shut up."

They waited for almost two minutes. It seemed like a lifetime. Chaney was about to light another match when he heard the rustle of branches and noise outside. He looked up and saw a man's face beaming back at him from beyond the bars.

"What the hell took you so long?" said Chaney.

"There was a car coming. Here, take this." The man outside was breathless. He passed Chaney a small walkie-talkie attached by wire to a headset.

"We got cars at each end of the street. They're both on channel seven. They see any movement outside, cars coming by, guards nosing around, they'll let you know. Cover the flame. You got it?"

"Got it," said Chaney.

"Here. Now don't drop it." The guy outside carefully slid the carrying case with the Victor torch through the bars. He had tied the handle of the case onto a rope so that he could retrieve it if for any reason they weren't able to get out that night.

"If you need anything, holler into the headset. I'll be in the car at the corner." Before Chaney could say anything, the guy was gone.

He left the other end of the rope coiled on the ground outside and headed back to his colleague in the car. For this he walked a very careful route, one that they'd mapped out earlier in the week.

Outside the jail was a video surveillance system. Cameras mounted on rotating motors were erected under the eaves of the building and monitored by guards at a station inside.

The system had only one problem: a noticeable blind spot in the area outside of the ground floor cell that Chaney had muscled away from Tattoo and Homer. It might have been a relatively new county jail, but it wasn't Pelican Bay or the federal prison in Atlanta.

Chaney got the sparker out of the box, adjusted the oxygen and acetylene for the right mix, and sparked the torch. He adjusted the nozzle until there was a blue flame and the steady hiss of gas.

Inside the box was a set of welder's glasses. Chaney put them on and went to work. It was a long and awkward reach, eighteen inches up into the open well of the window. He stood on the rim of the commode that was directly beneath it, and several times almost slipped and stepped into the open toilet.

Chenko held a blanket over the window in the cell's door so the flash of sparks from the torch cutting steel wouldn't be reflected outside into the partially dark corridor. Occasionally he peeked behind the blanket to be sure the guard wasn't making his rounds.

Smoke from the torch began to waft back into the cell and up toward the ceiling. Chenko looked nervously at the smoke detector wrapped in toilet paper and hoped that it would hold.

"Are you almost finished?"

"Shut up and watch the door," said Chaney. He'd cut through one of the bars and was halfway through another when the guys outside in the car whispered into the headset of the walkie-talkie.

"Cool it. Pedestrian coming up the street."

Chaney removed the torch from the window and held it down near the floor so that it wouldn't be visible from the outside. He waited a couple of minutes until he was given the "all clear."

Chaney was hoping the guys outside had remembered to bring the pry bar. The plan called for Chaney to cut through each of the bars one time near the bottom. Using the pry bar, they would then bend the steel bars out of the way, enough so that Chaney and the Russian, using the bars as handholds, could shimmy up and out through the window.

He hadn't quite finished the second bar when the torch began to sputter and showed a yellow flame. The first acetylene bottle was empty. Chaney began to worry that maybe he hadn't brought enough. If they couldn't cut the other bars, he would have to push all the tools out through the window, have the guys in the cars pick them up, then put the acrylic screen back in place and wait until tomorrow night to finish. If the guards checked the window and saw the burned bars or checked the acrylic screen, it would be all over.

He disconnected the first acetylene bottle and hooked up

the second, sparked a flame, and went back to work. Chaney was almost through the third bar when Chenko snapped his fingers twice. "Guard."

Chaney whipped the torch out of the window and doused the flame. He dropped the torch into its case and with one foot kicked the whole thing under the bunk.

The Russian pulled the blanket off the window and dove for the upper bunk as Chaney replaced the acrylic screen. He didn't have time to mess with the screw heads. He fell on his bunk just as the guard's flashlight beam reflected off the glass window in the cell door.

Chaney lay like a dead man in his underwear on the bunk as the guard's light flashed around the room and flickered off the acrylic panel in the window. He prayed that the guard wouldn't notice that the six screw heads were missing.

Chaney's head was turned away from the wall toward the door. His eyes were open enough for peripheral vision to pick up something on the floor. It was a loop of red rubber hose from the torch, sticking out from under the bunk.

The flashlight beam moved around the walls of the cell like Tinker Bell. Chaney flopped over on the bed as if shifting in his sleep, dangled one arm over the edge of the bunk, and with his hand scraped the floor, catching the hose in a single fluid motion, sweeping it under the bunk.

The flashlight traced his movements just a half second too late to pick up the hose, which by then had disappeared under the blanket hanging over the edge of Chaney's mattress. He held his breath as the light swept the wall above the bunks. It passed over the toilet paper cocoon covering the smoke detector so quickly that the guard didn't notice. He also failed to pick up the hazy cloud of smoke that floated lazily just beneath the ceiling of the cell like mist over the Blue Ridge Mountains. The guy was either blind or going through the motions of a bed check while his mind was off duty, probably thinking about humping his wife or his girlfriend or somebody else's wife.

The light disappeared from the cell door window. Chaney and the Russian waited several seconds until they heard receding footsteps back down the corridor outside.

Chaney got up and checked the window. "Go."

The Russian grabbed his blanket, jumped off the bunk, and

covered the window again. This time he kept a careful eye peering behind it.

Chaney went back to work with the torch. "Just one more." He cajoled and coaxed the little torch, babying it to conserve fuel. He kept checking his watch. Eighteen minutes later, he was through the last bar.

"Done." He whispered into the mouthpiece of the headset and a second later heard a car door slam some distance away outside. A minute later there was rustling in the bushes beyond the window and Chaney saw the business end of a long steel pry bar poking into the window from outside. Using the hard frame of the masonry around the window, the man outside leveraged his weight against the cut bars one at a time until each of them was bent almost ninety degrees and lay nearly flat against the well on the inside of the window.

"Time to go," said Chaney.

Chenko went first. He didn't bother with clothing. In his underwear he put one foot on the edge of the commode, then pulled himself up using the bars inside the window. He slid through the window easily and disappeared through the bushes outside.

Chaney started to go, then looked back. He stepped back down off the commode, disconnected the twin hoses from the bottles of oxygen and acetylene, and flipped the bottles up and out through the window. Then he assembled the torch back in its box and placed it on top of the commode. Only then did he pull himself up through the window and out. He used the rope on the outside to lift the case with the torch out through the window. There was no sense leaving it behind for the cops to trace. A Victor Portable torch was an item that a hardware dealer would remember selling. He might remember Chaney's face. Why have a bad portrait hanging in the post office when you didn't have to?

TEN

YEKATERINBURG

It appears the problem may be double what we originally thought." Gideon van Ry found himself shouting into the mouthpiece of the telephone. "No, I said double." He worried that his accent along with the bad connection was making it more difficult for him to be understood back in Santa Crista, where Caroline was taking notes.

He also spoke in cryptic terms. He was sure they were listening somewhere, probably down the hall from Mirnov's office.

"Yes. Yes, that's what I said." He was hoping Caroline would get the message without his saying it: that whoever took the devices took two of them. He worried that if he got too specific, the Russians would cut the phone connection. He'd already lost contact twice. Gideon waited for the deadening click, but it didn't happen.

Mirnov looked at him from across the desk. Gideon offered a harmless smile, shrugged his shoulders as if to say "bad connection."

"Oh, they're being very helpful. The Russian government is most cooperative," said Gideon. He hoped this might buy more time on the line. For the most part, it was true. The problem was that in the new Russia no one quite knew precisely where to draw the line on security.

"The facility here is everything we thought it would be," said Gideon.

This had a double meaning. He and Caroline had discussed what they knew about Sverdlovsk before Gideon left Santa Crista, and it was not good.

"Yes, you can put that in the report," he told her.

Mirnov smiled at him, and Gideon smiled back. He would call her once he left Russia and edit the report before it was released; otherwise they would never allow him back in. Diplomacy was always important if you wanted continued access to information. While sunshine was the institute's business, they were not out to embarrass the Russian government. Poking the light of public awareness into dark crevices containing arsenals of mass destruction was the institute's stock-in-trade. There was nothing the Russians would hear or read that they did not already know. Parts of their weapons storage and disposal system were in serious trouble. The problem was that neither the Russian nor the American governments were telling their people about this.

"One other note," said Gideon. "The items in question. They were not taken at the same time." He listened. They did not cut him off.

"That's right. Both of them shipped through Vladivostok. Right . . . Say again? . . . No. No. Different bills of lading. Both labeled machine tools. Some ultimate point of delivery. Yes."

Caroline was now probing him, trying to get everything she could. In an hour, the bare outline of information would be on their database. The details they could disclose publicly would follow in a few days. Clients around the world would be on the alert, mostly government security services. They would want as much information as possible. No doubt they would be querying the institute by phone, fax, and E-mail. It was a major story for a very select audience.

"Let me spell it. That's Belden Electronics. B-E-L-D-E-N. A Washington State address. Check with information," said Gideon. "It appears to be incorporated, if the address means anything. It's a P.O. box. A place called Friday Harbor. Probably an address of convenience. You can be sure they did not ship the devices there. That's right." He held one hand over his other ear to hear better over the faltering phone line.

"What? Say again? . . . Do I know when the last device was taken?" Gideon looked over at Mirnov. His superiors had instructed him to cooperate as much as possible. The Russian shrugged his shoulders. He wasn't sure. Or perhaps he was just in shock. No doubt he would be on a plane to Moscow by nightfall to answer a lot of questions.

"We cannot be sure when the last one was taken . . . Specifications, you say?"

Caroline wanted to know precisely the type of devices missing.

"Artillery shells. One-hundred-and-fifty-three-millimeter artillery. Hello. Caroline, are you there?"

He listened for a second. "Hello. Hello."

Apparently he'd gone too far. He could hear clicking on the line. They'd cut him off.

He held the receiver away from his face for a second and looked at it as if Caroline might actually crawl through the wire. Then he placed the phone into its cradle on Mirnov's desk.

"Ah. Telephone service. What can I say?" said Mirnov. "Like everything else in the new Russia. Only the new entrepreneurs have good phones."

Gideon looked up at the ceiling in frustration and ran the fingers of both hands through his long blond hair. It was usually parted in the middle and full. This afternoon it was a mess. He hadn't shaved or showered in more than two days. He and Mirnov had been camped at the Russian's office trying to assemble what information they could. Mirnov was constantly called out to confer with superiors. Gideon wondered if he was being told everything.

He worried that maybe the Russians would hold him, if not here, then upon his return to Moscow. The Russian government might be the least of his concerns. There were darker forces at work in Mother Russia. The Mafiya, as it styled itself, was more violent there than anyplace else on earth. They did not mind murdering foreigners, particularly those who threatened their interests.

Gideon pushed himself off the corner of Mirnov's desk, where he'd been leaning on the edge since his call went through to Caroline.

"We'll have to wait and see if our people can put the call through again," said Mirnov.

"Two devices," said Gideon.

"Yes." Mirnov lit a large Cuban cigar and offered one to Gideon.

The tall Dutchman shook his head. "Both artillery shells," he said. "I understand why they would take two of them. They could sell them both on the black market, Libya, Iran, Iraq. There are plenty of potential buyers. But why ship them to the same point of destination? That does not make sense," he told the Russian.

Even if there were two targets in North America, Gideon was convinced they wouldn't send a second device by the same route. The risks of surveillance were too great.

"You would send them to separate destinations, so that if one was discovered, the other might get through."

"Unless . . ." said Mirnov.

"Unless what?" Gideon looked at the Russian.

"These are old weapons we are talking about. Some of these artillery shells date back to the mid-sixties. Their nuclear cores are aging. The high explosives surrounding the plutonium pit are old. The detonators, which are critical, may not have been checked in years. They have been in storage for two, maybe three decades. We do not have the maintenance records. I checked. I suspect that Dimitri had looked as well."

"What are you saying?"

"What you call nuclear shelf life," said Mirnov. "If you were purchasing a nuclear device on the black market, paying top prices, would you not want some assurance that it would function?"

"I would," said Gideon.

"What better way than a second device?" said Mirnov. "Remember they have Chenko." Grigori Chenko was the Russian technician who disappeared about the same time as the first device.

"He would know if the first warhead was defective. Perhaps they found a problem after it was shipped. That would account for why they did not take them at the same time.

"With a second warhead, you have spare parts. Even if both were defective in some way, Chenko could probably make one good bomb. And perhaps increase its yield."

There were two basic types of nuclear weapons, so-called gun devices that used high explosives to propel a projectile of highly enriched uranium into a larger core target of the same. The resulting collision, assuming there was enough velocity, would split the atom, releasing massive amounts of energy and setting off a chain reaction.

The second type was more sophisticated. The so-called implosion device was constructed of a plutonium sphere in thirty-two individual pie-shaped sections. This was used to surround a beryllium/polonium pit in the center. The entire sphere was wrapped in conventional high explosives, a form of plastique, and set off by multiple simultaneous detonators. The uniform force of detonation, critically timed to one-ten-millionth of a second around the entire outer portion of the sphere, would drive the plutonium into the beryllium core, setting off the nuclear chain reaction.

The implosion device was more powerful, generating more atomic yield. The two artillery shells in question were of this type.

The elaborate nature of the implosion design also presented a problem. It required more maintenance. The timing of individual detonations around the outer sphere required exquisite precision. Without this, all that resulted was a dirty bomb, radioactive debris blown into the air by the explosion. By itself this could kill a few thousand people if they inhaled the dust. But if there was critical mass, if there was enough plutonium for a chain reaction and the device worked as designed, then in the flicker of an eye a major population center, hundreds of thousands, perhaps millions of people would be incinerated in a matter of seconds.

"Am I correct in assuming there are no safety devices for these shells?"

"What you call permissive action links?" said Mirnov.

"Exactly."

"No. They are too primitive for that."

The devices in question were small, and old, with a definite shelf life. They were not something that would find its way onto the shopping list of some rogue state for their own arsenal unless they had no other choice. It would be easier and more effective to purchase fissile materials and design their own bomb.

The artillery shells in question would be the weapon of choice only for a calculated act of terror. They were easily armed and transported. Whoever had taken them had gone to the trouble of coming back for a second device, evidencing some concrete plan. Everything Mirnov was telling him led to one unassailable conclusion: whoever bought the weapons had a clear target in mind.

He looked at the scrap of paper in his hand, the notes he'd made for his phone call to Caroline. He could catch a flight east across the Bering Sea, make a connection in Fairbanks. In ten hours, maybe twelve, he could be in Seattle. He wondered how long it would take him to get from there to this place on the note—this Friday Harbor.

ELEVEN

SEATTLE, WA

A sign on the wall with an arrow pointing left said:

GRAND JURY ROOM

Joselyn and Belden headed down the carpeted corridor in silence.

The place had a hushed feeling of unfettered power. Joselyn had never been partial to the federal side of the law, where cold formality seemed to hold sway. Just being here sent a chill down her spine, the kind experienced by nearly even every citizen when you mention words like "Internal Revenue Service."

Federal buildings were temples to power, where judges were appointed for life, and U.S. attorneys possessed the prosecutorial powers of warlords.

The reach of federal criminal statutes was troubling to Joselyn. They had become so broad that they virtually mimicked every state crime. The protection of double jeopardy had become a joke. If a defendant was acquitted at the state level, but the crime violated notions of political rectitude, the defendant would be tried again at the federal level. This was now done routinely in high-profile cases where political points could be made by a president or his attorney general.

While Belden may not have been concerned, Joselyn was. She knew that a determined federal prosecutor could indict nearly anyone they wanted for virtually any act of human conduct. Whether they could get a conviction from twelve unbiased citizens on a trial jury after they heard all the evidence, and not just hearsay that the government chose to dish up, which was the case before grand jury, was another matter. Even if you were innocent it could take a half million dollars and two years of your life to prove it.

In the distance, she could see a blue-blazered security man sitting behind a desk, just beyond a door with a frosted glass sidelight. On the glass the words GRAND JURY ROOM were etched in black letters. There was a line of wooden chairs backed against the wall in the corridor, hard and foreboding.

Joselyn was hoping to see other witnesses, someone Belden might recognize, to confirm that it was as he said, Max Sperling and his escapades of larceny that had brought them here. She was disappointed. The chairs against the wall were all empty.

Joselyn took the lead as they entered the door. She talked to the guard. With a pleasant smile, she handed him her business card.

"I'm Joselyn Cole. I'm here with my client, Mr. Belden. He's been subpoenaed to testify today."

The guard returned the pleasantries, but his gestures and movements were automatic, like a robot's. He looked at the card, then opened the desk drawer and pulled out a clipboard. He held it so that Joselyn couldn't see what was printed on the pages clipped to the board, and he checked something in pencil.

She assumed it was the witness list and hoped there were other names on it for this particular case. From what she knew of federal grand jury proceedings, they handled a vast mix of cases. The jury might hear bits and pieces of evidence on a dozen different and unrelated matters in a single day, most of it hearsay from government witnesses: the FBI, ATF (Alcohol, Tobacco and Firearms), Customs and Immigration, the IRS, and the DEA (the Drug Enforcement Agency).

Some of these might be long-term investigations involving complex criminal matters that could go on for months or even years. Some of them never resulted in indictments after prosecutors discovered that allegations were founded on nothing but rumors. Too often they made this determination after they called most of the target's friends and all of their business associates before the grand jury for a good grilling. The subject of the investigation might not be convicted, but their reputation would certainly be destroyed.

Other cases, the vast majority, were clear-cut: a bank robbery with a dozen eyewitnesses, for instance. These would usually result in an indictment after half an hour of testimony from two witnesses. Joselyn had no idea which of the two extremes might be involved in the Sperling case.

"I'd like to talk to the assistant U.S. attorney before my client testifies," said Joselyn.

The guy looked at the clipboard again. "That's Mr. McCally. I'll see he gets the message." He wrote a note on the back of Joselyn's business card.

They took a seat outside on the hard chairs, and killed time counting the dimples in the plastered wall four feet away on the other side of the narrow hallway. A number of people filed by, looked at the two of them sitting there, passed through the door, said hello to the guard, and disappeared into the jury room. After the first few went by, Belden shot Joss a quizzical glance.

"Jury members," she told him.

Another ten minutes passed and a few more jurors arrived. A door opened behind the glass sidelight, and a shadow appeared on the other side of the frosted glass. Undertones of a male voice could be heard talking to the gatekeeper at the desk. They heard Belden's name mentioned.

He got up.

"Sit down," she told him. Joselyn stepped around the door and came face-to-face with a tall man in a gray pinstripe suit. He had dark brown hair with some gray creeping in above the ears and deep-set eyes behind angular wire-framed glasses. His complexion was pale, like someone who has been indoors squinting under fluorescent tubes too long.

"Mr. McCally?"

"Yes." There was nothing friendly about the man. The quintessential prosecutor. He was stone-faced, almost icy.

"I'm Joselyn Cole. Mr. Belden's lawyer." She smiled and extended a hand hoping to crack the cold veneer.

It didn't work. He took her hand. "How do you do?"

"Can we talk for a moment before my client goes into the jury room?"

"Sure." He didn't move from the area directly in front of the guard's desk. The marshal just sat there looking at them, expecting to be the third set of ears in the conversation.

"I meant someplace private," said Joselyn.

"If you like." McCally had a file under his arm, quite thick, with the edges of paper sticking out, but nothing Joselyn could read. He led her down a short hallway behind the guard's desk to a room, where he opened the door and flipped on the wall switch. Fluorescent lights flickered on and hummed overhead.

Inside was a small metal conference table with four chairs, two on each side, and a telephone on one corner of the table. The walls were bare, painted pea green. It was very institutional.

They stepped inside, and McCally closed the door behind them.

"What is it you'd like to discuss?" He apparently had no intention of sitting down.

Joselyn was becoming concerned. If Belden was an uninvolved witness, the prosecutor's demeanor certainly did not reflect it. Maybe it was just the hard-nosed edge of federal authority showing, a display of who was boss, but Joselyn's antenna was up.

"My client received a subpoena to appear. He has no idea of the subject matter or what this involves."

"Is that right?" McCally almost seemed amused by this.

"Yes, it is. It would be helpful if you would give us some indication of what this is about?"

"I'll bet it would," said McCally. "Have you ever appeared with a witness before a federal grand jury before?"

Joselyn squirmed. He was checking her credentials.

"Not federal," she said. "I've accompanied witnesses at the state level."

"That's what I thought," said McCally. "Let me give you a little advice. I am not at liberty to discuss the subject matter or content of a grand jury investigation."

"So this is an investigation, not an indictment, at this point?"

"At this time, that's correct."

"Is my client a subject or target of the investigation?"

"Did he receive a target letter?"

"No. Not to my knowledge."

"There's your answer."

"That doesn't tell me much."

"Sorry about that, but it's all you're going to get."

"Can you at least tell me how many witnesses are being called besides my client?"

"No."

"Are any charges pending against anyone in connection with the investigation?"

"You don't appear to understand English."

"I represent a client who is being compelled to testify with no indication of the subject matter. You expect me to allow him to walk into a room without legal counsel to be grilled by God knows how many federal prosecutors and an army of grand jurors, and you won't give us a clue as to the subject matter?"

"Welcome to the real world," said McCally.

"My client doesn't have to testify. He can take the Fifth." She was testing the water, to see if she could walk on it. How badly did they want Belden's testimony? Maybe she could draw McCally into a discussion of immunity.

"He can take the Fifth," said McCally. "That's his right. However, I would point out that in long-term investigations it's often better for a client to stake out his turf before others give us their side of things. Mr. Belden could come up on the short end."

"What are you saying? That he is a target?"

"I didn't say that."

"What are you talking about? You just threatened him."

"I didn't threaten anybody. I just explained how the system works."

"In other words, if some other witness comes before the grand jury and lies through his teeth, you'll focus suspicion on my client because he exercised his constitutional right to remain silent?"

"He has an opportunity to dispel any suspicion by testifying."

"And if he doesn't?"

"Well. That's his decision, isn't it?"

Joselyn could feel the blood boil like molten lead in her veins, fired by the heavy hand of the federal government.

"You've already focused suspicion on him."

"No, I haven't." He smiled as if to say, "Prove it."

"If you want him to testify, we want a grant of immunity."

"Forget it." He turned toward the door as if to leave, then turned to face her again. "Tell your client he can expect some more mail." He was clearly implying a target letter.

"Wait." Now he had her attention. "You're telling me that if he doesn't testify you're going to aim this thing at him?"

"What I'm telling you is that he can help himself or hurt himself. It's up to him."

"What kind of government is this? You won't tell us what the hell is going on, and now you're telling me that if my client doesn't waive his right to remain silent you're going to indict him."

"I've got nothing more to say. Tell your client to make his decision."

"Wait a second. There's no way we can talk about this?"

"That's the process. Take it or leave it." McCally started for the door again.

"Let me talk to him."

He turned. "I would have thought you'd done that before you came here."

Whatever McCally thought Belden had done, he clearly thought Joselyn knew about it. She bit her tongue, afraid that what might come out of her mouth at this moment would only cause her client more grief. It seemed he was already in trouble. Her advice would be that he take the Fifth. But she wanted to keep open the lines of communication with the prosecutor.

"I'll have to talk to my client."

"Do it." He looked at his watch. "How long do you need?"

"I don't know. Give me ten minutes."

McCally was out the door, leaving it open behind him and Joselyn in the room alone. She knew Belden was in trouble. What she didn't know was why. It wouldn't have been the first time a client had lied to her.

She waited for a moment, so that McCally would not be loitering in the hall when she talked with Belden. She heard the door to the jury room open and close. Then she went out past the guard station and through the frosted glass door to the row of chairs against the wall. They were empty. There was no sign of Belden. She looked down the long corridor. Nothing.

She stood there frozen in place and for a moment wondered if McCally had pulled one on her, if during the confusion of their conversation he'd taken her client inside the jury room. *Even the Feds wouldn't do that*, she thought. Still she asked.

She turned to the guard behind her at his desk. "Did Mr. Belden go into the jury room?"

"No."

"Do you know where he went?"

"He's not out there?" The guard looked puzzled, stood up and came to the door, took a look for himself.

"Maybe the men's room," said the guard.

She turned and looked down the hall in the direction indicated by the guard. It was a long stretch leading to the solid oak double doors of one of the courtrooms at the other end.

"Unfortunately I can't check," she told him.

He gave her a look, like he really shouldn't leave his post, but he did. He walked quickly down the corridor, with Joselyn following behind him. The guard went into the men's room, and the door closed behind him.

She waited outside pacing back and forth, running the fingers of one hand nervously through her hair. She looked at her watch. Seconds seemed like minutes. Finally the door opened. She spun around expecting to see Belden. Instead, it was the guard. He was shaking his head.

"Nobody inside."

"Where could he have gone?"

"I don't know."

"You're sure he didn't go inside the jury room?"

"Yeah. Mr. McCally went in, but nobody else. You want me to check with him?"

"No." That was one thing Joselyn didn't want. Next he'd be issuing a subpoena for her. McCally was already wound and wired for action. If he found out that Belden had gotten cold feet and boogied, it would only serve to confirm whatever suspicions he already had.

"Maybe he just went out to get a breath of fresh air," she said. "I'll check."

Joselyn was getting that sick sense, the kind you get when you realize your client has lied to you. She wondered if there was a Max Sperling or if Belden had made him up. Still, why would he come all the way to Seattle with a lawyer and then run? It didn't make sense.

"Are you sure you don't want me to get Mr. McCally?" The guard pulled her from her reverie.

"No. That's all right." Joselyn quickly headed down the hall toward the elevators, leaving the guy standing outside the men's room door. All the way there she wondered what she should do. She could withdraw. After all, she hadn't made a formal appearance. It wasn't like a trial. She'd have to give Belden his money back, at least the part she hadn't already earned. If he wasn't going to tell her the truth, she couldn't represent him.

She could always buy time, tell McCally that her client had had a change of heart. That he'd decided to assert his Fifth Amendment rights. Maybe McCally wouldn't ask to see him. If he did, she could tell him he'd already left the building. Still, that might infuriate the prosecutor. McCally gave all the appearances of possessing a short fuse. He might apply to the court for a bench warrant and have Belden arrested for failure to appear. In the meantime, Joselyn would have spun a yarn to a federal prosecutor. She wondered if that would constitute obstruction of justice? A million thoughts raced through her mind as the elevator seemed to stop at each floor to pick up and deposit passengers. Finally she got to one, stepped out, and checked the lobby. There was no sign of Belden.

They had entered from the Fifth Street side of the building, so instinctively she went to that door.

Maybe he was outside having a smoke. Did he smoke? She couldn't remember. He chewed gum. He'd offered her a stick, outside the courtroom. It began to settle on her that she knew amazingly little about this man. He had paid her fifteen thousand dollars in retainers, and all she had was a post office box for an address and a phone number someplace in Kent. It was funny the things that money made you do—like stop thinking. Joselyn had accepted him as legitimate. Why? Because he came up with the cash? So could most drug dealers.

Her mind began to reel with the possibilities. What if he disappeared? Then she'd have his money. She could write to the court and tell them she couldn't find her client. Yeah, given McCally's mind-set he'd believe that!

She looked at her watch. She had told McCally ten minutes. It had taken her almost five just to get to the Fifth Street entrance.

She stepped outside the door. It was like a meeting of the fallen angels at Smokers Anonymous, the acrid odor of burning cigarettes. A dozen people stood around, hands in their pockets, shuffling and looking down at stamped-out cigarette butts on the ground, as they added to the carnage in their lungs. None of them was Dean Belden.

Joselyn raced down the stairs toward Fifth Street, looking both ways. There was no sign of him. It took her five more minutes to wave down a cab. She looked at her watch as she climbed into the backseat and gave the driver directions.

"There's an extra fifty bucks in it if you can get me there in under ten minutes," she told the driver. By now McCally would be looking for her, asking the guard where she went.

The acceleration of the taxi almost gave her whiplash. It drove her back into the seat, her hands scrambling for the seat belt. Fifty bucks was extravagant, but right now she was angry that Belden had misled her. She would pay some of his money for a fast taxi ride to rip into him. Why he had bothered to fly down she wasn't sure, but there was only one place he could be. If he got cold feet, he would go back to the lake and the plane. Joselyn hoped she could get there before he left.

The driver weaved in and out of traffic and took a course that looked nothing like the one she and Belden had taken earlier that morning. The taxi went under I-5 and climbed the hill on the east side. It took a left on a narrow residential street and then picked up speed. The taxi must have been doing seventy, the driver slowing to fifty for peripheral glances at the cross streets.

Joselyn was afraid to look. If anybody opened a door on a parked car, it was likely to end up in the next country, along with the driver, or at least his hand. She was about to relent, to tell the taxi driver to slow down, when he took another left on two wheels, throwing Joselyn against the corner and the door.

Then she saw it—Lake Union. It was less than ten blocks away on the other side of the freeway.

They headed down the hill. Joselyn fished in her purse for the money and came up with three twenties, then looked at the meter and grabbed a fourth. She was going to make the driver's day. Joselyn had no time to haggle over change. She wondered how long it took to prepare a floatplane for flight. Maybe he'd have to refuel? That would give her plenty of time to catch up with him. She hadn't spent that much time talking to McCally. Even if Belden had left the courthouse immediately after she'd gone into the room with the prosecutor, he couldn't be more than ten minutes ahead of her. Unless his taxi driver had his own private turnpike, he couldn't have gotten to the lake any faster than she did.

They ran a red light and sped along the east shore of the lake.

"It's about a mile up. On the left." Joselyn unbuckled the seat belt and was leaning over, hanging on to the front seat as best she could. She saw the restaurant, Chinese, or Japanese, the words KAMON ON THE LAKE in neon scrawled on a large sign. The seaplane dock was just beyond the restaurant. She remembered it.

"There." She saw Belden's plane. It was at the dock, but somebody had turned it around, and the engine was running. She could see mild ripples on the water being churned from the prop wash. There was no sign of Belden, but he couldn't be far.

"Stop here. Let me out." She almost threw the money at the driver. The car was still moving when she opened the door. It skidded to a stop on the graveled pavement of the parking lot, and Joselyn jumped out. Struggling for a better grip on her briefcase and purse, she nearly tripped.

"You want a receipt lady?"

She ignored the driver. Her thoughts were on the plane, its engine idling a hundred yards away at the end of the dock. She had to negotiate around a wooden planter box, through a white picket gate covered by an arbor.

Joselyn had just cleared the gate when she saw him. Belden was putting his wallet in his hip pocket. She was right. He had to refuel. He was walking toward the plane as if he didn't have a care in the world. He'd stood her up, left her talking to an angry prosecutor at the courthouse, and now he was going to head home as if nothing had happened.

Anger flared like molten lava. "Hey." She yelled at the top of her voice, but it was swallowed by the rumble of the engine.

He stepped across onto one of the pontoons.

She yelled again, but he showed no sign of recognition, his back still to her.

She dropped her briefcase and purse on the dock and started to run, hands cupped to her mouth yelling for him to stop. The heel of one of her shoes caught in the gap between two planks on the dock and snapped.

"Damn it." Her best pair of dress shoes. She took off the broken one, started to hobble, and nearly tripped. She ditched the good shoe, throwing it ahead of her on the dock, and ran in stocking feet, yelling Belden's name along with unmentionable epithets through cupped hands.

The constant rumble of the engine grew louder as she drew near. She was sure he couldn't hear her. He loosened one of the lines securing the plane to the dock, and then for some unfathomable reason, Belden turned, his gaze rising to meet her on the dock.

Joselyn stopped in mid-stride, out of breath, the nylons on her feet shredded. Standing on one pontoon, directly below the plane's open door, Belden looked directly at her, a studied expression as if at first he wasn't sure it was her. Then the sign of recognition, he waved. The fucker actually waved at her and smiled. She couldn't believe it. There was no remorse, not the slightest expression of atonement for the fact that he'd left her holding the bag with an angry prosecutor at the courthouse.

She bent over, hands on her knees, still catching her breath. She was furious. She wanted to kill him. She looked down at the shredded nylon on her feet. Then heard the roar of the engine as it revved-up.

Joselyn looked up, startled. He'd released the aft line, pulled himself up into the plane, and was pulling away from the dock. After all of this, Belden was going to leave her standing there. Over her dead body. She grabbed the first thing she saw—her single good shoe on the dock—and ran headlong toward the plane. She reached the edge of the dock and threw the shoe as hard as she could. It struck the metal aileron on the plane's tail and dropped into the water.

She stood there at the edge of the dock, perspiration running down her face, frustration boiling over. The bottom of one foot throbbed and bled where she'd picked up a splinter. She watched as the plane made a wide, sweeping turn beyond the boathouse at the end of the dock and passed out of sight. The roar of the engine was muted by the wooden facade of the building. Still she could hear him throttling up for the channel and his takeoff, and she could do nothing.

She walked slowly toward the end of the dock, furious. As she reached the corner of the boathouse, Joselyn heard the engine gain an octave in pitch and a hundred points on the decibel meter. Suddenly the plane emerged from behind the far corner of the building. Tail down, engine at full throttle, it roared across the water.

Joselyn stood transfixed as if witnessing the emerging geometric shapes of a kaleidoscope, as the propeller shot forward and skipped across the water like a stone. The wings seemed to lift in a single unified piece, separated from the plane's fuselage by an emerging orange flash, a brilliant burst that seared the optic nerve, delivering intense pain to her eyes. An instant later, the pressure wave hit Joselyn, throwing her onto her back on the dock. Her last memory was one of intense heat as the shock wave passed over her body. The spreading flare of exploding aviation fuel shot a hundred feet into the sky. Small bits of the plane floated in the air like leaves in an autumn gale.

TWELVE

The White House Working Group had tentacles into the National Security Council, eyes and ears at the CIA, the FBI, the Justice Department, and a dozen other federal agencies. They were the clearinghouse for information on domestic terrorism. The group had been formed after the bombing of the federal building in Oklahoma City, and since that time it had convened once a week in the Old Executive Office Building unless there was some urgent business, in which case they could be called together on a half hour's notice. This was not a regularly scheduled meeting.

"What is this about?" Stuart Bowlyn was the chairman of what was known as the Working Group. Its more formal name was the Coordinating Subgroup on Counterterrorism. The panel was designed to try to ease the turf wars that erupted every time Congress threw more money at the war on terrorism.

The attorney general wanted to make sure the State Department wasn't sticking its nose under the lawyers' tent on matters of criminal prosecution. The State was perennially pissed off at the National Security Council for making foreign policy. The FBI and the CIA had their own forms of tribal warfare, and the Department of Defense had only one concern: that nobody, including the president or Congress, screwed with its budget. Dropping money into this pit was like chumming with bloody bait in a tank full of sharks.

Bowlyn had his work cut out. He was an assistant to the national security adviser and closer to the seat of power than anyone else on the panel. Seated with him at the table were an assistant director of the CIA, a high-ranking official of the FBI, and an assistant attorney general. The other members came from Military Intelligence; Alcohol, Tobacco and Firearms; and the Protective Intelligence Division of the Secret Service. They all had high-security clearance.

The deputy director of the CIA handed Bowlyn a report in a folder marked TOP SECRET. Bowlyn opened it and read, then closed the file and looked up.

"Who's up and running on this?"

The CIA nodded toward a man in a naval uniform wearing the rank of captain on the shoulder boards of his white dress uniform shirt.

Bowlyn nodded. The officer got out of his chair and moved around the table toward a large map of the world that was pulled down in front of a chalkboard. He picked up the pointer.

"About a week ago, Naval Intelligence started picking up a lot of frantic transmissions from a Russian military installation in Siberia. A place called Sverdlovsk, here." He pointed to a location on the map in central Russia. "And their Pacific Fleet Command, here." He pointed again. "At the port of Vladivostok. We didn't think anything of it, but we continued to monitor. Most of it was encrypted. But some of it wasn't. Some of it was over phone lines that weren't secure."

"They were talking in the open?" Bowlyn seemed surprised.

"Yes. That got our attention, too. It was as if they wanted us to listen in."

Bowlyn nodded to him, a signal to go on.

"One word kept cropping up in the conversations and transmissions—*Isvania*. We weren't sure what to make of it. We pumped it into one of the military intelligence databases, and two days ago we made a hit. The *Isvania* was a Russian factory trawler. According to our information, it went down in the eastern Pacific sometime earlier this month."

The naval officer moved the pointer on the map again, this time to the U.S. side of the Pacific.

"It sank here, about sixty nautical miles due west of the Strait of Juan de Fuca, off the coast of Washington State. A Coast Guard C-130 spotted the oil slick about ten days ago. A Dolphin helicopter launched from the Coast Guard cutter *Regal* recovered small pieces of wreckage. A marker buoy, a flotation bag, and a partially inflated life raft."

"No survivors?"

"No." The officer picked through a file he'd put on the table until he found the photographs he was looking for, then passed them around the table toward Bowlyn.

"Stenciled on the side of the raft was the name *Isvania*. According to the Russians, the ship was slated for scrap. It was supposed to be headed for Bangkok."

"What was it doing off the West Coast?" said Bowlyn.

"We don't know," said the officer. "Neither do the Russians."

"At least that's what they're telling us." The man from the CIA apparently had his doubts about Russian candor.

The Navy man ignored him. "There were heavy seas in the area but no distress calls. The Russians acknowledge that it is possible the ship was involved in smuggling."

"Smuggling what?" said Bowlyn.

"That's the part they're not telling us."

"And we know why," said the CIA. "Because they know more than they're willing to admit."

"The wreckage we recovered wasn't much," said the Navy man, "but it was enough to give us a hint that whatever it was, the crew of the *Isvania* didn't want us to find it. The marker buoy contained a marine transponder. It emitted a signal that could be picked up on a Russian military frequency. It's an older system. Had a range of no more than about a hundred miles. The flotation bag was the kicker. It was filled with a hundred gallons of diesel fuel."

"What for?" said Bowlyn.

"A submersible lift, to assist the buoys. The buoys would float on the surface, one of them emitting the signal. Whatever the cargo was hung from a line below the bag of diesel fuel. You wouldn't be able to see the bag or the cargo from the surface. The whole thing was pretty ingenious. It was designed to go to the bottom if whoever was supposed to pick it up didn't get it within a few days. There was a small valve on the flotation bag. And a timer set to open the valve. Once the diesel oil spilled out into the sea, the cargo would have pulled the buoys to the bottom. The only reason we got it was that the cargo had been removed. The buoys kept the empty bag near the surface.''

''Any idea what the cargo was?'' said Bowlyn.

''It weighed roughly two hundred pounds.'' Now it was the FBI's turn. ''Our lab analyzed the bag and the marker buoy. Assuming there were two other buoys. We found three severed lines. If they were the same size, and given the capacity of the flotation bag, we worked backward and determined the weight of the load. And there's something else you should see.''

He passed a copy of the lab report to Bowlyn, who looked at it quickly, flipped to the second page, and stopped halfway down.

''You're sure about this?''

''Tested it twice.''

''What else do we know?'' Bowlyn looked around the table.

''We've continued to monitor the Russian communiqués out of Sverdlovsk.'' This from the CIA deputy director.

''We haven't been able to decipher all of them, but what we have indicates a considerable degree of anxiety at fairly high levels of the government.''

''This could come from the place Sverd—''

''Sverdlovsk,'' said the CIA. ''Yes. Underground bunkers. We've got satellite photos if you want to see them.''

Bowlyn shook his head. ''You think something got away from them?''

''It would appear that way,'' said the Navy man.

''Tell me about this place Sverdlovsk.''

''Nearest city is Yekaterinburg. It has a highly developed criminal subculture. There has been considerable violence there in recent years, most of it by organized gangs. Several local officials have been assassinated. One of the key prizes between the warring underworld factions is viewed as the armaments facility at Sverdlovsk. The various criminal groups vying for dominance see the facility as vital turf.''

''That coupled with the fact that the place has piss-poor security,'' said the CIA. ''From what we hear, the gangs in the area see themselves as major players in the world arms market. As far as they're concerned, the Russian government is merely storing the stuff for them, until they can find buyers.''

"We know that the Iranians and Iraqis have been over there trying to shop," said the Navy officer.

"Maybe they've made a purchase," said the CIA.

"Is there evidence of state involvement in this shipment on the *Isvania?*" asked Bowlyn.

"Not so far," said the Navy officer. "But we're still looking."

Bowlyn took a deep sigh.

"It gets a little worse," said the CIA.

"What do you mean?" Bowlyn looked at him.

"Some of the encrypted transmissions between Sverdlovsk and Vladivostok have been decoded. A name has popped up."

"What name?"

"A forged waybill for a shipment of machine parts out of Vladivostok, shipped by a Russian company called Blue Star Enterprises. The trawler *Isvania* left Vladivostok four days before the communiqués started flying back and forth."

"Wonderful," said Bowlyn.

"The CEO of Blue Star Enterprises is Viktor Kolikoff."

Bowlyn's gaze suddenly went cold as steel. He said nothing but sat there looking at the CIA deputy director. This went beyond mere security clearances. They would have to clear the room before the discussion went any further.

THIRTEEN

Lake Union, Seattle, WA

Joselyn winced just a little as the emergency medical technician maneuvered his forceps and plucked another wooden splinter from her forearm. In reflex, she had shielded her face from the force of the blast. The plane's explosion had shattered a piece of wooden railing, showering her with small splinters.

Thankfully the front edge of the blast had put her down flat on her back on the dock, so that most of the flying shrapnel and bits of debris from Belden's plane sailed past, embedding themselves in the wall of the wooden boathouse behind her.

"I hope you know you were very lucky." The EMT didn't look at her as he continued his work.

"Lucky. Right."

"Hang on. I've got a couple more here." He gripped another splinter with the forceps and plucked it like a feather from a bird.

"Ow."

"Relax. Just a few more." The EMT held up the splinter. It was half the size of a toothpick. "I can leave 'em and let them fester. You won't like it much."

Joselyn's arm looked like it had been peppered by a porcupine. "Go ahead. Just be a little more careful."

"Maybe we can talk while he works." McCally wasn't happy. He had arrived at the dock just forty-five minutes after the explosion. Now he was standing outside the back of the open ambulance with an FBI agent in a blue windbreaker, the letters stenciled across his back, and another guy in jeans, running shoes, and a dark sweatshirt with a hood.

"Tell me," said Joselyn. "How did you guys get here so fast?"

"We had your client under surveillance." The guy in the windbreaker spoke before McCally could keep him quiet.

"Thank you, Mr. Larkin," said McCally. "Why don't you go over there and look for pieces of Mr. Belden before the seagulls find them all."

The guy accepted the rebuke, looked down at the dock, but didn't move. Joselyn assumed that the other one in the sweatshirt was a federal agent as well. He was mostly bald and well built, like an athlete, with darting eyes that didn't settle on anything for very long. He had the wary look of some of the criminal clients she had represented down in California.

"You mean you had my client under surveillance the entire time he was under subpoena to appear before the grand jury?"

"Never mind that," said McCally. "You saw him get on the plane, is that right?"

"I already told the police what I saw. You can get whatever information you need from them." Joselyn had identified Belden as being on the plane. As far as she knew he was alone.

"We'd rather get it from you. We've already talked to the police," said McCally. "According to them, you flew down in the plane with him. Why weren't you on it for the return trip?"

"You sound like you're upset that I wasn't."

McCally said nothing. He looked at her waiting for an answer.

"It so happens he didn't tell me he was leaving the courthouse. When I discovered he was missing, I knew he had to come back here. I took a taxi and got here just as he was pulling away from the dock. You can find the cab driver if you don't believe me."

"We'll do that," said McCally. "Why would your client come all this way, fly down here, go to the courthouse, and then without talking to you, without any explanation, run?"

"Maybe he just got cold feet," she said.

"Hmm." His expression indicated he didn't buy it.

"Where did he get the plane?"

"How do I know?"

"You were his lawyer."

"I suppose he bought it."

"No," said McCally. "He didn't. We got a list of his assets. There's no plane."

"You seem to know more about him than I do. If you were watching him so closely, how did he get himself blown up?"

McCally looked at the other guy in the sweatshirt. It seemed neither of them had an answer for this.

"Why, if you'd focused so much attention on my client, didn't you send him a target letter?"

"You're not here to ask the questions," said McCally, "but to answer them."

"Oh, am I? I was under the impression I was here to receive medical attention. If you had him under surveillance, we had a right to a target letter."

"Maybe yes, maybe no," said McCally.

"What's that supposed to mean?"

"It means maybe yes, maybe no," said the agent in the sweatshirt.

"Does the name Harold McAvoy mean anything to you?" McCally changed the subject.

She thought for a second. "No."

"Or James Regal?"

"No."

"What about Liam Walker?" This time it was the agent in the sweatshirt asking.

"What is this, twenty questions?"

"Just answer."

"I've never heard of any of them."

The agent and McCally looked at each other. They moved a couple of steps away and whispered to each other so that Joselyn couldn't hear.

"Tell me what's going on," she demanded.

McCally looked at her as if it was against his better judgment. She heard the agent speaking to him. "It's not likely we're gonna be getting any answers from her client. She's the next best thing."

McCally thought for a second, then finally caved in.

"The three names are aliases," he told her. "Just like the name Dean Belden."

"What are you talking about?"

"These are all names used by your client in various countries where he's worked over the last two years. He has at one time or another possessed passports under each of them."

"Belden wasn't his name?"

"No."

"And electronics wasn't his business," added the man in the sweatshirt.

"What was his business?"

"He was a kind of specialist," said McCally.

"You might say transportation is his main field," said the agent. "Though he's done other things over the course of his career. Usually whenever he showed up, people started dying."

Joselyn listened but didn't say a word.

"He hired himself out to various clients. Businesses, sometimes governments, groups out of power who wanted back in. As far as we know, this is the first time he's ever worked in this country."

"You're telling me he was a hired assassin?"

"Nothing so modest," said the agent. "Mr. Belden, or whatever name he was using on a given day, dealt in group discounts. Why murder one person when you can do a few hundred, maybe a few thousand."

"What are you telling me?"

"The Kurds in northern Iraq. Your client provided some of the services."

"And some villages in Croatia," added McCally. "He didn't use bullets or guns. No explosions. It was all very neat, except for the bloated bodies in the streets."

"His specialty," said the agent, "was moving dangerous cargos. As far as we know to date, he'd confined himself to chemical weapons. What we're worried about is that he may have been branching out."

"That's enough," said McCally.

Joselyn guessed they were now getting into areas that might compromise the grand jury investigation.

"You still want to know why we didn't send him a target letter?" asked McCally.

"Given the outcome, it looks like we saved the taxpayers the cost of a first-class stamp," said the agent.

"I suppose you had me under surveillance as well?" said Joselyn.

McCally didn't respond, but from the look on the other guy's face he didn't have to.

"You still haven't explained how, if you were watching him so closely, somebody was able to get to his plane with explosives."

"Did they?"

"I'd say so." Joselyn looked at the scattered pieces of debris out on the water.

"And who might they be?" said McCally. "These other people who got to his plane?"

"How would I know?"

"You worked with him."

"I was his lawyer."

"Fine," said the agent. "And now he's dead, so you won't mind telling us whatever it is you know about his business dealings?"

"I don't know anything except what Belden told me. And according to you, that is probably all a lie."

"Humor us," said McCally.

Joselyn looked at the two of them but didn't say a word.

"Maybe you'd like to lawyer up?" said the agent. "Want us to read you your rights. Get you a lawyer."

"Let me get this straight. Am I under arrest?"

"No," said McCally. "Not for the moment anyway."

"Good. Then what I have to say is going to be very short and to the point. I don't know a thing about any of the activities you've mentioned. I don't know if Belden was his name or what he did for a living. All I know is what he told me, and if the two of you are telling me the truth . . ." She looked at them as if perhaps she had some doubts. "Then the information he gave me was a crock."

"And what was that?" said McCally.

"That he wanted to set up a business on the island. Something about electronics and switches. He wanted me to form the corporation for this business. That's all I know."

"And you didn't ask him anything else?"

"What else was there?"

"How did he pay you?"

"By check. Drawn on a personal account."

"Did you ask him where he came from?"

"He told me somewhere near Seattle. Kent, I think. But if what you tell me is true, then he probably lied about that as well."

The two men looked at each other, but from their expressions Joselyn could tell that what she'd told them was no help.

"Why did he pick you to do his legal work?" asked McCally.

"He told me it was a referral. A local banker."

"What was the banker's name?"

"I can't remember. I might have written it down somewhere."

"We'll need the name."

"I'll look when I get back to my office."

"How much did he pay you?" asked McCally.

Joselyn wasn't anxious to answer, but she knew they could access her bank records with a subpoena. "A ten-thousand-dollar retainer for the business work. Another five thousand for accompanying him down here for the grand jury thing."

The agent rolled his eyes. "Is that normal?"

"Dream on," McCally answered for her. "And this didn't give you some clue that Belden might have problems? When did he call you on the grand jury subpoena?" He asked another question before she could answer.

"Late last week."

"And what did he tell you?"

She told them about Max Sperling, though by now Joselyn was convinced that Belden had fabricated that as well.

"And you accepted all of this at face value?" said McCally.

"Why wouldn't I? A client comes to my door, tells me he needs legal services . . ."

"And pays you fifteen grand," said the agent. "Don't forget that."

"What other records do you have?" said McCally.

"Wait a second," said Joselyn. "You think I'm going to turn over client records just like that?"

"Your client is dead," said McCally.

"I'm not sure the privilege died with him."

"We can debate the point in front of a federal judge," said the prosecutor. "Or perhaps the grand jury."

"I'm not under arrest, just under suspicion, is that it?"

"You could cooperate," said the agent.

"I have. I've told you everything I know."

"Maybe Belden just liked lawyers who wore skirts," said the agent.

"For most men it beats the alternative," said Joselyn. "No offense."

"None taken," said the agent. "Did the two of you get it on?"

"Ask your people with the field glasses," she told him.

"They say no."

Now she was getting angry. "There you go," she told him.

"You are aware," said McCally, "that attorney-client privilege does not apply if you are in any way involved in furtherance of your client's illegal activities?"

"Why would I be worried about that? I've got the best alibi in the world. Just ask Peeping Tom there."

"Hey. I can't vouch for your every minute." The agent was the kind of in-your-face civil servant that gives government a bad name.

"I see, just the bathroom and the bedroom," said Joselyn.

"Enough," said McCally. He gave the agent a stern look and the guy backed off.

"Then there's nothing else you're going to tell us?"

"There's nothing else I can tell you," said Joselyn. "I represented the corporation Belden Electronics. While Mr. Belden or whatever his name was may be dead, the corporation that he formed is not. My obligations as a lawyer run to that corporation."

"We've checked the listing of corporate officers," said McCally. They already knew about the corporation.

"It shows Belden's name, yours, and a woman named Samantha Hawthorne. Who is she?"

"It's a usual practice," said Joselyn. For purposes of formation, lawyers often listed themselves and their employees as corporate officers. Samantha, her landlady, had agreed to be listed. "She and I were to be substituted out for other officers at the first meeting of shareholders."

"I take it that never happened?"

"No."

"Were there any other shareholders besides Belden?" This was something McCally couldn't get from public records, but he could subpoena it from her files.

"Not that I know of."

Before they could ask another question, another agent wearing a dark blue windbreaker, the letters ATF stenciled on the front and back, came up to McCally from behind, whispered in his ear, then handed him something. Joselyn couldn't see what it was, something small enough to be concealed in his closed hand.

McCally talked to the agent in street clothes. The three men took a few steps back so they could confer in private and not be heard. The EMT started to go to work on Joselyn with his forceps again.

"I think I'll keep 'em, as souvenirs," she said. Before the guy could get a grip, she rolled down the sleeve of her blouse. It was torn and spotted with blood.

The FBI agent in the blue windbreaker was the only one standing close enough for idle conversation. His two colleagues were locked in some mortal disagreement. She could see the one in the sweatshirt waving his arms intensely. He was losing the argument with McCally. Joselyn guessed that the agent wanted to take her into custody.

"So tell me. How long have you guys been following Mr. Belden?"

The agent in the windbreaker just looked at her, smiled, and said: "Right. Like I'm gonna tell you."

McCally walked back toward them.

"Are you finished with me?" Joselyn asked.

"One more question," he said. "What do you know about this?" he opened the palm of his hand. In it was a small piece of white plastic about an inch square. It looked like a tiny white picture frame with what appeared to be off-colored gray paper in the center.

"What is it?" she asked.

"Agents found it floating in the water out there. You've never seen it before?"

"No." Joselyn didn't recognize it until McCally put it up against the lapel of his suit coat, like a badge. Then suddenly it clicked. She'd seen them on the white coats of lab technicians in hospitals, people who worked in radiology.

"It's called a dosimeter," said McCally. "It registers doses of radiation, to make sure that people who come into contact with it don't absorb too much. Why would your client have one?"

"I don't know."

McCally looked at her like maybe he didn't believe her.

"A word of caution," said the prosecutor. "Do you have any idea as to why your client was killed?"

"Not a clue."

"If I had to guess," said McCally, "it's because we got a line on him. These are people who live in the shadows. Your client, Belden, whatever his name was, and his associates are people who live under rocks and slither out at night. When we subpoenaed him, he was suddenly caught in the headlights. His friends saw him as a threat, a weak link."

"What's that got to do with me?"

"Perhaps more than you think. Maybe you're telling us the truth. Maybe you don't know anything about your client's activities. On the other hand, it's not what you know, but what they think you know that could get you killed."

"What are you saying?"

"I'm saying that if they'd put the bomb on that plane for your flight down from the islands, we wouldn't be standing here talking now."

It was something Joselyn hadn't thought about, until McCally said it.

"I'm telling you that if you know something, now's not the time to keep it to yourself."

FOURTEEN

PADGET ISLAND, WA

Scott Taggart stood on the dock and watched as the small boat cut a swath of white water across the San Juan Channel and toward the island. No one came to the island unless they were invited. There was no ferry service and no mail delivery. Letters were sent to the post office at Friday Harbor, a four-mile boat ride across tide-ripped waters.

The island was less than a mile from tip to tip and only seven hundred yards at the wide point. It had been owned by a sheep farmer at the turn of the century, a place where he could raise livestock without worrying about predators. In 1927, the island's only well ran salty, and except for a few seasonal streams, there was no other water on the island. The rancher gave it up.

The next owners didn't worry about water. They shipped in whatever they needed by boat and made a fortune running Canadian whiskey across the border during Prohibition. It was less than twenty nautical miles across the Strait of Georgia to the Canadian side. It was a feature that commended the island to Scott and his group.

They had set up in the old lodge house built by a bootleg baron in the early thirties. The ground floor was constructed of stone and heavy timbers. The house overlooked the dock from the crest of the hill.

It was guarded by men packing Barret fifty-caliber semi-automatic rifles. These were legal weapons unless converted to full-automatic. They were accurized and scoped for precision, some of them mounted on fixed tripods. Their bullets penetrated the sound barrier with a distinctive crack and struck with the impact of a small cannon shell. They could penetrate light steel armor as well as the more modern ceramic plate that was favored by the military for its light patrol boats.

The clips for these guns each held eleven rounds. There were hundreds of clips, all loaded and stored in bunkers around the island. Each bunker had a commanding view designed to establish a cross fire against anyone attempting to land on the island.

The committee had been here for nearly a month. It was one of the conditions that was laid down by the man who called himself Thorn. Their food was brought in on their own boat, and water was provided by a large catchment basin built in the 1980s by the island's current owner, a wealthy Belizean who Scott figured was probably heavily invested in narco-traffic. Thorn had made the arrangements. He seemed to be well connected internationally.

Scott watched as the boat slowed its speed and cut a wide "J" through the tranquil water of the bay. It pulled alongside the floating dock and a single occupant got out. He grabbed a bag handed to him by one of the others and started walking toward Taggart at the other end of the dock.

They had met three times, twice in a cabin in the mountains of Idaho almost six months ago. Scott recognized the walk, like he had a ramrod up his ass. Thorn had a military bearing that was unmistakable.

"Mr. Taggart, is it?" Eyes like an eagle, even in the half-light of dusk.

Through the mist, Scott could see the broad outlines of his face, a kind of coercive grin under sandy-colored hair. Thorn's military training came from South Africa. Scott had learned at least that much.

Thorn wore a neoprene dive suit, the hood folded back off of his head. As Thorn drew close, Scott could see the most distinctive characteristics of what was admittedly a handsome face: deep-set piercing green eyes. Thorn had used many aliases over the course of his career. The most recent was the name Dean Belden.

"I didn't expect you to be on the reception committee. You could have sent one of the men." Thorn climbed the ramp from the floating dock made more steep by the ebb tide, lugging the heavy bag at his side.

"If there was bad news, I wanted to be the first to hear it," said Scott.

"No bad news. You worry too much. You have to learn to be more positive. Look on the bright side. How many people would have given us even odds that we'd have gotten this far? You think your federal government has any idea?"

"You tell me."

"Not a clue," said Thorn. "As we speak, they are dredging the bottom of that lake for shards of metal no bigger than this." He held his thumb and forefinger about two inches apart, like a caliper. It was what a pound of C-4 could do when it was properly placed near a tank of high-octane aviation fuel.

"As for the body, they'd do as well to look for the remains of the Lord Himself, all the good it will do them."

"Good."

"You have to learn to calm down," said Thorn. "You get too intense, and it can take a toll on the ticker. Learn to savor the moment."

"I'll savor the moment when we're done," said Taggart.

"Oh no. You have to learn to take pleasure from each step along the way. For the time being, take consolation in the fact that the only thing worse than being chased by your government is working for it."

"How's that?" They started walking toward the house.

"Right now all those civil servants are up to their government service honkers in cold water looking for things that the fish ate two hours ago."

Scott couldn't help but smile. There was something about Thorn, a certain affable gleam to his deadly edge.

"Now, tell me about the accommodations," he asked. "I hope there's some good showers. I could dearly use one."

"Good showers. As for the place, I'm hoping we won't have to be here that much longer."

"Like I said, patience." Thorn stretched his back as he walked and groaned a little. "I'm getting too old for this. The ride was a little choppy. Hard on the low back and kidneys.''

"We would have sent a bigger boat, but we didn't want to draw attention.''

"Exactly right." Thorn stopped, took out a pack of cigarettes, and offered one to Scott.

"No, thanks.''

He lit up and took a deep drag while he surveyed what he could see. "How many men have you got?''

"Twenty-eight. Enough for around-the-clock shifts. Food and water for eighteen days. That's what you said, isn't it? Eighteen days?''

"That's what I said." He flicked a little hot ash onto the dock. "Your people, you haven't told them anything?''

"They know something's up. They don't know what.''

"Let's keep it that way.''

"They're all handpicked," said Taggart. "Kept in the dark as to their destination until they arrived on the island. So their families don't know where they are. Only two of them are allowed off the island. I'll vouch for both.''

"Yes, you will." Thorn looked at him. "With your life if you are wrong.''

Scott didn't answer him.

"We did everything exactly the way you told us. We brought them in from different groups around the country. They are the cream. All have prior military training. Half of them have seen combat in the Gulf War, four of them in Panama. One is a former Navy SEAL. We checked them out. None of them have been members of their units for less than two years. They are all committed. They will fight. If necessary they will lay down their lives.''

"Well, let's hope it doesn't come to that.''

Scott guessed that Thorn looked down his nose at these men. Thorn was a professional soldier, a hired mercenary with an obvious history of combat under his belt. Unless Scott was wrong, most of it paid for by the highest bidder. He came with the ordinance, the Moscow connection. If Scott and his group wanted the device, there was one condition: Thorn came with it. The sellers couldn't take a chance that some foreign government would trace it back to them. The cost in reprisal would be too severe. Scott had anticipated someone with a thick Russian accent. Thorn had none. His English was perfect, clipped and precise.

He had a number of aliases and could be contacted only through a mail drop in Ontario, Canada. Even that was a forwarding address. Where he lived no one knew for sure. But he apparently lived well, if his fees were any indication.

"They will fight."

"Hmm." Thorn looked at him. "Oh, I'm sure they would if necessary." He didn't seem entirely convinced. It wasn't their bravery he was concerned with. It was their organization, and the assumption by Taggart that his ground had not already been penetrated by the government. The FBI had written the book on undercover ops. They had infiltrated the Mafia with its culture of *omerta*—silence or death. An institution as old as the Borgias, in which blood kinship was the key to acceptance, had been riddled like swiss cheese in less than a decade. They would have done it sooner except that J. Edgar Hoover had been on such friendly terms at the racetracks with some of the bosses. Thorn assumed that Taggart's organization was already compromised. He would operate on that basis. None of them would know what he was doing at any given time.

"You've said nothing to any of your people?" he asked.

"Not a word."

"Reduced nothing to writing?"

"No."

"Good. There is no need for them to know what we are about. Their job is to maintain security on the island, simple as that. Yours is to wire the funds in the agreed-upon amounts at the times stated, into the properly numbered accounts. If that happens, everything will go smoothly. The rest of the plan is mine. If you are taken by the government at any time, I reserve the right to terminate our arrangement. If the money is not wired at the times required, our arrangement is terminated, all funds paid to that point are forfeit, and the device disappears with me. Do you understand?"

"We've been over all of that."

"Yes. We have." Thorn took a quick survey of the area around the dock, as much as the limited light of dusk would allow.

"Looks like you've got everything pretty well secured."

"We got it covered."

"I would throw up a few pine bows for a blind. Your man out on the point there." Thorn gestured with the glow of his cigarette toward the tip of land that jutted out into the channel. It provided a sheltered bay for the dock.

"You can see the cannon your man is carrying from a mile out. There's no sense advertising. You don't want some pain-in-the-ass member of the Audubon Society calling the Coast Guard to come and take a look. Bald eagles and all that."

"I'll see that it's taken care of."

"Good." Thorn was smiling again. He put his arm around Scott's shoulder. He was now in charge, and they both knew it. Scott was the ideologist, the man that other true believers would follow. He'd spent three years after Kirsten's death in the mountains of Idaho, living alone in a cabin and making contacts with people who shared a single common interest— an abiding hatred of the federal government. Many of the people he met were racists. Scott did not encourage or participate in their rantings on this subject. There were times when he felt shame for listening and not speaking up as they lanced this boil and spread their poison.

But as months turned into years, Scott found himself talking more and listening less. He was steeped in the history of the country, better educated than any of the men with whom he associated.

He traveled the backcountry and spoke in barns and metal buildings, to men in dirty overalls and cotton flannel shirts with frayed sleeves. The lucky ones wore the dust of their jobs on their faces. The rest looked for work in a lumber industry now decimated by federal timber policies.

They listened wide-eyed as Scott told them about Jefferson and the rights of man, the god-given prerogative to pursue their dreams free from the tyranny of an overbearing government. It was Jefferson who warned that "the tree of liberty must be refreshed from time to time with the blood of patriots and tyrants."

There was a moral reckoning to Scott's words and the way he delivered them that erased any doubt as to the rightness of their cause.

In time these men came to trust him. Trust became leadership, not because he could handle a gun, but because he spoke to their concerns, their fears for the future. They viewed themselves as the victims of a political aristocracy, a ruling class that had forgotten about its own people. Bureaucrats with lifetime tenure ran their agencies like warlords, unaccountable to anyone, including elected officials.

Their view of the federal government was of a parent who devoured its own children. Its only real constituency was foreign governments or multinational corporations willing to pay for what was euphemistically called "political access." Good-paying jobs were shipped to Mexico or Asia where they could be downgraded to sweatshop wages while the president made empty gestures about job training and touted the benefits of the global economy. It didn't matter whether they were Republicans or Democrats, they all sang the same song. Scott Taggart knew the melody and could explain the lyrics.

The two men, Taggart and Thorn, were now inextricably bound.

Thorn stamped out his cigarette. They turned and began walking up the hill toward the house. Its windows had been blanked out by heavy drapes to prevent prying eyes with high-powered optics from observing the inhabitants or taking pictures.

"Where's the device?" asked Scott.

"In a safe place."

"I thought we were in this together?"

"We are."

"Then why the Chinese wall?"

"Because our success does not depend on your knowing where the device is. Suffice it to say that I do. And that it will be delivered to its ultimate destination at the appointed time. That is all you need to know."

"And the detonation. How will you accomplish that within the stated time parameters?"

"Again one of those worrisome details that you need not trouble yourself with."

"I always worry about the loose ends."

"I can tell," said Thorn.

"Like Belden Electronics."

"They can rummage through Mr. Belden's affairs all they want. They won't find a thing."

"What about the woman? The lawyer?"

"She doesn't know a thing. But just to be safe, we're about to tie up that loose end as well."

Scott looked at him.

"What do you mean?"

"There's no sense taking chances," said Thorn.

"Is that necessary?"

"There are documents in her office that are best disposed of in the flames of a hot furnace. If we take them, she will notice. Then she will start thinking, putting two and two together." Thorn stopped, turned, and looked directly at Scott. "You tell me. Is it necessary?"

Taggart hesitated only an instant. "Yes. I suppose."

"You sound reluctant."

"I take no pleasure in killing innocent people. It's why I selected the time and place."

"A virtue not shared by your government," said Thorn.

Scott looked at him and wondered. He had never told Thorn about Kirsten or how she had died. Could he know? Thorn was not the kind of man with whom you wanted to share your most intimate secrets, the things that propelled you through life and motivated your actions. Whatever inhabited that dark space behind those cold eyes left little doubt that it would use such information for its own purposes. He wondered if Thorn knew about Adam and Kirsten's parents in Seattle. For the first time since starting down this twisting path, Scott Taggart began to question what he was doing.

"Not to worry," said Thorn. "The woman is not your concern. She will be taken care of."

"When?"

Thorn looked at his watch.

"Soon."

They walked on in silence toward the house. It troubled Scott that innocent people had to die. But there was no alternative. Scott was not a soldier, but he knew the lessons of combat. Whether the federal government knew it or not, they were now at war.

FIFTEEN

ROSARIO STRAIT

Even if Joselyn wanted to cooperate with McCally and the federal probe, she had a problem. She'd told him the truth. She didn't know anything. She searched her memory for bits and pieces of information, anything that Belden might have said in her office or on the plane. Joselyn was no legal virgin. She'd had enough criminal clients lie to her over the years to know that among the lies there were at times a few kernels of truth. Maybe in Belden's lies there was some thread of information, something she might key on.

His business was electronics, at least that's what he had told her. Maybe the name Max Sperling was real, even if the story about him wasn't. She would look at her files when she got back to the office. Maybe there was something in her notes.

By the time McCally and his agent had finished with her on the dock, it was dusk. She was dirty and tired. She had been standing for hours in the chilly air. Her arm was now throbbing where the medical technician had plucked splinters and wrapped her with a heavy gauze bandage. By this hour, there were no ferries to the San Juans from Seattle. The only regular service left from Anacortes, a ninety-minute drive north by car.

She called a cab and had the driver take her to the nearest discount store, where she bought a pair of slip-on sneakers and some socks to replace her shredded hose and broken shoe. Then she went to a car rental agency. She had no choice. She would have to pay the hefty drop-off charge on the island and bill it to Belden's account.

As she drove, she wondered what she would do with the rest of his retainer. How would she return the unused portion? It was the kind of thing only a lawyer would think about. But she had a business to run. She would have to find some way to wind up Belden's corporation, to dissolve it, and to get her name off of the documents of incorporation. She thought about publishing a notice, going through the formality of searching for heirs. If McCally was right about Belden's past, it was not likely anyone would come forward. Presumably the money, any unearned fees, would escheat to the state after a period of time.

The concussion from the explosion had left an incessant ringing in her ears, and her body now started to feel the soreness of having landed on the hard dock after the pressure wave had knocked her off her feet. Her joints and muscles had the aching tenderness she'd experienced only once, following a minor auto accident.

Fifteen minutes after leaving the freeway, she rolled down the main drag of Anacortes, took a left at the light, and drove toward the headlands. Sleep now began to tug at her sleeve. She passed through the residential area of town and hugged the bluffs above the water. She could see the lights of Guemes across the narrow inlet. Occasionally, through a break in the trees, she could see the glow of the bright vapor lights from the ferry terminal as they bounced off the underside of a few wispy clouds floating overhead.

One of the ferries, with its cavernous open car deck lit up, its portholes and windows aglow like a Christmas tree on the water, was making a wide turn as it approached the dock a half mile out. Joselyn hoped it was the ferry to Friday Harbor.

She wound down the steep grade toward the terminal and saw that the parking lot was nearly empty. Two truck and trailer rigs and a handful of cars waited in line. Whatever rush hour existed for the islands was over for the day, and the tourist season was still months away.

She paid for a ticket at the tollgate.

"What time's the next ferry to San Juan Island?"

"That's it coming in."

A pickup with a camper on the back pulled up behind her, its bright lights beaming through the back window of her rented car. There was another big truck behind him. The last-minute rush. People in the islands lived and died by the ferry schedule. At night trucks often made their deliveries to avoid the heavier ferry traffic of the day.

The woman in the booth gave Joselyn the cash register ticket and her change and glanced back at the parking lot.

"Take lane four. They'll be boarding in just a couple of minutes."

By this time in the evening the ferries were usually late, losing time on every run during the day. Joselyn knew they wouldn't waste any time at the dock. She pulled into lane four and went all the way to the front, turned off her lights and engine, and waited. There were a few cars in the lane next to her, no more than a dozen in all. The ferry would be nearly empty.

She watched as the vehicles, their headlights gleaming, streamed off the boat and passed her on the exit road heading up the hill. Traffic from the islands was mostly one-way this time of day, some late stragglers headed for home.

Five minutes later, they were waved onto the ferry. Joselyn drove her small rented car directly into the main bay and up to the bow. She could hear the wind whistling through the open car deck. When they landed she would be the first one off. She couldn't wait to hit the soft flannel sheets of her bed and pull the covers over herself, a refuge from the nightmare that had been her day. Sleep was fast overtaking her.

The few other passengers left their cars and headed to the upper decks, the cafeteria, and the lounge. Joselyn pushed the toggle switch on the door that said "lock" and the buttons on both doors snapped down. She pulled the lever on the side of the driver's seat and reclined until it wedged against the back-seat. She close her eyes and wished she had a blanket.

She drifted into another world, only vaguely aware of the boat's movement. The vibration of the massive diesel engines stirred her only a little. The gentle swaying in the troughs as the vessel glided out away from the dock acted as a sedative.

The wind picked up and whistled past the closed windows, causing the small car to shudder, as the ferry turned and headed out through the Guemes Channel and into Rosario Strait. Four miles of open water until they reached the narrows of Thatcher Pass. Wind wiped froth off the crest of small whitecaps. Occasional small waves crested and crashed against the steel bow of the ferry, sending droplets of seawater splattering against the windshield of Joselyn's car.

The noise caused her to open her eyes halfway, to gaze up through the tinted windshield. It was a clear, brilliant night, the kind that brings the heavens to life with flickering stars, pinholes of light against the black backdrop of space. Joselyn drifted in that netherworld between sleep and consciousness. She gazed up through the opening between the wings of the passenger deck one level above. Tonight the two wings that projected out over the bow of the ship were empty. It was too cold. The few passengers onboard were huddled inside, warming their hands around cups of hot coffee or sprawled out sleeping on the benches beneath the windows.

Somewhere in Rosario Strait, Joselyn drifted into deep sleep, swayed by the gentle rocking of the great vessel and the occasional gust of wind that shook her small car as it swept through the car deck like a giant ghost.

She was lost in the rumble of the engines and dreamed of Belden and the small plane, the flash of brilliant light, and the explosive force that followed an instant later. Luminous, blazing lights, piercing the shield of her closed lids. Her eyes began to ache, and slowly Joselyn opened them to realize that she was not dreaming at all. Someone behind her in a vehicle had switched on their headlights, bright, piercing high beams. They filled the rear window of her car with a painful luminance like the sun. The reflection from her rearview mirror was blinding.

Joselyn shielded her eyes. "Turn them off," she muttered to herself, half asleep. Then she heard the rumble of the engine, deep and guttural, a heavy diesel starting up. Maybe he needed to charge a battery or refrigerate a load. She couldn't see a thing in the rearview mirror, the bright lights blinding her. She would wait a second and see if he turned them off and shut down. If not, she would go topside to escape the noise and the lights.

Then she heard the grind of gears and an instant later the hiss of compressed air. The driver had released his brakes.

Joselyn looked into the rearview mirror in stark terror as the headlights behind her began to move, closing in on the rear of her car. Suddenly the bright beams were no longer in her mirror. They flashed over the top of her roof, and all she could see was the massive grill and the huge steel bumper, with its metal studs. It made contact with her car at the level of the trunk and instantly there was the grinding sound of metal crushing metal. The trunk folded up like paper.

Before Joselyn could think, the truck driver gunned it. The car began to crumple like a crushed soda can. Joselyn went for the handle of her door. It wouldn't open. The frame of the car had bent. The door was jammed. She lunged for the door on the other side. Same story.

She heard the crunch of glass as the rear window exploded, shooting pellets of safety glass into her hair and over the front seat. The small car began to move relentlessly forward, its tires sliding on the ferry's smooth steel deck. The webbed safety net that spanned the ship in front of her car began to stretch, then rip as the diesel truck and trailer rig pushed her car like a steam-powered piston into the net. She could hear the driver double-clutching. This was no accident. Whoever was in the truck was trying to kill her.

Joselyn frantically looked up through the driver's-side window for help, her fingers pressed against glass. The ship's two passenger wings from the upper deck were nearly behind her now. They were both empty. No one could see her. She pressed the electric button trying to open the driver's window. It didn't work. She pounded on the glass to no avail. Desperate, she swung her legs around the steering column and pressed her feet against the windshield. With her back wedged against the seat she pressed with all of her might trying to break the windshield out. It didn't work. She was entombed in metal and glass, being crushed and pushed toward a watery grave.

Even with the brake set and the transmission in "park" Joselyn's car was no match for the huge truck. The small Chevy moved toward the open bow, and the deep, green water was now rushing toward her. She pressed on the brake pedal to no avail. The wheels continued to skid across metal. She leaned on the horn. Finally, something worked. At least it made noise. Someone should hear it.

The safety net shredded, and the single steel cable across

the top rode up over the hood of Joselyn's car, slid up across the glass of the windshield and onto the roof. Now there was nothing between her and cold, deep water of the sound.

She reached for the door handle one more time and laid her shoulder into the door as hard as she could, but it wouldn't open. She tried the electric opener on the window one more time, then suddenly realized. She turned the key in the ignition, pressed the button, and the window began to come down. Wind rushed in through the opening.

Joselyn reached out with both hands for the roof of the car and turned her body sideways to pull herself out. The front wheels of the car went over the edge. The vehicle tilted forward, gravity taking hold, bumper down; the small car teetered toward the onrushing water, white foam boiling off of the ferry's massive steel hull.

———————

"STOP ALL ENGINES." The captain of the *Tillicum* laid his hand on the red button on the console in front of him and leaned on it. The huge airhorn on the deck above the bridge pierced the cold night air like a knife.

The movement on the bridge was frantic. The first mate grabbed four levers on the console and pulled them back until they were straight up in the neutral position. The vibration of the engines stopped, but the ship continued gliding forward, cutting through the water, propelled by its own momentum.

"Hard to starboard."

The crewman brought the wheel over hard, but without the propulsion of the engines forcing water over the control surfaces of the rudder, the ship turned but very slowly.

The captain watched helplessly as the massive weight of the diesel truck pushed the small car over the edge.

"Engines full back."

———————

WITH HER LAST ounce of strength, Joselyn reached out, her body halfway through the open car window. The grip of one hand filled with nylon mesh, a piece of shredded safety net. The car tilted forward. A hundred tons of white water hit the hood, snapping the little car down into the sea. The violent force ripped Joselyn through the open window and left her dangling in space, her feet running along on air, just inches above the lapping bow wave.

She could hear the wail of the ferry's horn, and she twisted by a single hand from the frayed remnants of the nylon net. The joint of her shoulder was racked with pain. She couldn't hold much longer. Joselyn reached with the other hand, trying desperately to control her spinning body. She lashed out and felt the net with her other hand. She grabbed it and held for her life. Looking down, she saw the rush of white water under the bow and felt the momentum of the ship as it began to slow. It seemed to take forever. She got a single foothold and clung to the net, spinning in the wind, the icy sea lapping at her feet.

ORDINARILY HE WOULD have reversed the engines to bring the vessel to a stop in the water, but he couldn't. The captain of the *Tillicum* knew that if he did, the small car would pass under the hull only to be shredded by the massive bronze propellers.

He prayed that there was no one inside the vehicle. He could hear it bouncing, metal against metal, under the hull as the ship passed over it. Air trapped in the vehicle would keep it near the surface, at least for a few seconds. The two men ran to the wing of the bridge and watched as the dark green water glided past the ship.

The captain grabbed the swivel light mounted on the railing, swung it around toward the water, and flipped it on. A powerful beam of light penetrated the darkness, reflecting off the rippled surface of the sea.

The first mate ran back inside, grabbed the microphone for the hailing system. "Man overboard. All crew to the railing. Man over." He could hear the powerful speakers overhead echoing his voice. He repeated it two or three times, then hung up the mike. He'd barely returned to the wing of the bridge when one of the crewmen hollered from below. "There off the stern quarter."

The captain swung the light out, searched the water. Someone flung a life ring on a line as far out as far as it would reach. The captain followed it with his light until it hit the water, then kept moving the beam of light outward over the dark shimmering surface of the sea.

"There." He steadied the light, though the continuous movement of the ship made it difficult.

Barely recognizable, the pulverized vehicle bobbed a few inches above the surface. It was the twisted and battered roof of the small car, held up by a bubble of air under its dome. The mangled metal danced just a few inches above the surface of the sea as water lapped greedily around the edges. A small ripple swept the water driven by a gust of wind, and from the open driver's window, there was a gush of bubbles. Suddenly the car was gone.

They swept the water with lights. Now three of them, powerful spots operated by the crew. There was no sign of anyone in the water.

THE TORN AND tattered nylon mesh of the safety net hung over the front edge of the ferry like a broken spiderweb, and Joselyn hung from it. She looked up, wondering if the net would slip and drop her into the sea. The ship had slowed, but still it moved fast enough to take her under the massive hull if she fell. There were tons of water and cold steel, giving her little chance of being found in the dark water.

The wind whistled through her clothing, sending a chill through her body. Her hands were numb. Joselyn's grip on the netting was beginning to slip. In shock, she hung like a rag doll. She tried to clear her mind, to focus. Using her legs she tried to twist her body so that she would be facing the bow of the ship. She tried to reach with her feet for the steel plates at the ship's bow to get leverage. But the plates curved back and under the overhanging deck forming a prow, before plunging straight down into the water below. It was like trying to climb under an overhanging ledge on a sheer mountainside.

With one desperate grab, she reached up for another piece of netting with her right hand and snagged it. Now she hung as if on a cross, her arms spread. Somehow she managed to hook her other foot through a piece of the open webbing. She clung there, waiting for help, but no one came. It dawned on her that they couldn't see her. The crew and passengers were focused on the stern, looking for the car. No one paid attention to the ripped safety net. They were looking for survivors.

Joselyn could see reflections off the water, beams of light as they made a wide arc over the water and disappeared toward the stern. She could hear voices shouting. The onrushing water at the bow began to slack, as its momentum over the water slowed. The bow wave disappeared, and the rush of white water against steel slowly evaporated. The wind against her back slacked.

With her foot wedged firmly in the webbing of the net, Joselyn pushed with one leg and climbed hand over hand up the netting. A few passengers were now out on the wing over the car deck. She could hear their voices, asking each other if they could see anything. But no one looked down onto the car deck.

They were leaning over the railing looking to the starboard side of the ferry as Joselyn clawed her way onto the deck.

She lay prostrate and exhausted a few feet from the edge of the bow, her face turned sideways, her cheek against the cold steel deck. It took a moment to focus. Then the object she was staring at registered. What filled her line of vision was black rubber, the massive front tire of the diesel truck and trailer rig that had pushed her car into the sea. It was less than six feet away. She scrambled to her knees and looked up at the driver's door that loomed open, above her. Slowly she stood, eyes fixed on the open cab of the truck six feet up. There was no one inside, behind the wheel or on the passenger side. Whoever had tried to kill her had vanished and now mingled with the other passengers. As Joselyn stood gaping through the open door, she heard footsteps approaching on the deck.

She quickly moved to the other side of the truck and ducked down between two cars in the next lane.

Two crewmen started to examine what was left of the safety net. One of the other crewmen climbed up into the seat of the truck. "No key." He looked under the dash and pulled some loose wires down. Somebody had hot-wired the starter.

"Don't mess with it. Let's get the driver down here and see if he can back it up to balance the load. Did anybody call the Coast Guard?"

"They called from the bridge." Several crew members now

mingled and talked among themselves, taking charge. No one seemed to notice Joselyn.

She quietly started to walk up the car ramp to the staircase that led to the passenger deck. The concrete deck felt icy. Joss looked down and discovered she had lost her second pair of shoes while struggling to climb back up the safety net. Her purse and her briefcase were still in the car, sinking down to the bottom of the sound. Her clothes were torn where she had been peppered with the splinters from the explosion.

She opened the door at the top of the staircase and saw the women's restroom right across the corridor. She slipped into a stall and locked the door.

Whoever drove the truck into the back of her car thought Joselyn was dead. Her mind was confused. She was still in a state of shock, but her better judgment told her that at least for the moment, it was safer if she remained dead.

SIXTEEN

It was now after midnight. The Capitol dome was lit up. Bowlyn could actually see it from the office window that belonged to Sy Hirshberg in the White House's West Wing. Hirshberg was the national security adviser to the president. He had bags under his eyes and was wearing a black bow tie and a tux as he slouched in his chair behind the big cherry wood desk.

Bowlyn had snagged him as he headed home from a party at the Kennedy Center following a performance. He had thought better of discussing his problem with other members of the Working Group before giving his boss a heads-up. No doubt what Bowlyn was about to tell him was going to ruin Hirshberg's day.

"Can we make this quick? I've got a seven-thirty meeting tomorrow morning and a flight out to New York at ten." Hirshberg was on his way to meet with some of his counterparts from Europe at the U.N. to discuss Bosnia and the Middle East.

Bowlyn took a long, deep breath, then spoke: "We have information that Russian arms merchants may have shipped a nuclear device to clients in the U.S."

Hirshberg sat on the other side of his desk, his gaze fixed on his assistant as if he were in a trance. The only sign that he was conscious was the deepening furrows over his brow that set like concrete. Before his boss could speak, Bowlyn anticipated his first question.

"The device may have already been delivered," he said.

By now he had Hirshberg's undivided attention.

"We think the weapon was transshipped by vessel across the Pacific. The ship itself sank, possibly in a storm. The Coast Guard has confirmed that much."

"If the ship sank, how do we know the weapon didn't go down with it?"

Bowlyn opened his briefcase and pulled out a copy of the FBI lab report. He passed it across the desk to his boss.

Hirshberg opened it and read. It took several minutes to absorb the salient portions of the report. There were two key items of critical evidence. The first was that the tattered cargo lines that had linked the cargo to the diesel-filled flotation bag above had been cleanly severed, probably by a knife, according to the laboratory report. This was a clear indication that someone had cut the cargo free from its flotation, probably after pulling it aboard a vessel, and then jettisoned the flotation bag and the buoys over the side.

The second finding in the report was vastly more critical.

"Refresh my understanding of physics. It's been a long time," said Hirshberg. "A *rad*, as I recall, is the basic unit of radiation absorbed by the human body."

"That's correct."

"And the outer skin of this flotation bag contained enough radioactive contamination to cause cancer in a thousand people?"

"According to the analysts," said Bowlyn. "As soon as they found out, they shipped all of the recovered items from the *Isvania* to Oak Ridge for final examination and disposal. They had to decontaminate the lab at Quantico.

"Based on what they've seen, the device in question contains aging weapons-grade plutonium that has been exposed to the air for some time. It's begun to oxidize. Still, the physicists tell us that plutonium would not be emitting these levels of gamma radiation. There is something else there. We don't know what. The Coast Guard tried to decontaminate the chopper that picked the stuff up. When they couldn't, they simply pushed it over the side. Gave it to Davy Jones. The flight crew and everybody else who came in contact with the items have been quarantined. They're under observation.''

Hirshberg went back to the report. The analysts suspected that whoever took the device from the Russian munitions bunker had dismantled it before shipping. They had exposed the plutonium core to the air and possibly wrapped it in the deflated flotation bag before crating it up. The bag itself registered exceedingly high levels of radiation. He laid the report on the desk.

"Do they have any idea of the size of the bomb?" asked Hirshberg. "Any sense as to its destructive force?"

"No. Only that there's a danger of contamination. Whoever shipped it apparently didn't know what they were doing."

"Let's hope they're equally ignorant about detonation," said Hirshberg. "What are the Russians saying?"

"Dan Murphy at State has some of his people checking with their Ministry of Defense. The problem is that what little we know comes from intercepts, some of them on commercial telephone lines. We can't very well tell the Russians that we've tapped into their domestic phone system. We're not sure what they'll tell us publicly. We're hoping they'll cooperate. CIA has dispatched an agent to the facility in Siberia to see if he can find out anything. We've been working on decoding some of the intercepted transmissions, but so far nothing."

"So what can I tell the president?" said Hirshberg.

"That's the problem," said Bowlyn.

"What do you mean?"

Bowlyn took a deep breath. "We have reason to believe that the weapon in question was obtained by the Russian Mafiya, a group out of Yekaterinburg in Siberia. It was stolen from a government arsenal in that area. The documentation for a shipment of machine parts, which we think was the weapon, was made out in the name of a Russian corporation. That corporation is operated by Viktor Kolikoff."

Hirshberg turned his face up toward the ceiling and paused a long moment before he exploded. "Son of a bitch. I knew it." He shook his head, got up out of the chair, and began to pace toward the big window with the Capitol view.

"We warned him. We told him not to get involved with the guy. And what does he do? He invites him to the fucking Oval Office and shakes his hand in front of cameras. Invites him to dinner, sits down with him at coffee klatches. Does everything but give him the key to the front door of the White House.''

"He gave the money back," said Bowlyn, trying to look on the bright side.

"Yeah. Right. After the *Post* drove twelve inches up his ass on the front page.''

The problem was that the president had taken $240,000 in the last election, money that was ultimately traced to Kolikoff and was laundered through straw donors. When party officials got caught, they returned the funds. Kolikoff was a foreign national. To knowingly take political contributions from him was a crime. But they couldn't prove the president or any of his people knew the money was from Kolikoff.

"No one's going to prosecute him," said Bowlyn.

"Certainly not that rube of an attorney general," said Hirshberg. "Besides, the president has sold the public on the principle that if it isn't a crime, it's fine, and even if it is, it might be OK," said Hirshberg. He looked at Bowlyn. "Don't you get it? The voters have given the president a complete pass on matters pertaining to ethics, both in and out of government. Now they may get a slow nuclear burn in their beds for the favor.''

Bowlyn looked nervously around the room, wondering if it wasn't bugged and cabled for cameras. He knew the White House Situation Room was. Hirshberg had a temper, and when he lost it, all judgment flew out the window.

"Problem is," said Hirshberg, "the public's bought off on all of it. This country's in for a hell of a future.''

"It's not the president. It's his political handlers," said Bowlyn.

Hirshberg looked at him and arched an eyebrow. "If you want my job you'll have to speak a little louder into the pen set on my desk," Hirshberg told him.

Bowlyn's face flushed. "You have to admit Williams is a snake. To get caught with some hooker while he's talking to the president and have the gall to continue offering advice as if he were indispensable . . .''

"I give you Williams and the rest of that nest of vipers.'' Hirshberg lifted a glass of water from the desk and took a drink as if in toast. "But I ask you, who is it who has his lips wrapped around the flute playing music to coil by?''

Hirshberg looked at him through the glass of water. Bowlyn didn't have a reply.

"He was warned by the CIA and the State Department. Both told him before he ever met with Kolikoff that the man had ties to organized crime in Russia, that he had links in the illicit arms trade. Did he listen? No.''

Kolikoff had gotten more than the usual grip-and-grin photo session with presidential handlers telling him where to stand, like a cardboard cutout. He had spent days in the White House, filling the president's Rolodex with phone numbers and addresses of hefty contributors. The State Department and even the CIA had cringed. The president didn't care. All he wanted was the campaign cash, and he was willing to do anything to get it.

"Now, if there is a weapon of mass destruction on U.S. soil and Kolikoff is involved, I guarantee you that our commander in chief is not going to want to hear about it.''

"He's going to have to do something," said Bowlyn.

"I remind you," said Hirshberg, "this is the administration that led the charge against private ownership of guns, that made the NRA a four-letter word. Have you forgotten?" said Hirshberg. "Our president is for children, education, and the environment, children and social security, children and Medicare, and children.

"How can a man with that kind of a political mantra tell the public they might wake up tomorrow and find one of their cities missing, their children dying of radiation poisoning, that is, if they weren't incinerated in their beds? Oh, and by the way, your president took money from, and shook the hand of, the man who delivered the device to your doorstep.''

SEVENTEEN

FRIDAY HARBOR

A ferry with an accident overboard is like a small village. The rumors quickly spread from the crew to the passengers. They couldn't find anyone belonging to the car that went to the bottom. Consensus was growing that there may have been a fatality.

Joselyn wanted to tell the captain the truth, but she had no idea who'd tried to kill her. Whoever it was was still on the boat. She'd be putting her life in the hands of an unarmed crew, perhaps putting them in jeopardy. It seemed much safer for the moment to remain dead.

The truck driver whose diesel had run her car off the ferry's bow apparently was having a cup of coffee up in the cafeteria when someone borrowed his truck. Five witnesses saw him there.

The ferry crew searched the water for twenty minutes with lights, until a Coast Guard boat showed up and took over. Two of the Coast Guard officers boarded the ferry to interview the crew and any witnesses. The *Tillicum* slowly picked up speed and motored for Friday Harbor. It took nearly forty minutes.

Joselyn waited in the restroom until she felt the ferry dock. Walk-on passengers were always the first off as the crew readied the car deck for off-loading. As she left the restroom, the passenger deck was empty. She quickly made her way down the stairs to the car deck. The crew was busy removing the chocks from the car wheels as Joselyn walked off the ferry. She held her breath, waiting for someone to call out, to try to stop her. No one noticed her.

The sigh of relief was almost palpable as she headed up the dock toward Front Street.

She hoped the Coast Guard wouldn't spend too much time out on the frigid waters looking for a body. Still she had no intention of being dragged in by the authorities tonight. She was exhausted, both mentally and physically. She would stop in the sheriff's office in the morning and tell them what happened. There would be plenty of time for them to pick up the pieces of the investigation then.

Joselyn walked quickly to the end of the dock and took a right toward the Spring Street Landing. Vehicles coming off the ferry would have to make a sharp right along Front Street for a block before making a left up Spring Street to pass through town. On the waterfront, it was a one-way street. They would have to drive under bright streetlights before heading up the hill. Joselyn could get a good look at the drivers and passengers under the lights.

She wished she had a pencil and something to write on. The only thing she had at the moment were the clothes she was wearing. She fished in her skirt pocket looking for change, something to make a phone call. Nothing. She would have to bum a phone call from somebody, maybe one of the restaurants down the street. Call Samantha to come pick her up.

She looked at her watch: nine-thirty. It was possible Sam might still be at the office. She often worked late.

Joselyn hunched down in the shadows under a tree and sat on the end of a wooden bench outside the offices of Western Princess Cruises. Everything in town was closed, except a few of the night spots. She could hear muted strains of music coming from a tavern down the street.

Slowly vehicles began to emerge from the ferry, one at a time as they cleared the checkpoint set up by the Coast Guard. This made it easy for Joselyn to study each of the cars and their occupants. She wasn't exactly sure what she was looking for, perhaps anything out of the ordinary, somebody that stood out, who wasn't a local, not that it would be that easy to tell. She had one advantage: there weren't many cars on the ferry.

Whoever had tried to kill her was still onboard. Of that she was sure.

The first two vehicles had Washington plates, one belonging to a family with small children. The other was a pickup truck with a local business name and phone number on the door, a masonry contractor. She dismissed them both.

The third vehicle drew her attention. It was a late-model white sedan with two men in the front seat. They were dressed in business suits and the passenger was talking on a cell phone. It wasn't until they made the turn up Spring Street that Joselyn saw the federal license plate over the rear bumper.

She looked intently at the car for a moment as it disappeared up the street, then she dismissed the thought. If McCally was going to have her followed, the FBI wouldn't have used a car with government plates. Or would they? The two guys were probably agriculture inspectors here to roust some dairy farmer on the island.

Her attention was quickly distracted by the next car, an older-model sedan with a lot of rust and dents. It had seen better days. Joselyn squinted under the bright lights to get a look at the driver. It was an old woman, a lot of gray hair with a bandanna holding it in place. She took the next car in order. There were kids in the backseat.

In all she counted eighteen cars and the diesel truck. She saw the driver, got a good look at him. Maybe he was lying about being up in the cafeteria. Still, if what she heard on the ferry was correct, there were witnesses who saw him there.

Her thoughts returned to the car with the federal plates. If McCally had had her followed, why hadn't the agents helped her? They must have been watching, unless they figured she couldn't go anywhere on a ferry and went upstairs to get coffee like everybody else. At the moment, she had a lot of questions and no answers.

Without wheels, Joselyn hoofed it toward her office near the courthouse. It was only a few blocks from the ferry dock through downtown Friday Harbor. She could hear strains of guitar music coming from Herb's Tavern on Spring Street, some loud conversation from a few patrons inside.

As she walked, her mind swarmed with a dozen thoughts, none of them related. Belden was dead. What few notes or documents she had concerning his grand jury appearance were now at the bottom of the sound. There was probably nothing there. Still she would have killed to get one last glimpse at them.

She'd have to get a new driver's license, call the credit card companies and have them issue new cards. What else was in her wallet? Her state bar membership card. She made a mental note to call the bar.

She hoped Sam was at the office. At least she could get a ride home. She turned down First Street, past Christy's and the Clay Café, then left on Court Street, and walked quickly across the road and in front of the county courthouse. As she cleared a few trees and the corner of the building, she could see lights on upstairs under the covered walkway in front of Sam's office. She was in luck.

Joselyn picked up her pace and looked at the lights. She was halfway across the street directly in front of the office when she realized it wasn't Sam's office that was lit up—but her own.

She was sure she hadn't left the light on in her office. Maybe the janitor was inside cleaning.

Given the events of the day, she was taking no chances. She walked past the building and approached from the rear, through the small garage on the ground floor. It was deserted. Sam's car wasn't there.

Slowly and very quietly, she took the passageway that led to the wooden landing and the stairs, then began climbing, two half-flights, to the outside corridor that ran in front of the doors to the office suites on the second floor.

There was a beauty salon on the ground floor at the front of the building. Joselyn could see the reflection from a display of flickering lights in the window as they flashed on the grass and a few shrubs near the sidewalk out near the street.

She stopped at the top step, pressed her back against the stuccoed wall, and took a deep breath, then a quick peek around the corner and down the corridor. The overhead lights were out. Usually they were left on all night. Joselyn realized that it was the dark corridor outside that made the light in her office so visible and obvious from the street. Why would someone go to the trouble of turning off the outside lights to break into her office and turn on the office light? It had to be the janitor.

For a moment, she hesitated. She thought about running down the stairs to the sheriff's office near the courthouse. Somebody would be on the desk. She could wait there for a patrolman to check her office. And what if it was the janitor? She'd look like a fool. Worse, she'd have to tell them what happened on the ferry; otherwise she'd have a hard time going to them with the truth in the morning. They'd haul her back to the dock and the Coast Guard, and she'd be into it for a million questions. She'd spend half the night under bright lights. The U.S. Attorney's Office would get wind, and McCally would be in her face again. This time he'd be sure she knew something she wasn't telling him.

The thought caused her to edge her way past the last step, around the corner, and down the corridor. She hugged the front wall of the building, so if there was anybody inside she'd see them first. She passed two locked office doors, came up to Sam's door, and tried it. It was locked. There wasn't much chance she'd be inside with the lights out, but Joss had hoped.

She stopped and listened. She couldn't hear anything, but the door to her office was partially open, and light was streaming out onto the dark decking outside. It wasn't until she took another step that she felt something under her bare feet. Joss looked down and realized it was the crunch of glass. The lights overhead hadn't been turned off after all. They had been broken. At the same instant, she lifted her eyes and saw the frame of the door to her office. The wood was splintered, and Joselyn could see the tool marks in the paint where a pry bar had been inserted.

With this realization, Joselyn started moving away from the open office door and the light. She retreated three or four steps and felt the crunch of glass followed by a sharp pain in the heel of her right foot. She hopped, trying to catch her balance, and finally steadied herself against the wall. A razor-thin shard of glass from one of the broken bulbs had penetrated her sock and buried itself in her heel. She scratched gently with her fingernail, trying to pluck it out, and felt a warm trickle of blood on her fingers. A quick-moving shadow broke the shaft of light behind her.

Joss tried to run, but as soon as she put weight on her foot her knee buckled in pain as the glass was driven deeper into her foot. She collapsed on the wooden decking, turned, and saw the towering silhouette of a man backlit in the open door of her office.

"Don't touch me. I'll scream."

"Please. Do not be afraid. I'm not going to hurt you."

"Stay away from me."

"Are you all right?"

"I'm fine."

"Let me help you up."

"Leave me alone."

He ignored her and stepped forward, but instead of grabbing her, he reached gently for her foot with one hand. "That looks bad. You are bleeding. Here, let me help you."

The gentleness in his voice calmed Joss, but she was still wary. He was huge, at least six feet five, perhaps taller. In a single fluid motion, his arms were under her, cradling her back and under the bend of her knees. He lifted her as if she weighed nothing, turned toward the lighted doorway, kicked it fully open, and carried her through into her own office.

He placed her gently on the couch against the wall in the reception area, then turned, and headed for the door. He started to close it.

"Don't," said Joselyn.

He didn't turn around but looked at her over his shoulder. "I thought you might be cold. I will leave it if you wish." He left the door open and in three steps crossed the room to where she lay on the couch.

"That does not look good." He was foreign, had an accent. Joss wasn't sure from where. The blood from her heel was soaking into her sock, turning it a bright red. "I'll have to take that off to get at the glass." As he gently removed the sock, he caught the edge of glass in the fabric and she winced in pain.

"Sorry. If you lie still, I think I may be able to get it." As he studied her foot, Joselyn got her first good look at the man. He had fair skin, wavy blond hair, and broad shoulders. The features of his face were sharp as if etched in stone; a straight nose, high cheekbones, full parted lips.

He reached into his pocket and pulled out a four-inch folding knife.

Joselyn's eyes went wide, but before she could speak he plucked a tiny pair of tweezers from the handle of the knife and laid it on the small end table at the foot of the couch.

He looked at her. "Very handy little things," he said.

Joselyn smiled nervously and nodded.

"Think about something pleasant and don't look at your foot," he told her.

That was not going to be easy. She lay back and looked up at the ceiling. She felt the tweezers at work, but his large hands were amazingly gentle. Then sharp pain. Her leg jerked uncontrollably.

"Easy. I got most of it. Let me see."

She looked down at him as he studied intently the underside of her foot.

"Did you cut your knee when you fell?"

"What?" Joselyn looked down.

There was blood running down her leg from her knee. The adrenaline rush on the ferry caused her to not even notice until now.

"An earlier accident," she told him. Joselyn had cut her knee to the point of bleeding while clawing her way back onto the deck of the ferry.

"You lead a hazardous life," he said.

"You have no idea," she said. Joss was beginning to relax. If he wanted to kill her, he could have done it by now. "What are you doing in my office?"

"This is *your* office?"

"That's right."

"Then you are Joselyn Cole?"

"Who are you?"

He didn't answer her but adjusted the light from the table lamp at the end of the couch. "One thing at a time," he said. "I should concentrate, or the glass in your foot may require a visit to the hospital."

He picked at her again with the tweezers, and she flinched in pain, forgetting for the moment questions about the man's identity.

"There. I think that is all of it. That I can see anyway. You will know in a day or two if I have missed any. It will begin to fester. Very painful," he said.

"That's encouraging."

"I'm not the one who was running through glass in my stocking feet."

"Let's get back to what we were talking about," said Joselyn. "Who are you and what are you doing in my office?"

"Ah, yes." He reached into an inside coat pocket and came out with a business card. He handed it to Joselyn.

"My name is Gideon van Ry."

She read the business card. "What is the Institute Against Mass Destruction?"

"We are what you call a think tank dealing with international relations. Specifically the institute monitors fissile materials, missile systems, weapons of mass destruction. We publish reports, a database."

She looked at him, taking it all in, nodding almost as if in a daze.

"Why did you break into my office?"

"Oh, I didn't." He looked up and saw that she was focused on the door and its splintered wooden frame. "I found it that way." He raised one hand as if taking an oath. "I was looking for you. Found your office. I discovered the door as you see it."

"And you just let yourself in?"

"It was open. I thought perhaps someone was inside."

"Was there?"

"No. Whoever did this had already left."

"It's not going to be cheap to get that fixed," Joselyn was looking at the door again.

"Unfortunately whoever did that did not stop there."

"What do you mean?"

"The inner office," said Gideon.

She tried to get up off the couch.

"Easy." He pressed her back down gently and dabbed the blood off the bottom of her foot with his handkerchief one more time, then tied it around the wound.

Joselyn swung her legs off the couch and stood. She took one step and began to hobble as if she might go down. He grabbed her arm and steadied her, helping her as she hopped on one foot to the door to her office.

When Joselyn got there, she just stood in the open doorway, looking. The desk was turned over. Her two filing cabinets had been pulled over on their faces, the drawers pulled out and the contents thrown all over the floor. The glass in the frames holding her degrees and licenses had been smashed, though two of them still hung on the wall behind broken splinters. Whoever had vandalized her office had done a world-class job.

The light from the office's reception area and the open door offered a clear line of sight, even from across the street with the driver's window rolled up. With a rifle, he could have taken both of them right there. But Thorn insisted it had to look like an accident.

The car was rusted out, its motor idling. The driver reached up with one hand and grabbed the bandanna. The gray woman's wig slid off his head with it. His eyes never left the two figures standing, centered in the doorway of the second-floor office. He had to admit that from behind she had a nice body. She also had nine lives. He was sure he'd gotten her on the ferry. He wondered who the blond giant was standing next to her. He dreaded his next task: telling Thorn that she was still alive.

EIGHTEEN

WASHINGTON, DC

Hirshberg reported to the president in a written memo, sealed and marked, FOR THE PRESIDENT'S EYES ONLY. The memo was brief, discreet, and factual, reporting only what had been confirmed so far: that a Russian ship had gone down off the coast of Washington State, that it was believed to have been carrying fissile materials, perhaps a nuclear device, and that the device or materials were unaccounted for. He held the information on Kolikoff's involvement to a single line at the bottom of the memo. It was sealed and hand-delivered to the president by one of Hirshberg's aides.

Three minutes after the president slit the envelope and read the memo, he was on the phone to his national security adviser.

"Sy. Who else knows about this?"

"You mean the Russian ship, Mr. President?"

"And Kolikoff's involvement." The president cut right to the chase.

"CIA, FBI, and Military Intelligence know about the ship, the fact that it was carrying fissile materials."

"And Kolikoff?"

"Only myself and the CIA deputy director." Hirshberg could hear a palpable sigh of relief at the other end.

"Which deputy is that?"

"Malcolm Sloan," said Hirshberg.

"Oh, yes. Sloan. He's a good man." Interpretation: Sloan was ambitious and could be reached by the White House for the proper spin on the story if it became necessary.

"I'd like you in my office in ten minutes to discuss this."

"Would you like me to call Sloan, or Director Gentry?" Kurt Gentry was director of the CIA, and Sloan's boss.

"No. I don't think there's any need for Gentry to know anything more at this point. He knows about the Russian ship, I'm sure. I'll call Sloan myself," said the president. The president was busy trying to narrow the circle of knowledge. Information in politics was power, and compromising dirt on a president was the ultimate form.

"Don't talk to anyone about this. Do you understand?"

"Yes, sir."

FORTY MINUTES LATER, Hirshberg and Sloan had their preliminary rewards for silence and discretion. They were named to chair the special crisis task force appointed by the president to look into the ship *Isvania*, its cargo, and whether the incident posed any imminent threat to national security.

Assigned as staff were all of the people in Hirshberg's working group. Notably, their bosses had all been cut out of the loop. Hirshberg and Sloan were to report directly to the president. If their bosses, the directors of the CIA, FBI, or Joint Chiefs of the military interfered, Hirshberg and Sloan were to report the matter to the president.

Both men were given special passes, issued by the president himself and authorizing them to interrupt presidential business if at any time, in their judgment, there was a need. It was something sure to cause rancor within the White House pecking order. The president's chief of staff, the principal gate-keeper, jealously guarded his prerogatives, foremost among which was access to the Oval Office. Now he would be left to stare at the president's signature on the special passes and wonder what it was that Hirshberg and Sloan knew that he did not.

To identify the group they borrowed an acronym from the FBI: ANSIR. It stood for "Awareness of National Security Issues and Response."

The ANSIR team convened for their first meeting less than

two hours after Hirshberg and Sloan left the Oval Office. Each one of the members was reassigned on a temporary basis to full-time duties with the ANSIR team. Any questions on this assignment were to be referred to the White House—more fuel for the fires of political envy.

"We are going to have some structural and support problems," Hirshberg told the group. "None of the Cabinet secretaries have been told about this."

Heads turned and looked around the table at one another. "Why not?" Finally one of them spoke up.

"Those are our orders," said Hirshberg.

"There's no sense starting a panic." Sloan from the CIA put a better spin on it. "The more people who know, the more chance of a leak to the press. If it gets in the media that we suspect a nuclear device is in the hands of terrorists in this country, all hell could break loose. It's on a need-to-know basis, and they don't need to know right now."

Once the Cabinet-level officers became involved, the bureaucracy would take hold. News would filter through the various agencies and before long mid-level bureaucrats would be talking over coffee about how the president compromised himself with Kolikoff. From there it was only whispering distance to the *New York Times* and the *Washington Post*. As a consequence, the limitations on the ANSIR group were severe.

Hirshberg sat at the head of the table, flanked by Sloan, who saw the entire exercise as a fast elevator to the penthouse of power. The very surroundings confirmed his sense in this regard: the White House Situation Room with its proximity to the president.

"Here are the ground rules," said Hirshberg. He read from hastily written notes prepared during his meeting with the president.

"All discussion of the device, its alleged smuggling into the country, and steps to discover its location or to secure and disarm it if it was in the country, are to be confined to members of this group, at least until further orders."

He looked around the table to be sure that this was understood.

"Assets for any investigation will include only military intelligence."

Hirshberg tried to go on.

"Excuse me." It was the representative of the FBI. "The bureau has principal responsibility for domestic terrorism. I can't just go behind my director's back. I would at least ask to get clearance. To discuss it with the director."

"I'll look into it," said Hirshberg. "I'll talk to the president. But for the moment you are to say nothing. Understood?"

"Yes."

"For the moment the president, as commander in chief, wishes to deal with this issue through the military chain of command. Therefore for the time being we are to rely principally on Naval Intelligence." There was a muted but obvious smile from the naval officer at the other end of the table. What it boiled down to was that the people who already knew about the Russian ship, and the name Kolikoff, had now been effectively co-opted by the president.

The FBI interceded again. "The problem is we have contingency plans for these situations. This effectively makes those plans worthless."

"Sorry. But that's the way it is," said Hirshberg. "At least for the moment." Hirshberg agreed with the FBI. The problem was, the president saw it differently.

"What we can all do to alleviate the situation is to work quickly," said Hirshberg. "If we can confirm that there is no device in the country, that it went down with the ship, then there won't be any further need for this group to meet or for further action to be taken, other than perhaps to recover whatever is out there. For the moment, we can't be sure there was a device.

"If on the other hand a device is in the country, then I will prevail on the president to put all of our resources to work. I'm sure he will see the wisdom of bringing in the Cabinet and all the appropriate agencies at that time." Actually Hirshberg wasn't sure of this at all, but he would do his damnedest to convince the man.

"Where do we go from here?" Hirshberg looked at Sloan.

"I think it would be best if we start with an analysis of what we already know. In the last twenty-four hours we've gathered new information which indicates that the device or devices in question . . ."

"There's more than one?" The FBI was asking questions again.

"We're not sure," said Sloan. "There may be."

The FBI started searching other faces around the table for support but didn't get it.

"As I was saying, new intelligence reveals that the devices in question may have been paid for, at least in part, by a rogue state, possibly Iraq. According to our reports, they're keeping their distance. It's likely that the people involved at this end don't even know about the outside support. They're merely being used to achieve a mutual goal. If the reports are correct, the Iraqis may have put up considerable cash to obtain the device and are probably paying a middleman to facilitate assembly and transportation."

"The middleman. Do we know who he is?" asked the FBI.

"No. Unfortunately we have no information, but we're following it up. We do have solid information that whatever it was that was shipped out on the trawler in question was obtained by the Russian Mafiya, specifically a corporation founded by KGB money as the Soviet Union collapsed. It is now run by former rogue agents. Its CEO is Viktor Kolikoff."

Sloan shot a sideways glance at Hirshberg. He didn't intend to get into the finer details of Kolikoff, though most of the people in the room had read the newspapers and could fill in the blanks for themselves. The president's political predicament was going to make their job much more difficult.

"Do we know if there is verifiable state sponsorship for these activities?" It was the man from the State Department asking.

"You mean Iraq?" said Hirshberg.

"Yes."

"Why?"

"If so, the administration is on record. It has not ruled out a nuclear strike in retaliation for such an attack."

"And your point is?" said Sloan.

"It's vital that any foreign state actively involved with domestic terrorists understand the risks to themselves."

"You're suggesting we contact the Iraqis?" said Hirshberg.

"If we have incontrovertible evidence of their involvement," said the man. "It's possible that we can peel them away from whomever they're dealing with in this country if the risks to themselves are made readily apparent. A full-out nuclear attack," said the man.

Sloan looked over at Hirshberg and wrinkled an eyebrow. It wasn't a bad idea. "Who knows, the Iraqis might give up whoever is working at this end if they know their own ass is in the flames," Hirshberg said.

"Thank you. We'll see if we can firm up the Iraqi connection." Sloan made a note. The item was now firmly in his own quiver of ideas, the ones he would fawningly present to the president. Sloan wouldn't remove lint from the shoulder of a friend's coat unless he got credit.

"There's another aspect to this whole thing." This time it was Navy Intelligence.

"What happens if a device is detonated in a major American city? How could we be sure some other power doesn't panic and launch a full-out preemptive strike out of fear?"

"Why would they?" said Sloan.

"He has a point," said the man from the State Department. "Another nuclear power, Russia, China. Even if they're not involved, if they think there's a chance we might suspect them, they could launch before we have a chance to quell their fears."

"You mean a full-out preemptive strike?" said Hirshberg.

The man from the State Department nodded his head. They all knew that the Cold War might be over, but the risks of nuclear annihilation were not.

"The problem with the Russians," said the naval officer, "is that their early warning system is shredded. There's no money for maintenance, and their stations in Latvia are gone. They're a nuclear giant stumbling around blind. If there's a detonation somewhere in a population center in this country, their first inclination may be a preemptive launch rather than waiting to see if we sort things out."

"That shouldn't be a problem," said the FBI. "The president made a statement six months ago that Russian missiles were no longer aimed at American cities."

"They're not," said Sloan.

"Then we would have time to contact them and give them assurances," said the FBI.

"You don't understand," said Hirshberg. "Russia's nuclear missiles are configured in such a way that even if the

Russians removed the targets from the missiles' computerized guidance systems, if they're launched, the missiles are programmed to immediately reacquire their last known targets.''

The president's assurances aside, they were living in a fool's paradise.

NINETEEN

Joss stood looking at the mess in her office, this time in the cold light of morning. If anything, it looked worse than the night before.

By nature she was not well organized. She generally worked from piles of papers that to the average eye might appear disheveled. It was her own kind of filing system. Usually these stacks rested on her desk and any other flat surface that was available. She knew where everything was and could usually stick her hand in any of a dozen of these document heaps and come up with whatever was needed. The problem now was that these stacks had been scattered all over the floor, some of them torn up.

"What in the world?"

Joss turned to see Samantha outside, standing in the doorway. She was examining the splintered wood around the lock of the office's front door.

"I had visitors last night," said Joselyn.

"I can see." Sam wandered in looking at the tall blond guy standing in the reception area, holding some loose pieces of paper he'd picked up off the floor.

Joss made the introduction. "Samantha Hawthorne, Gideon van Ry."

They shook hands. Samantha eyed him, making a careful

and slow appraisal, then looked around the office again. "They really did trash the place."

"Sam's my landlady," Joselyn told Gideon.

"You have my condolences," he told her.

"I hope insurance will cover this. What happened?"

"I came back from Seattle last night and found it as you see it. Somebody broke in," said Joss. "Trashed the place and left."

"Kids, you think?" said Samantha.

"I doubt it."

"You sound like you know who did this."

"Not really," said Joss.

"Have you called the sheriff?"

"A deputy just left. He took the report. Of course they'll investigate."

"We'll need it for insurance if nothing else," said Sam. She was still surveying the damage. "Is anything missing?"

Joss gave her a shrug, like she couldn't be sure. She had also used the opportunity with the sheriff's deputy to report the incident on the ferry the night before. When she did, the cop looked at her askance, like this clearly wasn't her day. Still he didn't seem driven by the coincidence to link the two events or ask many questions. Joselyn was sure she would be hearing more from them, but at least for the moment they seemed satisfied.

Gideon had spent the night in a small motel by the airport just on the fringes of town. Given the events of the day, they agreed that it was not wise for her to go home. She took a room just a few doors away.

Van Ry seemed straight-arrow. That morning Joselyn had slipped away from him long enough to call the phone number down in California that was on his business card. They vouched for him and provided information about the institute, which seemed to correspond with what he'd told her the night before.

Now he disappeared into her inner office and was lifting the two filing cabinets off the floor and positioning them against the wall where they belonged.

"Who is he?" Samantha whispered in Joselyn's ear.

"He's here about Belden's business."

Sam looked at her as if the name didn't register.

"The guy with the desperate phone calls."

"Ah. That one."

Samantha craned her neck to peek around the doorway for one more look at Gideon. "Not bad," she whispered. "You can send him to my office to clean up when he's finished here."

"He's here on business. Belden's dead."

This took Samantha's attention away from the doorway and the tall blond. She looked at Joselyn wide-eyed. "How did it happen?"

Instead of answering, Joss unfolded a copy of the Seattle paper with the story on an inside page. It was sparse on details and attributed Belden's death to an accident that was still under investigation.

"You flew down on this plane with him to Seattle?"

Joselyn nodded.

Sam slumped into a couch in the corner. "You could have been killed."

"That's not the worst of it."

Sam looked at her.

"His death was no accident. I can't tell you anything more. Not right now."

"He was murdered?"

"It looks that way."

Suddenly the light clicked on in Sam's eyes. "You think this is connected?" She meant the tossing of Joselyn's office.

"I don't know."

"You should go to the sheriff. You told them that he was murdered, didn't you?"

"No. I don't have any evidence."

"Start with this, what happened to your office, the fact that your client is dead, the fact that you were on the plane with him earlier in the day. I think they'll be able to connect the dots."

"I don't want to get into it right now. Can we talk later?"

"Sure, if that's what you want. But I'll tell you, I wouldn't wait. Can I help you clean up?"

"It's pretty much a one-person job. And I've got . . ." Joss gestured toward the door to her office and Gideon. She could hear metal drawers sliding into their hardware.

"Call me if you need me. I'll be right next door." Sam

took one last look at her, then slipped down the corridor to the next office.

Joss headed toward her office and the mess that was inside.

"I am just putting all the files in a stack on your desk." Gideon looked up at her. He was on his hands and knees behind the desk.

"There's no need for you to do that."

"As long as I'm here, I may as well be of some help."

"Really." She went over behind the desk and started taking the papers and folders out of his hand. "I can do this. Please."

He got up from behind the desk.

"Tell me," said Joselyn, "how did you get my name?"

He picked up her office swivel chair, which was flipped over behind the desk. "You were listed as one of the corporate officers for Belden Electronics—with your State Department of Licensing."

"Of course. The corporate formation." Suddenly Joselyn started wondering. If van Ry could find her from the documents of incorporation, so could anyone else. Belden's associates, the ones McCally warned her about. Maybe that's how they found her on the ferry and located her office.

"I assume you were simply acting for your client?" said Gideon.

"Hmm?"

"In creating the corporation."

"Of course."

"So you weren't involved in any actual management activities?"

"No."

"What do you think they were looking for? The people who did this?"

"I don't know. Maybe they weren't sure themselves."

"Ah, what do you call it?" Gideon thought for a second. "A fishing expedition."

She nodded but didn't look terribly convinced.

"I would say you are in a great deal of trouble," said Gideon.

"Why?"

"Because the people who did this are very dangerous," said Gideon. "I do not think they were on some idle search for the unknown in your office."

"All of my papers relating to Belden and his business went to the bottom of the sound with the car." She had told him about the incident the night before. "Maybe that's what they were looking for."

"It's possible, but I doubt it."

"Why?"

"Put yourself in their shoes. You go down to represent your client Mr. Belden before the grand jury. You would take the Belden file with you, wouldn't you?"

She nodded.

"They would figure that much out themselves. They attempt to kill you on the ferry. As far as we know, they are satisfied that they succeeded. You are silenced. The file was with you in the car. They can surmise as much. And still, they come here and do this." He wrinkled his eyebrows. "The question being, why?"

Joselyn shook her head. She didn't have a clue.

"Let's start with your client's business."

Joss was no longer in the mood to protect client confidences. She wondered if she'd made a big mistake in refusing to cooperate with McCally. She wasn't going to make the same error twice.

"He said he was in electronics. I had no reason to question it."

"What kind of electronics?"

"Something about switches. Programming for security systems or something. I don't remember all the details."

"Did he ever take you to his place of business?"

"No."

"Did he give you an address?"

"He said he was just getting set up. I'm not sure he'd found a place." Joselyn slumped into the swivel chair behind her desk as Gideon pushed one of the client chairs into position across from her and took a seat.

"In other words, you're not certain he was in business at all."

She shook her head. "Why would he come to me to set up a business if he didn't need it?"

"Why indeed?" said Gideon. "What did he look like?"

She gave him a quick description and then told him about the investigation by the U.S. Attorney's Office and McCally's warning that Belden had used many aliases, that the government believed he was involved in moving dangerous munitions. Gideon took it all in, made a few notes, and didn't look up at her until she mentioned the small plastic device that the authorities found floating in the water at the site of Belden's plane crash.

"What did it look like?"

"Small, white, about the size of a square wristwatch."

"And they said it was for measuring radiation?"

She nodded.

"A dosimeter," said Gideon.

"That's it."

"Did you get a good look at it?"

"He showed it to me."

"The paper inside the square," said Gideon. "Was it discolored?"

"I don't know. I don't remember. I didn't look that closely. Besides, they pulled it out of the water."

"Yes. That could have affected it. Also the heat of the blast. You said the plane exploded?"

"The biggest damn fireball you ever saw," said Joselyn. "I've got melted nylons to prove it."

"So we are back to where we started."

She shot him a quizzical look.

"What were they after? The people who did this." Gideon was glancing around her office again like he coveted whatever it was they were looking for, the missing piece to a puzzle.

"Like I said, there was nothing here to find."

"My guess is that if you did not know the item or items were significant, you would not have hidden them. They would have been in your files or on your desk." He ignored this disclaimer and seemed to think out loud to himself. "That means that whatever it is, they probably found it. So we are left with a simple process of elimination."

"What are you talking about?"

"We account for all of your files and materials. And whatever is missing . . ." He looked at her from under arched eyebrows.

"Read my lips. There was nothing here. Besides, going through all the files would take all day."

"You have other things to do today?"

Based on the mess in her office, the answer was obvious.

"So the sooner we get started . . ." Gideon was back down on the floor, rummaging around, picking up files and loose papers from the floor, trying to figure out which papers went with which files.

She took them out of his hand and put them on the desk. "You stack. I'll sort," said Joss.

TWENTY

DEER HARBOR, WA

The pit was composed of less than thirty pounds of pure plutonium, surrounded by a casing. Grigori Chenko worked in a tent shrouded by heavy-mil plastic. In the roof was a vacuum hose and high micron filter intended to create a slight negative air pressure inside the enclosure. This would keep any of the friable particles of plutonium from escaping, hopefully trapping them in the filter.

To protect himself the Russian wore a hazmat suit of yellow neoprene. It was equipped with a breathing apparatus containing fine micron filters. Chenko was sweating inside the hot suit, the plastic face piece continually fogging over. It was not the kind of forced-air breathing apparatus they used at Sandia and other high-tech labs but something Chaney had acquired on the open market.

He took a break, stepped outside the tent, and removed the headgear so he could clear it to see. His hands were sweating inside the neoprene gloves, his back aching from bending over the small table he'd set up inside. The work was slow and tedious, punctuated by moments of intense anxiety as when he removed the plastic explosives from around the core.

The garage had been evacuated and Chenko's footsteps cast an eerie echo from concrete floor to metal walls as he paced about and stretched to loosen his body. The others waited outside until he was finished and the device was secured in its new metal casing.

Chaney had fabricated the casing from pieces of two old military fighter wing tanks that he found in a scrapyard on the mainland. Working from photographs of the original device, Chaney demonstrated his skill with a welding torch, reshaping the metal and adding touches like rivets for realism. The Russian could not tell the reproduction from the original on display. They were peas in a pod from a large photograph that had been taken a month earlier and brought back to the island by Thorn himself. The plan was ingenious.

He donned the headgear and ducked back through the slit in the plastic tent. To the untrained eye, the device on the table looked like a soccer ball. It was composed of thirty-two individual pie-shaped pieces of plutonium. Each was cut at a forty-five-degree angle. These were formed into a sphere and surrounded a beryllium/polonium core.

The entire package was wrapped in conventional plastic explosives that contained multiple detonators. It was this, the plastic explosives and the detonators, that drew Chenko's attention. They were old and presented the greatest risk of failure. The simultaneous timing of the detonators was critical. The nuclear reaction was a given, an immutable matter of physics, but only if the plastic explosive that triggered it was timed to one ten-millionth of a second. The pressure giving rise to implosion would have to be precisely uniform around the entire outer ring of the sphere. Only then would critical mass be achieved, setting up the nuclear chain reaction.

It was a small bomb, as nuclear devices went, but at its core, at the instant of ignition, temperatures would reach one million degrees, hotter than the surface of the sun. The high temperatures would release massive amounts of electromagnetic radiation. Objects in the immediate vicinity would be vaporized instantly.

The radiation would be absorbed by the air immediately around the bomb. This in turn would be heated to incandescence, creating a fireball that would expand at velocities approaching the speed of light until its temperature dropped below 300,000 degrees. Then it would slow to the point where the mammoth shock wave created by the compression of air in the atmosphere would overtake the fireball, flattening structures and knocking down trees. Within a second, the fireball would reach the same area, igniting every flammable surface, melting metal, and turning human bodies into instant steam.

The shock wave would travel more than two and a quarter miles in ten seconds and result in maximum devastation of the affected area. The luminosity of the fireball would fade. The violent overpressure of the shock wave would pass. Out of the violent sphere of fire, the forbidding mushroom cloud would raise its deadly head toward the stratosphere, cooling as it climbed, creating its own violent convections of air. There would be lightning from within, and if conditions were right, a deadly downpour of highly radioactive particles, a rain shower of agonizing death.

It took Chenko more than two hours to check and replace detonators. He did this by cannibalizing and using the spare parts of the other device, the first one the fishermen brought in, missing its deadly plutonium core.

He then took the assembled device and bolted it into the open half of the bomb casing that Chaney had built. He stepped out of the plastic tent and lifted the hood of the hazmat suit from his head. Sweat dripped down his forehead into his eyes and ran in rivulets down his neck into the suit.

He walked toward the large sliding door of the metal garage and slid it open with a rattle. The men outside turned from their conversations to look. A few of them dropped cigarettes into the dirt and stamped them out.

Chaney and Thorn were off to one side, by the old battered pickup truck Thorn was using. The Russian joined them, unzipping his suit as he walked.

"It is finished."

"Good," said Thorn. "And the lead wires for the electronic detonator?"

"As you requested. I have left them exposed through the small opening near the tail fins. You can replace the hatch cover when you are finished. Touch up the paint, and it is ready."

"Excellent. You do good work."

The Russian smiled.

They went inside, and Thorn went to work. He set up at a workbench against the back wall of the garage, opened a briefcase, and pulled out a small computer. He attached a microphone and began speaking into it, reciting only two words: "Critical Mass." The sound of his voice was registered in spiked lines similar to a graph on the computer's screen. He did this several times until he got a voice test he wanted. Then he saved this onto a computer disk. He removed the disk and punched it into another small computer-like device known as a "blue box." It had a keypad similar to a computer and terminal ports. Thorn punched the keys and delivered the information on the computer's disk to its destination. He then carried the small plastic package over to the device.

By now, Chaney was finished fastening the two halves of the bomb casing together. He and two other men had it on a hydraulic floor jack, rolling it on wheels toward the truck.

They stopped a few feet from the vehicle and Thorn did the final preparation. He connected the wires to a switching device capable of sending a powerful electric charge to the detonators set into the plastic explosives inside the bomb. The receiver and its wires were then carefully fitted into an area near the bomb's large square tail-fin assembly, where the battery pack would also be placed before the device was delivered to its ultimate destination. The tail-fin assembly had been fabricated by Oscar Chaney using precise specifications from photographs taken of the original. Even the olive-drab paint had been matched with care.

The fifteen deadly tubes that would surround the core of the device rested with their lethal liquid contents, sealed in a special lead-lined vault deep in the bowels of the truck's tank. These would be inserted later, once the device reached its destination. They would require great care in handling and the use of a C-suit and breathing apparatus, all of which Thorn had placed into special compartments in the tank of the truck.

"Done." Thorn wiped his hands on a rag and turned to Chenko. "You're sure the device is properly assembled?"

"Absolutely."

"No last-minute adjustments required, anything like that?"

"No. Connect the lead wires according to the schematic I have provided, install the batteries, and it is armed."

"Good," said Thorn. "Let's you and I go outside, have a beer."

The Russian smiled.

"Oscar. Go ahead and get it inside the truck," Thorn yelled

to him across the garage, and Chaney gave him a thumbs-up.

Thorn and the Russian went outside to the old pickup truck, where Thorn reached into the back and opened a small cooler, pulling out two glass bottles of ice-cold beer. He twisted the cap off of one of them and handed it to Chenko, then opened the other for himself.

Inside the garage, Chaney was busy with two other men, rolling the large bomb across the concrete floor on a hydraulic alligator jack. They maneuvered it under the tank that Chaney had welded onto the bed of the truck. Then Chaney pumped the long handle of the jack, raising the bomb up into the opening under the belly of the tank. It was bolted into place and secured, and the false steel panel under the tank was put back in place.

In ten minutes they were finished, and Chaney began pumping raw sewage from the portable john into the separated upper compartment of the tank, in case they were stopped.

Chaney had welded a solid plate of steel, lined with lead, separating the truck's tank into two compartments: a lower section for the bomb and an upper section for raw sewage. Conventional satellite surveillance would be of little use in detecting the truck. Plutonium gave off only mild gamma radiation, which could be shielded by a piece of paper. Thermal detection at checkpoints, if the Feds had time to set them up, could be more problematic. Thorn had taken the precaution of having Chaney line the bomb compartment with a quarter-inch lead liner. The absence of any signature from the device, coupled with the obvious presence of actual sewage in the truck, would likely cause authorities to wave them through without much question. They were counting on the normal human reaction to recoil from thoroughly inspecting such cargo. Besides, who would suppose that a septic-tank truck would be hauling an atomic weapon?

Outside, next to the pickup truck, Thorn watched as Grigori Chenko twitched on the ground. He was in the final tremors of death. His eyes rolled back into his head like two cherries in a slot machine. Potassium cyanide worked very quickly, especially in a dosage as strong as that which Thorn had added to the beer he'd given to the Russian. Chenko's job was done; one more loose end eliminated.

TWENTY-ONE

It was after four in the afternoon, and they were both tired. Out of the corner of one eye, Gideon watched Joselyn Cole as she arranged the files on her desk. She was an attractive woman, blue-eyed with shoulder-length sandy-colored hair. Her body was well proportioned and curvaceous, and she had a tawny complexion that the tall Dutchman found pleasing.

She also had a core of iron. After the events of the previous day, many people would have gone to bed and pulled the covers over their heads for a week. But Joselyn remained focused on the job at hand.

She looked up at him. "Thank you for your help today," she said.

"I must admit to a certain selfish motive," he told her.

"What's that?"

"You are the last lead I have for the two forged waybills." He had told her about the shipments out of the port of Vladivostok. There was a grave tone in his voice. "I cannot impress upon you enough the seriousness of why I am here."

"Maybe if you told me a little more," said Joselyn.

"If I am correct, your client Mr. Belden was involved in a very dangerous matter, a matter that could have devastating consequences for your country, and perhaps for the world."

"What consequences?"

What he had discovered at Sverdlovsk could start a public panic if it were published. The fear that a nuclear device might be in the country, in the hands of terrorists, could result in wild speculation as to a target and mass migration of hundreds of thousands of people clogging highways and overrunning airports.

"Until I know more," said Gideon, "I can't be sure of my information. I can tell you this much. What I know would seem to be consistent with the information given to you by the prosecutor in Seattle. It is possible that this man who called himself Belden was involved in transporting weapons of mass destruction."

"And you think these weapons are here, in this country?"

"I don't know. Perhaps what they were looking for here in your office will tell us that."

Joselyn returned to the documents on her desk, looking through each more carefully now, mystified by what could possibly be contained in her files that would confirm van Ry's suspicions.

"I was curious as to why you omitted to tell the local authorities that the incident on the ferry was an attempt on your life," said Gideon. "You told them it was an accident. Why?"

"Because I have no proof," she told him.

He engaged her eyes from the other side of the room as he put the final touches on one of the filing cabinets, pushing it against the wall.

"Do you really think it is coincidence that your client is killed in the afternoon and that night someone tries to push you and your auto off of the ferry?"

"It could happen."

"I see," said Gideon. "And you attribute all of this sudden misfortune to an unusual episode of bad karma?"

She gave him an irritated expression but didn't respond.

"You might wish to check the alignment of the planets before you venture out onto the street again."

"You seem to have all the answers. What would you have me do?"

"You could have told the authorities about your conversation with the prosecutor in Seattle, about Belden's death. The two incidents, the plane exploding and the fact that you were driven off the ferry only a few hours later. I suspect they might have seen some pattern here.''

"Fine. And what would have happened then?''

"I suspect they would have provided you with some protection.''

"Great. Wonderful,'' said Joselyn. "So they put a sheriff's deputy outside my office door. That's going to do wonders for my practice. 'Mr. Jones, I'd like you to meet Deputy Smith. He's going to be watching over us while we talk, just in case someone makes an attempt on my life during client consultation.' To say nothing of the chilling effect it would have on clients in criminal cases.''

"They would certainly know you have influence with the sheriff's office,'' said Gideon.

Joselyn stifled a laugh. "Besides, if McCally found out about the ferry incident, he'd drag me before the grand jury for sure. Probably have me taken in federal protective custody.''

"Why not?'' said Gideon. "You would at least be safe.''

"Just what I need, cops outside my door, or a cell, courtesy of the federal government. For how long?'' she asked.

"Until this is over.''

"And how long will that be?''

Gideon couldn't answer this. The expression on his face said as much.

"Precisely,'' said Joselyn. "In the meantime, whatever meager practice I have here disappears.''

"You would be alive.''

"You call that living?''

"It may be better than the alternative,'' said Gideon.

Joselyn didn't argue the point.

"Why in the world do they want to kill me?''

"Because you know something.''

"I don't know a damn thing.''

"They think you do, and for the moment that is the same thing,'' said Gideon. "I suspect that the answer is somewhere there, in front of you.'' He gestured toward the papers on her desk. She returned to the task, this time with more energy and interest.

"Is there anything this man Belden told you?''

"I've already been over all of that, with McCally and the FBI."

"Yes, but their powers of perception may not be as finely tuned as mine."

Joselyn looked up at him, cracked a smile, and they both laughed.

"OK, Sherlock. What do you want to know?"

"When did Belden first come to you as a client?"

"Less than two weeks ago."

"And how did he find you?"

"A referral from a banker in town. At least that's what he told me. It was probably a lie."

"I suspect you are right," said Gideon. "Did you have any special expertise that he might have been looking for?"

"We talked about that," said Joselyn. "In fact, it was just the opposite. He could have hired a hundred lawyers down in Seattle who knew more about business law than I did and not paid them a dime more in fees."

"So we know that he wanted something else," said Gideon. He looked at her with an appraising eye, so that she could read his mind.

"I don't generally discuss my sex life with strange men, but if you have to ask, the answer is no, we didn't. Not even close," said Joselyn.

"I didn't think so," said Gideon.

Joss feigned hostility. "And why not?"

Now his face turned a shade of red she had not seen before.

"It's just that . . . ah . . . Belden being a client and all," said Gideon.

"What's that got to do with it?" She looked at him steely-eyed, unwilling to let him off so easily.

"All I meant was that it wouldn't be the professional thing," said Gideon.

"And you see me as the consummate professional, is that it?"

"Absolutely," said Gideon.

"Gid. Can I call you Gid?" said Joselyn.

"Whatever you want to call me is fine," he told her.

"If that's the case, then for the moment I'll just call you a bull-shitter."

Gideon tried to maintain composure but could not. The red

veins in his neck began to stick out, and he started to laugh. "What is it they say? Takes one to know one."

"That's what they say," said Joss.

He settled into one of the client chairs across from her desk. "We know one thing."

"What's that?"

"There is clearly some connection between what happened in Sverdlovsk and whatever is going on with your grand jury down in Seattle."

"Why's that?"

"According to the prosecutor, your client, Mr. Belden or whatever the latest name he is using, was expert in the handling of certain large-scale weapons. It cannot be a coincidence that fissile materials are missing from a Russian storage facility, traced to the port of Vladivostok, and that forged waybills show a shipment to Belden Electronics. I would think the prosecutor knows something."

"Maybe he does, but you can be sure he's not telling us."

"Perhaps not," said Gideon. "But he might tell someone else."

"Who?"

"His own government."

She looked at him quizzically.

"We have some contacts in the intelligence community. I will call my director at the center and see if perhaps we can float some balloons, do some checking. If it is a matter of national security, the Justice Department might contact the National Security Agency."

"What good would that do us?"

"At least we would know that intelligence agencies are, as they say, in the loop. And after all," said Gideon, "we do have information to trade."

She looked at him questioningly.

"What I learned in Sverdlovsk," he said. He clearly had more confidence in government than she did.

Joselyn was holding a single piece of paper in her hand, searching the surface of the desk for the appropriate file as he spoke. She had been looking at it intermittently, trying to find the file it belonged to. Suddenly she realized the file wasn't on her desk.

She stepped across the room to the filing cabinet that Gideon had straightened against the wall. Joselyn opened the second drawer and thumbed through the files. She turned and looked at him, a troubled expression on her face.

"What is it?"

"Are all the files back in the cabinet?"

"Except for the ones on your desk."

She retraced her steps and checked the surface of the desk one more time. It wasn't there.

"What is it?"

"It doesn't make any sense," said Joselyn.

SEATTLE, WA

Thomas McCally flipped through the pages of the report. Only three pages long, it was lean on many details. The FBI was still investigating, but two federal prisoners awaiting trial had escaped from the Kent jail. One of them was of particular interest to McCally. Oscar Chaney was a bank robber with no prior criminal history but a colorful military record. He had been trained by Army Special Forces in what was euphemistically called "special ops" and had participated in what the report called "operations other than war." McCally was no military tactician, but he knew what this meant. These were insertions into other countries that were never publicly reported, sometimes into hostile Third World countries, sometimes into the territory of allied nations. The purpose might be to gather intelligence on the ground or deliver arms to insurgent movements or to destroy some strategic facility, a radio station or fuel depot. The people who did this work were highly trained. Oscar Chaney had done this and was also active in the Gulf War. He'd cashiered out of the military, and for the past five years he had lived abroad. According to the State Department, he traveled in Europe, Africa, and Latin America. More important, information obtained by the FBI from European intelligence sources indicated that Chaney had been involved with Harold McAvoy, alias James Regal, alias Liam Walker, alias Dean Belden.

The report provided clear evidence of outside help and extensive planning in the jailbreak that sprang Chaney. The FBI had already arrested one of the men assisting from the outside.

The man arrested had extensive contacts with a local militia group.

"It looks like they wanted Chaney out, and they came well prepared." As McCally read the report, the FBI agent who had delivered it paced the office in front of his door. "They cut the bars with a torch," said the agent. "We didn't find it, but the thermal marks on the steel are unmistakable. We also found a small portable wire transmitter. According to the one arrested, there were three others helping from the outside."

"The one you picked up. Is he giving up any information on Chaney's whereabouts?"

"I don't think he knows. He says he was drafted for the job by higher-ups in his militia cell. He doesn't know the names of the others involved in the break. My guess is they all came from different cells, and if we go up the food chain, we're going to find out that the people who tapped them for the job don't know any more than they do."

"How did we arrest the one guy?" said McCally.

"He was shootin' his mouth off in a bar about how easy it was, the jailbreak," said the agent. "Like he was looking for more clients."

"If the information in this report is accurate, he's not the kind Chaney would run with or trust very far," said McCally. "Which brings us to the question of why Chaney was robbing banks."

"And doing it so poorly," said the agent.

"What do we know about the local militia groups?" asked McCally.

The agent gave him an expression as if to say, "not much." "Mostly situated up north and on the other side of the Cascades. Rural counties. They operate in leaderless action cells— small, loosely organized units. There's not a lot of contact between the cells. Nothing you could call organized command and control. It's mostly a mixed bag of nuts, some with racial motives, some just hate the government, and a lot of wannabe soldiers. Almost all male. Mostly in their thirties and forties."

"Have we been able to penetrate any of the cells?"

"Not a problem. Just go to weekend war games and bring your own rifle. Problem is because of the small size and lack of cohesion between the groups you'd need a thousand agents in war togs and face paint to cover them all. For the most part, the ones here in Washington have generally been satisfied with hating the world and shooting at cardboard targets. Not that violent.''

To McCally it sounded like the agent might want to join them.

"Define violent," he said.

"Most serious is recreational explosives. Stealing a rifle from a National Guard armory's the equivalent of earning your bones in the mob. They consider it big-time. We can usually pick them up in a local bar bragging about it. Not what you'd call a well-planned conspiracy.''

What the government had learned in Oklahoma City is that intelligence against such groups is almost useless. The most dangerous among them often acted alone or with one or two other friends. The first wind of any activity came with the pressure wave of an explosion.

McCally thought for a moment. "Doesn't sound like an organization that could get up to speed on weapons of mass destruction.''

"You thinking chemical or biological?" said the agent. "Not unless they could make it in somebody's garage.''

"What I'm thinking of they couldn't make in a garage," said McCally. "I'm thinking nuclear. Remember the little piece of white plastic—the dosimeter we found in the water after Belden's crash?''

"I hear Russia is a major shopping center for nuclear arms. But how would they get the money? That would cost a bundle. Even Iran and Iraq haven't been able . . .''

"As far as we know," said McCally. "Let's assume for a moment they found an open channel for such a weapon. Then they would need help. Professionals who knew how to arm and transport such a weapon.''

"That would explain Belden and Chaney," said the agent. "But how would they get the money for a bomb, to pay people like Chaney and Belden?''

"Raise it. They have a network. Bogus check-writing schemes, a little fraud here and there, sell securities in the Comstock Lode to the aged.''

"That might raise a few hundred thousand, maybe a million if they're playin' the market. But we're talking multiple millions here.''

"They could have a secret investor," said McCally.

"Whaddaya mean?"

"I mean what if you were Saddam and you were itching for a little revenge, but you didn't want to be *it* in a game of nuclear tag?"

"A rogue state?"

"Working from the shadows. I can think of a half dozen regimes that would love to blow the shit out of a major American city, especially if they could deflect blame to one of our own homegrown groups. Such a government might come up with a little subsidy to make a device available."

The agent thought about this.

"They might even steer a little technical help in their direction," said McCally. "Suddenly Mr. Belden and his colleagues are knocking on your door, courtesy of Saddam or Muammar."

"You think . . . ?"

"I don't know," said McCally. "But people like Belden, and Chaney, are here for a reason. It is possible that they came as part of a package, attached to some kind of a device."

For a moment they simply looked at each other, each knowing the question but declining to put it into words: was it already here?

"The militia groups up north," said McCally. "Are they at all tied in with the bunch out on the island?"

The FBI and ATF had identified a sizable contingent of well-armed militia members on a small private island in the San Juan chain just south of the Canadian border.

"Not as far as we know. The group on the island came in from Idaho and Montana."

"What are they doing out there?"

"We don't know, but they're armed to the teeth. ATF has spotted some major ordnance."

"Anything we can move in on? Get a search warrant?" asked McCally.

"Not without the Marines." The agent arched his eyebrows as if to emphasize the point. "We don't know if the weapons are legal. We've taken some long-range photos, but we can't tell."

"No full-automatic stuff?"

"Haven't seen or heard any bursts."

Possession of fully automatic weapons was illegal without a special license issued by the federal government. Evidence of such might be enough for a search warrant.

"They're under twenty-four-hour surveillance?"

The agent nodded.

McCally took a deep breath. He knew they were on the edge of something, but what? Without a warrant he couldn't search the island, and without Chaney he had no one to squeeze for information. He didn't want to look like a fool by going to intelligence agencies, but he had decided one thing. It was time to share what information he had with superiors in the Justice Department. Let them make the call.

"Let's assume Chaney's involved with the ones on the island," said McCally. "The local militia could be providing logistical support. Helping to spring him."

"That would demonstrate a lot more organization than we've seen before," said the agent.

"Let's just suppose something big, very big, is in the works," said McCally. "The people in charge have secluded themselves on the island."

"Why?"

"To stay out of reach, to prevent us from infiltrating, from getting information until whatever it is they're planning is finished."

"So why do they want Chaney out?" said the agent.

"Maybe he's key to their plan."

"And who killed Belden?"

"I don't know," said McCally. "Maybe Chaney. He had a lot of explosives training in the military."

"But why?" said the agent.

"What, do you think I've got a Ouija board?"

The agent sat in one of the client chairs across from McCally's desk and rocked his head back, counting ceiling tiles as the lawyer finished scanning the report on the jailbreak.

"What's this?"

"Hmm?" The agent brought his gaze down and looked at him.

"It says here this wasn't the cell Chaney was assigned to."

"Yeah. Can you beat it? Jail staff lets 'em move wherever they want within the unit. Fucking five-star hotel, and we get handed the bill."

"Who's this guy, Chenko?"

"He's the other one, got out with Chaney. We're probably lucky they didn't allow a slumber party in the cell. We'd be hunting for fifty of 'em," said the agent.

"It wasn't Chenko's cell either," said McCally. "Says here he was in on an immigration violation."

The agent shrugged his shoulders as if to say, "So what?"

"So what do we know about him?" Suddenly McCally sat upright in his chair.

"Nothing beyond what's in the report."

McCally looked at him. "You still don't get it?"

"What?"

"Why would Chaney rob a bank and accept a packet of bait bills from the teller normally reserved for the mentally impaired, then within twenty-four hours after getting busted pick up with some guy in the county jail who speaks pidgin English and who's in the country illegally?"

The agent shrugged his shoulders. "I don't know."

"They weren't after Chaney," said McCally. "Get me everything you can find on this guy Chenko. If you have to, contact authorities in Moscow. Do it. See if he has any prior record. Find out his occupation."

FRIDAY HARBOR, WA

George Hummel's file was missing. Joselyn was back at the open filing cabinet, rifling through it for records relating to other fishermen.

"Who is George Hummel?" Gideon was behind her, looking over her shoulder.

"He's one of my clients. There are five of them," said Joss. "All local fishermen with similar medical symptoms. I was looking for some kind of industrial causation, a link that would explain the condition and provide some financial recourse."

What Joselyn held in her hand was a medical report. It had come into the office late the previous week. She hadn't had time to file it or to call Hummel. She had thrown it into a basket on her desk. Whoever trashed her office apparently had missed it, but the Hummel file was gone; so were the files of the other four fishermen.

"Can I see that?" Gideon gestured toward the paper in her hand, and Joselyn gave it to him. It was no time to make a stand at the bulwark of client confidence.

He read it quickly, then looked up at her. "When did these clients first come to see you?"

She thought for a moment. "I don't know, maybe two months ago."

He looked at the medical report, the brief description on the piece of paper under the heading SYMPTOMS: *Initial nausea and vomiting, anemia, rapid hair loss, intermittent and repetitive bleeding mostly from the gums and mucous membranes, periods of unquenchable thirst.*

"Where do these people work?"

"They're sport fishers. Some of them own boats; others work as chartered skippers."

"They all work here on the island?"

"As far as I know."

"And the boats, where are they kept?"

"Docked down at the harbor," said Joselyn. "Why?"

"Your clients are suffering from radiation poisoning," said Gideon.

"How would they . . . ?"

"I don't know. But you said this man Belden came to you out of the blue. You said you wondered why he hired you, why he picked you when he could have gotten a more experienced business lawyer down in Seattle."

"That's right."

"Maybe he didn't want an experienced business lawyer," said Gideon. "Maybe there was something else you had that he wanted—information about these clients. Maybe what he wanted to know was whether you had discovered the source of their illness."

Joselyn thought about it. She remembered that Belden had asked her questions the first day she met him. George Hummel had been in the office, and Belden had seen him. He had asked her about him and had tried to pry for details.

In an instant, their eyes locked. "We take my van," said Gideon. "I have some equipment." Before he finished the words, he was headed for the door with Joselyn at his heels.

TWENTY-TWO

WASHINGTON, DC

The president put the pen to paper and formed a single letter of his name. The motorized clicks of a hundred cameras echoed like crickets in the Oval Office.

With a smile, he handed the pen to one of the congressmen standing behind his chair, picked up the next pen, and repeated the performance. The last pen was presented to the attorney general, who thanked the president graciously, stepped back, and began the round of applause that brought the chief to his feet with a broad grin and handshakes all around.

"Mr. President, if you have a moment when we're finished," Abe Charness, the attorney general, whispered in his ear. He got a smile and a nod from his chief.

The little performance was the final chapter in a legislative package that did virtually nothing but was being hustled to the public as the administration's centerpiece for campaign finance reform. It would give folks back home the cozy feeling that something good was happening in Washington.

At the moment, the president was riding high in the polls, taking credit for an economy over which he had virtually no control. As a politician, he followed the first rule of medicine: do no harm. He coupled this with a lot of smiles and promises of vague new programs.

Two of his military aides and a couple of White House

ushers herded the press toward the door. After they left, the president took a couple of minutes and chewed the fat with some congressmen. Photos were taken of them, shaking hands with the president in front of his hand-carved cherry desk. They would use the pictures in their upcoming campaigns. The last congressman smiled, then took his leave. Finally they were alone.

"Have a seat, Abe." The president loosened his tie and undid the top button of his shirt. He was back in his doughnut phase, having put on twenty pounds since the last election.

"Someday I'd like to get a golden screen," said the president, "so I could lounge behind it in pajamas like the Empress Dowager, and whisper what I wanted done to some eunuch out front."

"I'll build you the screen, Mr. President. But I draw the line at cutting off my pecker."

The president laughed. It was what he liked about Charness. What little ceremony the man stood on was grounded in some crude Georgia clay. They were both sons of the South, raised in families that eked out a living on the upper edges of poverty.

"Sit. Sit," said the chief. They took up the same ends of opposing sofas across the coffee table in front of a fire that was still crackling.

"How's Jenny and the kids?" asked the president. The two men hadn't seen each other in three weeks. Charness had been in The Hague for a conference and had traveled through Europe meeting several of his counterparts.

"Oh, they're fine."

"I imagine the kids are getting big."

"John's taller than I am," said Charness.

"Makes us all feel like we're getting old."

"You bet."

"Well, what is it?" The president could tell something was bothering Charness.

"It's ah. It's one of my assistants. Jim Reed. I think you know him."

The president arched an eyebrow and thought for a second.

"Tall man, slender. A little sparse at the tree line," said Charness.

"Oh, yeah. Sure. You brought him by for a Cabinet meeting a few months ago."

"That's the one."

"Is there some problem?"

"I don't know. It seems Jim has been assigned to some team or special task force during the time that I was away. No one back at the office seems to know much about it, and when I talked to Jim, he indicated he wasn't at liberty to discuss it."

"What kind of team?"

"From what I understand," said Charness, "it was authorized by you."

The president looked at him with an expression of surprise on his face. He shook his head as if he were at a loss.

"I think it operates under an acronym, ANSIR. I don't know what it means," said the attorney general.

"Ah. That," said the president. Suddenly he was filled with recognition, a hearty smile, a lot of bluster. "I didn't know what you were talking about. I'd forgotten all about it."

Charness looked at him, an expression of interest filling his eyes. "I figured there would be some explanation, Mr. President. You can imagine my surprise when he told me he wasn't authorized to discuss it with me."

"Oh, it's nothing. Nothing," said the president. "Probably be wrapped up in a week or so."

"Can I ask what it's about?"

"Oh, one of the national security types brought something to his boss. It required a number of reviews, including legal. I figured your people would be the best for the job, so I just told them to tap whomever they needed. I guess this Reed fellow was drafted."

"It would have been nice if maybe I'd gotten a memo or something," said Charness.

He was worried about turf, the eternal battle of every bureaucrat. "Yeah, well I borrowed a few people from a dozen agencies. If I took the time to send memos to all of them, the task would be done before the memos went out. If your man Reed is taking too much time off the job, I'll tell them to let him go, find somebody else." The president started to get up off the couch.

"No. No. That's not necessary, Mr. President. I mean, if you need him, that's fine. Not a problem. We can pick up the slack." What Charness really wanted to know was what was going on.

"Well, good." The president wasn't telling him. "Listen, we're gonna have to get together for dinner over here, just the two families," said the president.

"We'd love it," said Charness. The president had changed the subject, leaving his attorney general with nothing but heightened curiosity. He would have to pump other Cabinet members to see if they knew anything, who on their staffs had been tagged for the ANSIR group.

"Is there anything else?" asked the president. He smiled. The last one he needed with his nose under this particular tent was the attorney general. He was already aware of the president's false steps with Kolikoff, the acceptance of campaign money and the photos in front of his desk. Knowing Kolikoff, those pictures were probably already being used on labels to hustle some cheap brand of vodka in Moscow.

Charness looked at the floor, then at his hands, which were on his knees. He was hoping that if he sat there long enough, the president would tell him why he was using one of his assistants.

The president looked at his watch. "Got a reception in half an hour. Jesus, I wish I could get that screen. You sure you won't reconsider?"

Charness laughed and got up off the couch. The two men moved toward the door, the president with his hand on the attorney general's shoulder, making sure that he kept moving in the right direction.

"There is one òther thing," Charness added, as if he just remembered it himself.

"What's that?"

"It's probably nothing," said Charness. "Something that crossed my desk this morning. A report from my office in Seattle. Seems they've got an investigation going, dealing with some militia groups out in the Northwest."

"What else is new?" The president edged him toward the door, trying to get rid of him.

"This one may be a little different," said Charness. "There seems to be some basis to believe these people are shopping for weapons, something big, maybe out of the FSU."

Like a flashing red light, reference to the term FSU—Former Soviet Union—stopped the president in his tracks.

Suddenly Charness could tell that he had the boss's undivided attention. There was finally something he had that the man wanted to know.

"Like I say, it's probably nothing," said Charness.

"No. No. Tell me about it."

"Not much to tell. Just a brief report."

"What did it say?"

The attorney general scrunched up his face, like he was trying to remember. "Oh, some group is holed up on an island. They seemed to be armed and waiting for the second coming. Probably just another group of nuts. As long as we don't overreact, wait them out, I'm sure it can be handled."

"Is there a Russian connection?" said the president.

"Not with their government," said Charness.

"That's not what I meant. You said there was information that this group might be trying to get weapons out of the former Soviet Union?"

"Well, yeah, there seems to be some information that some of the people involved might be hired professionals."

"What kind of weapons are we talking about?"

"One of these people, a mercenary of some kind, was killed in a small plane crash. They found a small item floating with the wreckage. Something called a dosimeter."

The president gave an expression as if it meant nothing to him.

"It's what radiologists wear. That little piece of plastic with paper in the frame that they wear on the lapel of their lab coats. It's used to measure doses of radiation," said Charness.

The president nodded.

"Like I say, it probably means absolutely nothing, but it was passed up the chain, and I thought I'd mention it." Charness started to move toward the door.

"Maybe I should see the memo," said the president.

"I can send it to NSA," said Charness. He was talking about the National Security Agency. "I don't want to bother you with it."

"I think it might be a good idea. Why don't you send it over here. Fax it back when you get to your office. I'd like to look at it before we forward it on."

"Sure. If you think it's important enough." Charness opened the door and was headed out, past the little cubicle occupied by the president's secretary.

"And, Abe."

The attorney general turned around. The president was standing in the open door.

"Keep me posted if you hear anything more about this."

FRIDAY HARBOR, WA

It was now dark. The only light came from a few vapor lamps that threw a yellow haze over the mist as it rose from the still waters of Friday Harbor. The ferry boat dock was empty. There was one late-night run, but it wasn't due for more than an hour.

Over the last decade, the commercial fishers had been decimated by fished-out salmon runs and large factory trawlers that prowled off the coast. The few sport fishing boats that were left clung to docks in slips out at the end, beyond the pleasure boats with their bright canvas dodgers and gleaming fiberglass hulls.

Gideon parked his van at the end of Front Street, across from the small building with a sign over the door: PORT OF FRIDAY HARBOR. The building was dark, except for one light outside over the door.

"These fishing boats that belong to your clients. Do you know where they are moored?"

"A general idea," said Joselyn. She started to open the door to get out.

"Let me do this."

"Why you?" said Joselyn.

"Because it may be dangerous." Gideon moved quickly out of the vehicle and around to the other side.

"Tell me what you think is out there." Joselyn wanted to know what they were facing.

"I don't know. I can't be certain."

"But you have some idea."

"It is based only on the information I have from my travels in Russia."

Joselyn looked at him, waiting for an answer.

"We may be dealing with old nuclear devices. If I am correct, they date back to the early nineteen-sixties. Such weapons can be very dangerous."

"You're talking about an explosion?"

"It is not what I am worried about." Gideon knew that if some group intent on an act of terror had gone to the trouble of smuggling nuclear weapons into the U.S., they were not going to waste them on some isolated islands in Puget Sound. They had a more strategic target in mind. The question was where?

"I am concerned about oxidation," he told her. "Plutonium, when it is exposed to the air, turns to a fine powder. This powder is very radioactive. It can be very dangerous."

"And yet you're going to go out there."

"I know what I am looking for. Besides I will take precautions."

He opened the sliding door to the van. He had borrowed the vehicle from a friend who worked for the University of Washington, someone in the radiation lab he'd met years before. With the information he had gathered in Sverdlovsk, he knew he might need the equipment, and it was the only local source. Inside were a number of large metal boxes. On a hook was a yellow suit with a hood and what appeared to be a breathing apparatus that attached to the face mask.

"I only have one of these," he said, pointing to the suit. "Besides, if I get into any trouble out there, I will need someone back here on the docks to call for help."

Joselyn looked at the boxes and the suit inside the van. She didn't like it, but what he said made sense.

"I'm coming at least inside the gate on the dock. I want to get as close as I can."

"I want you out of harm's way," he told her.

"I can't help you if I can't see you."

Gideon agreed. Then he opened one of the boxes and took out a flashlight and another small device. Joselyn instinctively knew what it was, even though she had never seen one up close: a Geiger counter. He slung it over his shoulder by the strap attached, then grabbed the suit off the hook and slid the door to the van closed. He started to walk toward the dock.

"What about the suit?" said Joselyn. "Aren't you going to put it on?"

"Not yet." He headed across the street and Joselyn followed him.

WASHINGTON, DC

It was nearly one in the morning when Sy Hirshberg reached the security kiosk leading to the West Wing of the White House. The uniformed Secret Service agent waved him through, and Hirshberg parked his car and walked quickly to the entrance.

There were a few lights on, even in the middle of the night. The West Wing never shut down completely. Hirshberg didn't stop at his office but headed to the southeast corner of the ground floor. A Secret Service Agent stepped from the shadows of a room directly across from the Oval Office. He recognized Hirshberg, greeted him by name, but stood in the way until he checked a clipboard showing appointments for the president. This one showed that the president himself had cleared the appointment an hour earlier. The agent tapped on the door to the Oval Office.

"Yes."

The tone in the president's voice was not pleasant. Hirshberg had detected an air of crisis when the president called him at home after midnight. He sensed that whatever it was, it was important, and probably not good.

"Mr. President."

"Sy. I'm glad you got here."

The agent stepped outside and closed the door to the office. Hirshberg had expected to find a dozen people, high-level advisers closeted in crisis mode inside the Oval Office. Instead the president was alone, sitting in front of the fire, reading papers, and making notes on little Post-its.

"What is it, Mr. President?"

"A problem. A big problem." Without looking up at Hirshberg, the president flipped a piece of paper from the top of the stack to the other end of the couch. Hirshberg crossed the room, picked it up, and read. It didn't take long.

"What I want to know," said the president, "is why I have to find this out for myself. You've got a team of people, all the resources of intelligence, the military, and law enforcement, and I have to find out by myself about this band of crazies holed up on an island in Washington State shopping for nuclear bombs."

"Where did you get this?" said Hirshberg.

"From the attorney general. Seems they've had an investigation going on out in Seattle for some weeks now, based on information that home-militia groups were attempting to obtain a weapon of mass destruction and that criminal elements in Russia were attempting to fill the order."

The president had a pile of paper in his lap. "Grand jury transcripts," he told Hirshberg. "It makes very interesting reading. It's too bad the various agencies of the executive branch aren't sharing information. It's just a goddamned good thing I happened to meet with the attorney general today."

Hirshberg bit his lip. He wanted to defend himself, to tell his boss that if he hadn't been so intent on covering his tracks following the embarrassment with Kolikoff, the Cabinet would have been alerted. The Justice Department through the attorney general would have known about the sinking of the Russian ship off the Washington coast, the suspicion that it might have been carrying one or more weapons, and no doubt would have linked it with the information in their grand jury probe. Hirshberg looked at the date of the Justice Department report. They had now lost vital time.

"I want you to get your people on this now," said the president. He lifted the mass of transcripts so that Hirshberg could gather them up. They were trailing paper onto the floor.

"Does this mean that we can come out in the open, involve other agencies, local government?"

"Hell, no," said the president. "I want you to read this stuff before morning. Call in whomever you need from your team. I want a briefing at eight o'clock in the morning, here. I want to know if Kolikoff's name appears anywhere in that transcript. Do you understand?"

Hirshberg was stunned. They were confronted with the possibility of a nuclear device loose somewhere in the United States and the president's first concern was whether it might lead to a political scandal in the White House.

"Mr. President, I think we have to call in all of the appropriate civil authorities. There is a protocol that's been established for this very kind of situation."

"No." He looked at Hirshberg through intense, narrow slits of eyes.

"But, Mr. President, knowing what we now know, there is

a good chance that these people have in their possession . . ."

"I said no. I'll be damned if I'm gonna have this thing splashed all over the front pages and played on an endless tape every half hour on CNN. We don't know any such thing. All we know is that Justice has some kind of investigation going on out on the coast that may or may not lead anywhere. It's under investigation."

"Mr. President, we know that wreckage from the Russian ship was highly radioactive. We know that it went down somewhere off the coast of Washington State. We know from Russian sources that there has been a tremendous amount of radio traffic from this Siberian arms depot to Moscow and back. Now we have this." Hirshberg cast a glance at the reams of paper that were now weighing him down. "I think that we can be reasonably well assured that there is cause for serious concern. That some action is essential. At least let's find out what this militia group is doing out on the island."

"You think the weapon might be on the island?"

"It's a possibility."

"We need a map." The president was up off the sofa, grabbed the phone, and dialed the number for the Situation Room. "Who's the duty officer tonight?" He spoke into the receiver, then waited a second.

"Monagan, this is the president. Get me a map. I'm in the Oval Office. I'm looking for an area around North Puget Sound in Washington State. There's an island." He snapped his fingers twice and pointed to the papers in Hirshberg's arms, the grand jury transcripts, then put his hand over the phone and spoke to his national security adviser.

"The name of the island? It's in the transcript. I marked it with a purple margin sticker."

Hirshberg fingered through the pile of paper until he found the marker. "Padget," said Hirshberg.

"Place called Padget Island," said the president. "Get me everything you can on it and deliver it here in five minutes." He hung up the phone and headed back to the sofa.

"We gotta be careful here, Sy. I don't want to go off half-cocked. We can't even be sure there is a device." The president was in denial.

"According to Oak Ridge there was enough contamination on the junk from that Russian ship to keep the glow on

Yeltsin's nose going for the next thousand years," said Hirshberg. It was a hard fact to ignore.

The president looked down at the carpet and took a long, deep sigh. "OK. All right. We'll put the island under surveillance."

"Watching it through binoculars is not going to tell us what's going on," said Hirshberg.

"What do you recommend?"

"We need to get somebody on the island. Eyes and ears," said Hirshberg.

"I don't want some shoot-out, another Waco or Ruby Ridge."

"I understand," said Hirshberg. "But we don't move now and they have a device and they move it . . ." He didn't have to finish the thought.

They had worried for years about people like Saddam and Qaddafi getting their hands on weapons of mass destruction. Sail a nuclear bomb into Seattle on a cargo ship or, better yet, up the East River and park it just off the U.N. Plaza and you could destroy half a city and cut off the head of the United Nations at the same time. Such a message would have a clear impact on world policy and the willingness of nations to form a united front.

The maps came from the White House Map Room, and a military aide spread them on the president's desk.

The president thanked the aide, and the marine left the room. The president and Hirshberg scanned the map and found Padget Island.

"It's not very big," said the president. The map did not show any structures or streets. "We could get aerial surveillance, some satellite photos."

"It wouldn't do us any good. If the device is there, it's probably pretty small. Not likely we'd be able to see anything. And it would take time, and that we don't have. If the device is there, we have to confirm it quickly and bottle up the island as fast as possible."

"So what do we do?"

"I would suggest, Mr. President, that we send in a small contingent, a platoon. Probably Navy SEALs," said Hirshberg. "We have them plant listening devices and cameras and then we take them off. A quick insertion, in and out. If it's done right, the people on that island will never know we've been there. Then we'll know what the hell's going on.''

The president had a long, drawn expression on his face. If shooting broke out on the island, he had visions of news crews with live cams on yachts taking it all in for CNN and the networks. Things could get quickly out of his control. Congress would start asking questions, and before he knew it Kolikoff's name would surface in connection with a nuclear bomb. Considering the lack of alternatives, however, there wasn't much choice.

''I don't want to go through the Joint Chiefs on this,'' said the president. ''All we need is a story about some loose nukes in the country, and the Pentagon will be using it to beat me over the head with Congress to reinstate budget cuts.''

The administration had spent four years reducing the defense budget and closing bases around the world. Since the collapse of the Soviet Union, the military brass had been forced to sit quietly on the sidelines and take it. But there were those among the Joint Chiefs who would relish the opportunity to roast the administration for its lack of readiness. They would serve the president up on a platter to the press if they had a chance.

''This insertion on the island. Can you arrange it through your Navy rep on the ANSIR team?''

Hirshberg didn't like it. Presidential concerns over a scandal were now driving military policy. What if shooting did break out? What if it turned into a rout on the island and Navy SEALs were killed? The military leadership in the Pentagon would be outraged and rightly so.

''The man's only a captain,'' said Hirshberg.

''That's all right. I'll give him whatever authority he requires.''

''We'll need the cooperation of the SEALs down at Coronado. SEAL team one,'' said Hirshberg.

''That can be arranged.'' The president had him boxed. It was against Hirshberg's better judgment, but it was either avoid the normal chain of command or do nothing. They had to find out quickly if the devices were in the country and, if so, where.

''If we're going to do it, we need to go in and set up intelligence on that island in the next twenty-four hours,'' said

Hirshberg. ''I don't know if they can be ready.''

"Let me handle that," said the president.

Time was running out. If there was a device, and the militia group on the island had time to move it, the chances of finding it again were slim.

The president looked at him with a reluctant expression, took one more deep breath, then nodded. ''Then we're agreed. Twenty-four hours,'' he said.

TWENTY-THREE

FRIDAY HARBOR, WA

The damp night air seeped through Joselyn's clothing and chilled her to the bone as she and Gideon made their way to the gate leading out onto the floating dock at Friday Harbor.

Gideon kept a close eye on the Geiger counter's meter and listened for the telltale clicks of danger. So far all he got was mild background radiation, nothing that would indicate the presence of fissile materials.

At the gate, he stopped her. "I want you to stay here."

"The boats are way out there." She pointed out into the dark distance. "You won't know which boats to look for."

She had given him the names of the vessels and a general description of their location on the docks. They would be with the sport and commercial fishers out near the end, near open water.

"It is too dangerous," said Gideon. "This is my job." He was adamant. "There is a cellular telephone in the van. If I am not back in ten minutes, call this number." He pulled a card from his pocket and circled one of the telephone numbers on it with a pen.

"It is a special twenty-four-hour number at the institute. Use my name. Tell them what we know, about the sick fishermen and the boats. They will know what to do. Then call the police and have them cordon off the docks. Tell them not to allow anyone on or off and to wait for help."

"But you'll be back by then," said Joselyn.

"Perhaps."

The way he said it caused Joselyn to think she might not be seeing him again. There was more danger than he was admitting.

"If you have to wait for these people from the institute to come up from California, that could take hours," said Joselyn.

"Trust me. They will know who to contact up here."

"Shouldn't the sheriff come out and get you?"

"No. Just do as I ask. Please."

"I will."

"If I do not come back immediately, it may be because I do not want to spread further contamination. Not to worry," he told her. "I will move away from the source and wait for help. No one should be allowed to enter or leave the dock until the decontamination team arrives. Do you understand?"

"Yes."

"Good." He flipped on the flashlight and checked it. Then looked at her one more time. "If there is no problem, I will be back as quickly as I can."

He headed down the ramp toward the slips farther out in the harbor. In his hand he held the list of the fishing vessels' names printed in pencil by Joselyn on a scrap of paper she found in the van during their ride to the docks: *Martha's Desire*, *Skip Jack*, and *Float Me a Loan*.

Joselyn stood on the dock, watching as he disappeared into the darkness beyond the reach of the big vapor lamp on the power pole overhead. When she could no longer see him, she began to pace the dock and wrapped her arms against her sides, hugging herself against the chill of the damp night air. Every few seconds, she would stop and strain her eyes for any glimpse of Gideon among the forest of masts and sea of boats. Less than a minute had passed since he left the gate and already it seemed like forever.

She looked at Gideon's van parked at the curb and tried to remember if they had left the door unlocked. If not, she would have to find a pay phone.

She looked at her watch again. She was worried that he would get lost out on the labyrinth of floating docks. She wondered why he hadn't put on the protective yellow suit before he headed out onto the docks.

She tried to take refuge in the fact that he knew what he was doing, that if there was anything out there, the Geiger counter would pick it up. By now, if there was radiation on the docks, the instrument should be recording something.

She waited a few more seconds, then looked at the van. She checked her watch. Three minutes had elapsed. She could hear nothing except the creaking of the docks, the straining of mooring lines, and the occasional clang of hardware or the gong of a small bell somewhere in the distance as the boats bobbed in their berths.

THE DOCKS FORMED a labyrinth of dead ends out on the water. Anchored in place by old wooden pilings, they rose and fell with the tide. What light existed was cast by the few boats that were live-aboards, inhabited year-round by their occupants. For the most part, the floating docks were lost in pools of darkness.

Gideon's flashlight had begun to flicker; perhaps the batteries were bad. He stopped for a second and checked the Geiger counter. It was still reading only mild background radiation. He tried to get his bearings and wondered if maybe he made a wrong turn at one of the intersections where the floating docks joined. He seemed to be mired in a sea of tall masts from sailboats and large, extravagant craft, some of them more than fifty feet in length. Most of the boats were dark, though in the distance he could hear the sound of a television set and see muted light from a salon belowdecks. It gave him a sense of confidence that at least he wasn't totally alone on the docks.

He looked back toward the port building. Situated as he was, behind a row of boats, he couldn't see the gate where he had left Joselyn, though he could see the halo of light from the large overhead streetlamp.

He checked his watch. He had six minutes to find the boats or else get back to her before she called the institute. He tapped the flashlight against one of the pilings, and it flickered a little brighter.

He slung the yellow neoprene suit with its hood over his

free shoulder. He wouldn't put it on until he had to. The
hooded visor limited visibility and would quickly fog up with
exertion. If he stepped off the dock in the dark, it would fill
with water quickly and take him to the bottom.

Gideon moved as fast as he could down the dock, counting
boats as he went, straining his eyes and searching the distance.
When he got to eighteen, the beam of his light ran out of
concrete and suddenly reflected off of water. He'd come to the
end. There were no sport fishing boats on this dock, and none
of the vessel names he was looking for. He had to go back.

He checked his watch. Five minutes to go. Nothing on the
Geiger counter. Gideon began to run, stepping over power
lines that fed heat to the boats and kept them from freezing in
winter. At a dead run, he jumped the small cracks between the
floating sections of dock and in less than a minute found himself at the main crossing dock.

Now he could look back up the dock and see Joselyn. She
was still at the gate, though now she was pacing, not looking
in his direction. He tried to catch her attention with the flashlight, but it was flickering, the batteries quickly dying. He
turned it off to save power, then looked in the other direction
out into the dark distance. The docks seemed to stretch forever
before disappearing into inky blackness. Beyond, he could see
the lights of houses on Brown Island, tiny and flickering in
the cold night like stars in the heavens.

For a moment he hesitated, wondering if it wouldn't be
wise to return to Joselyn up on the docks. He could get batteries for the flashlight and tell her to give him more time. The
thought died in his mind as he transferred the strap of the
Geiger counter from one shoulder to the other. The instrument
suddenly picked up a slow rhythmic click as it cleared his
body. The reading was coming from somewhere out in the
darkness, toward the end of the dock.

BY NOW JOSELYN was freezing. She kept a constant eye on
her watch. If he didn't return in four minutes, she would make
the call. She assumed Gideon was looking at his own watch,
that he knew how much time had elapsed and that if he didn't
find anything he would come back before ten minutes were
up. That was a big assumption, and Joselyn knew it.

She looked at the gate leading down the ramp and toyed with the latch. Maybe she should join him on the docks? She hesitated. He had told her to wait. The tall Dutchman seemed to know what he was doing. If she went out there, she would only end up putting both of them in danger. She was torn. Joselyn wanted to help but couldn't. She was getting more angry with herself by the minute. Why hadn't she seen through Belden? He was the kind of man every woman should be able to read like a book: full of hype, full of himself, full of lies. God knows she'd had enough clients who had lied to her over the years. She should have seen Belden coming in a minute. He was too good to be true.

Suddenly Joselyn realized what it was that she liked so much about the tall Dutchman. She had known him for little more than twenty-four hours, but the difference was like day and night. Gideon van Ry was the very antithesis of Dean Belden: self-confident without being arrogant. He took the time to explain to her what he was doing and why. He didn't tell her what to do and try to manipulate in the way that many men do but reasoned with quiet persuasion, the kind of logic that could not be denied. It was not his looks so much as the way he treated her that made her suddenly wish he was standing back here on the docks next to her again.

She strained her eyes for any glimpse of the moving flashlight out on the docks. "Where is he?" Without thinking she spoke the words out loud to herself and heard the echo of her voice off the wooden siding of the port building. It was followed an instant later by what sounded like leather scraping gravel. She turned and looked toward the building, but couldn't see a thing. She was bathed in light from the vapor lamp, and the building was lost in shadows. She shaded her eyes but still couldn't see anything.

"Hello." She waited an instant. Nothing. "Is somebody there?"

No one responded. She was like a child in the dark; her imagination was now playing tricks.

She turned and looked back down the dock for Gideon. He was out there somewhere. She checked her watch; two more minutes and she would make the call.

––––––––––––

THE REGISTER ON the Geiger counter was now giving up a steady stream of clicks, getting louder and more constant as Gideon moved down the dock toward open water. There were sleek pleasure craft, gleaming *Grand Banks* and *Island Gypsies*, a large *Ocean Alexander* that rested at the dock and looked like the *Queen Mary*. There were private yachts that Gideon could not even dream of owning. As he moved farther out on the docks, they gave way to small craft, working boats with wooden hulls stained by rusted bolts and aging fittings. The floating docks changed from concrete to wood, some of the planks split and stained by oil. The neatly coiled power cables disappeared, as electric power was no longer present to fuel the boats' heaters. Most of the vessels were small, under forty feet in length, many of them with open cockpits and large live-bait tanks centered in the stern.

The meter on the Geiger counter was now registering a virtual constant flow of ionizing radiation. Gideon had to turn the volume down to hear himself think.

He was in little danger, at least for the moment. There were three principal means of protecting himself: time, distance, and shielding. He had the protective C-suit, which would provide shielding if he needed it, so now he had to factor in the other two—time and distance. Looking at the gauge on the Geiger counter, Gideon estimated that he should spend no more than four, possibly five, minutes in the area.

The radiation seemed to get more intense as he moved toward the end of the dock. Now, even in the darkness, he could see the last four boats, each tied neatly in its slip. Across the long end of the dock on the outside, as if crossing the T, was a larger commercial fishing boat, a steel vessel that Gideon estimated to be close to fifty feet long.

The first boat in the slip to his right caught Gideon's eye. It was backed in and tied securely with a spring line. On its stern the name in stenciled black letters: FLOAT ME A LOAN.

Gideon spun around and quickly looked at the small boat in the slip across from it: MARTHA'S DESIRE. And next to it a small vessel, barely twenty feet long, the name SKIP JACK lettered on the bow.

By now the Geiger counter was clicking incessantly, its meter tripping at times off the top end of the scale as Gideon moved it around over the surface of the dock. There were

significant traces of radioactive contamination of the wooden
dock itself. Gideon knew that the levels of radiation being
recorded on the Geiger counter were not coming from plutonium. There was something else on the boat, something emitting deadly levels of radiation, which compounded the dangers
of the device. He did not want to stay here long.

He moved the instrument toward the stern of *Float Me a
Loan*. He was surprised when it failed to measure any increase
in the count. Gideon moved along the side of the boat on the
slip and the reading on the Geiger counter actually diminished.

He moved back toward the center of the dock and tapped
the flashlight on wood trying to obtain light to read the meter.
He got a flicker, a weak beam of light, and moved toward the
other two boats. Neither vessel seemed to register higher readings as he moved toward the slips and between them. Then
the needle soared as Gideon came back onto the main dock
and took a few steps toward the end. He looked up. There in
front of him was the steel fishing trawler, her name in chipped
and faded paint on the bow: DANCING LADY.

JOSELYN WAS FREEZING. It had begun to drizzle, and she'd
taken refuge under the eaves of the post office building. She
strained for any glimpse of Gideon out on the dock but could
see nothing except a forest of aluminum masts swaying in the
quickening breeze, their halyard lines clanking against metal
as the boats rocked. She had been here long enough to get the
feel of the islands. A weather front was moving in.

She looked at her watch. Twelve minutes had now elapsed.
She had given him two extra minutes. She prayed that he
would come back, that she wouldn't have to make the call.
She wanted to shout, to pull him back.

Joselyn was beginning to feel incredible guilt. There was
no way she could have known Belden was involved with nuclear weapons. Still, she had allowed him to use her name and
the address of her law office, and in this way Gideon had been
bound up in Belden's web.

Now whatever was out on that dock was Joselyn's fault.
She had, through her own stupidity and greed, brought whatever it was into the quiet tranquility of Friday Harbor.

She checked her watch once more, then reluctantly headed

toward the van and the cellular phone. She turned one last time in hopes that maybe she would see him coming up the dock. Her mind was filled with thoughts of regret. *I'll give him one more minute*, she thought. *Then I'll give him a piece of my mind.* He had no right to put himself in danger. There were people who were paid to do this, people who worked for the government. The thought had barely entered her mind when regret followed it. She was thinking of these as nonentities, people who worked in dangerous jobs to protect the rest of us. They had families, too, people who cared for and loved them. She could feel the pulse in her throat and the pounding in her ears. Sensory perceptions were dulled by the feelings that raged within her so that she failed to comprehend the movement of shadow behind her, just beyond her shoulder at the corner of the building.

GIDEON STEPPED OVER the railing near the stern of the *Dancing Lady* and onto her deck. A huge reel of netting occupied the fantail, and overhead two large booms forked high in the air and flared to either side of the vessel.

The meter on the Geiger counter spiked as Gideon moved forward around the wheelhouse. He took two more steps toward the forecastle area up on the bow, all the while watching the meter closely. The Geiger counter was now pulling in consistently high radiation readings. The audible clicks were rapid, constant, and loud, even with the volume turned down. Something had happened on this part of the deck that had turned it into a hot zone. If the device was armed with a beryllium-polonium core, the radiation readings he was picking up from the boat were from something else. There was something besides the nuclear core with that bomb.

Gideon backed away, turned off the flashlight and set it on the deck, then began to put on the yellow C-suit. It was arranged like a jumpsuit. Gideon stepped into the pants, then pulled the top up and slid his arms into the sleeves. After he wrestled it over his shoulders, he zipped it up the front, then finally put the hood over his head, sealing it with strips of Velcro around the neck.

The suit was not one of the more advanced models with a self-contained air supply under pressure. Now breathing became an exercise in endurance. Every breath had to pass through the fine micron filters that were built into the face mask. Carbon dioxide had to be expelled and oxygen forced in. Gideon began to sweat, and the visor in the face mask began to fog.

There was a single hatch cover, closed and latched on the forecastle deck. Whatever was in there, or had been in there, was the source of radiation. Gideon was sure of it.

He looked down, searching for the flashlight he had laid on the deck. Visibility through the mask was now a problem. There was no peripheral vision at all. He stopped over and felt around with his hands on the deck and finally located the flashlight. He pressed the button to turn it on and got nothing, then tapped it hard on the stainless steel railing in an effort to revive it.

That was when he heard it: a metallic clank that echoed his own, like something hitting against the hull of the boat. He stopped in his tracks, stood still, and looked back at the wheelhouse. He couldn't tell the direction from which the sound came. He struck the railing with the flashlight again and within three seconds heard a reply. This time it was sharper, more pronounced, metal-on-metal coming from the aft part of the vessel somewhere below decks. On the back side of the wheelhouse, facing the aft deck, was a cabin door. He guessed that this led down to the engine room and whatever accommodations passed for living quarters.

Quickly he moved to the cabin door, opened it, and shined the feeble beam of the flashlight on the Geiger counter. It was registering only half of the radiation he'd picked up on the forecastle deck. Here he was shielded by the steel structure of the wheelhouse. Inside was a ship's ladder, leading down into the bilge and engine room.

Gideon cast the beam of the light down in the direction of the ladder and peered into what seemed a bottomless pit. Between the faltering batteries of the flashlight and the fogged face mask, he was nearly blind. He gripped the railing on the ladder, stepped over the threshold, and began to climb down. He went down only one step and turned, then felt around with his hand on the inside of the bulkhead near the door. If there was a light switch, it would be here. He found it mounted on the bulkhead and turned it. Nothing.

Someone had either turned off the gen-set, or else it had run out of fuel. Without a generator or shore power, there were no lights. Gideon knew just enough about boats to know this was trouble. If there were no lights, there was no power for the bilge pumps. Vessels always took on water somewhere, slow leaks in the packing around the drive shaft and through the hull fittings. Depending on how long the power had been out, the bilge and lower holds could be filling with water.

Being blinded and weighted down by the suit could be a problem. He looked down the dark ladder and then proceeded slowly, a step at a time. He held the flashlight out in front of him, not that it was much use.

A dense cloud of blue vapor danced in the beam from his light and settled just under the overhead deck. Gideon put the Geiger counter up toward it and took a reading. The needle on the gauge didn't move. It was holding steady in the low to mid ranges, nothing as hot as the forecastle deck and the sealed hold up front.

Tentatively Gideon broke the seal on the Velcro around his neck and lifted the lower flap of the hood. What he breathed was not fresh air, but it was more cool than the CO_2 trapped under the stifling hood. It was tinged with a foul stench of diesel fumes.

He lifted the hood off his head and directed the beam of his flashlight down the ladder. It shimmered off the surface of oily water.

''Hello. Is anybody here?'' Gideon's voice echoed off the walls of the steel chamber.

Instantly the reply came, again in the clang of metal against the steel hull. It emanated from somewhere behind him toward the stern.

He stepped down into the water, still clinging to the ladder, standing on rungs. With the light, he could see only a few feet out in front of him. Gideon looked down onto the oily surface but couldn't tell how deep it was. Now the neoprene suit presented a hazard. If he slipped, and fell in over his head, or stepped into an open and flooded hatch, the suit would quickly fill with water. In the dark, without a clear sense of direction, weighted down by the suit, he could quickly drown.

He stepped down one more rung, still no bottom, then another. On the third step down, he finally hit a flat surface. He was now well above his knees in water. With one hand still clinging to the railing of the ladder, he took a tentative step away. He appeared to be in a narrow companionway that spanned the center of the vessel from bow to stern.

Gideon took a chance, let go of the ladder, and began sloshing toward the stern, down the short companionway in the direction of the last metallic echo on the hull.

"Hello." He listened. The signal of clanging metal was now being repeated as if in desperation, though the rhythm seemed erratic and without energy.

"Here." Gideon could hear a voice, weaker than the beam of his own flashlight but still audible.

"Where are you?" He called back.

"Here."

Gideon took a reading on the Geiger counter. It was well below what he'd received on the forecastle deck; still, time was running out. By now Joselyn should have made the call. He'd been wise to leave her behind. Help was on its way.

To the right along the companionway was a cabin door.

"Keep talking so I can find you." Gideon listened. Nothing.

He looked with the flashlight as far as he could see down the companionway before the beam disappeared in a film of fumes and darkness.

"Here." The voice was breathless but close. It came from farther down the companionway. A few feet farther on was an open door. Gideon peered inside and flashed the light around. It was a small galley, a table that was just above water and a propane stove with two burners. Water sloshed around inside, and remnants of food, some water-logged slices of bread, floated on the surface.

He headed back down the companionway. Within five feet he came to another door. This one was closed. He tried the handle. The water had swelled the wood in its frame and jammed the door. He put his shoulder into it and heard the wood panel in the center of the door begin to splinter. He hit it again, this time with his full weight. The door buckled and broke. His foot hit the threshold, and Gideon nearly fell through the opening into the water on the other side. Somehow he managed to stay upright and flashed the light inside. He peered through the darkness. In the distance, against the bulkhead on the far wall, was a double bunk bed, upper and lower. The lower bunk was several inches under water.

As he watched through the flickering beam of light, a form moved under the blanket on the top bunk. Quickly Gideon stepped over the threshold and sloshed his way across the cabin.

He held up the flashlight and lifted the blanket back. Gideon wasn't ready for the vision that awaited him. It was only arguably human. The hair was completely gone from the head and lay in tufts like molting fur on the pillow. There was a stench emanating from the bunk that overpowered even the fouled air of diesel fumes. Gideon wanted to put the hood back over his head, but he knew if he did he wouldn't be able to see.

The pathetic form on the bed was bleeding from the mouth and nose, dark frothy blood that Gideon knew was coming from deep in the lungs. It formed a pool on the mattress in which the man now rested.

His eyes looked pleadingly up at Gideon. "Water. Water." He seemed able to repeat only the one word.

Gideon was no physician, but it did not require a medical degree to tell that this man would never make it to a hospital. He was dying. Gideon knew he had no more than a few minutes.

"Who are you?"

"I need a drink. Water."

Gideon looked quickly around the cabin. In one corner was a table, high enough to be above the water. On it was a stainless steel pitcher. He made his way to it around a pillow and small stool floating in the water.

Suddenly he felt a lurch as the vessel tilted toward the stern, the weight of the engines drawing it down. She was taking on more water. The *Dancing Lady* was slowly sinking.

There was no water in the pitcher. Quickly Gideon made his way through seawater that was now creeping up his thigh. He moved from the cabin down the companionway and back to the boat's galley. The fresh-water tanks should still be watertight, he thought. The question was how he would get water without a functioning pump. He turned the tap and gravity emptied enough water from the pipes into the pitcher to put about three inches in the bottom. It was not much more than a small glass. More than that would probably kill the man in any event.

Gideon made his way back to the cabin. When the man saw the pitcher of promised water, he expended his last spark of energy, straining toward the pitcher and trying to raise his body.

"Easy. Easy," said Gideon. "Slowly." He knew the man would choke to death if he swallowed too quickly, and there was no more to give him once this was gone. He held the man's hands down and fed him a few drops of water slowly from the pitcher.

The man began to hyperventilate and cough.

Gideon removed the pitcher from his lips just in time to prevent being flooded with a froth of dark venous blood.

This dripped down the man's chin, and Gideon wiped it gently with a corner of the blanket.

"Who are you?" asked Gideon.

"My name is Jon Nordquist. My boat," he said. He was breathless. "Water."

"In a moment. Where is the device? Is it up forward in the hold?"

The man used what energy he had to turn his head slowly from side to side only once. "It's gone."

"Where?"

"I don't know."

"What happened?" said Gideon.

"It . . ." His voice faded. He regrouped. "It opened. The casing."

"The fissile materials were exposed to the air?"

The man lowered his chin as if to nod. "Yes."

"They took it in that condition?"

"Water."

Gideon was now using the pitcher as incentive, trying to keep the man alive long enough to find out what had happened. He gave him a few drops of water.

The man choked them down and coughed up a little more blood.

"Did the men who took the device handle the fissile materials inside?" If they had, Gideon knew they would be in the same condition as Nordquist, perhaps a few days less advanced but dying nonetheless. If they were lucky, any plan they had for a bomb might die with them.

"Did they handle it?" Now Gideon pressed.

"No. Over the side," said Nordquist. "My son put it over the side."

"Where?"

"At sea. Broke open on the deck," said Nordquist. "My boy is dead."

It was a cryptic picture, but Gideon understood. Somehow the casing of the Russian artillery shell had broken open. Plutonium, along with the beryllium reflectors inside the bomb, had toppled out onto the deck. Beryllium was a magic metal, lighter than aluminum, stronger than steel, and very expensive. It was prized for its role in inducing critical mass in a nuclear weapon. A beryllium reflector used to surround the plutonium core would reflect neutrons back toward the core, multiplying the chain reaction and hence the power of the bomb.

They were only fishermen, with no training in the handling of nuclear weapons. Beryllium dust in the lungs was deadly. It resulted in berylliosis, in which the lungs closed down and the victim choked to death. Under the circumstances, the fishermen had the presence of mind to do the only thing they could. They put the nuclear core over the side.

"Is that why the forecastle is radioactive?"

"Rolled around," said Nordquist.

That explained part of it. The device had probably already started to oxidize in the bunker at Sverdlovsk. Once it was free, rolling on the deck, abrading against the rough surface of the wooden deck, it would have left a trail of plutonium dust like a snail's track. The crew had breathed it in, along with beryllium dust, trying to catch the elusive silvery sphere as it rolled around the pitching deck. But there was something even more deadly present. No amount of salt water or solvent could cleanse the boat, not with the readings that the Geiger counter had detected.

"More water," said Nordquist.

"Was there a second device?" said Gideon.

"Water."

Gideon gave him a little more, and Nordquist lurched into a coughing spasm. For a moment, Gideon thought he would expire. He put one hand behind the man's back and eased him up so that gravity might help clear his lungs and the blood might run to his stomach. It took several seconds but it worked.

"Were there two bombs?" asked Gideon.

The man was breathless, his eyes glazed. Gideon had seen the pallor of Nordquist's face only once in his life, on a cadaver in a science course in college.

"You must tell me. Was there a second bomb?"

Nordquist struggled to breathe, speaking only as he exhaled, between parted and parched lips the word that Gideon dreaded: "Yes . . ."

"Where is it?"

Nordquist was suddenly silent.

Gideon moved the pitcher to his lips, but the water merely formed a rivulet down the man's chin onto his chest. Van Ry studied the man's open eyes and realized that he was staring from the fixed gaze of death.

SHE HAD GIVEN him almost twenty minutes. Joselyn couldn't wait any longer. He had a watch and a flashlight. She had to assume that whatever he found out on those boats was not good, otherwise he would have signaled her from the docks or come back. She was worried that perhaps she had already waited too long.

She turned and headed for the Dutchman's van at a run. She skipped over the curb and passed the corner of the port building. The only sensation was the sweep of air an instant before the leaded-leather sap connected with the base of her skull. Joselyn never felt the impact of the concrete as her head hit the sidewalk.

TWENTY-FOUR

INBOUND, SAN JUAN ARCHIPELAGO

Captain William Conners didn't like it. The orders had not come down through the SOC (Special Operations Command), the normal chain. Instead they had been routed out of Washington, high up in the Pentagon.

Conners had never seen anything like it before. In his view, it was not only unusual but dangerous. Still, nobody was asking for his views. He wondered who in the chain of command knew what was happening.

He and the other four men on his team would have no real logistical support. There would be no patrol boats for insertion and extraction. A slow fishing trawler was supposed to pick them up, a vessel that couldn't move faster than nine knots if it came under fire.

Conners looked at his watch. The Lockheed C-130 Hercules was five hours into its mission, out of the Naval Air Station in San Diego. Three of his men were asleep in reclining flight chairs, the same kind used on commercial jets, only in this case they were bolted to the floor up front in the cargo bay, down under the ladder leading to the flight deck.

Another thirty-five minutes and they should be over the drop zone.

"What's the weather looking like?" Conners cupped a

hand to his mouth and shouted over the roar of the four huge Allison turboprops.

The flight engineer had just come down the ladder. He was doubling as load master for this trip and getting things ready for the drop.

He gave Conners a thumbs-up. ''Clear. Light winds at the surface. Shouldn't be any problems.''

That was easy for the flight crew to say. They didn't have to jump out into a jet black sky at twenty-thousand feet over open water cold enough to induce hypothermia in a matter of minutes. If his men couldn't find the inflatables in the dark sea, they would drown, even with tanks and fins and clothed in wet suits. Whoever planned this one had shit for brains, and Conners knew it.

The so-called HALO (High Altitude–Low Opening) jump was something that might provide great cinematic effect in a James Bond flick. But Navy SEALs who put their bodies on the blocks in combat knew it was insane, especially at night.

''What are you calling light winds?'' said Conners.

''Five, maybe seven knots,'' said the engineer. He was now busy with the gear, unlashing it and getting it near the rear cargo ramp.

Conners followed him. ''Seven knots!''

''Tops,'' said the guy.

Conners knew that this could be enough to whip up whitecaps on the surface. He checked his tide charts. The northern reaches of Puget Sound could be treacherous. The tidal pull in the narrow channels between the islands could suck a man out into the Pacific quicker than some cruise liners.

Calculating the tides and currents and the wind drift during free fall, Conners estimated their drop point to be a quarter mile west of Padget Island. If they hit it within half a mile, they would consider themselves lucky.

The island was a dot of land, a half mile wide by a mile long. There was a single rocky beach on its western shore. The other three sides faced the water with sheer cliffs that would require climbing gear. This was not included in their equipment or their briefing, leaving little margin for error.

The plan called for using the tidal flood to reach the island. Motors were out; too much noise. Timing was critical. The incoming tide would last for only two more hours. If they missed it and failed to reach the island before the tide turned, the outgoing flood would pull them toward the Strait of Juan de Fuca. There would be no way they could paddle fast enough to stay out of its grip. Beyond the strait was the North Pacific, one of the roughest bodies of water in the world. It was not something you wanted to ride in in an open inflatable raft.

"What's the drop altitude?" asked the engineer.

"Seventeen thousand," said Conners.

"And your opening?"

"Three hundred feet."

"They couldn't pay me enough," said the engineer. He adjusted the altimeter on the large cargo parachutes, so that they would trigger to open at five hundred feet. Deploying at five hundred, the chutes would not open fully for another two hundred feet. If the loads hit the water too hard, it would dislodge the flotation, sending the packages to the bottom, perhaps leaving the men to die in the water.

In the dark, dropping like bullets through the cloud deck, none of them would know where the rest of the team was. Breathing from their scuba tanks, they would free-fall at speeds approaching 130 miles per hour for more than a minute and a half. At three hundred feet, they would pop their chutes and drop into the sea. They would have just enough time to slow their descent before hitting the water. They would be visible in the air for less than ten seconds. The plan was intended to minimize the chances of detection by sentries on the island. It also increased greatly the team's risk factor. Night drops into the sea often met with casualties. Usually these were the result of accidents rather than combat.

The cavernous cargo bay was nearly empty, except for the two small pallets containing the inflatables and the listening gear along with cameras to be planted on the island. There were small arms, automatic weapons, and supplies of ammunition in the event of trouble, though Conners had been briefed. He knew that in a firefight they would be outgunned. The men on the island had fifty-caliber weapons. It wasn't known whether they were full automatic.

The pallets were dragged to their position near the rear ramp. The men themselves would jump from one of the two doors on either side of the aircraft behind the landing-gear fairings.

With eight minutes and counting, Conners got his men up and started final checks on their gear, the regulators on their tanks, the seals around their face masks.

At six minutes, the warning light on the cargo bay bulkhead went on and the flight engineer donned his face mask for oxygen. The team would breathe from their compressed-air diving tanks.

Conners tapped the altimeter on his wrist and checked his compass.

At three minutes, the whine of hydraulic motors kicked in and a yawning ramp at the rear of the plane opened. As the shape and control surfaces of the giant C-130 changed, it began to buffet, porpoising through the thin, high atmosphere.

The flight engineer opened one of the side doors and removed it. Now the rush of wind filled the cargo bay. Conners lined his men up at the door. Then the green light. One by one, they jumped from the door, falling like stones through the cold night air.

Conners was the last. He felt the cut of air like a dozen knives as it hit the flesh of his face and forehead between the diving mask and the hood of his wet suit. He tried to breathe normally from the mouthpiece as his body experienced the giddy weightlessness of free fall. In the dark, with no point of reference, it was easy to relax, to go too far and blow past the safety point. If it happened, the jumper would never know it. Hitting the water at more than a hundred miles an hour, the human body would explode like a water balloon hitting concrete.

Conners kept a tight eye on his altimeter. He heard the pop of a chute, like a rifle shot, as he flew past and continued to drop. If his altimeter was working, they were at two thousand feet. They hadn't hit the water, and already there was a problem. He wondered if it was one of his men or one of the giant cargo chutes.

He dropped through the cloud deck, and suddenly there were lights. In the distance he could see the glitter of a small town spread out in front of him. He checked his compass. He was facing east. He bent his knees and dropped his torso, spinning his body half a turn. Now he was facing Padget Island. All he could see below was the darkness of the sea. Off in the

distance were the lights of a large refinery. That would be
ARCO. It was a marker for the pilot.

Six hundred feet. He put his hand on the rip cord. Three
seconds later he pulled it. The black Jedi Knight chute exploded above his head, jerking his body to a stop like a rag
doll. The delta canopy overhead, with its steering shroud lines,
allowed him to maneuver, if only for a matter of seconds.
Conners used the time to orient himself toward the island. He
was looking at his compass, then suddenly saw the fluores-
cence of the sea an instant before he hit the water.

He went under immediately. The trick now was not to get
tangled in the chute or the shrouds. In the water, with any kind
of current, it could drag you down. Even with the right gear,
using engineered releases, it was possible to be dragged
through the water by tidal rips and towed into deep, pressure-
crushing trenches by falling cold-water currents.

Conners hit the release on his harness. It popped open.
Quickly he swam away from the lines. The chute was weighted
around the seams so that it would slowly sink.

Conners got to the surface and cleared his mask. He tasted
the brine around his mouth as he spit the mouthpiece out and
bobbed in the water. There were small whitecaps forming,
wind blowing in a westerly direction. He could hear one of
the men calling. Each of them had a small light mounted on
the shoulder of their suit. It emitted an intense halogen beam.
Conners could see two flickering beams, like Tinker Bell bobbing in the distance. He lowered his mask and bit into the
mouthpiece, then lowered his face in the water and began to
kick. It took him several minutes swimming against the current
to reach the other two men. They were struggling with one of
the floating cargo pallets. It was still attached to the cargo
chute.

Conners lifted his face mask and spit out his mouthpiece.

"What's the matter?"

"We can't get it to release."

The parachute had filled with water and was acting as a
massive sea anchor. It was going down and hauling their gear
with it. The men were hanging on, trying to buoy it.

Conners pulled his diving knife from a sheath on his ankle,
grabbed some of the shroud lines in a bundle, and cut them.
The chute immediately released its load of water, like a sail

spilling wind, and the floating pallet righted itself.

One of the SEALs opened a canister and removed the metal oars while Conners cut the line binding the inflatable raft and the other man popped the pin. In less than a minute, the raft filled with compressed air.

By now they were all bobbing in the sea, whipped by wind-driven whitecaps. Two of the men tumbled into the raft while Conners lashed the floating pallet with the gear to an aft line and climbed aboard. They stowed their tanks in the bottom and removed the fins from their feet while they continued to scan the sea for the other two men.

There was nothing but the dark sea and the black night sky. Conners looked at his watch.

"How long can we wait?" one of them asked.

"We can't," said Conners.

"But they're out there somewhere."

"I know."

"They could be in trouble."

"I'm aware," said Conners. He looked in the direction of the island. He could see a dim outline in the distance and hear the crash of a mild, wind-driven surf on rocks or a beach. Soon the emerging rays of dawn would silhouette the island and light up the surface of the sea.

"If they're behind us, we can't get to them. If they're between us and the island, they should be all right." Even without the raft, Conners was confident they had come very close to the drop point. They could swim to the beach if they had to.

They continued to scan to the east for flickering signs of the halogen shoulder lamps. But there was no sign.

"We can't stay here, and we can't go searching for them." Conners knew they would only exhaust themselves paddling against the tide, searching in the dark. When the sun came up, they would be caught out on open water. If the men on the island were as dangerous as Conners had been led to believe, three divers in an open raft would be dead meat. The rest of the team would have to find the other raft and make it on their own. The three men in this raft were now a SEAL team, and they had a mission.

"We'll find 'em on the beach," said Conners. "Now let's paddle."

SAN JUAN CHANNEL

Joselyn was bleeding from the nose, and the base of her skull had a lump the size of a goose egg. Even without touching it, she could feel it as her head bounced against something hard. She came to in the bottom of a small boat running at high speed on choppy water. Her hands were tied behind her back, her eyes covered by a cloth blindfold that did not entirely do its job. She could peek under the corners and get glimpses of the dark space into which they had jammed her body, a kind of cuddy cabin belowdecks. The pressure of the knot from the blindfold at the base of her neck caused even more pain in her head.

Periodically she could hear male voices somewhere outside, shouting above the roar of the engine as it churned and whined through the swells.

Joselyn had lost all sense of time. She had no idea how long she'd been unconscious. She was lying in bilge water and breathing gasoline fumes. Between the throbbing in her head and the ceaseless motion of the boat, nausea began to overtake her. Joselyn was ready to retch when suddenly the engine eased and the boat began to surf in its own wake. A couple of seconds later there was a solid thud against the hull. The boat stopped dead in the water, its only motion now caused by its own wake as it bobbed against a dock, or a larger boat. Joselyn wasn't sure.

"Where is she?" This time the voices came from outside the boat.

"Down below."

"Bring her up to the house. We don't have much time. Only twenty minutes before Thorn and Taggart have to leave. Thorn doesn't want to go before he knows what's up."

Joselyn heard something like a cabinet door open somewhere behind her, and suddenly the murmur of voices got louder. She went limp as if still unconscious.

Something poked or kicked her. It felt like a foot.

"Come on. Get up." He poked her arm.

She still didn't move.

"She's still out. Sure you didn't kill her?"

"I didn't hit her that hard."

"That's fine. You can carry her."

Someone grabbed her around one ankle and dragged her several inches across the rough wooden bottom of the boat. Joselyn offered no resistance though the wood caused an abrasion on her arm.

"You get her arms. I'll take her feet."

"Just pick her up. She can't weigh more than a hundred twenty pounds." The other voice sounded exasperated.

Suddenly Joselyn felt a strong set of arms behind her knees and across her back. She went limp in the man's arms, and he lifted easily. She allowed her head to hang back, though the pain was intense. Her mouth was open, her eyes only partially closed under the cloth that covered them. As long as they thought she was unconscious, Joselyn sensed she was safe. They wanted her for a reason, information they thought she had; otherwise they would have dumped her body over the side out in the sound.

Whoever was carrying her moved quickly. With her head hanging back, draped over the man's arm, she was able to catch glimpses of light and see figures passing as she heard his footsteps move along the wooden dock.

"They're waiting up at the house."

"They're gonna need smelling salts." The man carrying her was talking now.

"Maybe they got some ammonia."

"Look and see."

They started to climb stairs, stone or concrete, Joselyn wasn't sure, but they were steep and there were a lot of them. The man began to breathe heavily. She could hear more voices now, and see lights. Under a corner of the blindfold, she caught a passing glimpse of a porch under a roof and lighted windows, lots of windows.

Somebody got the door for them. She couldn't see who without moving her head, but when it opened the voices got much louder. There was a lot of shouting.

"Listen, don't you tell me. I was the one who said we should deep-six the trawler and the fishermen with it."

"Yeah, right, Charlie." Now that he was in the room, the guy carrying her was getting into it. "You were the one said he drowned the woman here. On the ferry, remember?"

"I pushed her off. Whadda ya want?"

"Heaviest fuckin' ghost I ever saw." The man carrying her was huffing and puffing.

"I got the goddamn car."

"Well, shit, let's call the auto club and report the crime."

"Listen, asshole, I suppose you coulda done better."

"My six-year-old niece coulda done better."

"Now we got the Feds crawling all over the docks, talkin' to God knows who . . ." Now other men in the room were getting into it. Joselyn couldn't see their faces.

"We don't know it was the Feds."

"Who the hell else would it be?"

"Where do you want me to put her?" The guy carrying Joselyn was still trying to catch his breath.

"Put her in the bedroom at the end of the hall."

As he carried her down the hall, she could hear the argument continue.

"Why didn't they get the guy?"

"He was out on the docks."

"What, you're afraid to go out there?"

"Damn right. Fuckin' stuff'll light you up like neon. You haven't seen the fishermen coughing up their lungs, have you?"

"Show some hair, why don't ya."

"I don't mind showing it. I just mind losing it."

"I told you we should have got some of those rubber suits."

"You and your fuckin' rubber suits."

"I'm telling you we ought to get the hell off this island before the Feds show up. You can be sure they know what's goin' on."

"And how would they know that?" This time it was a different voice. Suddenly there was silence in the room down the hall, like someone had thrown water on a fire.

"I just meant we should get off the island while we still have a chance."

"You sound like maybe you know something the rest of us don't." It was the voice that had quelled the argument. There was something strangely familiar about it. Joselyn couldn't see his face without moving her head to look down the hall. She was playing opossum as long as she could.

"No. I don't know anything."

"You seem to be awfully worried about the federal government," said the voice.

"There is reason to be worried. This woman . . ."

"The woman is not with the federal government."

"Yeah, but the guy with her."

"I doubt if he's with the federal government either."

"How do you know that?"

"If the federal government thought there was a weapon of mass destruction out on that dock, do you think they would have sent one man to check it out, with a woman to stand guard at the dock?"

"I don't know."

"Trust me. There would be two hundred armed troops on that dock and two dozen men in hazmat suits crawling all over every boat moored out there. What we have here is the stuff of amateurs."

Now there was some chuckling in the room.

"You worry too much. You should learn to relax. You'll live longer."

"Yeah, Charlie. Relax."

The voices receded into the background as Joselyn was carried down what seemed like a long hallway. The man wedged her body against a wall and leaned against her with his weight as he freed one hand and opened the door.

He crossed the room and dropped her on the bed like a sack of potatoes. She fell limp and loose bouncing with the springs. She heard his footsteps recede across the room toward the door.

"You musta fuckin' brained her." Another voice in the doorway. "You better hope she's not dead. Thorn wants to talk to her."

"Fuck Thorn and the horse he rode in on. I'm getting a little tired taking all his crap."

"Well, maybe you should tell him."

They closed the door, and Joselyn heard the key turn in the lock. She lay still on the bed for almost a minute, listening to the voices in the other room. Every once in a while, she could make out a word or two.

The room was dark. She could see little triangles of wallpaper and part of the ceiling through the space under the blindfold where her cheek met her nose. She lay motionless, listening for the sound of breathing to make sure she was alone in the room before she moved on the bed.

Finally satisfied, she rolled over, hooked one leg over the edge of the bed, and with some effort sat up. By tilting her head back, she could scan the room from under the blindfold. It was a large bedroom, and whoever owned it had money. There was an adjoining bathroom and what looked like a marble floor.

Joselyn stood up. For an instant she began to weave in circles, dizzy from the blow on the head. She steadied herself by bracing her legs against the side the bed. She slowly took a step, then another. She made her way across the bedroom, her head tilted back, peeking under the blindfold so that she didn't run into a wall or trip over furniture.

She stopped in the bathroom doorway. She could see a light switch, a large plastic toggle with its own light built in so you could find it in the dark. She could have hit it with her shoulder, but they might see the light under the door or through the window on the porch outside.

Joselyn moved to the sink and turned her back. With tied hands she pulled open the top drawer. She fished around inside: a comb, a brush, something that felt like a mirror.

She turned around and peeked down into the open drawer. Somewhere there should be a pair of scissors, anything sharp to cut the cord around her wrists. She couldn't see well enough in the dark.

She heard footsteps coming down the hall. Joselyn slammed the drawer shut and in five giant steps raced back to the bed throwing her body onto it and turning her head to the wall an instant before the key turned in the lock. The door opened and later the light came on.

"Leave me alone with her." It was all he said before the door closed.

She waited. It seemed forever. Joselyn didn't move, but lay as if she was unconscious on the bed. Then she heard his footsteps moving closer to the bed. She felt his weight on the mattress as he moved behind her and untied her hands. She closed her eyes tight, and he undid the knot on the blindfold and slipped it from her face. It wasn't until he ripped the tape from her mouth that she moved.

"You can open your eyes now."

That familiar voice. He knew she wasn't unconscious. The game was up. She turned her head and squinted in the light, having difficulty focusing, and moved one hand up to shade her eyes. He appeared as a dark silhouette, the features of his face lost in shadows cast by the bright overhead light in the room.

She rubbed her eyes. He stepped back from the bed. Joselyn fought the dumbstruck expression as it crept across her face. He was staring at her with that same smile—the arrogant grin he had left her with on the dock as he climbed into the plane.

"You are surprised to see me?" said Belden.

"You were . . ."

"Dead?"

She nodded.

"The brain accepts what the eye beholds," said Belden.

"But I saw the plane."

"I had to do something. Your government had a great many questions to which I did not have very many good answers. You can appreciate my predicament. It seemed the easiest thing was to become dead."

"But the plane?"

"A simple matter of electronics, some explosives. Of course I had to wait until you reached the dock. You did take your time. For a while there, I was afraid you weren't going to come. It wouldn't do to have an explosion without a witness. Someone who actually saw me climb aboard, who could identify the victim for the police. Who better than my own lawyer?"

"That's why you hired me?"

"No. No. You should have a higher regard for yourself than that. I came to you because you were a good lawyer. In fact you were a little too good. You were getting a bit too tenacious on behalf of some of your clients."

She looked at him with a puzzled expression.

"The fishermen. We knew they were sick. What we didn't know was whether they had information as to the source. Whether they knew about the *Dancing Lady*."

"The what?"

"Of course," said Belden. "You don't know about that. No doubt, by now your friend out on the dock does, however. By the way, who is he?"

"Someone who is going to get you into a great deal of trouble," said Joselyn.

"Oh. I am relieved. I thought perhaps he was trouble himself. No doubt, you heard our discussion in the other room."

She shook her head.

"Oh yes. I forgot. You were sleeping." He smiled at his own humor. "Can I get you something to drink?"

She shook her head again, though she was dying of thirst.

"There is no need for us to make this unpleasant. Some of the men outside are, shall we say, not in a good mood. They have concerns about your friend, the tall blond one on the dock. I thought perhaps you could allay their fears."

"No problem," said Joselyn. "He's with the Marines. The rest of them were busy getting their helicopters warmed up."

Belden gave her an expression of regret. "Is he with the government?"

"Yes."

He reached across the bed and slapped her across the face.

"No."

He slapped her again with the back of his hand.

"Maybe."

He slapped her again, this time much harder.

"Who is he?"

She didn't respond.

Belden sat on the edge of the bed, grimaced a bit, then reached into his pants pocket and removed a handful of items that had created a bulge: keys, a folding knife, some scraps of paper, and a business card. He put these on the bedside stand.

"These other men outside. They are not as nice as I am. You should learn to trust me."

"I see. They don't draw the line at beating women."

"No, as a matter of fact they don't."

"The last time I trusted you, you left me at the courthouse all alone talking to a federal prosecutor."

"Yes, well, he had all those pointed questions," said Belden. He looked at his watch. "I would love to discuss this at length, but there really isn't much time."

"And I suppose if I tell you what I know you're going to let me go?"

"No."

"I didn't think so."

"But there are many ways to die," said Belden. "Some of them are actually quite painless."

"I'm sure you'd be the expert on that," said Joselyn. "So what are you saying? You're going to let me pick my own poison?"

"If you like."

"Fine. I want to die in a plane crash by remote control."

Belden laughed. "Ah, if we'd only met under other circumstances. Another time, another place."

"But you've got such a busy schedule, moving all those bombs."

Belden looked at her. For the first time the smile was gone.

"Who told you that?"

Joselyn didn't answer.

"Your tall friend?"

She just looked at him.

"Or was it the federal prosecutor?" He leaned on the bed with one hand.

"Tell me." His voice lifted a little at the end.

While Joselyn was still looking at his face, the back of his hand caught her full force on the cheek snapping her head to the left. The pain exploded like a star burst. For an instant, Joselyn thought she might pass out. She tasted the salty tang of blood inside her mouth and tried to focus her eyes.

Now he was smiling again. "You can tell me. After all, you are my lawyer," said Belden. "We really shouldn't have any secrets."

She could tell he was starting to get off on it. Fire was forming in his eyes. Hitting women was something he enjoyed.

"After all, I did pay you a fee," said Belden. "Maybe it wasn't enough?" He caught her with the hand coming back the other way, and the pain in her head ratcheted up one more notch.

"Don't we have some kind of confidence or something here? Maybe I should file a complaint with the bar," said Belden. "My lawyer won't tell me what's going on."

He reached over like he was getting ready to smack her one more time when the door opened. Joselyn looked through glazed eyes at the man standing in the open doorway. She could feel blood running down her chin from the corner of her lip.

The man in the doorway was small, with soft brown eyes and dark thinning hair. He was carrying a suitcase and dressed in a sport coat and slacks, like he was ready to travel. For an instant, his eyes met Joselyn's. There was something in his expression that provided a sense of sanctuary, as if suddenly something human had entered the room. It was an expression of compassion. It was quickly coupled with regret.

Belden stopped in mid-slap and dropped his arm. "Ah. Mr. . . . ." He almost said the name but then stopped. "I'd like you to meet my lawyer, Ms. Cole. We were just having a frank exchange of views."

"It's time to go." The man did not acknowledge her presence but broke eye contact and turned away. At that moment, Joselyn knew she was dead.

Belden picked up the items from the bedside table, all but one. The business card he left, dog-eared and frayed, and replaced the rest of the items in his pocket.

"I wish it could have been longer," said Belden. "But all good things must come to an end."

"Until the next time," said Joselyn. Blood trickled down her cheek and fire filled her eyes. If he'd given her an opening, Belden would have been sporting permanent scars and speaking with a much higher voice. She might have paid the price, but he would have known he'd been in a fight.

"Unfortunately not," said Belden. He took one last look at her, crossed the room in three strides, closed the door, and was gone.

TWENTY-FIVE

PADGET ISLAND, WA

Conners could no longer feel the tips of his fingers. They were numb from the fifty-degree water. The three men struggled with the inflatable raft, pulling it up onto the rock-strewn beach. In the dark, with no clear landmarks, Conners couldn't even be sure if in fact they had landed on Padget Island. He looked for landmarks. A jagged rock cliff on the left seemed right. The swale cut by a small creek that drained on the beach matched the map he'd studied on the plane.

The beach was nothing like the sandy dunes around San Diego where they trained. The three men slogged up to their knees through the mud of a tidal flat, their feet slipping on moss-covered boulders and slick seaweed. They struggled to pull the raft with its floating pallet of equipment above the incoming tide line.

Conners huddled with the other two men in the lee of a large boulder and scanned the beach with night goggles for any sign of thermal images.

"You think Scofield and Reams made it?" One of the others looked at Conners. The kid was no more than nineteen years old. His first time in anything approaching combat, and he was scared.

"I don't know."

"Shouldn't we look for 'em?"

"Break open the gear," said Conners. "Get me the radio."

They took their gun-metal diving knives to the black neo-prene cover over the pallet, sliced it neatly, and popped the lid off of one of the metal containers inside. Within a few seconds, they found the small handheld radio set. It had a range of only about a mile, but it used secure low-range frequencies.

Conners took it and checked the power switch, then hit the transmit button and held it down. "Gopher, this is Gopher One. Do you read?"

He let the button up. All the heard was static. He turned the squelch dial up to kill the sound, so sentries in the bunker on the bluffs wouldn't hear the noise.

"Gopher, this is Gopher One. Come in. Do you read?"

More static.

"Maybe we should check the beach for them. Maybe they got separated from the pallet and lost the radio."

"We don't have time," said Conners. "If they're on the island, they'll find us."

"If we stay here, the people up there are gonna find us real quick." The third SEAL was older, more experienced than either Conners or the other man. He had seen action in Panama and the Gulf. He knew what Conners suspected; a night dive over pitch-black water, you could expect fifty-percent casualties to be delivered by the forces of nature, tides, weather, and the sea.

"Right now, we've got to find that sentry post up on the bluff," said Conners.

"But Richie and Jason . . ."

"Richie and Jason knew what they were doing," said Conners. "We can't help 'em, and we can't go looking for them. Do you understand?"

The kid didn't like it, but he understood.

"According to the map, the militia has a fifty-caliber gun mounted in a bunker somewhere up here in these trees." The three men looked for landmarks that offered some clue as to the location.

Normally SEALs would take any sentries out, either with a silenced round or a knife. But the rules of engagement in this case made that impossible. They were to fire only in self-defense. The mission was classified as an "operation other than war," an event that if it went right, would never be reported. Their job was to get in, plant their equipment—mini-ature cameras and listening devices along with a small microwave transmitter—and then get out, and to do all of it undetected.

They opened the watertight arms container from the pallet and removed the small arms. Each pallet contained six weap-ons, two M-16s, and M-14 for distance and penetrating power, an MP-5 submachine gun, and two handguns—nine-millimeter Berettas, each with a silencer. If they had to shoot, the plan was one shot, one kill. They would aim for the high chest or forehead. Unlike the movies where emptying a full clip in a single burst made for action, the SEALs had limits. Ammu-nition was heavy. Pulling too much of it behind you on a pallet in the open water was like dragging a sea anchor. Unless they got into a full-out fire-fight, three-round bursts were the limit.

There had been one M-60 light machine gun included with their equipment. Along with the loss of two of his men, Con-ners now discovered that the M-60 was missing.

"It musta been on the other pallet."

"Check the electronic gear," said Conners.

One of the SEALs popped the metal lid off the other con-tainer, while Conners and the other man checked the ammu-nition. Quietly they slipped loaded clips into the receivers and pulled the bolts back, chambering rounds.

Each man took a rifle. Conners took the MP-5 and tucked one of the Berettas into a pack.

Into the pack, they loaded five small microphones along with miniature cameras, each with a fish-eye lens that would allow wide-angle shots at short distance.

Into a separate pack they loaded a base-station transmitter, a small metal box weighing fourteen pounds with its own col-lapsible dish. This would be placed at a high remote point on the island, facing the southwestern horizon. It would transmit both audio and video signals on a special subsonic frequency to a satellite in space. In turn, this would be relayed to the naval base in Everett, forty miles south, where agents of the FBI and Military Intelligence would monitor the signals.

"Check the batteries," said Conners.

The SEAL flipped a switch on the transmitter and watched as the tiny pinhead lamps flashed on. "It's good."

They cut the line tethering the equipment pallet to the inflatable raft, then punched holes in its rubber flotation wings with their knives. They stripped the flotation off the pallet and buried it in some loose gravel under a rock. Anyone finding the pallet would think it was mere flotsam, washed up on the beach.

Then the three men muscled the inflatable raft along with their air tanks and diving gear farther up the beach. They hid the raft and tanks under some brush and cut a few low boughs from the trees to cover it all.

They smeared their faces and the backs of their hands with jungle-green and black-sand-colored grease paint to repair the camouflage that had washed off in the water.

Conners checked his watch. They had less than two hours before the first rays of dawn crept over the mountains to the east. Using hand signals, he directed the man with the M-14 and the other silenced pistol to take point. The three of them began to scale the high bank toward the bluff.

WASHINGTON, DC

Sy Hirshberg was camped in the Situation Room in the basement of the West Wing. He had been there all night, waiting for word from the naval base in Everett. It was now after seven in the morning on the east coast, and Hirshberg was worried.

"What are we hearing?"

Hirshberg turned and saw the president as he entered the room.

"Nothing. Not a word since the plane left the drop point last night."

"It's still early," said the president.

Hirshberg looked at his watch. "We should have had radio communications by now."

"You think something went wrong?"

"It's possible. I think we should have provided some contingency plans," said Hirshberg. "If those men get in trouble . . ."

"They'll be all right. The SEALs are the best," said the president. "I don't want to overreact. You remember what happened at Waco. We don't want a repeat."

Hirshberg didn't like it. The SEALs were under-gunned, out-manned, with no backup or fast boats to extricate them if trouble developed.

"I think we made the right decision," said the president.

Hirshberg grated in silence at the use of the plural pronoun. "I'm sorry, Mr. President, but I have to disagree. I think we should have sent in troops."

"More troops just draw more attention. We'd need a staging area."

Hirshberg knew the president well enough to know what he was really afraid of. The media would pick up on it.

"No. I'm satisfied that this is the right way to go about it," said the president.

"And if it fails, we will have lost any element of surprise," said Hirshberg. "If they have a device and if it's ready to detonate, what then?"

This actually stopped the president for a moment as he considered the consequences. "If it must be, better there than some major population center."

Hirshberg couldn't believe what he was hearing. The expression on his face betrayed his thoughts.

"Listen, Sy, I'm not at all convinced there's anything to this. You want my personal view—I think we're all running around chasing our tails. I don't think there is a device. I don't think there ever was one."

"What about the debris from the Russian trawler?"

"Yes, well, who knows where that came from. Maybe they used the ship to refuel some of their subs at sea. You know the Russians. They're not exactly careful the way they handle and transport the stuff. Stone-age safety systems. Remember Chernobyl?"

"Can we afford to take the chance, Mr. President?"

"That's why we're sending in the SEALs. To check it out."

Hirshberg knew what the president was afraid of. If he sent in forces he would have to explain why, the nature of the threat. This would be followed by a lot of questions from the press and Congress that would inevitably lead to Kolikoff and his corporation, questions the president would rather not get into.

If anything went wrong, Hirshberg suspected that the White

House was already prepared with the usual litany of lies for the public and the press. A tragic accident had occurred on the island during a training exercise. The president knew nothing about it but was getting the facts. He would be calling the next of kin to commiserate with them. He and the first lady would be flying west to meet with the families in San Diego. It wouldn't be the first time some screwed-up covert ops got passed off as a wayward training exercise.

The question in Hirshberg's mind was what the president would do then. Would he agree to throw a ten-mile cordon around Padget Island and send in troops, or would he continue to deny until a mushroom-shaped cloud formed somewhere in the sky over the Northwest?

"Mr. President, we have to assume that if the people on that island have a bomb, they will use it. We may only have one chance to stop them and that's to act now, swiftly and with maximum force to seize the device before they know what hits them."

"If the people on that island have a bomb, my first objective is to isolate it. Keep it where it is. Bottle 'em up, and then talk 'em to death," said the president.

"Negotiate with terrorists?" said Hirshberg.

"I didn't say negotiate. I said talk, until we wear them down."

"And what if we don't wear them down? What if they decide to push the button?"

There was a long, deep sigh from the President. "We're not talking New York or Boston or even L.A.," he said. "We will have confined the damage maybe to a single island."

"That assumes the bomb is on the island."

"That's why we sent in the SEALs, to find out. Now let's not argue about this anymore. I've made the decision." The president wandered to a side table where there were some Danish pastries and a pot of coffee. He poured a cup and picked through the pastries. "What is this—can't we get anything hot?" He looked at the Marine aide who immediately took his order, bacon and eggs with toast.

"Sy, you want anything?"

"No, Mr. President." Hirshberg had lost his appetite. He was beginning to envy the litany of aides who had bailed out on the administration as it neared the end of its first term.

"Something coming in, sir." One of the communications staff was talking to the officer in charge, a Marine lieutenant.

Hirshberg got out of his chair and practically flew to the area over the soldier's shoulder, looking at the computer screen.

"Is it from Everett?" The president put a half-eaten pastry down on the side table as he chewed and swallowed.

"No, sir."

He went back to his pastry.

"I think you better see this, Mr. President." Hirshberg was reading the screen.

The president grabbed his coffee and walked over toward the computer station.

There on the screen was a communiqué. It was not from the naval base at Everett, but from the Department of Energy, marked

TOP SECRET, RD (Restricted Data) URGENT!

CIVILIAN SOURCES CONNECTED WITH THE INSTITUTE AGAINST MASS DESTRUCTION (SANTA CRISTA, CA) REPORT EXISTENCE OF HIGHLY RADIOACTIVE DEBRIS ON VESSEL, LOCATED FRIDAY HARBOR, SAN JUAN ISLANDS. CONTAMINATION BELIEVED RELATED TO NUCLEAR DEVICE. REQUESTING DISPATCH OF NEST.

The acronym referred to one of four Nuclear Emergency Search Teams. Their role, though they had never been called up in an actual event, was to respond to nuclear emergencies, including terrorist devices brought into the country. The teams had conducted mock emergency exercises in the early 1990s with less than satisfactory results.

"Did they find a bomb?" asked the president.

"Sir, it doesn't say. Only that they believe the contamination is related to a nuclear device." The young lieutenant at the monitor looked back over his shoulder at the president.

"Well, get some clarification. Call somebody at DOE." The president's words sent the military aides in the room scrambling.

"Mr. President, we can't afford to wait."

"What?" The president looked at Hirshberg.

"It's no coincidence, sir. The militia on that island. The discovery of radioactive debris on a vessel."

The president looked at a map of Puget Sound that was already projected on a large screen on the wall. Padget Island was circled by a slow flashing ring of light, indicating the area of operations by the SEAL team. Hirshberg grabbed a laser pointer from a podium below the map and hit Friday Harbor with a red arrow.

"It's less than twelve miles."

Even in a state of denial, the president could no longer avoid the obvious.

"There's a small force of Marines at Everett. They can be airborne in choppers in less than a hour." Hirshberg had done his homework. He had, through the Joint Chiefs, put the Marines on alert.

"Cordon off Friday Harbor," said Hirshberg. "Hit Padget Island with everything we've got and hope we find the device."

"We should wait for confirmation," said the president. "What do we know about this institute, this place in California?"

"They produce a database. Information on weapons of mass destruction. Several of our agencies subscribe. CIA, DOE. Some of their people have participated on U.N. inspection teams."

"Their information, is it usually accurate?"

"Yes."

There was silence in the room, a look of grim resignation on the president. The ultimate fear of every man of power: his options had suddenly been limited by events he could not anticipate.

"Sir, the longer we wait, the greater the risk that they could move the device," said Hirshberg. "If they do, it could be very difficult to find it again."

The president said nothing.

"Sir, the Marines will need time to muster."

SAN JUAN CHANNEL, WA

They turned toward Iceberg Point, and Thorn, alias Belden, pushed the throttles forward on the twin-engine outboard. The bow lifted out of the water and the boat began to plane out across the sound. The harbor at Cap Santé was at least an hour away even in good weather and at top speed.

The sea picked up a chop as dawn approached. Taggart settled into the seat across from Thorn and zipped his jacket, turning the collar up against the cold, damp air. His gaze fixed upon a distant island in a daze as if there were nothing there.

At the moment, his mind was occupied with thoughts of Kirsten. Increasingly, in the last days, he had spent more time thinking about her and wondering what their lives would have been like had she lived. He could see the features of her face as clearly as if she were standing in front of him. At times when he was alone, he would actually speak to her, confident in the belief that she was with him wherever he went. And he worried about Adam, who was now five years old. He wondered what kind of a world he would be leaving to his son.

"What time's your flight?" Shouting over the noise of the engines, Thorn interrupted Taggart's thoughts.

He looked at his watch. "Eleven-forty."

"You'll have time to drop me off," said Thorn. "You've got your ticket?"

Taggart nodded.

"When you transfer planes in Denver, call for further instructions."

"I know."

"Use the cellular number."

"We've been over all of that," said Taggart.

"Just checking," said Thorn. "You've got the cellular number?"

"I've got it."

Thorn was a definite type-A. He was neurotic. He believed that unless he said it out loud, it wouldn't happen.

Then out of the blue. "You're not planning on contacting anybody else?"

"Who would I be calling?"

"Maybe not a phone call," said Thorn. "I was thinking maybe a letter."

Taggart reached into his inside coat pocket. The letter he'd written the night before to his son Adam, something for the boy to read when he got older, some explanation from his father. The letter was gone.

When he looked over, Thorn was holding the envelope between two fingers. It was stamped and sealed. At least he hadn't read it.

"Give it to me."

"I took the liberty of checking your coat just before we left."

"Give it to me."

Thorn didn't say a word, but just held it up in the wind as the boat skimmed the water.

"I suppose you went through my bags as well?"

Thorn made a face of concession. "I understand the urge to let your boy know something about his father. But I couldn't take the chance that you might have mentioned my name."

"I don't know your name."

"Good. At least something's secure. It's only natural," said Thorn. "You want to explain to him why you did what you did. Hell, if I killed a hundred thousand people and had my name attached to the act, I'd want the entire world to know why."

"My son's the only audience I care about."

"It won't do to have this floating around in the mail." With that Thorn let loose of the letter.

Taggart lurched from his chair and tried to grab it, but he was too slow. The envelope flipped up into the wind like a leaf, then landed on the churning prop wash behind the speeding boat. Taggart stood and watched as it disappeared in the distance.

"I wasn't gonna mail it now." Taggart shouted above the wind and the noise of the engine.

Thorn was hunkered down behind the boat's windscreen.

"I was gonna wait until we were done. Until the last minute," said Taggart.

"And when would that be?"

"I don't know. You haven't told me."

"Precisely," said Thorn. "And for very good reason. The fewer who know, the better. You would have mailed that letter from the target city. If the authorities got their hands on it before we had a chance to detonate the device, they would have been able to piece together the target and concentrate their forces. You don't give them an edge. Not if you're smart.''

"That assumes they would have been able to intercept the letter.''

"Oh, they'd have found the letter all right. Your boy is staying with relatives, right?''

Taggart didn't have to respond. Thorn already knew the answer from the address on the letter.

"Your wife's parents?'' Thorn didn't wait for an answer. He knew he was right.

"You're not doing them any favors by sending them mail from the grave. The government will be all over them when this is over. Anybody you've ever talked to—your friends, family, girlfriends you haven't seen in twenty years. They will all be getting visits from the FBI. There will be search warrants for their homes, any property they own. They will ransack their lives looking for evidence. A letter like that will only cause your family more trouble.''

Taggart didn't say a word. Anger consumed him. Almost a minute passed in strained silence as the two men looked straight ahead through the windscreen.

"If you want to talk to the boy, leave a tape-recorded message.'' Thorn reached into his pocket and pulled out a small microcassette recorder. He reached over to hand it to Taggart, who remained stone silent, looking at the man who had just destroyed the last words his son would ever receive from his father.

"Take it,'' said Thorn. "I'll see the tape gets delivered. In a way that the government doesn't find it, after this is all over. You can tape it in the car when we get to Cap Santé.''

"Why would you care about my son?''

"Call it an inoculation against disaster. Human nature being what it is.'' Thorn shouted above the noise of the engines. He looked straight ahead at the swells as they slammed under the bow of the small boat. "If I didn't give you a way out, you'd just write another letter.''

"How do I know you'll deliver the tape?'' said Taggart.

"You don't. But you can be sure of one thing. If the government gets its hands on anything you write, you can be sure your boy will never see it. And they'll probably twist whatever you say for their own purposes.''

He had a point. The government probably already had Taggart's name on a list, taps on his in-laws' phones, and court orders to monitor incoming mail. It was why the men on the island had cut themselves off from the outside world. Taggart took the tape recorder.

''Now tell me,'' said Taggart. ''A question I've been itching to ask. How much are you getting paid for all this?''

''You ought to know. You're paying the freight,'' said Thorn.

''Don't insult my intelligence. You're gonna tell me there was a white sale on nuclear bombs? You got a discount at the home show? We tried for three years to make contact, even to get a price. We never got close. Then you show up and, just like that, magic. For a long time we thought you were the federal government.''

''How do you know I'm not?''

''Because the radiation on those boats was real. As well as the guys coughing up their lungs.''

''Let's just say you've got friends,'' said Thorn.

''Who?''

''Your government has managed to piss off half the world. Take your pick.''

''And how much are these people paying you?''

''You're being well subsidized. Don't tell me this offends you. Undercuts your pride of anarchism. You can be sure you'll get all the glory,'' said Thorn.

''And what's in it for them?''

''Cover. It's very simple. Your goals are entirely mutual. You want to destroy your government. So do they. You want the world to know you did it. They want the world to believe it. To that end they will waste no resources, spare no expense. Witnesses, documents. It's all been arranged.

''All they want is to avoid retaliation,'' said Thorn. ''Your government is on record. The use of weapons of mass destruction by a foreign state against U.S. interests will be met with nuclear retaliation. If on the other hand what is left of your government can be convinced that it was entirely a domestic matter, what are they going to do—bomb Seattle?"

"So you just brokered the deal?" said Taggart.

"That's my business. I must admit, it is the biggest deal I've ever done. In the end, your government will thank us for blaming you."

"Why's that?"

Thorn was amazed. As bitter as Taggart was, he was naive.

"You think the politicians are going to be anxious to start World War Three? Why do you think they centered on Oswald so quickly after Kennedy was shot, and why they insisted that he acted alone? They were shitting little green apples for fear that the Russians might be involved, and that they might have to do something about it.

"You pull this off, and they're not going to be looking very far for answers. They're gonna be bending over, grabbing their collective asses, and trying to figure ways to keep a grip on power. To demonstrate that they're on top of the situation. What they'll want are some heads they can roll quickly. I'm not particularly interested in offering mine, and if we're successful, yours won't be available. They'll take what they can find and call it justice," said Thorn.

"Not if we're lucky," said Taggart.

"And what's gonna stop them?"

"The people."

"The people?" Thorn was now laughing out loud. His hair blowing in the wind. "Right. The people. I forgot about the people."

"If they act quickly, they'll have a chance," said Taggart. "They'll respond."

"That assumes they can find the off button on their remote controls. Within twenty-four hours, there'll be a thousand experts getting face time on the tube, all analyzing the nuclear cloud and offering bullshit as answers. Geraldo can show pictures of fried politicians with lard melting off their bones like a barbecued roast, and everybody can argue whether Democrats or Republicans smell worse when charred. Within forty-eight hours, the public will be bored with the story and flipping channels again. Take my word for it. The only thing this is going to do is up the ante in the ratings war."

Thorn didn't have much confidence in "the people." He also knew that once they detonated the device there were not going to be a lot of places to hide. He had spent twenty years working for dictators in banana republics and kings who'd traded in their camels for armor-plated Mercedes. This job was the capstone of his career, one final and great shake of the money tree. The men involved could never work again. They would be international outlaws. No country on earth would dare to give them asylum. It was why Thorn, in his incarnation as Belden, had gone to great lengths to die and to do it in such a public way. It was why the woman, Joselyn Cole, had to die—to keep his secret.

Suddenly Thorn's gaze out through the boat's windscreen became focused and hard. He squinted into the early morning dawn. Then without saying a word he turned the wheel and brought the vessel into a curving right-hand turn. They cut a wide arc, sweeping across the open channel.

Taggart was jostled in his seat and looked over at him. "What's wrong?"

"I don't know." Thorn was peering into the distance.

The water's surface took on the heaving silvery hue of mercury under the breaking dawn. For a second Taggart thought it was just the cresting tip of another wave. But as the water shifted, the object took on a permanence, dark and angular. It was something floating on the surface, caught in the pull of the tide, being carried toward the straits.

Within seconds the boat overtook it. Taggart grabbed a boat hook from a tray that ran along under the gunnel. He tried to snag whatever it was but missed.

Thorn maneuvered the boat in a wide turn to take another pass. This time he pulled alongside and cut the engines completely. He left the wheel and took the boat hook. He reached over the side and snagged a line.

It was connected by a metal hasp that joined a number of lines. The lines ran to the water and disappeared into inky darkness. Thorn knew instinctively what floated beneath the surface. Without saying a word, he pulled a folding knife from his pocket and cut the shrouds to the parachute, then ripped open the protective rubber covering the floating pallet.

"What is it?" said Taggart.

"It's trouble." Thorn reached in his pocket for the cell phone and punched the auto dial button for the number on Padget Island, then hit the "send" button. He had programmed the number on the island into the phone but never called it for fear that the government had a tap. Now he had no choice.

It rang once. Then again. "Damn it. Pick it up."

"Hello." Finally somebody answered.

"Thorn here. You've got company on the island." He could hear laughter and a lot of bluster on the other end. No doubt they were all in from their bunkers, getting coffee and warming their feet in front of the fire.

"Quiet." The man on the other end was hollering for them to shut up so that he could hear.

"Get the men into the bunkers," said Thorn, "and send out patrols."

"Is it the military?" asked the voice on the other end.

"We got an M-60 machine gun floating in a package out here," said Thorn. "What do you think?"

The voice repeated everything he said at the other end and now the sounds coming from the house on the island were the sounds of panic.

"Get to those bunkers," said Thorn. "And listen." He couldn't tell if the man on the other end had dropped the phone.

"Are you there?" said Thorn.

"Yeah, I'm here."

"The woman. Kill her. Now."

TWENTY-SIX

Joselyn heard the phone ring. A moment later there was a lot of shouting coming from the other room. She was tied and gagged, lying on her side on the bed. One of the men guarding her had gone the extra yard of tying her feet and looping the rope through the one on her wrists, pulling it tight so that her body was now strung like a bow. He hadn't bothered to replace the blindfold. Joselyn took it as an ominous sign.

She struggled with the knot on her wrists, trying desperately to free her hands. She couldn't tell what was happening outside, but something was causing a lot of excitement. Men were running around, the sound of heavy boots on the wooden deck of the porch. Somebody was shouting orders from outside the window to the room.

"Who's got the B-A-R?"

"Tom, I think."

"Tell him to get his ass down on the beach. How many Brownings we got?"

"Two. One of 'em's out of commission. Bent firing pin. I been telling Thorn to get it fixed for a week. Where's Oscar?"

"He left this morning, right after Thorn."

It sounded like two men had closed the distances, so that their voices now dropped to conversational tones right outside the window.

"That was Thorn on the phone. Says we got company."

"Locals or Feds?"

"He found a pallet floating in the straits. An M-60 and a lot of other gear. You figure it out."

"I'm surprised they waited this long. Do we know how big the force is?"

"No. I want you to get the men on the beach and keep 'em busy. Break out the two Brownings that are still working, and make sure they got plenty of ammo. The Feds want fireworks, we'll give 'em a fifty-caliber light show, followed by one big fucking bang."

"Where's the boat?"

"Tied up in the cove on the west end."

"None of them know about it?"

"No. And let's keep it that way unless you want it to look like the Cuban boat lift. Thorn made it clear before he left. Any trouble, we get off the island, make for the truck, and get the thing moving. Oscar left early this morning. He's already headed that way. To get it ready."

"What about these guys?"

"Dead bodies tell no tales."

"What are you talking about?"

"Thorn had me wire the bunkers last night. Those crazy fuckers are gonna be shootin' from on top a pile of C-4. One round in those sandbags, and God's fringe element's gonna get some heavy reinforcements."

"What about the woman?"

Joselyn stopped struggling with the ropes on her wrists and did some heavy listening.

"Like I said, the dead tell no tales. Now move. And if shooting starts, don't go diving in any bunkers."

Now she was frantic, struggling with the ropes. She heard someone come back inside the house. The front door slammed shut. There were footsteps, heavy boots on carpeted wood. Then she heard it: the slide and click of metal. Joselyn was no firearms expert, but she knew the sound of a gun being loaded with a clip and chambered with a bullet.

Now she could hear the creak of footsteps coming down the hall toward the room. She rolled on the bed toward the wall until her back slammed against it. She tried to wedge her body between the bed and the wall. A key turned in the lock.

The knob moved, and the door started to open.

Joselyn wiggled her hips and pressed down hard with the weight of her body. Her eyes bulged as she saw the shadow come through the door. She never looked at his face. Instead she was mesmerized by the pistol in his hand, a semiautomatic with a bore the size of an elephant gun.

His head centered down the sights as he took aim.

She moved violently on the bed, trying desperately to make a bad target. Joselyn drove her hip into the crack between the wall and the mattress. Something moved.

She squeezed her eyes shut tight and prayed, an out-of-body experience, waiting for the bullet to rip into her.

The force of the concussion registered behind her, hitting the wall with a thud, a vibration that passed through her body. The blast resounded in her head nearly puncturing her ear-drums. It hit the wall like a bowling ball. Joselyn waited for the searing pain to register. A shower of dry plaster peppered her face.

When she opened her eyes, she realized she was no longer on the bed but down on the floor. Her last wild gyrations had shifted the mattress. Joselyn had gone between the bed and the wall. The bullet had hit just above the edge of the mattress, punching in the drywall a hole the size of her thumb.

Now she saw his face, flushed with anger.

"Goddamn it." He took aim a second time. She could see his eye leveled on the sights as he lined up and carefully angled the muzzle over the edge of the mattress. Joselyn was trapped, unable to move, wedged against the wall.

The explosion was muffled, almost quiet. It sounded like someone popping the tab on a beer can. A red dot appeared on his forehead just above the line of the sights on the gun. It expanded like red ink on a porous paper, then ran down his nose in a rivulet. A quizzical and vacant expression spread across his face. His eyes open, the man with the gun toppled onto the bed and bounced on the mattress.

Joselyn issued a muted scream through the gag in her mouth. She lay trapped on the floor between the bed and the wall and watched in horror as the man's hand twitched on the bed just inches from her nose.

Suddenly there was automatic weapons fire outside the house. Glass shattered in the window, breaking the pane.

He was wearing a black neoprene wet suit and came through the window, a single leg followed quickly by his head and shoulders. In a fluid motion, he hit the floor, turned, and began firing out through the broken window, rapid coughs from the tiny machine gun in his hand. It had a bulbous black cylinder over the end of the barrel. The shots came in staccato bursts.

Bullets punctured the wall around him and ripped through the wood frame of window. Several more shots punched through the shade. Exploding glass from the upper pane sprayed the room. The man dropped to the floor of the bed, and for an instant Joselyn thought he was dead. He turned his head and looked at her.

"You all right?"

All Joselyn could do was stare at him bug-eyed and nod. Quickly he got to his hands and knees, then removed the gag from her mouth, and in a single motion produced a knife from somewhere near his ankle and sliced the rope from her wrists and legs, freeing her body.

"I'm OK." She rubbed the chafed flesh of her wrists.

Another volley of bullets ripped into the window. This time the shade fell to the floor and sunlight streamed into the room.

"We can't stay here. Green Giant's gonna shred this place in a minute." He grabbed her by the arm and led her across the floor, both of them crawling on their hands and knees as fast as they could go. Bullets punctured the wall above them and smashed into a mirror over the dresser. Shards of slivered glass showered down, catching in Joselyn's hair and nicking the flesh on her cheek.

"Who are you?"

"No time for that now," he said.

She wiped the blood from her cheek absently with the back of her hand, then saw it. Joselyn crawled toward the window where the bullets were hitting.

"Not that way."

She ignored him, then reached up and grabbed the business card Belden had left on the bedside table. Joselyn scampered back across the floor.

"Lady, you're out of your mind. You're gonna get shot." He crawled toward the door, and she followed him. The man in the wet suit opened it a crack and stuck the fat cylinder of a muzzle through, then peeked out. The fact that he didn't fire told her it was clear.

He threw the door open and crawled through. She followed him closely until they sat propped against the wall, shoulder-to-shoulder in the hallway outside. There were no windows here, no other opening except the end of the hall that emptied into the living room. He kept his gun pointed in that direction as he pulled a canvas bag from his shoulder and reached inside.

When his hand came out it was holding a pistol, small and black with a tube on the end.

"Have you ever fired a handgun?"

Joselyn shook her head.

"If I get hit, you may have no choice. Listen up." He unscrewed the tube from the end. "I'm taking the silencer off. It'll be loud. It's better. They're more apt to keep their distance." He figured the chances of her hitting anything were slim. The noise might provide some cover.

"There's fifteen rounds in the clip. The little red dots on the side." He pointed to them. "When they're uncovered—when you can see them—it means it's ready to fire. When you can't see them, it means the safety's on." He clicked the safety back and forth several times so she could see how it worked. Then he handed it to her.

"You got it?"

She nodded like she understood.

"When you put the safety on, the hammer goes down automatically. In order to fire, you just take the safety off, cock the hammer back, and pull the trigger. Aim before you do it. Every time you pull the trigger after that it will shoot."

Joselyn was nodding at every word, but he could tell by the dazed look that she probably was not going to get it right. He pulled the slide back and chambered the first round, then handed it to her. "Keep it pointed away from me."

They were shooting up a storm outside, bullets hitting metal with a dull thud, the clink of broken windowpanes. The curtains in the living room danced as if inhabited by ghosts.

He checked his watch. "There's a gunship coming in in three minutes. They're gonna shred this place. It's ground zero. We gotta get the hell out."

"Who are you?"

"Navy SEAL. Time for introductions later." He went into

overdrive and started crawling on his hands and knees down the hall toward the living room.

Joselyn looked down at the gun in her hand, made sure she couldn't see the red dots, then followed him so that the highest points on each of their bodies were their hind ends, like two hounds sniffing the carpet.

———————

COLONEL, PLEASE TELL me what your plan is?'' Gideon yelled over the *thwop-thwop-thwop* of the helicopter rotors as the chopper approached at slow speed, three miles out from Padget Island.

''We've got to wait until they soften the place up.'' The Marine officer in charge was juggling incoming messages from the other choppers in formation, a few Black Hawks, but mostly older HI-1 Hueys from the Air National Guard that had been grounded for inspections. They were now pressed into service by executive order, the only means of close transport that they had. The entire force had been patched together at the last minute. It was all they could assemble on short notice from Everett.

He'd managed to dig up two Cobra gunships, one of them an AH-1G left over from Vietnam, nearly an antique, to provide covering fire when his men hit the ground.

''We don't know what they've got down there. I'm not sending my men in to get killed on the ground. I've got a handful of non-coms with combat experience, and that's it. Most of these men have never seen any fighting.''

''Could you not get more experienced men?'' said Gideon.

''There wasn't time,'' said the colonel.

''I understand, but I am still worried about Ms. Cole.''

''You think she's on that island?''

''That is my guess. The sheriff back at Friday Harbor found the piece of paper with the telephone number, the one I had given her before I went out to the docks. It was on the ground in the parking lot. He also found minute traces of blood next to it.''

''She's probably dead,'' said the colonel.

''I don't think so.'' Gideon had to shout to be heard above the rotor wash and the noise of the engine. ''Why would they carry away a dead woman? If they took her and if that island is the center of their operations, my guess is, she is down there.''

The colonel didn't turn to look directly at him, but Gideon could read his pained expression even in profile.

"I'm afraid I've got my orders, Mr. van Ry. There are protocols for dealing with this kind of scenario, NBC's, nuclear, biological, and chemical. That island is off-limits to anything that moves right now. Nothing goes in. Nothing comes out. And we're about to unleash hell on them.''

"What kind of hell?" said Gideon.

"As you can see, I don't have much by way of firepower with me. A few old choppers to transport my men. No artillery and no armed vehicles. I could use a couple of Bradley fighting vehicles, but getting them here and down onto that island in the face of fifty-caliber machine gun fire is another story. I've got to silence those guns before we do anything.''

Gideon shook his head and gave the Marine a quizzical look like he didn't understand.

"We're lucky," yelled the colonel. "We had some equipment out here on the coast for testing.''

"What kind of equipment?"

"It's a palletized gunship. C-130. Those people down there are about to get a lesson in modern urban warfare. Hundred-and-five-millimeter howitzer rounds, precision-guided and very deadly. I've got to bust up those bunkers before we hit the ground.''

"I'm very worried about Joselyn Cole," said Gideon.

"We will do our best to confine our shots," said the colonel.

"Colonel." The chopper pilot turned his head toward his commander in the jump seat behind him. "We got contact.''

"Lemme have the headset." The colonel held the earpiece in place with one hand and talked into the mouthpiece.

"Able, this is Charlie. Where are you?" He listened for a second.

"Good. Test your guns out over open water, then check back. And don't sink any fishing boats out on the sound." He handed the headset back.

"Jolly Green Giant," said the colonel. "You know what that is?''

Gideon shook his head. "I think you should wait, Colonel."

"Why?"

"Because if one loose round hits that device, you could get a very dirty explosion."

The Marine officer now turned and looked at Gideon over his shoulder with a quizzical expression. "What are you talking about?"

It was the only reason he'd brought the Dutchman along. The NEST team couldn't move north fast enough. It would be three hours before they arrived at Friday Harbor with their equipment. Gideon was the only nuclear expert on site. The military needed him in case they found the device.

"That Russian artillery shell is very old," said Gideon. "It's a style of munitions made in the early nineteen-sixties. It contains conventional high explosives wrapped around a core of plutonium. We cannot be sure how old those high explosives are. They could be quite unstable due to age. If you hit them with a round, a piece of shrapnel, anything hot, they could explode." The Dutchman said this in a matter-of-fact manner that caused the colonel to sit up and take notice.

"That'll set off a nuclear blast?"

"Probably not," said Gideon.

"Then what's the problem?"

"An explosion like that could pulverize the plutonium core. It could turn it into dust and send it into the atmosphere. I would not want to be downwind if that happens."

"Radiation?" said the colonel.

Gideon nodded.

"How far could it travel?"

"That depends on the prevailing winds, how high the dust is carried. It could certainly reach the mainland, parts of Seattle, Victoria, Vancouver, depending on the direction of the winds."

This gave the colonel something to chew on. A possible international incident. He thought for a second. Then tapped the pilot on the shoulder. "Gimme those photos."

The pilot handed him a file from the rack on the inside of the door. The colonel opened it and looked at the pictures inside, satellite reconnaissance photos of the island.

"It's the only sizable building," he said. He showed the

pictures to Gideon. "If the device is on the island, chances are it's inside that house. They wouldn't put it in one of the bunkers unless they were crazy."

"Perhaps," said Gideon.

The colonel tapped the pilot one more time, then snapped his fingers for the headset.

He held it up. "Able, this is Charlie. Change of plans. Scratch the house. Do you read?" He waited for the response, which Gideon could not hear over the engine and rotor noise.

"Do not hit the house. Everything else is fair game. Do you read?" He listened again. "That's affirmative. You can go in but don't hit the house." He handed the headset back to the pilot.

"That plane's got a palletized hundred-and-five-millimeter howitzer. Fires terminally guided munitions. It can put a round through a fart from ten thousand feet, before the gas comes out your ass."

Gideon wasn't sure about the metaphor or the wisdom of the man's actions. "Colonel, if they took Ms. Cole, she's alive and she's on that island."

"That may very well be, Mr. van Ry. But I've got my orders. I've got men on that island, too. We're not going in there until we've pulverized those bunkers."

"We'll leave the house alone and hope for her sake that she's inside."

ALTITUDE FOURTEEN THOUSAND FEET: SAN JUAN CHANNEL, WA

It emitted a streak of fire that looked more like a flamethrower. Four rounds thundered through the airframe of the reserve KC-130 in less than two seconds.

They tested the gun out over water. Four distinct plumes rose thirty feet in the air like white feathers all in a line, as the rounds hit the surface of the sound and exploded.

The targeteer checked the coordinates from the global positioning satellite, as well as the link to the mission data computer.

"We're set. Take her in on a left-hand orbit, maintain one-four triple zero."

If they flew at fourteen thousand feet in an orbit that would not cross over the island at any point, the men on the ground would never hear the plane. Their first clue would come in the form of bunker busters, high-explosive shells that could be pinpointed, designed to rip into revetments and tear up sand-bagged emplacements. Not knowing where the rounds were coming from, and with no enemy to shoot at, was a prescription for panic. The ground war in the Gulf proved that even trained soldiers would throw down their weapons and run when faced with an enemy who was killing them with invisible precision.

Once this occurred, phase two would kick in. The bunker busters would be followed by antipersonnel rounds. When these hit the ground, they would release small baseball-sized bomblets that would bounce ten feet up before exploding. Fired in rapid four-round bursts, they would spread a carpet of death, sending out thousands of ball bearings, ripping into flesh and tearing up everything in a radius of hundreds of feet.

The gunship would take the starch out of anybody on the ground who wasn't sitting in a concrete bunker ten feet down. By the time the Hueys swung in over the beach to off-load their troops, the people on that island would be running in panic, tripping over their weapons, and looking for anybody who would take their surrender without killing them. It was mismatch—a total turkey shoot.

GUEMES CHANNEL, WA

As the motor launch skimmed over the waters of the channel, Thorn stayed to the far side, away from the ferry landing at Anacortes.

"Here, take it." They changed seats and Taggart took the wheel. "Keep her straight down the channel."

Thorn got the field glasses out of a case in the cuddy cabin. He trained them on the docks and focused. Two Coast Guard patrol boats were moored a hundred yards off the docks.

"What's wrong?" Taggart looked over at him.

Both of the state ferries were tied up, and a line of traffic snaked up the hill and out onto the highway.

"What do you make of that?" said Thorn.

Taggart squinted. Even without glasses, he could see the traffic. "Pretty busy, even for a weekend."

"Busy, my ass," said Thorn. "Take a better look." He handed the field glasses to Taggart, who held them to his eyes with one hand while he steered with the other.

"What am I supposed to be looking at?"

"The shoulder of that road coming down to the ferry terminal."

Taggart let go of the wheel long enough to focus the glasses. There, off to the right of the road, was a string of dark, olive-drab vehicles each with a distinctive white cross painted on the top and sides.

"Humvees," said Taggart.

"Not just any kind," said Thorn. "Military ambulances. Looks like they're expecting patients. And they've stopped all ferry service."

"What do you make of it?"

"I'd say it's obvious," said Thorn. "They're not interested in having any civilians out on the waters in the San Juan Straits, at least not today. I'll bet there're military vessels patrolling. We might have just made it past them. They don't want the good citizens getting in the way, maybe seeing something they shouldn't."

Thorn looked at his watch. His worry now was Oscar Chaney. If he was on schedule, he would already be onboard the *Humping Goose* along with the tanker truck. It would be an unremarkable sight out on the waters of the sound: a small private working ferry with a septic pumper on its open deck, shuttling between the islands, or in this case between the island and the mainland.

Thorn unrolled a small laminated chart of the islands from inside the cuddy cabin. "If he's on time, Oscar would be right about here, heading down the Rosario Straits." He traced it with his finger on the chart. "Two hours would put him off of Whidbey, another half hour to Keystone."

"If there are military vessels patrolling out there, there's a good chance he won't get through."

Thorn knew that this was the most problematic part of his entire plan. Until he broke out of the sound, onto the mainland with the truck and the device, he and his entire project were in peril.

"I'm banking that they've got their hands full, concentrating on that island for the next several hours. If your people hold up their end.''

''My people will hold up their end. They will die holding up their end.''

''Then by the time the Feds figure out the device was never there to begin with, it will be too late. Oscar will have the truck on the mainland. They won't know what to look for. A million miles of road to cover and a nuclear device they can't be sure where. With every hour, the circle to be searched will grow, and with every mile, the odds shift to our side. They have no description of the vehicle, and if they are lucky enough to corner him, they have to worry whether he'll detonate it.''

''He won't, right?'' Taggart was adamant. ''Not until we reach the target. This is not now some blind act of vengeance. We have a purpose, a goal. If we don't reach our objective, we don't detonate. That was understood from the beginning.''

''Agreed,'' said Thorn. ''But they don't know that.''

Taggart wasn't sure he believed him. The council, the militia leadership, had offered a bonus of a million dollars if Thorn met the target date. There was no way he could make the deadline, so Taggart was worried that Thorn and his cadre might set off the device in some city or town along the way— cut and run. The group had lost financial leverage by transferring the final payment the night before they left the island. It had been done through numbered accounts in Europe, and Thorn had confirmed the payment. Those had been his terms. He was taking no chances.

Now Taggart didn't have a choice. ''I am authorized,'' said Taggart, ''to offer you an incentive to deliver the device to the appointed site even though you missed the date.''

Thorn looked at him but didn't say a word. The prospect of more money. ''I thought you guys were belly-up. Financially, that is.''

''We have half a million,'' said Taggart.

''Oh.''

''A contingency fund.''

''And what exactly is the contingency in this case? You don't trust me?'' He smiled.

Taggart didn't say anything.

"Half a million would buy some more trust, I suppose."

"And how much trust is that?"

"Half a million's worth." Thorn smiled and looked straight ahead down the channel. "Half now, half when it's delivered," said Thorn.

"All of it after it's delivered." They had already been down that road.

Thorn laughed out loud, the kind of mocking chuckle a man makes when he's already had you once. Then he made a face of acceptance. "That makes a bonus of a million and a half if I meet the target date."

"Dream on," said Taggart.

"The date has not yet come and gone," said Thorn.

"Fine. A million and a half. We both know you're not gonna drive that truck across the country in three days."

Thorn didn't say a thing, but merely arched his eyebrows as if this were a matter of opinion. "Take my advice," said Thorn. "You should operate as if everything is on schedule."

"Right. Even if it isn't," said Taggart.

"You hired me to deal with the details."

"I didn't hire you at all. You came with the device."

"For good reason," said Thorn. "Learn to have some faith."

Faith was not the first thing that came to Taggart's mind when he thought about Thorn.

"Don't go spending the bonus money," said Thorn. "I still have three days."

PADGET ISLAND

Pinholes of light punched through the walls of the living room, as bright sunlight broke over the dock and the front of the house. The noise of the shots was distant but Joselyn could hear the distinct and repetitive impact of the bullets as they pierced the front wall of the house and lodged in the wall on the other side.

She followed the man in the wet suit on her hands and knees, then took his lead and went to her stomach. They hugged the floor and shimmied along the back of the couch under a horizontal rain of death. Windows and mirrors shat-

tered. A table lamp over her head disintegrated in a shower of
clay shards. The paneling on the kitchen cabinet doors came
apart like tree limbs run through a shredder. The stacked dishes
on the shelves exploded in a thousand pieces of fired ceramic.

He had made it to the back door when it hit him, low in
the back, lifting him off the floor and spinning him in agony.
The wet suit erupted in blood.

Joselyn was in shock. She dropped the handgun and
crawled toward him.

"What can I do?"

The man didn't respond. All that passed from his lips was
a groan of agony.

She lifted his head and looked down at his stomach. The
bullet that struck him in the back had passed through his body.
Blood was pulsing from the wound.

She crawled on her hands and knees without thinking,
headed for the kitchen and the towel that was draped over the
oven door. The snap of bullets breaking the sound barrier an
inch from her head brought her back to her senses. She hit the
floor and crawled on her stomach. Joselyn grabbed the towel
and three seconds later was back at his side. She pressed the
towel to the open wound with as much pressure as she could
muster lying on the floor.

She looked into his eyes. They were half open, half closed,
staring at nothing. Though Joselyn had never seen the trance
of death, she recognized it, held a finger to his nostrils in hopes
of feeling some sign of breath. There was nothing.

Her hands were covered with blood. She looked around her
on the floor. The pistol. She grabbed it. The man in the wet
suit had said something about Green Giant. Gonna shred the
place. Had to get out.

Joselyn reached up far enough to grab the knob on the back
door. She turned it and opened the door an inch. Like an invitation to a convention of hornets, a score of rounds hit the
door turning what was left into splintered firewood.

Her face shielded in her hands, Joselyn looked at the small
machine gun on the floor next to the dead sailor's hand. She
didn't know if she could figure out how to fire it. She had
seen him do it in the room. She picked it up and looked for a
safety catch. There was a small lever on the side. She flipped

it up and saw a painted red dot on the black metal. Now the question was: were there any bullets in it?

Carefully, as if not to hurt him, she pushed against the dead man and rolled him over, then eased the canvas satchel off his shoulder.

She looked inside. There were black metal clips like the one in the machine gun. Joselyn pulled one out. It was heavy and she saw the copper heads of bullets stacked inside. And there was something else, smooth and round, the size of a large metal egg. She had seen pictures of grenades that looked like pineapples. This was different. But it had a metal clip along the side and a pin connected to a round ring, holding the clip in place. She lifted it in her hand to get a sense of its weight, then wondered how anyone could throw the thing. It weighed as much as a cast iron pan.

Carefully she put it back in the bag and moved the articles around with her hand. There was a compass, a shiny metal mirror, a drab green can of what looked like food. That was it.

She tried to figure out how to get the clip out of the machine gun. She pulled on it but it wouldn't come. She saw a button on the side and pushed it, and the clip fell out onto the floor. There were bullets in it but she couldn't tell how many. Assuming the one from the bag was fully loaded she slid it into the gun and hit the end of the clip against the floor. It clicked into place. She flipped the lever on the side until the red dot appeared, then pointed the fat muzzle toward the wall on the far side of the room. She flinched and turned her head away as she squeezed the trigger gently. She was startled only by the near silent vibration in her hands as a dozen bullets riddled the wall.

So much for target practice. She grabbed the satchel and edged her body toward the door. If the house was a target for something called Green Giant, she had to get out.

She flattened her body to the floor and with one hand swung the door open. Another flurry of shots rang out. Bullets snapped the air in the open doorway. She slid the muzzle around the edge of the door frame, and without looking she pulled the trigger. Once, twice, three times. She tried a fourth but it wouldn't fire.

Joselyn pulled the gun back in before they shot it off. She

pushed the button and the clip fell out. It was empty. She reached into the satchel and found another and slid it into the gun. Quickly she stuck the muzzle out the doorway and pulled the trigger. Nothing.

She looked at it, slapped it on its side, hit it on the floor, and tried it again. It wouldn't fire. If they realized she had a broken gun, they'd be on her in a second. She reached for the pistol in the bag and pulled it out.

Suddenly she remembered. The sailor had slid something back on the top of the pistol when he loaded it. She looked. There was nothing like that on the machine gun. Then she saw a small knob on the side. She hooked a finger over it, pulled hard, and slid it back. When it got to the farthest point, the knob slipped out of her finger and slammed forward. She reached for it again and without thinking squeezed the trigger. Bullets ripped the wall six inches away.

"Fixed." It scared the hell out of her, but at least it worked. She stuck the muzzle out the door and fired again. Within seconds the clip was empty.

She couldn't hit a damn thing, and she knew it. Joselyn looked in the satchel. There were only two more clips, and the Green Giant was coming. She didn't have a clue as to what it was or how much time she had. For all she knew within a minute she would be lying dead on the floor next to the sailor.

She reached in the bag and felt around, found the small metal mirror. She loaded a fresh clip into the gun, then rolled over on her back so that she was flat on the floor with her head just inches inside the frame of the door. She held the mirror in her left hand and slowly eased it past the edge of the door. Finally she could see who was shooting at her. Four men behind a wall of sandbags, their rifles resting on top. They were maybe fifty feet away. Joselyn had been shooting into the dirt.

BUCK THOMPSON HAD his own rifle, a .270 Winchester with a scope and a kick like a mule. It had a Remington bolt action, and he couldn't fire rapidly, but he could thread the needle at two hundred yards. He had arrived from down in California only the day before, carrying a satchel of cash from their fund-raising activities back to Taggart. Now Thompson was in the thick of it.

"How many you think are in there?" He looked at the guy next to him behind the sandbags.

"One. I think." The guy was reloading a clip from an M-16, sitting in the bottom of the bunker with his back against the sandbags. "There was another one, but I think we got him."

Thompson peeked over the top of the bags. He could see a bright reflection off a piece of metal or glass. "Son of a bitch is checking us out with a mirror."

The other man slammed the clip into his rifle and came up next to him. Soon there were four heads peeking over the top.

"He's laying with his head against the wall, just to the right of the door at the level of the floor. Let me have one shot at the mirror," said Thompson. "That'll force him to lie still flat on his back. Give me a count of three, then concentrate your fire right at the level of the porch floor, just to the right of the door. Put enough rounds there, we'll get him in the head."

Thompson slid the bolt back on his rifle and brought it up to the top of the sandbag.

SHE'D BEEN LOOKING at the image in the mirror for several seconds, taking it all in before it finally registered: the four men were standing in a bunker.

One of them took aim. Joselyn pulled the mirror in a half second before he fired. The round smashed into the wooden threshold at the bottom of the door and a spray of splinters caught the back of Joselyn's hand. She grimaced in pain, and pulled it to her chest. She took one long breath and then, without waiting or looking, pulled two splinters as long as porcupine quills from the back of her hand. Searing pain ran up her arm, but the rush of adrenaline and the fear of death worked like a narcotic.

She rolled on her side toward the door. She remembered the two men she had overheard talking about the bunkers being wired for explosives. Forming a mental image of the sandbags and their location, she stuck the muzzle out the door, holding it higher this time, and pulled the trigger. A dozen rounds rattled off, nothing.

Bullets smashed through the wall an inch behind her head, shattering the maple leg of the end table under the window and slamming into the dead sailor. His lower body danced on the floor like a marionette pulled by invisible strings.

Joselyn lifted the muzzle higher and pulled the trigger again, holding it down. She couldn't tell how many rounds she fired, but the gun stopped shooting just an instant before the concussion blew what was left of the windows out of the back of the house. The superheated air of the blast rushed through the open door like a firestorm. Joselyn could feel the radiation on the side of her face. One of the sandbags came down, slamming through the roof over the porch. It landed with a thud two feet from the open door. Joselyn could see the scorched fabric of the bag still smoking.

Now there was silence, broken only by the crackle of flames somewhere outside. Carefully, Joselyn peeked around the door frame. The bunker was a scorched ruin. There was no sign of any of the men. She wasn't going to wait for their friends to show up. She dropped the pistol and the mirror into the satchel and picked it up. Then scurried to her feet. She took one last look at the dead sailor on the floor, then ran as fast as she could out the door, headed for the wooded high ground behind the house.

TWENTY-SEVEN

SITUATION ROOM, THE WHITE HOUSE

Hirshberg closed the door and left behind the acrid odor of coffee having cooked too long over a heated plate. The corridors in the basement of the West Wing were now bustling with people as the workday moved toward noon. As he passed the White House Mess, headed for the small flight of steps and the president's office upstairs, Hirshberg yearned for a fresh cup of coffee. But he didn't have time.

Hirshberg climbed the stairs two at a time and headed down the crowded corridor. Young interns and secretaries parted for him like the waters of the Red Sea. None of them knew precisely what was going on, but the president had canceled all of his meetings outside of the White House, and Cabinet secretaries and military personnel had been seen entering and leaving the Oval Office all morning.

It was a busy time of year. Preparation was ongoing for the State of the Union address, now just a few days off. But events in the West Wing had the smell of an international crisis, not the usual domestic soothsaying of growth in the economy and fine times ahead.

Hirshberg was growing double bags under each eye to match the double chin his wife had been warning him about. He was no longer a kid, and staying up all night had long since lost the excitement it held in his youth.

He didn't bother with formalities but walked into the Oval Office and closed the door behind him. The president was huddled with General Richard Skzorn, chairman of the Joint Chiefs, and two other military aides. They were seated on the couches near the fireplace.

The president looked up. "Any word, Sy?"

"Yes, sir. None of it good."

"Give it to us."

"Coast Guard cutters a mile off the island report gunfire, and one large explosion."

"How large?"

"Conventional," said Hirshberg.

There was a palpable sigh of relief from the president. "Any word from the SEALs? They're our eyes and ears. We've got to get information from them to know what to do."

"We have nothing from them directly," said Hirshberg.

"That means either the satellite station didn't function right, or maybe they lost it going in," said the president.

"They could have gotten caught in a firefight before they had a chance to set up," said the general.

"In any event, we're blind," said the president.

"That's not the worst part," said Hirshberg. "We now have casualties."

"Who?" said the president.

"The SEALs did make contact with one of the Coast Guard cutters on a military frequency. It was very brief and sketchy before their signal broke up. They were calling for boats to get them off. They were under fire. According to the information, two of the five-man team never made it onto the island. We think they were lost at sea in the night drop."

"Jeez." The president got up from the couch, hit his thigh with one hand, and turned his back to the men sitting across from him on the couch.

"How did we get in this mess? We shouldn't have gone in at night. That was a mistake. And there should have been a much larger force, more time for planning."

"Mr. President, you will recall that is what we recommended," said the general.

"I know. I know," said the president. "I made the call. The responsibility rests here. It doesn't make the pain any less." He turned to Hirshberg. "Do we have ships in the water, searching for those men?"

"It's pretty difficult right now, Mr. President. With incoming troops and a gunship in the air. Besides we're trying to screen vessels on the sound. Private pleasure craft, commercial fishing vessels. Just in case they got the device off the island."

The president took a long, deep breath and thought for a second. "Has the Coast Guard seen any traffic coming from that island this morning?"

"Not since oh-five-hundred when the blockade was put in place."

"Then let's forget screening the vessels. We can't cover everything on the sound. Let's assume that the device is bottled up on that island," said the president. "Get what boats we can spare to search for those men."

"Mr. President, I don't think we can take that chan—"

"Don't argue with me, Sy."

Hirshberg knew when it was useless, but he tried anyway.

"They couldn't survive in that water for more than two hours, Mr. President. Even in wet suits."

A new taste of reality for the equation.

"They can survive," said the president. "They're Navy SEALs. They're the best in the world. I will not have it said that I did not give them every chance. Stop screening vessels and get those ships into search-and-rescue mode, every available ship that isn't needed for the blockade. Is that clear?"

"We're very likely to have more casualties before the end of the day, Mr. President," said Hirshberg.

"Let's hope they're all on the other side," said the general.

"Hoping is not going to make it happen," said Hirshberg. "Most of our troops going in are green. Only the commanding officer and five of his non-coms have any combat experience."

"We've got firepower and training on our side," said the general.

"I certainly hope so," said Hirshberg. "Because we're going to need that, and a lot of luck, if we're going to find that bomb before they detonate it."

"Sy, see if we can make contact with the SEALs on that island. Tell them that help is on the way."

"They know that, Mr. President. The Coast Guard told them to stay away from the bunkers, that they were targeted."

"Good. That's something anyway."

"I'd better get back and see if there's anymore communiqués," said Hirshberg.

"Let us know the second you hear anything," said the president.

Approaching Keystone, Whidbey Island, WA

The Coast Guard vessel was showing red and blue lights, flashing like strobes over the roof of the bridge as its bow cut across the wake of the slower-moving LCS and pulled in behind it. It closed the distance quickly. The *Humping Goose* was no match for the fast and nimble Coast Guard patrol boat.

Oscar Chaney saw it in the mirror of the truck as he sat behind the wheel. He rolled down the passenger-side window and leaned low over the seat in order to look up at the wheelhouse.

The skipper slid open the window.

"What do they want?" asked Chaney.

"They want us to stop so they can board and inspect." Nat Hobbs leaned out of the wheelhouse window and yelled down to Chaney. Hobbs was wearing a Greek captain's cap that looked like it was molting little blue balls of fuzz. His face was smudged with oil and his jumper had seen enough sweat to stand in the corner without Hobbs in it.

Chaney looked at the ferry dock less than a quarter of a mile away. He noticed two State Patrol cars parked near the ferry building and what looked like an older blue Customs Department vehicle.

"I hope you're not on a tight schedule," said Hobbs. "I'm gonna have to stop."

"Gotta do what you gotta do," said Chaney.

"I could try and put in for the dock, but if I jack 'em around we may get the full nine yards. I'll be tied up at the dock for two hours for a safety inspection while they hassle the hell outta me with forms."

To Chaney it sounded like Hobbs might not pass. He didn't say a word but rolled up the window as if to say the call belonged to Hobbs. At the same time, he reached under the seat cushion on the passenger side of the truck and slid the .45 semiautomatic across the seat and into the belt of his pants.

He pulled his sweater down over the handle, then ran his hand along the back of his leg and into the top of his boot to feel for the hilt of the large Bowie knife inside.

He opened the door of the truck and stepped down. The Kalashnikov was under the seat, fully loaded with a fifty-round clip. It could be fired on full automatic, and there were six more loaded clips lying beside it, but it was no match for the mounted gun on the bow of the Coast Guard boat.

Chaney glanced with one eye behind the seat, just enough to catch a glimpse of the red metal ring attached to a light cable. The cable ran through a hole in the back of the truck's cab and from there into the welded tank on the back. It was connected to a timed detonator and eight pounds of C-4 plastique. This was mounted just underneath the device. If all else failed, Chaney could pull the ring. He would then have exactly ninety seconds to hit the water and swim as fast as he could, against the direction of the wind.

The explosion would not go nuclear, but it would blow the truck into the air, rupture the tank, and send highly radioactive plutonium dust into the wind. If he waited until the Coast Guard boat was tied up alongside, the ensuing chaos might give him time to get away. What he needed now was to stall for time, control of the boat.

Chaney closed the truck door but didn't lock it, then walked toward the stern of the *Humping Goose* and climbed the short ladder to the wheelhouse.

When he got there, Hobbs was on the radio.

"You guys just inspected me last month." Hobbs let up on the button to the microphone and turned to see his passenger.

"We see one truck onboard," said the Coast Guard. "How many passengers?"

"Just one. Just the one truck," said Hobbs.

"What's on the truck?" asked the Coast Guard.

"It's a septic truck. You wanna look inside?"

There was a delay, several seconds at the other end.

"We are under orders to board and search all vessels in this area. You are ordered to come to a dead stop and prepare for boarding. Is that understood?"

"Shit." Hobbs didn't press the mike button, but said it to himself.

"At least let me clear the channel to the ferry landing," said Hobbs. "Unless you want an accident."

Again there was a delay from the Coast Guard end.

"You better get down to your truck. Sounds like they're gonna want to look and see what's inside," Hobbs told Chaney.

"Affirmative," said the Coast Guard. "We will follow you into the channel."

Hobbs hung the microphone up on the radio receiver set, like he wanted to break off the knob that held it.

"Son of a bitch. They think I got nothin' else to do." He was now talking to himself. "I hope they bring their fancy white dress gloves." He kicked the two throttle handles for the twin diesels from idle to full-ahead, while he steered the *Humping Goose* back out into the open channel. He didn't pay any attention to the fact that Chaney was still behind him. "I guarantee you those dandies aren't gonna want to look inside your truck. One whiff, and they'll take their starched uniforms back to their boat and disappear. In the meantime, I'll lose an hour screwing around."

THE SQUARED-OFF BOW of the *Humping Goose* was designed to drop like a World War II landing craft. It formed a hydraulic bridge that allowed cars and trucks to drive onto a beach or more usually a private boat ramp. The captain of the Coast Guard boat watched as it plowed the water in its own ponderous way back out toward the channel and the rougher waters that fed the Straits of Juan de Fuca from the North Pacific.

In five minutes, they had gone more than a mile.

"*Humping Goose, Humping Goose*, this is the Coast Guard. How far out are you going?"

The Coast Guard captain released the mike button and listened. There was no response.

"Private ferry, do you read? This is the Coast Guard." The radio channel opened and all the officer heard was static. He was about to punch the button to speak one more time, when the frequency suddenly came to life.

"Coast Guard. This is the *Humping Goose*. I wanna get well clear of the channel," the voice came back over the radio.

"You're now in safe waters," said the Coast Guard officer. "Cut your engines and prepare for boarding."

Suddenly one of the enlisted men came onto the bridge. "Sir, communiqué from Everett." He handed the captain a slip of paper with a typed message.

The Coast Guard officer was still watching the stern of the old rusted-out LCS bearing the chipped green paint and the words *Humping Goose* across the broad transom. There was no sign that its engines were slowing.

The captain looked down and read the message in his hand, then fumed and shook his head. He opened the channel again. "To the working boat, *Humping Goose*, do you read? There has been a change in our orders. We are being diverted to air-sea rescue in the north sound. Thank you for your cooperation. You are free to put in at Keystone. Repeat. You are free to put in at Keystone."

"Thank you, sir. I appreciate it." The reply came back.

The Coast Guard boat cut a sharp swathe across the wake of the *Goose* and bounced into high speed as she overtook the slower vessel on her port side. The officers on the bridge didn't pay much attention to the working boat's captain with his greasy face and Greek sea cap as he waved and smiled at them from the open window of the wheelhouse. The Coast Guard boat sped away and cut across the *Goose*'s course two hundred yards ahead before making the turn back north.

OSCAR CHANEY TOOK the hat off his head and dropped it onto the deck of the wheelhouse as he steered a course south down the channel. Change of plans. He wasn't going to Keystone or any other public dock. They were looking for something, and Chaney knew what it was. He glanced over his shoulder at the river of blood that began to dam near the threshold of the wheelhouse door. The big knife had not only cut the jugular vein and carotid arteries, it had all but severed Nat Hobbs's head.

PADGET ISLAND, WA

The trees, large evergreens, some of them ninety feet tall, looked like the charred masts of a wrecked fleet. They had been limbed, some of them snapped in half by the aerial howitzer rounds from the gunship. Every third tree seemed to be missing its top. Many of them were still burning.

The howitzer had not been as effective as originally believed. The dense foliage had caused many of the rounds to explode high in the trees. Still there were bodies everywhere.

Gideon counted at least eight dead in the fifty feet around the area cleared for the helicopter landing pad. He jumped out behind the colonel and ran at a crouch until they cleared the rotor wash.

"I want you to stay here, Mr. van Ry." The colonel turned and looked at him. "I will leave one of my men with you. You do whatever he tells you. Do you understand?"

"Colonel, if the device is on this island, I would suggest that we get to it quickly."

"I understand. You're anxious to get at it. But we haven't rounded up all the terrorists. There's still a pocket of resistance down near the beach. Until it's safe, I want you here."

"What about Ms. Cole?" asked Gideon.

"I've passed the word to my men to keep and eye out for her. I don't want to be worrying about you as well. So you will stay here." It wasn't a question. It was an order.

Gideon nodded.

The Marine colonel looked like maybe he didn't trust him. "Corporal." He turned to one of the young Marines behind him. "I want you to keep an eye on Mr. van Ry here. If anything happens to him, I'm going to hold you personally responsible. Do you understand?"

"Yes, sir."

"Good. Now let's get down to that beach." The colonel headed out. "Where's my radio man?" A clutch of armed troops followed him as another helicopter came in. Another young Marine, with a radio strapped to his back and a coiled antenna looping over one shoulder like a wounded angel, loped up next to the colonel. He took the telephone receiver from the kid and started talking, but Gideon couldn't hear what he said. The sound of the rotors and the helicopter engine revving up for takeoff drowned out everything else. Dust kicked up, and Gideon and the corporal turned their backs to the landing zone and covered their eyes.

The helicopter swung up over the trees and out toward the water. It was followed by another incoming chopper.

"I think maybe we should get out of here," said Gideon.

The corporal didn't seem to object, so Gideon headed off toward a clump of burned-out trees on a high knoll overlooking the west side of the island. When he got far enough away that he was no longer deafened by the noise of the helicopters, he found a flat boulder, hefted the back-pack with his equipment off of one shoulder, set it down, and sat on the rock. He checked his watch. It was now after noon, and his empty stomach was grumbling. He had not eaten since supper the evening before, with Joselyn at her house on San Juan Island. He wondered if she was alive or dead.

The distant sound of the helicopters was now punctuated by the periodic sound of gunfire, single shots and short bursts, the echo of what sounded like machine gun rounds, some of it heavier.

The corporal brought his M-16 up across his chest. An expression of concern suddenly crept across his face.

"What is wrong?" said Gideon.

The soldier was standing on an outcropping of rock closer to the edge of the bluff and looking down at something Gideon could not see.

"I don't like this. We're silhouetted up here," said the Marine. "If there's anybody down there with a rifle, we'd make a pretty good target." He pointed and Gideon got up to take a look.

Below, nestled in the embrace at the bottom of the bluff, was a large building the back side of which was still smoking. He could see no movement, no signs of life. Beyond the house was a cove and what remained of a small dock, shattered and gone in places, some of its pilings charred to the waterline.

"Is that the main house?" said Gideon.

"I guess so."

"Do you have a map?"

The Marine shook his head.

Gideon turned and looked in the direction of the gunfire. "I take it the beach is on the other side of the island?"

"I think so."

"Then we're probably safe here." Gideon stepped back and reached into his pack. He pulled out the one piece of useful equipment he had thought to bring: a small pair of binoculars. The field glasses were not the best. They were underpowered for the distance.

He trained them on the house and focused. The place looked deserted. He held them as still as possible and watched for any telltale signs of life, anything that moved. The only motion came from wisps of dense black smoke that floated across his field of vision.

"See anything?" asked the corporal.

"No. Would you like to look?"

The Marine smiled, strapped his rifle over his shoulder, and took the field glasses. He started scanning from the corner of the house nearest the dock, trying desperately with compromised optics to check the windows for rifle muzzles. He did this slowly, scanning the house from one end to the other.

"Do you see anything?"

"No." The corporal still had a troubled look on his face.

"Why don't we go down there and take a look?" said Gideon.

The Marine gave him a sick laugh. "No way."

"Where is your sense of adventure?" Gideon smiled, the look of an older man challenging the other's manhood.

"I left it home," said the soldier.

He might be young, thought Gideon, but he was no fool.

There was a sudden respite from the noise as all of the helicopters moved offshore, a sudden lapse in the deafening sound that seemed to be replaced by a lot of shouting back in the clearing. The corporal turned to see what was going on, while Gideon took another look through the binoculars. When he turned, the Marine was totally distracted, his back to the bluff.

"What's happening?" said Gideon.

"I don't know. Something's up."

They could still hear more firing off in the distance. What sounded like heavier machine gun fire now.

Gideon turned and looked at the house once more. He wondered if Joselyn might be inside. He didn't know what other buildings existed on the island, but the house was definitely a candidate for the device. When he looked back at the corporal, the Marine was now totally occupied with the scene back at the landing zone. If the kid had an antenna of his own, it was now definitely up. Something was wrong.

"Maybe we should go find out what's happening," he said.

Gideon grabbed his backpack and followed the Marine back to the landing zone. By now Marines were coming up from the beach in groups of four and five, all with differing but dazed expressions on their faces. Some were running, others walking, but all conveyed a single uniform emotion—fear.

"What happened?" The corporal tried to stop one of them. The man ran right through his arms. "What the hell's going on? Somebody talk to me." Something had happened, and a contagion of fear was taking hold of the young Marines on the hill. Now they were coming up from the beach in larger groups. It looked like a wholesale retreat.

Gideon recognized panic when he saw it. He grabbed one of them by the arm. The kid dropped his rifle and looked at him with a vacant stare.

"You!" He looked down at the man with as stern an expression as he muster. "Tell me what's happened?"

"Hisss . . . his head. It it it it . . ."

"Whose head?"

"Co . . . Co . . . Colonel Simmons."

"What about Colonel Simmons?"

"His head's gone."

"What are you talking about?"

"The colonel's dead. They shot him in the head. It just . . . just . . . exploded."

"Who's in charge?" said Gideon.

"I don't know," said the Marine. Gideon released his hold on the man for an instant to collect his thoughts, and before he could grab him again the kid was gone, leaving his rifle behind him in the dirt as he ran down the hill in the other direction.

Gideon reached down and picked it up. By now the corporal that Simmons had left to watch him was caught up in the general panic that was spreading like a rash across the landing zone. They were in trouble, and Gideon knew it. Shots were still coming from the beach, heavy gunfire.

"Where's the radio?" said Gideon.

No one paid attention to him.

"Who has the radio?"

TWENTY-EIGHT

DENVER INTERNATIONAL AIRPORT

Scott Taggart reset his watch to eastern time, skipping the mountain zone since he would be there for less than an hour. He tried to calculate how many hours had passed since he dropped Thorn at the small private airport at Arlington in the Skagit Valley. While he wondered what Thorn was doing there, he knew better than to ask. Thorn was not one to share information unless there was a purpose. At that point, Taggart's job was to get to Sea-Tac and catch his flight to the east coast.

During a layover in Denver, he found a bank of phones and placed the call as Thorn had directed. He dialed the cellular number and heard it ring twice before a voice answered.

"Yes." It was Thorn. He was breathless, his single word muffled by what sounded like industrial noise in the background: heavy equipment, and the relentless peal of a safety bell as a truck or some other vehicle backed up.

"Taggart here."

"I was beginning to worry," said Thorn.

"I just arrived. The flight was ten minutes late getting in."

"Then you don't have much time," said Thorn. "Check inside your briefcase. You will find a key stamped with a red number. It fits a locker on that concourse. Go to the locker.

Everything you need as well as your instructions are inside. Do you understand?"

"Yes."

"Follow the instructions precisely," said Thorn.

"How will I contact you?"

"You won't," said Thorn. "Just follow the instructions." The signal at the other end went dead. Thorn had punched the "end" key on the cell phone before Taggart could say another word.

He hung up the receiver, lifted his briefcase onto the flat stainless steel surface under the phone, then spread it open and looked inside.

The leather briefcase had not been out of his possession since he packed it the night before. But there in the bottom was a brass key, the number C-142 stamped in red plastic. Thorn must have dropped it into the case on the boat that morning, when they switched seats so that Taggart could drive.

He grabbed the key and began searching the concourse for lockers. The first set he found didn't correspond to the number on the key. His flight had landed twenty minutes late. By the time he got off the plane, he was down to half an hour before the connecting flight departed. The phone call to Thorn had taken time. He checked his watch. He had less than eighteen minutes to find the locker and catch his connecting flight.

Padget Island, WA

Two helicopters were headed back in from the sound toward the landing zone. Gideon could see them coming in low over the water. Only this time they were not the ponderous, overburdened Hueys that had landed Simmons and his troops. These were smaller, with a sleek, black profile. Gideon recognized their dark silhouettes from pictures he had seen in *Jane's Defense Weekly*.

The two Cobra gunships swept in low over the landing zone at high speed, causing the Marines on the ground to flinch and duck. The two choppers swung toward the beach and the sound of the gunfire. It was clear that somebody in authority had found a radio.

Gideon didn't wait to find out what would happen. He knew that if he wanted to see what was in that house he would have to do it now. The corporal that Simmons had assigned to watch him was busy getting an earload: descriptions of death down on the beach.

Gideon picked up the Marine's M-16 from the dirt where the panicky kid had dropped it. He slung the gun over his shoulder, grabbed his backpack of equipment, and ran through a grove of burned-out trees down a dusty path that seemed to head in the right direction, toward the house on the cove.

In the star burst of figures fleeing the landing zone, Gideon was just one more running figure. In less than a minute, he had separated himself from the forces on the hill. He was alone, moving quickly down the dusty path.

He rounded a bend and could see the house, this time from a different angle. He stopped behind a tree and studied the front of the building again through the field glasses that he took from his pack.

Most of the windows across the front were shattered, blown out like the ones in the back that he and the Marine corporal had seen from the bluff above.

What looked like flyspecks all over the white paint under the overhanging porch on the front side, on closer inspection through the glasses, turned out to be bullet holes.

There had been a pitched battle at the house, and Gideon wondered what had caused it. Simmons had ordered the building off-limits to the gunship and its howitzer.

He scanned the area in front of the house. A sandbagged bunker appeared to be empty, though he couldn't see into part of it because of a corrugated metal roof.

He dropped the field glasses back in his pack and started back down the path.

Thirty feet down, he crossed a small creek. The path suddenly descended precipitously. His feet hit loose gravel, slipping out from under him. Gideon grabbed the rifle and managed to keep it out of the dirt, but slid on his side and began to roll down the steep incline.

He lost control and tumbled. Items came flying from his backpack. He lost his grip on the rifle. The sling wrapped around his arm, and halfway down the hill something hit the trigger. The rifle discharged. The shot didn't hit him, but the sound of the report close to Gideon's head nearly deafened him. He rolled down the hill but somehow managed to get control of the rifle again. He clung to it like a lifeline.

It wasn't until the tumbling stopped abruptly in the hollow of a small ravine that Gideon realized that he had never checked the rifle to see if the safety was on or if it was loaded. The fact that he hadn't shot himself was a miracle, though anybody within a half mile of the house now knew he was there. He lay there dazed for a moment, trying to recover his bearings.

Gideon felt a burning sensation along the side of his leg and looked down. His pants were ripped, and the skin that poked through on the side of his thigh looked like raspberries that had been crushed in a blender. His right arm was scraped and scratched from the wrist to the elbow.

He tried to collect himself, looked back up the hill, and saw items of equipment from his backpack strewn over the steep path. The pack was still wrapped around one arm, its strap twisted around his wrist. He unwound the strap from his arm and set the bag carefully on the ground to check what was left of its contents. The heavy Geiger counter was still in the bottom, though Gideon couldn't be sure after the pounding whether it would still function.

The binoculars and compass were gone. He looked with a pained expression back up the hill. He did not have time to go searching for them now.

Carefully, Gideon checked for a safety on the rifle, and found what he thought was it. Even though he was a weapons designer, he had little expertise in firearms. He flipped the wedge-shaped metal catch back and forth several times, until he satisfied himself as to which position was on and which was off.

He fumbled with the gun for a few more seconds and managed to detach the metal magazine from the underside of the weapon. He checked this for ammunition. The clip appeared to be full. He took one of the bullets out of the magazine.

Five-point-five-six-millimeter NATO rounds. The Netherlands was one of the charter members of NATO, though Gideon knew more about its organization than its small arms.

It was a small bottle-shaped round with a bullet roughly the size of a .22, but heavier in weight and longer. Gideon guessed that the bullet was probably fifty or sixty grains in weight and steel-jacketed. The rifle would be accurate out to maybe two hundred yards, that is, if you were a good shot, which Gideon knew he was not. Perhaps he could hit a large, still target at a hundred yards, if he was lucky.

He hoped he wouldn't have to use the gun at all. If he did, he would fire one shot at a time, and hopefully come close enough to discourage anyone from investigating him at closer range. He had no desire to kill anyone, and even less to be killed himself.

He pressed the bullet back in the magazine and carefully slid the clip back into the gun. Then he checked the safety one more time, slung the rifle over his shoulder, grabbed his back-pack, and stood up.

With the first step he limped heavily on the injured leg. Blood was spreading through the material on his pant leg, though the pain told him that the injury was not serious. He had no time to take care of it. He gritted his teeth for the first few steps and slowly lengthened his stride as his limbs loos-ened up and the burning sensation in his leg began to pass. A few more paces, and he shook off the stiffness. He moved in the direction of the house. It was maybe fifty or sixty yards away, across a small meadow.

He felt the percussion of the bullet as it passed an instant before the sound of the shot registered. Gideon hit the ground like a sack of sand.

DENVER INTERNATIONAL AIRPORT

Taggart checked two more alcoves off of the main con-course before he found the locker with the right number stamped on the metal door. He slid the key into the lock, and it turned. Carefully, applying pressure with one hand while he pulled gently with the other, he opened the small metal door just a fraction of an inch, just enough to allow a sliver of light to penetrate into the dark confines of the locker. Then he looked to see if anyone was watching.

The busy concourse was filled with travelers, most of them in a hurry. No one seemed to be paying particular attention to anything going on at the bank of lockers.

Taggart peeked inside over the edge of the slightly open

door. There was a piece of paper, what looked like a single sheet, folded inside on the bottom of the locker. It was a few inches back from the door. On top of it was a glass container, what looked like a classic bottle of men's aftershave. Next to these appeared to be a closed book of matches.

Taggart looked for wires or strings connecting the bottle to the door, any sign of a booby trap.

He had never trusted Thorn from the inception. The man had come into the deal, firmly attached to the nuclear device as part of the transaction. Taggart had never fully understood why, only that it was an immutable condition of the transaction.

The man had been paid a bundle of money by Taggart's group, money they had raised by highly intricate scams and a few violent robberies, mostly banks with large cash deposits.

For all Taggart knew, the nuclear device that his group had paid for might well be resting at the bottom of the sound, dumped there by Thorn at the first sign of trouble. He had seen the device only once, and then only briefly after being blindfolded and taken to an undisclosed location as a condition of payment.

If things had now soured, eliminating Taggart would be Thorn's first instinct. Why leave somebody behind who could identify him? After all, Thorn had killed the woman for the same reason.

Taggart couldn't see any wires or thin fishing filament connected to the door or running from the back of the locker to the bottle.

There was one other possibility. The bottle was large enough to contain an explosive accelerant, nitro, or something else equally potent. It might be set up to detonate by a photocell. When the door opened, and enough light reached the bottle—BANG.

Taggart carefully closed the door and leaned against it with his shoulder to keep it shut against the pressure of the slight back-spring. He took the handkerchief from his pocket and wiped the perspiration from his brow, then checked his watch. He was down to eight minutes if he was going to catch his flight.

Quickly he lifted his briefcase and reached inside. He grabbed a thickness of pages, eight-and-a-half-by-eleven sheets from a spiral notebook, and ripped them from their wire binding.

He dropped the briefcase and held the thickness of paper up to the edge of the locker door like a shield, then carefully opened the door, a fraction of an inch at a time.

Sweat ran down his upper lip. Finally with the door open just a crack, he slipped the flat of his hand through, holding the thickness of paper between his thumb and his palm. He then shut the door against his forearm and tried to seal off as much of the light as he could with his shoulder.

Feeling around inside like a blind man, Taggart inched his hand toward the bottle, careful not to jar it or knock it over. He got a grip on it and wrapped the paper around it. He tried to feel for any protrusions in the glass that might indicate the existence of a thin photocell cemented to the outside. He felt only the smooth symmetrical shape of the glass.

Still he took no chances. Carefully he lifted the bottle out, still tightly wrapped in its paper covering. Then he grabbed the piece of paper that was neatly folded and lying on the bottom of the locker.

Using his lips and his free hand, he opened the note and read. It was typed and very brief. His brows furrowed, and a smile curled on his lips as he digested the message. It was so simple it was brilliant. It gave him a whole new sense of appreciation for Thorn.

He was no longer worried about the bottle exploding. He carefully unwrapped it from the paper, then checked its cap to make sure that it was sealed tight. He gingerly set the bottle into the bottom of his briefcase and propped a few items against it for safety, so that it wouldn't break or leak.

The last instruction in the note he followed to a tee. He placed the note back in the locker, then looked to make sure that no one was watching. He picked up the book of matches inside and without removing his hands from the locker, struck a match and set an edge of the paper on fire. Closing the door only enough to confine the smoke and look over the top, Taggart watched the paper slowly turn to ash as the flame finished its work.

A light haze of smoke curled from the locker as he opened the door. No one else seemed to notice. He reached inside and swept the ash out of the locker and onto the floor, then checked his watch. He had less than five minutes to catch his flight. Taggart picked up his briefcase and ran for the gate. Thorn was about to make his bonus money after all.

PADGET ISLAND, WA

Joselyn edged cautiously toward the edge of the small grove of wind-dwarfed trees with the sound of the first shot. She had heard distant firing all morning, but this was different. It was much closer.

She waited and listened. She moved out of the brush, all of her senses sharpened like a cautious deer. Clutching the small machine gun from the dead Navy SEAL in her hands, she was now down to the last full magazine of bullets. She had stashed the satchel with the pistol and grenades in the hollow of a tree in the grove. It would be her last refuge if she were forced to retreat.

Joselyn had just cleared the edge of the small grove and was looking toward the path when she saw him, sitting on the ground a hundred yards away, looking at his pant leg, picking at it with the fingers of one hand. It was same tan pants and white shirt he'd been wearing the night before, when he left her standing on the dock in Friday Harbor.

The ungainly figure sitting on the ground looking at his leg was Gideon. She had no idea how he'd gotten to the island, and what's more, she didn't care. All she knew was that he had come for her, that she was no longer alone.

Without thinking, she dropped the gun and started to run.

Gideon didn't see her. He seemed focused on the backpack on the ground in front of him and the front of the house. He never looked toward the grove of trees set into the high bluff behind it.

Joselyn edged her way around giant boulders of sandstone, and into a small ravine running with water from a creek. She lost sight of him as she dropped down into the ravine and tried to climb up the other side. She couldn't. She kept sliding back down. She grabbed at some small roots growing from the side of the ravine, and they pulled loose in her hand. She turned and followed the ravine down, following the flow of the water, the course of least resistance.

She ran for what seemed like a minute, but was in reality

only seconds. Her head surfaced just above the edge of the ravine so that she could see Gideon once more, walking through the meadow, limping toward the house.

Joselyn raised an arm and was about to call to him, when the shock of the rifle butt against the side of her face drove her to the ground and back down into the ravine.

She had failed to see the man wedged in the rocks just above her. Joselyn got only a fleeting glimpse of his face, hideous and seared, as she hit the ground and rolled on one shoulder into the shallow channel of the creek. The only force keeping her conscious was the shock of the icy water and the flow of adrenaline coursing in her veins.

Dazed, she looked up and saw him as he took aim.

Buck Thompson was a crack shot, but his rifle had taken a beating, bouncing on the ground after the explosion had thrown him out of the bunker. He centered the crosshairs of the scope on the man's chest and squeezed the trigger.

UNABLE TO SHAKE off the effects of the blow or to crawl to her feet in the trickling waters of the creek, Joselyn heard the sharp peal of the rifle as the shot reverberated through the ravine. A second later he was on her, the barrel of his rifle waving in her face as she got to her knees, its tapered muzzle moving close to touch the side of her temple just below the hairline. Cold, hard, steel.

He worked the bolt and ejected the round, seating another. "Don't scream."

She tried to open her mouth, but nothing came out.

"Don't." His voice issued from twisted lips, burned crisp to a hideous black at one corner.

She knew from the way he fired and leaped from the crevice in the rocks that his shot had found its mark. Gideon was dead. The thought made its mark on her consciousness, but acceptance of the fact as reality did not.

She began to scream. Joselyn couldn't keep her eyes off of the man's face. It embodied every grotesque event of the last twenty-four hours. She screamed in a pitch of fright and revulsion at the death that lay about her.

The man's right eye seemed to be gone, the side of his face

had the texture and pallor of melted wax, part of it seared and blackened like meat that had been left too long on a spit.

Even in this form, she recognized him. It was the man with the scoped rifle, the one she had seen in the mirror, taking aim as she lay near the open doorway. How he'd survived the blast in the bunker Joselyn had no idea.

His one good eye darted between Joselyn and the edge of the ravine over which he could no longer see. He rapped her on the head with the barrel of the rifle, not hard, but with enough force to get her attention, to stop her screaming, which pierced his open sinus cavity like a knife.

Joselyn looked at him in stark horror, but she stopped screaming.

He lifted the muzzle of the rifle and grabbed Joselyn roughly by the arm, pulling her to her feet. Then he pushed her ahead of him, down toward the shallow end of the ravine, where it poured into the open meadow.

They entered flat ground near the side of the house, Joselyn in front, the steel barrel of the man's rifle in the small of her back.

Keeping her between himself and his dead quarry, the man kept peeking over Joselyn's shoulder with his one good eye, trying to locate the body on the ground. Grass and wildflowers now formed an impenetrable horizontal sea, a foot deep and a hundred yards wide across the meadow. Having given up the high ground, the gunman could no longer find his target. He wanted to put one more bullet in him just to make sure.

As they walked along the side of the house, he pulled Joselyn in close to his body like a shield.

She could smell the odor of singed flesh hanging over her shoulder, the whistle of heavy breathing through the edema of burned airways.

"Slow down." There was fear in his voice.

Joselyn knew that any second he could pull the trigger, sending a rifle bullet smashing through her body.

He held her tight in front of him as he pressed his back against the wall at the side of the house, forming his own kind of human bunker.

"What was in that?" He whispered into her ear.

"What are you talking about?"

"The sandbags, behind the house? What was in them?"

"I didn't do it," said Joselyn.

"Explosives?"

She nodded.

"Who?"

"The man they called Thorn," said Joselyn. "He had them wired."

"Why would he do that?"

"He didn't want any witnesses. He didn't want any of you to survive."

"I don't believe you."

"Shoot into that one." She nodded as far as he would permit her head to move, toward the sandbagged emplacement at the front of the house. It was no more than thirty feet away.

He glanced in that direction but held her close with a firm grip on her shoulder, as he pressed the barrel of his rifle against her back with his other hand.

"If you don't believe me, do it," said Joselyn.

"I've got a better idea," said the man. "Get over there." He let go of her shoulder and pushed the barrel of the rifle into her back hard.

Joselyn staggered forward several steps and stopped.

"Go on." He was breathless, almost panting.

Joselyn was thinking that if she could hang on, stall him just a few more seconds, he might pass out. She turned now and looked at him.

"You want to shoot me. Do it now."

"No. I want you over there." He motioned with the rifle toward the bunker.

"I told you the truth. I didn't do it."

"You fired into it."

"Only because you were shooting at me."

"Move," he said. Now there was anger in the single eye that peered out from the scarred face.

Joselyn backed up several steps, held her hands in the air, an emphasis that she was now disarmed. She could tell by the look on what was left of his face that it didn't matter. He knew the pain he was in, and he wanted revenge. She backed up a few more steps.

The barrel of the rifle began to wave in broad circles as he focused his good eye on her.

"More."

She took two more steps back, turned, and looked over her shoulder. She was less than five feet from the corner of the sandbagged bunker.

"Get up against those bags." He brought the rifle up to his shoulder and tried to sight through the scope. At less than thirty feet, it was a blur. Still, at this distance he couldn't miss the sandbags.

He brought the side of his body against the wall of the house for support and shielded himself from the blast behind the corner.

Joselyn backed up until the back of her legs and buttocks hit the bags. She pressed against them and prayed, "Dear Lord, let it be done."

A thin splinter of wood split from the molding at the corner of the house just at the level of his eyes an instant before the sound of the shot echoed off the bluff. The gunman stood as if suspended by some unnatural force, his rifle barrel dipping six inches before it tumbled from his hands. His knees buckled. Joselyn watched as the rigid lines of his body turned fluid and collapsed into the dust by the side of the house.

She turned and looked behind her toward the meadow. A tall, slender giant stood halfway to his knees in grass and wildflowers, a rifle in his hands.

Gideon looked at the sky and thanked God for a lucky shot.

TWENTY-NINE

PADGET ISLAND, WA

A Marine marksman examined the gunman's rifle where they found it lying in the dirt by the side of the house. He found that the scope had been jarred, probably by the explosion in the bunker, so that its mountings were forced slightly out of alignment. Buck Thompson's shot had missed Gideon by inches.

The Marines, with Gideon in tow, searched every structure on the island for nearly three hours. The Geiger counter clicked with only periodic surges of background radiation, but nothing more. They could find no sign of the nuclear device. The NEST team showed up shortly after noon and took over the search.

Gideon and Joselyn were put onboard a Marine helicopter and flown to the naval air station on Whidbey Island, where Gideon was taken in one direction and Joselyn in another.

Joselyn wanted to know why they were being held. No one would give her an answer.

She was allowed to shower and clean up at the base, constantly under the eye of a female Marine, then given a quick medical exam and treated for the multitude of bruises and abrasions.

The Navy doctor wasn't sure about Joselyn. He thought she might have suffered a concussion. The knot on the back of her head where the men had sapped her the night they took her on the dock, as well as the bruise on her cheek from Thompson's rifle butt, had swollen badly and was quite discolored. The physician wasn't sure about her ability to travel.

"Is it life-threatening?" asked a stone-faced FBI agent.

"Probably not, but I won't take responsibility," said the physician.

"She can travel," said the agent.

She was handed a blue Navy jumpsuit, in place of her soiled and torn clothing, and hustled aboard a small Air Force jet in the company of two agents. A moment later Gideon, also wearing a Navy jumpsuit and bent over so that he was nearly crouching to half his height, entered through the door of the small jet. He smiled when he saw her, bandaged and scrubbed, and wearing a jumpsuit two sizes too big for her.

"Lovely. It's good they had one in your color," he said.

"Sit down and buckle up," said the agent.

Gideon took the chair next to Joselyn.

They talked for maybe an hour until the drone of the jet engine finally put them both to sleep, her head tilted over onto his shoulder, his head against hers.

Gideon was awakened by the gradual decline in altitude and air pressure. Instinctively he looked for his watch and only then realized that it was gone. He'd left it with his clothes back on Whidbey Island. He shifted in his seat. Joselyn blinked her eyes and woke. She stretched and yawned.

"I think we're about to land." He told her. "Do you know what time it is?"

She looked at her empty wrist. "No." Then out the window, but she couldn't see a thing. They were flying through cloud cover thick as soup.

Ten minutes later, they felt the wheels of the jet as they skidded onto the runway. The plane taxied to a stop near a large hangar. All they could see out of the windows were military planes, jet fighters, and transports, lined up along the runway.

Gideon craned his neck to see out of the low windows. There was another large plane, blue and white with gleaming silver wings parked inside a massive hangar a hundred yards away. On the tail section was painted a large American flag, just above the tail number 28000. The words UNITED STATES

OF AMERICA were stenciled in clear, dark letters on the white upper portion of the fuselage.

"I think it is Andrews Air Force Base," said Gideon.

A dark blue government van pulled up on the apron next to the plane. Gideon had to manually unfold his legs, and even then he walked like a stick figure once he cleared the low door on the small Air Force jet. He felt as if he was coming out of a sardine can.

Joselyn got to the bottom of the steps ahead of him. On solid ground now and rested, she became more assertive and turned to one of the agents. "Where are you taking us?"

"You'll see." He opened the sliding door of the van and motioned for them to get in.

She didn't move, and when Gideon tried to, she stopped him. "Are we in custody?"

The agents looked at her, and then glanced at each other.

From the look, it was clear they weren't sure.

"If we're under arrest I want to see a lawyer, and I want to know what we're charged with."

"Later," said the agent.

"No, now." She had been shot at and kicked, threatened with a rifle, and nearly fried by an explosion. She wasn't going to move until she got some answers.

Gideon took one look at the stern expression on the agent's face. "I think that perhaps this is not the time to stand on legal principle," he told her. He took Joselyn's arm and gently gestured toward the van.

"Where are they taking us?"

"I don't know."

"Well, I'm not going. Not until I get some answers."

"I think if you do not, they may put you in the van forcibly."

"Listen to the man," said the agent.

"I want to talk to somebody in authority," said Joselyn.

"That's where we're taking you," said the agent. "To see the man in charge."

Joselyn looked at Gideon. She wasn't happy. She folded her arms and tapped her foot, but she didn't move.

"We could always call the Dutch ambassador," said Gideon.

She didn't look at him, but the stone slowly cracked around

her lips, she laughed, and the resolve was gone. They got into the van. The agent shook his head.

It took an hour in thickening city traffic before they started to see familiar landmarks. The Lincoln Memorial, Jefferson's in the distance on the other side, and the tall obelisk of the Washington Monument. Joselyn had never been to Washington, D.C., before, and she hovered like a tourist at the darkened windows of the van as they sped past each site.

Gideon seemed to take it in stride. The adrenaline rush of the previous day left him weary, even with the fitful sleep on the plane. He was jolted into full consciousness when the van turned and pulled up to the black iron gates.

The expression on Joselyn's face said it all. "Is this what I think it is?"

Gideon didn't say a word, but he was leaning forward, looking over the front seat between the two agents. In the distance, through the black wrought iron of the southwest gate, was the gleaming oval portico of the White House with its Doric columns.

One of the agents flashed credentials at a uniformed guard in the kiosk, and they waited while a phone call was placed. Seconds later the iron gates rolled back. The van drove up West Executive Avenue and turned right, stopping in front of a basement entrance to the West Wing.

Without ceremony, the van door slid open and two men in suits looking suspiciously like Secret Service agents helped Joselyn and Gideon from the back of the van.

Neither of the agents said a word but instead led the couple past a guard. They took the first right, down a few stairs. Joselyn could smell food. When they got to the bottom she could see the White House Mess, a kind of small cafeteria.

"Wait here." One of the agents stayed with them while the other went over to a large locked door. A Marine guard in dress uniform with a side arm was stationed next to the door. The agent worked the coded keypad next to the door, opened it, and disappeared inside.

The cafeteria seemed to be bustling. Young men in rolled-up shirtsleeves and ties, and young secretaries in short skirts, hustled back and forth on the stairs, each looking as if they were on a mission from God.

The plastered walls were painted a glossy white, with Colonial pediments over the doors.

No one seemed to pay much attention to Gideon or Joselyn. She felt like an itinerant in jail togs. She fussed with her hair a bit, wishing she had a comb and mirror and a little makeup.

A few seconds later, the door to the room opened again and the agent came out. He was in the company of an older man in shirtsleeves rolled to his elbows, his tie knotted halfway down his chest, and glasses, narrow cheaters propped up on his forehead like a visor.

He took the glasses from his forehead and held them in one hand a second before he reached them.

"Ms. Cole and Mr. van Ry, I assume." He extended his hand and the first smile either of them had seen from anyone in half a day.

"My name is Sy Hirshberg."

Gideon recognized the name.

"I am the president's national security adviser. I want to thank both of you for coming."

"I didn't know we had a choice," said Joselyn.

He ignored her. "Are you hungry? Would you like something to drink?"

"I'm dying of thirst," said Joselyn.

"What would you like?"

"A club soda, if you have it."

"Done. And you, Mr. van Ry?"

"Very good. Yes. The same."

With a look from Hirshberg, the Secret Service agent was suddenly transformed into room service. "And while you're at it, see if they can put together a couple of sandwiches."

"No meat," said Joselyn as the agent turned, headed for the Mess.

"If you'll come this way," said Hirshberg. "We have a lot of questions, and not much time."

He led them back to the door with the combination on it. Hirshberg opened the door and ushered them in. It was a conference room surrounded on three sides by two small offices, computer workstations, and little warrens filled with communications equipment. The main conference area was small and gave the appearance of being cramped, every inch being employed in some functional use.

There was a map projected on a screen hanging down from one wall. It was large-scale and very familiar. It showed in detail large sections of North Puget Sound, the area embracing the San Juan Islands.

There were a series of tables arranged in a rectangle with an open area in the middle, a few men and two women sitting around it. Some of the men were in uniforms.

There was intense conversation. They were in the middle of a meeting. A few people looked up, but no one paid particular attention to Joselyn or Gideon.

Gideon immediately recognized one of the women. Sheila Johnstead was the U.S. ambassador to the United Nations.

Joselyn's eyes were fixed on the man seated at the far end of the room. She couldn't help but stare, in the dim pools of light, at the president of the United States.

He didn't smile or acknowledge their presence; in fact he barely looked at either of them. He was locked in conversation with a man seated directly in front of Joselyn with his back to her.

"I cannot emphasize how important this is," said the president.

"Sir, I can appreciate that," said the other man.

She couldn't see his face, but the voice had a familiar ring. Joselyn thought maybe it was someone she'd heard interviewed on television.

They were ushered into chairs against one wall just inside the door. The room was crowded to the point of overflowing. Young aides stood against the walls with pads and pens, periodically scribbling notes. An air of tension hung over the place as palpable as smoke.

"Sir, I realize it is important, but evidence before a grand jury, if it is to mean anything, must be maintained in confidence."

"We have a crisis here," said the president. "Don't you understand?"

"Yes, I do." It was that familiar voice. Joselyn tried to edge around to see the profile of his face, but she couldn't.

"Then help us out," said the president. "You are the only one who has reviewed all of the evidence in this case. I am asking you in my official capacity, as president, to tell me everything you know concerning your investigation of this matter.''

"With all due respect, sir," said the man, "Rule Six of the Federal Rules of Criminal Procedure makes no exception for disclosure of grand jury information pertaining to national security."

It hit Joselyn like a lightning bolt. The man sitting in front of her was Thomas McCally, the assistant U.S. attorney from Seattle, the man she'd left waiting in the courthouse the day Belden ran.

"Well, if the law doesn't provide such an exception, it should," said the president.

"That is a matter, sir, between you and Congress," said McCally.

Joselyn arched an eyebrow. McCally was clearly swimming in deep political waters.

The president flipped a pencil into the air. It landed in no-man's-land between the tables.

"He's yours," said the president. "You deal with him." He turned to Abe Charness, the attorney general, who was seated two chairs away.

Charness offered an uncomfortable smile to McCally and ran one hand through his thinning gray hair, disheveled and falling out faster by the minute. His shirt showed signs of perspiration under the arms, where it was bunched up by the thick suspenders that looped over his narrow shoulders.

He was not a big man, but Charness mustered all the authority he could in his voice. "Son, we don't have the time to go through the grand jury transcripts. We assume that if you had uncovered anything regarding the smuggling of a nuclear device into the country, you would have alerted all of the appropriate agencies, the National Security Council, and the military."

McCally nodded.

"So we assume that you did not uncover such information."

"That's correct."

"Fine. The president has a simple question. It goes to issues of policy concerning this administration. We need to know whether the name Viktor Kolikoff ever surfaced in connection with testimony by any of the witnesses in your investigation."

"That I cannot tell you," said McCally.

Charness looked at the ceiling and fumed. He did not want to get into the specifics, not in front of staffers and military brass. Members of the Cabinet knew or guessed what the problem was. The president couldn't be sure if Kolikoff's name had surfaced. If it had, and if indictments were later handed down in connection with militia activity in Washington State, and if Kolikoff was involved in brokering a weapon of mass destruction to the group, nothing the president could do would keep it under wraps.

If on the other hand Kolikoff's name hadn't come into the investigation, then a low-profile search for the bomb might be in order. If they could find it quickly and quietly, Kolikoff's connection to the device might never become public. The president's acceptance of campaign contributions would be a minor blip on the screen.

"Are you telling us that you don't know?" said Charness.

McCally said nothing.

"Are you telling us that you can't remember whether you ever heard that name in connection with the investigation, Mr. McCally?"

"I'm telling you that I will not get into the substance of grand jury testimony in a room filled with people who are not authorized to receive that information."

"Then you would be free to tell the attorney general what you know concerning this matter in private?" said the president.

McCally paused for a moment and took a deep breath. "If I were assured that it would go no farther and that the disclosure was for legitimate law enforcement purposes," said McCally. "Solely for purposes of investigation and prosecution of crimes."

The president looked at Charness and smiled. Finally they were getting somewhere. Charness could go into a closed room with McCally, get the information the president wanted, then come out, and spill his guts to the president in private.

Charness did not look happy. Clearly what the president had in mind was the commission of a felony and the use of the Justice Department to do it. He had to know where Kolikoff was in the entire scheme of things before he charted his course and decided how aggressive to be in the search for the device.

"I'm going to suggest, Mr. Charness, that you confer with Mr. McCally in private." The president nodded. "You can use one of the small conference rooms." He pointed to what looked like a closet just off the Situation Room.

McCally saw Joselyn for the first time when he got up. He swallowed hard and found it difficult to maintain eye contact. Both of them knew the government's investigation was about to be compromised, that unless Charness was made of steel, the president would vacuum him like a rug for information the second they emerged from the conference room.

Joselyn had a whole new respect for people like McCally, working in the trenches.

She leaned into Gideon's ear. "Who is this guy Kolikoff?" When she looked at him he had an enigmatic smile.

"Arms merchant," he whispered. Kolikoff's name had appeared enough times in reports from the institute in Santa Crista that he was well known in circles concerning arms control.

Joselyn looked up at him. "Nuclear?" she whispered.

Gideon held one hand just off of his lap and waffled it a bit as if to say anything was possible.

"What about this other lawyer?" said the president. "This woman, what's her name?"

"Joselyn Cole." Hirshberg spoke up.

"Yes, Cole. Has anybody heard from her?"

"She's here, Mr. President."

"Oh." Suddenly the president perked up, looking around the room for a female in a business suit. "Where?"

Joselyn tentatively raised her hand. After seeing what happened to McCally, she wasn't sure she wanted to do this.

"Oh." He looked at the way she was dressed, the bruises on her face, then whispered to a man at his right shoulder, who passed him several sheets of paper and a small box. The president listened and nodded while he looked at Joselyn, the way people do when you know they're talking about you.

The president's brows arched and his forehead furrowed, some hint of surprise registering in his expression as he listened to the quick briefing. The aide straightened up, and the president squared his chair to the table again.

"Well, young lady, you've had a very harrowing couple of days. Please move up to the table. Gentlemen, make room for her. Find her a seat."

The waters parted. Suddenly she found herself headed for McCally's vacant chair. She balked and wouldn't go without Gideon.

"Is that your friend?" said the president.

"This is Gideon van Ry," said Joselyn. "He's the reason I'm here. Otherwise I would be dead."

"Please come forward. Mr. van Ry. You, too."

One of the men seated at the table got up and gave Gideon his chair. They moved forward into the chairs and sat down at the table.

"I trust you both understand the seriousness of the situation?" said Hirshberg.

"I think so," said Joselyn. "We don't know everything."

"I dare say you probably know a damn sight more than we do," said the president. He smiled, and there was some light banter around the table.

"That's why you're here. We need your help. We understand, Ms. Cole, that you represented this man, Dean Belden, before the grand jury in Seattle," said the president.

"If that was his real name," said Joselyn. "It appears he told me a good many things that were not true."

"I'm told that you believed he was dead, killed in a plane crash."

"That's correct."

"It seems that both you and the U.S. attorney were taken in by this."

"Yes."

"But he wasn't killed?" said the president.

"No. Somehow he managed to stage his death for my benefit, so that I would tell the authorities. You see he used me to identify him. He wanted to be officially dead, so that the government would stop looking for him. It was the only way he could finish whatever it was he was doing."

"And what was that?" said Hirshberg.

"I'm not exactly sure. He tried to kill me twice, the first time, the night that his plane crashed. I'm certain now that he tried to push my car, with me in it, off of a state ferry into Puget Sound."

"And the second time?" said Hirshberg.

"On the island," said Joselyn. "He left orders for me to be killed. The only reason I'm alive is that a Navy diver saved my life, and he paid with his own. A good many men died on that island. I saw the bodies."

"Yes. I know." The president seemed very uncomfortable with the thought. "These people. The people on that island. They may have a nuclear device. You understand that?"

She nodded.

"Do you have any idea where it is?"

"No."

The president looked at Gideon, who shook his head.

"You, sir. You're with the Institute Against Mass Destruction in California?"

"That is correct, Mr. President."

"I want to thank you for your help. We have been in touch with the director at your institute. He has been exceedingly helpful, very cooperative. We're aware of your travels in the former Soviet Union and of the information you turned up there. That was exceedingly useful, and we are all very thankful."

"Not useful enough, Mr. President."

The president looked at him as if he didn't understand.

"To keep the device out of your country," said Gideon.

"Oh, yes. Indeed."

Hirshberg interrupted. "Ms. Cole, you were on the island with these men. They took you captive, is that correct?"

"Yes."

"While you were there, did you hear anything?"

"I saw Belden. He came into the room where I was being held. I believe he went by another name as well."

"Yes?"

"Thorn. The men on the island referred to him as Thorn."

Notes were being scrawled on pads around the table.

"He seemed to be in charge," said Joselyn.

"We're trying to identify the bodies on the island now," said Hirshberg, "to see if he's among them."

"Don't waste your time," said Joselyn. "You won't find him there. He left the island with another man before the raid."

Joselyn's words inspired a flurry of eye contact among the

men around the table, along with more intense note-taking.

"We have a picture of the man we believe you call Belden," said the president. "Would you look at it for us and identify him?"

Joselyn nodded and an aide handed her a file with the photo in it. She opened it and looked.

"That's him."

"Good. Send that photo out to all state and federal law enforcement agencies," said the president. "Say that he is wanted for . . ." He looked down the table at the attorney general's empty chair. One of his assistants stepped up from against the wall, looked at the president quizzically, and said: "Kidnapping, murder of a federal officer, assault on federal officers."

"That's enough," said the president. "Let's not put anything in there on the nuclear device. At least not for now. We don't want to start a panic."

"Be sure and let them know he's extremely dangerous," said Hirshberg. "And if state or local authorities see him, no attempt should be made to take him. They should call the FBI immediately."

"Good," said the president. He turned back to Joselyn. "You say that he left the island with another man. Can you describe this man?"

Joselyn thought for a moment. "He was short, maybe five-foot-five, five-six. Thinning hair, brown, dark eyes, dark complexion. A kind of sad face."

"Could you help the FBI artists prepare a computer composite of the man?" This question came from an intense-looking man along the right side of the table.

"I could try."

"You say he was dark," said Hirshberg. "Could he have been a foreign national?"

"He didn't speak with any apparent accent."

"You heard him speak?" said the president.

"A few words. They were in a hurry. He came to the door of the room where I was and told Belden it was time to leave. That's all I heard."

"You were bound, gagged?" asked one of the other men.

"Tied up, on a bed. Belden had torn the tape from my mouth. He was questioning me."

"What did he want to know?"

"He wanted to know what I had said to the authorities after the plane crash. Who Mr. van Ry was. They had seen him down on the dock, by the boats at Friday Harbor the night I was taken. They thought he might be with the government."

"What did you tell him?"

"Nothing. There was nothing I could tell him. I didn't know anything. He already knew about my clients, the fishermen who had become ill. We thought it was an industrial injury of some kind."

"And what was it?" asked Hirshberg.

"Radiation poisoning," said Gideon. "The military confirmed that the docks and several of the boats were contaminated."

"How?" said the president.

"The device. The outer casing split open. The plutonium core somehow got loose on the deck during a storm. It abraded."

"What's that?" said Hirshberg.

"Plutonium is very soft," said Gideon. "If it is rubbed on a rough surface, it will turn to dust. If that gets into the lungs, it is usually deadly. But I do not think that was the only problem here. There was too much contamination on the boat that I found. I believe there was something else."

"What?" said the president.

"I believe that whoever engineered the device had in mind something particularly deadly. I believe they have combined the nuclear device with a quantity of cesium-137."

"Explain," said Hirshberg.

"Cesium is a particularly toxic material. A by-product in the refinement of plutonium. It emits very strong gamma radiation. It must be carefully handled in order to shield anyone from uncontrolled exposure. At room temperature it is a liquid, but it reacts violently to contact with other materials. It is soluble in water and a big worry for those who must dispose of it."

"Why would they be bringing what is basically a nuclear waste product on the boat?" said one of the military men.

"As insurance," said Gideon. "In case the device itself failed to reach critical mass, in which case there would be no nuclear chain reaction. Then at least the conventional explosive around the core of the device would vaporize the cesium, releasing it into the atmosphere. In sufficient quantities, it is very deadly. Carried on the wind, it would have killed thousands, perhaps tens of thousands.''

"If nothing else," said one of the other military men, "it would have been a hell of a message from Saddam or Muammar.''

"If that's who really is behind this," said Hirshberg.

"I believe there was a quantity of cesium on that boat, and that some of it spilled." Gideon ignored their obsession with fixing blame. The nuclear genie was coming home to roost.

"So essentially we have a dirty bomb?" said one of the military men.

"No," said Gideon. "A dirty bomb relies solely on nuclear fallout for its destructive force. I believe this is a nuclear device with cesium to make it more deadly. Wherever it is detonated, that place will become a toxic wasteland and deadly for decades.''

There was silence around the table, deep lines of concern etched in the president's face.

"It is the only thing that can explain the levels of contamination on that boat," said Gideon.

"How far would this fallout travel?"

"It would depend on the wind," said Gideon. "Whether there was rain.''

"Where is this boat now?" asked the president. "The boat that was contaminated.''

"It has been towed out to sea, along with several of the other fishing boats." One of the military men answered the question. "They are decontaminating the dock. They may have to remove part of it.''

"Have they analyzed what was on that boat?" said the president.

"I don't know," said the man in the uniform.

"Well, find out.''

"Ms. Cole. Did the men on the island ask you any other questions?"

She shook her head slowly. "Not that I can remember.''

"Do you know how Belden and the other man left the island?"

She shook her head and thought for a moment. "It was a

boat. I think the other man said something about a boat.'' She couldn't remember now whether she'd heard it or simply assumed it.

"Did you hear a boat leaving?"

She shook her head.

"Did they say anything about a destination?" asked Hirshberg.

She thought again. "No. Just that time was getting short. That they had to leave."

"Anything else? Any other names?" said Hirshberg. Joselyn searched her memory, racked her brain. "No. But the two men on the porch. They mentioned names."

"What men?" said the president.

"I don't know. I could only hear their voices, outside when the shooting started. They mentioned a name." She thought for a second. "Oliver. Edgar." She looked down at the tabletop. "Oscar." Suddenly she looked up. "That was it. Oscar. I remember because they said he'd left the island earlier that morning as well."

"With Belden and the other man?" said the president.

"I don't think so." Suddenly a look of revelation came over her face. "Oh, my God."

"What is it?" said the president.

"They were talking about the bomb," said Joselyn.

"What? Where?" said the president.

"The two men. They were out on the porch. There was a lot of confusion. Shooting. They had a boat tied up in a cove somewhere on the island. They were talking about escaping. It's how I heard about the bunkers' being wired for explosives. They said Thorn had ordered it done. They mentioned Oscar, said he had left that morning and that they were supposed to get off the island if anything happened. The two men. They were supposed to go to a truck. And get the thing moving. Those were their words."

"Does that island have ferry service for vehicles?" said Hirshberg. He looked at the people around the table. They were all scratching their heads and looking at one another.

"It did not." The voice that spoke up was Gideon's.

"How do you know?"

"I checked before I flew out of Friday Harbor on the Marine helicopter. I was supposed to help search for the device.

I did not want that weapon placed on a car-carrying ferry in the sound as we approached. There was no public ferry service to the island."

"Then it was never there," said the president.

"No," said Gideon.

"The Coast Guard threw a blockade around the island," said Hirshberg. "There's no way they could have gotten it off once the assault started."

"Unless the man Belden took it out on the boat with him."

"No. Not on a small boat," said Hirshberg. "Satellite surveillance would have picked up a vessel that big coming from the island. Especially if it was on a truck."

"That leaves one other matter," said the president. He opened the small box that had been handed to him by the aide when he first called Joselyn's name. He lifted the top and poured the contents out onto the table.

Gideon immediately recognized the wristwatch as his. Joselyn's was next to it. Everything from the pockets of their clothing, including wallets, scraps of paper, and change, was lying on the table. Someone had gone through their wallets: driver's licenses and credit cards landed on the table in a small heap.

"We have checked everything," said Hirshberg. He was speaking to the president. "There are only a few items that we have questions about. I hope you understand." He looked at Joselyn and Gideon.

Joselyn was angry. The authorities had gone through their clothing at the air station on Whidbey Island, searching through their wallets and pockets for information.

"It would have been nice if you asked," said Joselyn.

"There was no time," said Hirshberg.

"There was what, four hours on an airplane crossing the country?" she told him.

"Nonetheless, we have a few questions," he said. "These notes, the name Grigori Chenko in your wallet, Mr. van Ry. What is it?"

"Ah. Notes I took at Sverdlovsk, Russia."

"Ah yes. The information I believe came to us from the institute?" Hirshberg was checking with one of his assistants who nodded.

"Ms. Cole. These phone numbers on a note from your wallet."

"Those are friends down in California."

"I see. We can check them out." He handed the note to one of his assistants. He didn't believe her. She was now burning at the tips of her ears.

"And this?"

She looked at what he was holding in his hand but couldn't make it out."

"It's a business card," said Hirshberg. "Port-a-John Sanitation Service, Oak Harbor, Washington."

He drew a blank stare from her. Then suddenly she remembered. The business card that Belden had left on the bedside table. The one she picked up as the Navy SEAL tried to get her out of the room.

"I forgot all about it," she said. "Belden left it behind, in the room."

THIRTY

The FBI had the business card from the pocket of Joselyn's blouse for nearly seven hours by the time she reached Washington, D.C. They wasted no time checking into it as a lead.

Two agents drove to the small town of Oak Harbor on Whidbey Island, only a short distance from the base. They found the owner of Port-a-John Sanitation Service. The man was able to identify Belden from a photograph as one of several men at a site near Deer Harbor on Orcas Island. The man had rented them a portable toilet and delivered it, the kind usually used at construction sites and outdoor events.

"The reason I remember is 'cuz they were a little strange."

"In what way?" said one of the agents.

"There was a building there. You know. One of those fabricated metal jobs over a concrete floor. It was all closed up. When they heard me drive up, one of them came out through a side door and told me where to set the unit down.

"When I finished, I realized I'd forgotten to have him sign the paperwork. So I went in the door. Knocked on it, but nobody answered. I guess they didn't hear me. So I let myself in. I thought they were gonna kill me."

"Why?"

"I don't know. But two of 'em grabbed me and forced me

back out the door. Roughed me up. I had a good mind to put the unit back on the truck and take it away.''

"Could you see what was inside the building?''

The guy made a face, like "not much." "Some tools. A cutting torch. They pushed me outside real quick. They signed the papers, and I got the hell outta there. These guys were on the thin edge. You know what I mean? Why are you interested in them?''

The agent ignored the question. "Could you see what they were working on?''

"Oh, yeah. It was a truck. They were welding something on the back of it."

"What kind of truck?''

"Search me. I was busy being pushed out the door. But it looked like a tank."

"You mean an armored tank?''

"No. Like a small tank truck, the kind they use to haul chemicals. Like I say, I damn near put the john back on my truck and left. Not that they would have missed it.''

"What do you mean?''

"There was a perfectly good bathroom in the building. It was right by the door. I heard it flush when I was outside.''

DEER HARBOR, ORCAS ISLAND, WA

A score of high-powered rifles with expert marksmen from the Skagit County Violent Crimes Task Force, along with FBI agents and sheriff's deputies from Island Country, surrounded the place.

It was a fabricated metal building just as the man had described. Once they were set up with positions for covering fire, the tactical squad moved in. They hit the side door with a battering ram. The metal door took two shots before it gave, and officers with M-16s went inside.

They were there less than a minute before one of them came back to the door and gave them the all-clear sign. Handheld radios on secure frequencies announced that it was secure, that nobody was inside.

The FBI agents in suits moved in. The tac-squad started to cordon off the building and the driveway around it with yellow crime scene tape.

·

The building was deserted. There were a few tools scattered around on the concrete floor, what looked like an expensive portable torch and some wrenches. There was a makeshift bench set up near the center of the floor.

They were inside only long enough to take some quick pictures and get a reading on a Geiger counter. Radiation levels were high.

"I want everybody out now," said one of the agents. "Call the NEST team. Tell them we need them over here now."

The men started to move out. One of the agents kicked something with his foot, and it slid across the concrete floor.

It was a metal sign, the kind with magnets on the back used to display the name of a business on the door of a vehicle. He walked over and slipped the blade of a small penknife under the face of the sign and flipped it over so that it was faceup. On the other side was the name:

A-ONE SEPTIC
DENVER, COLORADO
LUCK. #CZ 14869

WASHINGTON, DC

The Justice Department was picking up the tab for accommodations, at least until they were released. Gideon and Joselyn were driven to the Hay-Adams Hotel on Sixteenth Street, not far from the White House. They were given fresh overalls, this time with "FBI" printed on the back, clean underwear, toothbrushes, a few toiletries, and adjoining rooms with two agents camped outside.

"For house arrest, it isn't bad," said Joselyn. She grabbed the robe from the back of the bathroom door as she talked to Gideon through the partially closed adjoining door to his room.

"I'm going to take a shower. Change my jailhouse jumpsuit. The sooner I get out of here, the better."

"Don't you like the White House?" said Gideon.

"The place is fine. I can't say as much for the people in it," said Joselyn. "That's why I need a shower."

She disappeared into the bathroom, dropped her clothes on the floor, turned up the hot water, and allowed it run over her body, like a waterfall.

With her eyes closed, the pelting beads of water hitting her bruised face, the events of the past twenty-four hours played themselves back in her mind like a bad dream. She couldn't get the dead Navy diver out of her thoughts. Five minutes under the spray, and she began to shake and cry uncontrollably.

The reality of what had happened suddenly hit home. It came with a force and permanence that Joselyn never expected. It wasn't a film or make-believe. A young man with his entire life in front of him had died before her eyes. His wife, if he had one, would never feel his arms around her again. His mother and father would in this world never set eyes on him. She did not want to think about whether the man had children. In less time than it took to blink, his life had been snuffed out by a bullet as he tried to save hers. She was crying not only grief but guilt. She was alive, and he was dead. If she hadn't been there, he might never have entered the building. He might still be alive.

The water poured down her body, mixed with her tears until she was drained. Exhausted, she leaned against the tile wall, steadied herself, and turned off the water.

Quickly she toweled herself dry, put on the clean underwear, a T-shirt in place of a bra, and the terry-cloth robe. She wrapped her hair in the towel turban-style and walked back out into the bedroom.

"How was it?" It was Gideon. He was standing in the door between their rooms.

"Great. I didn't realize how tired I was."

"Your eyes. They are very red."

"Oh." She took the pointed end of the towel that hung down from her head and wiped them. "I got soap in them."

"Ah. I see." Gideon could tell she had been crying. "Are you hungry?"

"Not really."

"We could raid the mini-bar," he said.

"What's in there?"

"Let's see." He took the key from the top of the bar and opened it. "We have peanuts, M&Ms, a chocolate bar."

"Sounds awful."

"How about something to drown your pain?" When he

stood up he was holding three tiny bottles with seals around their caps.''

''Now that sounds good.''

''Vodka, whiskey, or scotch?''

''Scotch. With a little soda if there's any in there.''

''Just the thing.'' He came up with a can of club soda.

''If we were in Amsterdam, I would give you something a little more potent. Something from one of the *brown cafés*.''

''What's that?''

He thought for a moment, while he popped the can and opened the bottle.

''I suppose you would call it a pub, or tavern, maybe a coffee-house. All three. They are very old. Some of them have been open for hundreds of years. You can find them on every street in the old part of town. And their walls on the inside are very brown. They are never cleaned or painted. They serve wonderful blends of coffee—along with mind-altering drugs.''

She looked at him and laughed.

''What's the matter, you don't believe me?''

''No. I believe you. It's just that I can't see you doing drugs.''

''It's the Dutch national pastime,'' said Gideon. ''By American standards, we are a sinful people. Very permissive. At least in Amsterdam. Drugs are considered a recreational necessity.''

''Try selling that one to the group we met with today,'' said Joselyn.

''Free sex is regarded as a constitutional right.''

''We are different,'' said Joselyn. ''Over here it's just one of the perks of public office.''

''Aw, empty.'' Gideon picked up the ice bucket, opened the door to the room, and stuck his head out.

''Excuse me, gentlemen.''

One of the agents came to the door.

''I think the ice machine is on the next floor. We are getting drunk. Would you mind?'' He handed the bucket to the FBI agent and closed the door.

He turned, folded his arms, and leaned against the door. ''Well. We have some time to kill. What shall we do?''

''I'm sorry, but I'm a little too tired. You'll have to exercise your constitutional rights with someone else tonight.''

Gideon laughed and blushed a little.

"I could mine your thoughts," said Gideon.

"You mean pick my brain?"

"Yes."

"That would be poor pickings indeed, at least tonight."

"You are not convinced that Denver is the target?"

The call from the FBI at Deer Harbor had come in when they were in the White House.

"It was that obvious?" said Joselyn.

"Well, when you told the president that he had his head wedged securely up his rectum . . ."

"I never said that."

"No. But the implication was quite clear."

"Well, if the hat fits," said Joselyn.

"How can you be so sure?"

"Because the Belden I knew is not a man to make mistakes. Not like that. A sign left on the floor?"

"As I recall, Denver was the scene of a major trial for domestic terrorism."

"Very convenient," said Joselyn. "I'm sure Belden thought of that. In the meantime, the FBI spends its time combing highways that cover half of the western United States, searching for a truck that may or may not exist."

"Ah. But the witness they talked to saw the truck."

"But did he see what was in it?" said Joselyn.

"A septic truck would be a perfect cover. Who is going to want to search it?" said Gideon. "And the tank on the back can be lined with lead. You are not going to pick up any emissions from the device, even if you run it through a portal monitor."

"Maybe," said Joselyn. "But if you want to know what I think."

"I do," said Gideon.

"I think Belden's not that stupid. I don't think he's the kind of man that makes that many mistakes. First the business card on the table, then the sign in the garage. Why did he leave them?"

"Maybe they meant nothing. Maybe they were in a hurry."

"No. He took everything out of his pocket because he wasn't comfortable sitting there slapping the hell out of me on that bed. He put it all on the side table, and when he was finished he carefully picked everything up, except the business card. He leaves that there.''

"He was finished with it," said Gideon.

"He was finished with me, but he wasn't gonna leave me lying around."

"You could identify him."

"So could the man who rented him that portable john."

Gideon thought for a moment. She had a point.

"Think about it. According to the agents, this guy drives up to the building and they immediately come outside. They don't stay with him and keep an eye on him. They don't ask if he has a receipt or anything to be signed. They tell him where to put it and then they go back inside. When he knocks, they don't answer. But when he opens the door, they allow him to come inside just long enough to see the truck before they make a big scene and throw him outside."

"What are you saying?"

"I'm saying that Belden wanted him to see that truck. The same way he wanted me to see his plane go up in smoke. To serve a purpose. Our port-a-john salesman just did. He has the federal government looking in all the wrong places."

"You have a very devious mind," said Gideon. "Are you always this paranoid?"

"Only after I've been pushed off a ferry, kidnapped, beaten, and shot at."

"Are you sure it wasn't simply because the president dismissed your views about Mr. Belden and his plans?"

"I grant you the president doesn't have a very high opinion of women or their views." They wouldn't listen to her, and she was angry. They weren't interested in her judgment, only the information she could give them. But she had dealt with Belden firsthand, the only one in the room with that experience. Joselyn was convinced that she was right.

There was a knock at the door. Gideon opened it.

"Thank you." He took the ice bucket from the agent, closed the door, and walked over to finish mixing the drinks. He handed Joselyn hers.

"Thanks." She sipped slowly from the plastic glass.

"It doesn't matter anyway," said Joselyn. "Tomorrow I'm outta here. It's their problem."

Gideon arched his eyebrows. "There's a nuclear bomb loose in your country and you don't care?"

"You haven't heard. Apathy in America is chic. As long as they don't set the thing off under my bed, it's none of my business."

"You really believe that?"

"Why not?"

"I don't think you do."

"What makes you think so?"

"Because I saw the way you looked when you talked about that sailor. Tonight when you told them how he died. I think it is easy to be apathetic when we think about death in the abstract. But a two-kiloton nuclear weapon is no abstraction. It would kill thousands of people. It would make what happened on that island seem tame. Entire families would cease to exist. They would die horrible deaths."

Gideon took a drink from his glass, swallowed it, and then chewed on a small sliver of ice.

"You know," he said. "There were people in Hiroshima whose shadows were printed by the blast on the concrete walls of buildings and pavement. These shadows can still be seen. Some of the bodies that made them were never found. It was as if they never existed. There are those who have seen these shadows scorched on the hard ground, to whom they are mere curiosities of history—images of a time that has passed. If that is all they have come to be, then they are indeed the angels of apathy."

THIRTY-ONE

SEATTLE, WA

Oscar Chaney pulled to the curb in a loading zone and turned off the diesel engine and the headlights. He sat quietly behind the wheel for almost a minute, checking the rearview mirror to make sure no late-night strollers or homeless vagabonds were wandering in the area.

It was now after midnight. A solitary street sweeper, its emergency light dominating the deserted lanes, was doing doughnuts down on Fifth Street cleaning the pavement, while the stoplights flashed red at the intersection.

Chaney could see the federal courthouse two blocks away. Its five-story block monolith was dimly lit by security lights, as janitors finished up their nightly chores.

With gloved hands, Chaney checked the passenger door on the truck to make sure it was locked, then opened the driver's door and stepped down onto the running board and from there to the curb. He checked the street one more time. The last thing he wanted was someone who might be able to link him to the truck.

He checked his watch. The meter maids wouldn't start patrolling the streets until just before rush hour. A large truck in a traffic lane, even at a loading zone, would be an item to draw their attention. Chaney wanted to make sure that they didn't simply tow it away to the city's impound yard.

He reached behind the seat and grabbed the two magnetic signs. They were identical to the one he'd left on the floor of the garage at Deer Harbor. The only difference is that these identified A-One Septic as being located in Bellevue, Washington. He pushed the locking button down on the driver's door and closed it, then placed one of the magnetized signs on the door. He went around the truck and put the other sign on the passenger door.

Chaney already knew that the authorities had raided the empty garage. One of his crew had stayed behind to observe and report on intelligence.

He knew that the minute the meter maids reported the vehicle for towing, police computers would go nuts. They would match the name on the truck with the name on the sign from the garage. The Feds would stop wasting their time and resources searching the highways between Washington State and Colorado, and turn their attention instead to Seattle. They would waste several more hours clearing the area and bringing in experts to check for radiation before they took the first tentative steps to disarm the device. It would be mid-afternoon on the west coast before they realized their mistake.

Chaney crossed the street and headed down toward the corner. He walked two blocks and allowed at least four cabs to pass, before raising his hand to flag one down. When it pulled over, he opened the door, slid into the back seat, and told the driver: "Sea-Tac Airport."

HAY-ADAMS HOTEL, WASHINGTON, DC

Joselyn heard a light rap on the door. It sounded distant and roused her only slightly from slumber, so that the voices of the men talking seemed like a dream, laid over sleep. She rolled over on the bed in the dark hotel room and looked at the illuminated digital clock on the nightstand. It was after ten. She assumed it was morning, though with the heavy drapes pulled she couldn't be sure.

She sat up abruptly in the bed, suddenly concerned that she might have slept away the day. She stumbled to the window with the comforter from the bed wrapped around her body and pulled back the heavy drapes. The brilliant sunlight blinded her, forcing her to turn her back and cover her eyes.

She had a massive headache and wondered if there was any aspirin in the small bag of toiletries the agents had given her the night before. Joselyn had killed all four of the tiny bottles of scotch from the mini-bars in both rooms. She drew the line at the whiskey and left the vodka for Gideon. She fumbled through the bag in the bathroom and found nothing that would take the edge off her head. She was headed to the mini-bar to see if there was anything there when Gideon came through the adjoining door.

"I thought I heard you moving around. Did they wake you up?"

"Who?"

"The agents at the door."

"That's who it was?"

"Yes. They are leaving. I've got your wallet, cash, and credit cards, along with my own, and the keys that were in your pocket."

"Then we're free to go?"

"No. They have asked us to remain in town until further word, in case they have more questions. But it appears that they believe everything you told them," said Gideon. "More important, they have found the truck."

Joselyn was on her hands and knees rummaging through the mini-bar on her quest for aspirin, the thick comforter wrapped around her like a bearskin. She turned and looked up at him, the obvious question written on her face.

"They found it in Seattle," said Gideon.

"Seattle?" Joselyn was surprised. "The bomb?"

"They are working on it now. The agents didn't have many details or if they did they weren't talking. It appears the authorities got some readings off the vehicle. High gamma radiation. Beyond that, they don't know anything more. It looks like you were wrong," said Gideon.

"Do you have any aspirin?" she ignored him.

"No. But I can run down to the package shop in the lobby and buy some."

She shifted the bed cover around her, adjusting it from under where she sat. "While you're at it, get me some new clothes and a bra and some makeup."

"We can go shopping after," said Gideon. He could tell

that her mind was on other things. "I wonder why they would go to all of that trouble to drive the device down to Seattle?"

She looked at him and nodded from sleepy eyebrows. "I just hope the people across the street are wondering the same thing."

SITUATION ROOM, THE WHITE HOUSE

There was an air of celebration in the Situation Room when the president came through the door, and even some brief applause.

"Let's not get carried away," said the president. "We still have a lot of work to do. What have we heard from the emergency team on site?"

"They have relatively high gamma readings but nothing above safe tolerances, which would be injurious to passers-by, people who came in contact with the truck. They think the device is shielded, probably inside a lead container in the tank."

"Do they have any estimates on how long it may take to defuse it?"

"They haven't actually gotten to the bomb itself. Right now they're trying to clear the area."

"They haven't made a public announcement?" said the president.

"No. No. We are telling the public that we have a gas leak in one of the major mains in the area. We're evacuating eight square blocks. It's gonna take time. We've shut down I-Five at the interchange and we've ordered all civilian aircraft out of the area."

"Good," said the president. "We don't need any pain-in-the-ass television crews in choppers over that truck."

The president didn't leave the doorway to the room but stood against the closed door, a sign that he wasn't going to be there long.

"Mr. President, I'd like to talk to you in private if I could." Sy Hirshberg had been trying to get into the Oval Office all morning. The president had been taking written communiqués from Seattle all morning from military aides but, other than that, had been incommunicado. He had been locked up, in preparation for the State of the Union that evening. There had been a constant shuffle of Cabinet secretaries into the Oval Office all morning, each trying to get last-minute items into the president's speech or to make sure that nothing from their A-list agendas had been taken out.

"Can this wait, Sy?"

"I believe it is important, Mr. President."

"Is there something having to do with the current situation I don't know?"

"No," said Hirshberg. "But something that we should talk about."

The president looked at his watch. "I'm sorry, but it's gonna have to wait for now. I've got at least two more meetings. These fanatics with their bomb could have waited a few days. It would have been a great deal easier to deal with. Education is due in my office now. The staff is waiting to put the final touches on the speech. And I need at least two hours to go over the final draft."

He looked at his watch. "I'll have some time around four-forty." Hirshberg knew that he would get the president's divided attention at best. "I'm only gonna have about five minutes," he told him.

Hirshberg nodded. He suspected that given the momentum of events, what he had to say to the president was likely to fall on deaf ears.

THIRTY-TWO

THE NATIONAL MALL, WASHINGTON, DC

Scott Taggart sat on a bench and watched as young people jogged along the broad gravel path that looped around the National Mall. Behind him was the Hirshhorn Museum and beyond that, across the curving street, was the red sandstone castle, the headquarters of the Smithsonian.

Its myriad museums, like copies of the acropolis spread out in every direction. At one end, sealing off the Mall, was the U.S. Capitol Building, with its imposing dome.

Less than a mile away, to the west, and across the Ellipse, was the White House.

Taggart put down the newspaper and checked his watch. The museum had been open for a little more than an hour. He got up from the bench, pulled a pair of heavy leather gloves from his pocket and put them on, then put his gloved hands into the pockets of the heavy navy pea coat. He started to walk in the direction of the Capitol. He crossed Jefferson Drive at Seventh Street and walked one block to Independence Avenue, where he turned left. Halfway down the block, he climbed the stairs in front of the massive building with its two-story glass front and followed a line of schoolchildren on a field trip into the National Air and Space Museum.

Directly in front of him was a large information desk, and

behind that, in the distance, a display entitled "Milestones of Flight."

For a weekday in the middle of winter, the place was crowded. The usual tours of children mingled with the retired and the growing number who took vacations in the off-season.

To the right, Space Hall was cordoned off in preparation for the party that night. Tables had already been set up and a raised dais was in the process of being erected.

Over Taggart's shoulder was the Wright Brothers plane from Kitty Hawk, and just beyond it was the *Spirit of St. Louis*, hanging from wires in the ceiling.

But today Taggart wasn't interested in history. The thought that preoccupied him at the moment was of a massive building three hundred yards to the north and a little west, well within the zone of maximum destruction. The offices of the Internal Revenue Service were across the Mall, wedged in behind the Museum of Natural History and the headquarters of the Justice Department. Within hours, all of these would take on the appearance of the burned-out concrete remnants of Hiroshima and Nagasaki after the blasts.

Taggart convinced himself that he harbored no ill will against the people who worked in these buildings but rather against the institutions themselves. It was the reason why the cesium was so important. Computer records and documents for every agency in the federal government would be instantly transformed into nuclear waste. There was no more effective way to kill the beast than to destroy the information that fed it.

The government was entrenched behind a Constitution that could not be amended by the people and that the politicians used at every turn to increase their own power. It could only be interpreted and constrained by judges who shared in the federal spoils system that was now expanding faster than the universe. The government grew like a tumor, engulfing everything in its path.

In Taggart's mind, America had reached the end of the line. It had killed Kirsten and given rise to a perpetual political class that was arrogant in its views and brazen in its corruption—a political aristocracy that displayed an indifference and contempt toward the public that was stunning. Now they would pay the price.

At the main concourse, behind the information desk, Taggart stopped for a moment and took a small vial from his inside coat pocket. Fumbling with his gloved hands, he removed a small capsule from the vial and placed it inside his mouth, between the cheek and gum. He threw the vial in a trash can, then turned to his left and walked past the history of "Early Flight" and "Jet Aviation."

He strode with a purpose through the thronged gallery, passing the ghosts of another era—the airships that carried America to world power. They were old now and obsolete, like the generation that made them and the men who flew them, symbols of past glory and honor that no longer had a place in America. They and he were irrelevant to the corrupt politicians who took money from foreign countries that were our enemies.

Taggart's mind raced as he walked, his hands plunged deep into the pockets of his coat. He walked with purpose, looking through people as if they weren't there. His focus was centered on the object in the far corner, on the north side the building, toward the Mall.

There were only a handful of tourists and sightseers gathered beneath the gleaming sheets of metal with their aviation rivets and the number "82" stenciled just under the huge nose canopy.

Like a laser, Taggart's concentration was fastened on the cylindrical object beneath the mammoth airframe near the open bomb bay.

Through the thickness of the gloves, he felt deep down in his pocket for the glass bottle, the one that Thorn had left for him in the locker at the Denver airport.

The bottle contained hydrochloric acid, with a dye capable of etching metal and staining it a blood-red color.

Taggart edged his way toward the barricade beneath the huge fuselage. He stopped and looked around to make sure that no one was likely to get in his way. Then without hesitation he stepped over the metal railing.

One of the guards, forty feet away, saw him. He started to react, but it was too late.

Taggart closed the distance quickly to the green metal cylinder under the fuselage, then pulled his hand from his pocket and flung the bottle at the olive-drab cylinder.

The glass shattered against the sheet-metal casing, exploding in a profusion of blood-red dye that covered the side of the cylinder and ran down onto the floor. Taggart covered his face to escape the vapors rising as the acid ate into the metal.

"America is a nuclear murderer!" Taggart shouted at the top of his lungs as tourists retreated from the airplane and guards moved in. They watched his hands for signs of a weapon but saw none.

The acid from the bottle was beginning to eat a small hole in the side of the metal display.

Taggart continued to shout. "America is a nuclear killer."

He lashed out with his foot, kicking the metal cylinder, and smeared the dye with his gloved hands.

Though seemingly hysterical, he possessed the presence of mind to strip the gloves from his hands before the acid could penetrate and dropped them onto the floor.

Before he could kick the metal side of the cylinder again, two of the security guards were on him. They wrestled him out beyond the barricade and within seconds managed to cuff his hands behind his back.

Before the guards could even lead him away, the staff of the museum had moved in to assess the damage. The gleaming fuselage, perhaps the most significant icon of the age of air power, was untouched. But the acid on the metal cylinder beneath it continued to send off noxious vapors.

Quickly two maintenance men bent low under the fuselage and pushed with their hands against the tail fin. Using the rectangular wheeled dolly that was part of the display and all of their strength, they maneuvered the green metal casing out from under the giant body of the *Enola Gay*. They wheeled the dolly toward the open door at the rear shop entrance to the museum and watched as the acid ate and etched the metal of the faithfully authentic replica of "Little Boy": the atomic bomb dropped on Hiroshima.

OVAL OFFICE, THE WHITE HOUSE

The president looked up from the thick sheaf of papers spread out before him on the desk. He was crossing out words and lines and inserting others with a pencil. Sy Hirshberg was standing in the open door to the Oval Office.

It was nearly five o'clock in the afternoon. "What is it, Sy? I don't have much time." The president was only four hours from the State of the Union address, and butterflies were beginning to gather in his stomach.

"Anything new from Seattle?" he asked.

"Not yet. They're trying to figure out how to get into the tank without applying heat to cut the metal. They've tried X rays to see inside, but there's a lead shield."

"Can't they just move the damn thing? Tow it onto a boat and take it out into the ocean."

"They're concerned that it might be booby-trapped."

The president took a deep breath and looked at the ceiling. "How in the hell am I supposed to go before two hundred million people and talk about the state of the nation while on the other coast we have men trying to disarm a nuclear bomb?"

"That's why I wanted to talk to you, Mr. President."

The president looked at Hirshberg.

"I think you should cancel the speech."

"What?"

"Just postpone it, Mr. President."

"What the hell. I can't do that. Not now. It's too late. We've given embargoed copies of the speech to the press. Do you have any idea what they would say if we canceled it. They'd want to know why."

"Maybe we should tell them."

"No!" The president was adamant. He swiveled around in his chair, so that Hirshberg was presented with the high leather back.

"There's no reason to cancel," he told Hirshberg. "If that bomb is safely disarmed, why should we needlessly alarm the public? And if it's not, canceling the speech isn't going to do a damn bit of good."

"And if it goes off during the speech, Mr. President? What then?"

"At least the president will be seen as engaged in the country's business, even in the face of a crisis," said the president.

"There is another possibility," said Hirshberg. "Much more serious."

"What's that?"

"That the device isn't in Seattle."

The president wheeled around in his chair to face him again. "What are you talking about? They found the truck."

"Yes. But they haven't gotten inside of it."

"They have radiation readings."

"That's true. But that doesn't necessarily mean that the device is inside. Remember, Mr. President, that there were much higher radiation readings on those fishing boats, the ones the Navy hauled out of Friday Harbor and sent to the bottom in the North Pacific. It could mean that the truck was used to transport the bomb. It is possible that the device could have been removed before the truck was ever driven to Seattle."

"What are you saying?"

"That the truck could be a decoy, Mr. President."

"Bullshit," said the president. "We have the device, and you know it. And if your people were smart they'd get it the hell out of that city before we have an accident."

"An accident?" said Hirshberg. "This is no accident. They are people bent on mass carnage. If there is a chain reaction, fifty thousand people could lose their lives. Maybe more."

"I thought you evacuated the area."

"Twelve blocks, Mr. President. If that device goes off, the fireball will take out the entire metropolitan area of downtown Seattle. The shock wave would cross the sound in less than three seconds and take out the eastern waterfront of Bainbridge Island, a major residential community. That would be awful," said Hirshberg. "But what if the bomb isn't there?"

"If it isn't there, where would it be?"

"Need I remind you, sir, that in four hours you are going to be assembled in the same building with every member of Congress, the Cabinet, except for a single member, the Supreme Court, the Joint Chiefs of Staff, the entire federal government under one roof."

"You've been talking to that woman," said the president. "What's her name?"

"Ms. Cole. No, I haven't seen her since she left the Situation Room yesterday. But I will tell you that what she had to say about this man Belden has been troubling me ever since. Why did they make the truck so easy to find?"

"It may have been easy to find," said the president, "but

they sure as hell haven't made it easy to get into it."

"No. Perhaps that's by design," said Hirshberg. "To keep us looking in the wrong place just long enough."

The president thought about what he was saying. "You think I should cancel the speech?"

"I do."

"What do I tell Congress?"

"Tell them you'll deliver it next week."

"Then what do I do, leave town?"

"That would be advisable. Perhaps Camp David," said Hirshberg. "Or some other secure military base."

"You haven't told the Secret Service about your concerns?"

"No."

"Thank God. They'd be hauling me away with a rope." The president held the pencil between two fingers and drummed the papers in front of him. It was a no-win situation. If he left the Capitol and didn't tell Congress why and word later got out, they would cut his political legs out from under him, even members of his own party. He would become known as the president who left the entire government sitting under the Capitol dome to face nuclear holocaust while he trekked off to Camp David to save his own ass.

"Jesus, Sy, if you thought this was a possibility, it would have been nice if you'd mentioned it a little earlier."

"Mr. President, until yesterday we thought that the device, if there was a device, was on that island. Now it appears that it was never on the island, and we don't know how long it's been on the loose. They could have had time to transport it."

"Maybe it doesn't exist," said the president. "Have you ever thought of that? After all, no one has actually seen it, have they?"

"No."

"Not the woman. Not her friend, what's his name? The Dutchman."

"Van Ry," said Hirshberg.

"Why don't you talk to them again? See if maybe we've missed anything."

Hirshberg could tell he was being sent on a mission of distraction, something to get him out of the president's hair so that he could avoid a decision.

"There is another possible way out. You could become ill at the last minute," said Hirshberg.

"NO!" He exploded, dropped the pencil on his desk, and stood. "That's all I need. Speculation that I've had a stroke or a heart attack. Hell, if I was the president of Russia I could just tell them I was drunk or better yet let the press figure it out."

"It doesn't have to be a stroke," said Hirshberg.

"You don't cancel the State of the Union for a cold. No. It's too late to cancel," said the president.

"But . . ."

"No. Now I've made a decision and it's final." He looked at his watch. "Is there anything else?"

"No, sir."

"Then if you don't mind," said the president.

Hirshberg turned and left the office.

The president's gaze returned to the papers on his desk, but his thoughts did not.

Near Silver Hill, MD

He had been in the air, on and off, for more than fourteen hours. The vintage DC-3 was slow and flew at a low altitude, but it was nothing if not reliable.

Thorn taxied up the runway in front of several small hangars. No one paid particular attention to the old plane, even in mint condition. Vintage planes were more common here than perhaps anywhere else except the annual Oshkosh Air Show.

The airport was only a few miles from Silver Hill, the home of the Paul E. Garber Restoration, Preservation and Storage Facility. It was the repair center and principal storage area for the Air and Space Museum.

Sitting on twenty-one acres and comprising more than forty thousand aviation artifacts, the Garber facility had a full-time paid staff and an army of volunteer aviation buffs, people who encompassed every aspect of construction and repair from the space shuttle to planes dating back to Kitty Hawk.

Thorn was counting on this volunteer spirit and the loose arrangement that existed between the museum and people who donated their time, some of whom worked at the Garber facility.

Before the plane's wheels even stopped rolling, a truck pulled out from behind one of the hangars. It was thirty feet long with a cargo box on the back, the kind of truck that furniture movers use. It pulled alongside the cargo door of the DC-3.

Thorn cut the plane's engines. Oscar Chaney jumped down from behind the wheel of the truck and threw two wooden chocks in front of the plane's wheels. He arrived at the rear cargo door just as Thorn opened it.

Chaney looked at his watch. "Right on time."

"Let's move," said Thorn. "We've got a lot to do."

Thorn had performed the "dirty work" at the small airport in Arlington, in Washington State, before he took to the air. He had donned the C-suit and breathing gear from the tank truck and, with great care, had inserted the small tubes of highly radioactive material into their holders surrounding the plutonium core of the device. It would not transform the guts of the two-kiloton artillery shell into a thermonuclear bomb, but would provide a nasty surprise to anyone trying to clean up the mess afterward. The contents of these tubes, when vaporized by the explosion, would transform everything for more than a mile around ground zero into a radioactive wasteland that would last for more than thirty years. Records and computers, files and documents, the vital essence of America's bureaucratic nerve center would become untouchable.

Chaney backed the truck around until its rear end lined up perfectly with the cargo door of the plane. He lowered the hydraulic Tommy-lift on the back of the truck so that it was out of the way, sliding easily under the fuselage of the plane. He climbed up into the DC-3 and, together with Thorn, fitted a heavy wooden ramp that had been predesigned to level and bridge the brief span between the slanting body of the plane and the bed of the truck.

In less than five minutes, using gravity and leverage, they rolled the cargo on its rectangular dolly and metal wheels over the ramp and into the truck.

Thorn donned a pair of blue overalls and a baseball cap with a logo above the bill that read I'D RATHER BE FLYING. He dropped down onto the concrete apron, then closed and latched the plane's cargo door from the outside.

Seconds later, he was in the passenger seat of the truck as it headed out toward the road that ran in front of the airport. They stopped at the front gate. Thorn got out and ran across the street to a pay phone at a gas station. He was inside the phone booth less than a minute. When he came back, Chaney had the radio on, tuned to NPR's "All Things Considered."

In less than three hours the president will address Congress and the nation. Among the items to be covered will be a major push toward national standards for education . . .

Thorn and Chaney looked straight ahead through the murky film on the windshield as the sun moved low in the sky. They followed the signs toward the interstate, onto the on-ramp heading northwest under the green highway sign that said "WASHINGTON, D.C."

Chaney put his arm out the window, signaling to the merging traffic, then allowed it to dangle, his fingers just inches above the magnetic metal placard on the door:

PAUL E. GARBER FACILITY
SILVER HILL, MD.

The director wanted the smoldering display of "Little Boy" off the museum grounds before guests began assembling for the party that night. They were the overflow crowd, the people who couldn't get seats in the gallery above the House of Representatives. Nonetheless, they were VIPs. Many of them were large contributors to the Smithsonian. Some of them were on the A-list in Washington, movers and shakers, but simply not quite high enough this year to get one of the coveted seats under the dome tonight.

They would watch the speech projected on a large sectional television screen in Space Hall, then drink cocktails and eat hors d'oeuvres. Afterward, the president's chief of staff and several other notables would visit, though the president himself had other plans.

"I want that thing out of the parking lot now. I don't care what you have to do with it. Call the Army and have it hauled away.'' The museum director was up to his ass in alligators, and someone was letting more water into the swamp. He had a thousand guests to worry about and less than three hours to get ready. He was standing just inside the barrier looking at the rust-red stains on the concrete floor.

''Will those come out?''

''We don't know.'' It was one of his maintenance supervisors.

''Well, don't make them any worse. Try to get something to cover it, just for tonight. And get that thing out of the parking lot.''

''What are we supposed to do with it?''

''I don't care. Just move it. I don't want people who park there looking at it.''

''We can't roll it into the shop. It's putting out some pretty heavy fumes.''

''Is it toxic?'' said the director.

One of the workmen looked at the other and wrinkled his eyebrows in a questioning way. ''Not if you don't touch it.''

''Is there any damage to the fuselage?'' asked the director.

''No. Just the stains on the floor.''

''Cover them and get the ropes back in place. People are going to want to tour the museum after the speech. They're going to want to see *Enola*.''

The director turned and headed back toward his office. He had a million things to do to get ready. Now they were having problems with the wiring on the big screen.

''What are we supposed to cover it with?'' said one of the workmen.

''Search me. Keep working, and I'll see what I can find.'' The supervisor disappeared in the direction of the shop.

The men continued to run wet mops over the floor, but the rust-red color wouldn't come out. It didn't look as bad as the blood-red dye on the casing of ''Little Boy'' itself, but still it was noticeable.

''What do you think that guy was on?''

''Who? The director?''

''No. The nut who did this.''

''I don't know. But he's lucky he didn't splash some of that shit on himself.''

"Yeah. Phantom of the fuckin' opera," said the other guy with the mop.

"Hey. Hey, you guys."

They turned and leaned on their mops to see the super coming back from the direction of the shop.

"What's up?"

"We're in luck. Somebody got hold of the facility out at Garber. Guess what? Seems they've got another one out there."

"What, some fucking nut?"

"No. Another mock-up of 'Little Boy.'"

The two guys on the mops looked at each other. "What are they doing with two of them?"

"I don't know. I don't care. All I know is it's on a truck and it's headed this way. According to Robbie, who took the phone call, the restoration people out there got the shade of green paint a little off on the first 'Little Boy' they did. I can see why, not havin' the real thing and all. Anyway they threw the fabricated casing in a warehouse out there."

"Maybe it's pea green," said one of the guys.

"Hey, right now I don't care if it looks like puke. It'll cover that stain on the floor."

"Shouldn't we tell the director?" said one of the workmen.

"Why? He told us to cover the floor with something. That's what we're gonna do. Besides he's up to his ass. We'll can tell him later. Right now we gotta push that thing in the parking lot outta the way, make room for the truck comin' in. If we're real lucky we can get 'em to haul that smoldering pile of crap outside back to Garber before OSHA declares this place a toxic waste dump."

THE TRUCK PULLED up to the back door of the Air and Space Museum ten feet from a pile of something that seemed to be smoking under a black plastic tarp. There were two smiling workers standing beside it.

Thorn looked over at Chaney behind the wheel.

"Looks like Taggart did a real fine job," said Chaney. "Wonder where he is now?"

"Not to worry," said Thorn. "The man was a true believer.'' He got out of the truck and smiled at the men by the plastic tarp.

"How ya doin'? I guess we got what you're lookin' for." Thorn nodded toward the box of the truck and pretended like he was chewing on gum.

"How do you wanna get it inside?" he asked them.

"You can back up to the dock there," said one of the men.

The other one went around to open the large overhead door. Chaney backed the truck up to the dock.

"Any chance of getting you guys to take this one away when you go? Take it back out to Garber?" said the supervisor.

Thorn and Chaney looked at each other. Thorn smiled. "Sure. Why not."

It took the four of them to roll the display out of the truck, groaning and grunting every inch of the way, even with the Tommy-lift to make a smooth ramp down onto the loading dock.

"Jeez. This one weighs a ton," said the super. "Why's it so heavy?"

"Musta used a heavier gauge metal," said Thorn.

"Yeah. And put concrete inside," said Chaney. The four of them laughed.

Once it hit the concrete floor, the metal wheels of the dolly began to roll with ease.

"Tell you what," said Thorn. He looked at the supervisor. "Why don't you help my friend George here?" He looked at Oscar. "He'll move the truck and the two of you can use the Tommy-lift to load the other one in the back of the truck. That way we can get outta here."

The supervisor was happy to oblige. In the meantime, Thorn and the other man rolled the mock-up of "Little Boy" out of the shop area and across the floor of the museum. By now, the Air and Space Museum was closing, people milling toward the exits. Some of them watched as the bomb rolled down the concourse toward the gleaming B-29.

"Damn shame," said Thorn. "You spend a lotta money doing all this, and some idiot with a loose wire comes in and tries to ruin it. Takes all kinds."

"You bet," said the other guy. "Shoulda seen our director.

Mad as hell. If he got his hands on the guy, I think he'd kill him.''

''Hmm.'' Thorn just looked straight ahead and smiled as they pushed the dolly toward the gleaming belly of the *Enola Gay*.

He could see the two-story windows looking out on the Mall, the only thing standing between ground zero and the Capitol Building.

The fireball would race down the Mall at the speed of light. It would vaporize every living thing within two hundred yards, and melt the bronze statute on the dome of the Capitol. An instant later, the blast would rip the copper sheathing off the roof and ignite every flammable surface inside. Temperatures would reach two thousand degrees within seconds.

The White House would be blown off its foundations. Even the underground bunkers would be heated to temperatures approaching incineration.

Thorn wondered whether Scott Taggart would feel any of it or whether Taggart had discovered the other item that Thorn had dropped into his briefcase along with the key; the small glass vial with a single capsule of cyanide inside.

THIRTY-THREE

HAY-ADAMS HOTEL, WASHINGTON, DC

Gideon and Joselyn spent the afternoon shopping for some clothes, the bare essentials to get themselves home. They caught a movie in the late afternoon and unwound in the cool, dark theater, some place where they didn't have to answer questions or look over their shoulders to see if they were being followed by the FBI.

Joselyn wondered if the government would pay for her airfare back to Seattle. It seemed the fair thing, considering the fact that she hadn't asked to come here in the first place.

By the time they got back to the hotel, it was almost eight o'clock. She dropped her shopping bags on the bed in her room and kicked off the new pair of shoes she had purchased. They were killing her feet.

Gideon rapped on the adjoining door. She walked over and opened it.

"I'm going to take a shower," he told her. "You want to get some dinner when I get out?"

"I'm exhausted. I'd rather eat in the room. Just relax tonight, get to sleep early."

"Why don't you order room service. Get something for me. A steak, medium rare, and small dinner salad."

"Where do you want to set up, my room or yours?"

"Doesn't matter," he told her, then disappeared to take his shower.

She studied the room service menu and called down for dinner. Gideon left the door to the adjoining room open, in case she had the waiter deliver it to his room. She could hear when he knocked on the outside door.

Joselyn wondered if she might be able to get a plane back to Seattle in the morning. She had talked about it with Gideon. One of the agents had told him that the FAA was screening flights into Sea-Tac, diverting some into other airports, until they were able to defuse the device in downtown Seattle. They were using the cover story that maintenance on one of the runways was causing a problem.

She could hear the water running in the shower and Gideon singing. He had a pretty good voice, though his tune at the higher register was a little off.

She smiled to herself and dropped onto the bed, grabbed the remote off the nightstand, and turned on the tube. She checked out the pay-per-view movies. It was a wasteland. She surfed the channels, CNN, and the weather. She found the local news, neighborhood shootings in the district and the plight of city government on the financial edge.

They were trying to buy off the mayor, to keep him from running for another term, with a six-figure appointment as professor emeritus at one of the universities. Joselyn was glad that she lived on an island.

She was about to turn off the set when they switched stories:

And there was a great deal of excitement at the Air and Space Museum today. For that story we go to Charlene Williams.

An attractive woman with a microphone in one hand and a notepad in the other appeared on the screen. She was standing on steps in front of a wall with large metal block letters:

NATIONAL AIR AND SPACE MUSEUM
Yes, Charlie. There was a great deal of excitement here today. Police arrested a man inside the museum after he threw a container of acid on one of the displays.

*No one was hurt, but an undisclosed amount of damage
was done to a replica of the first atomic bomb dropped
on Japan. A reproduction of the atomic bomb known as
"Little Boy," resting under the fuselage of the famous
B-29 Enola Gay was doused with acid. It had to be
removed from the museum because of highly toxic fumes
and damage.*

*A woman inside at the time of the incident caught these
pictures on videotape, moments after the man was hand-
cuffed by police and just before he was led away.*

The image on the screen broke up in diagonal lines for a
second as the videotape began to play. Joselyn was lying on
the bed with her head on the pillows, her mind beginning to
wander, thinking about dinner, when she saw his face on the
screen. Her eyes opened wide in disbelief as she sat up on the
bed.

She only saw his face for a second on the screen before he
was hustled away by police, but it was a face that was engraved on her mind's eye. It was the same face she had seen
in the house on Padget Island. The man standing in the doorway that morning telling Belden that they had to leave. She
had described him to the president, and to the FBI working on
a composite drawing.

She reached for the controls and turned up the volume.

*And the mystery deepens tonight. Police have reported
that the man (she looked at her notes), Scott Evan Taggart, died of an apparent heart attack shortly after being
taken into custody. Police are saying nothing more
about the incident, only that it is under investigation.*

They cut to the anchor:

*Charlene, do authorities have any indication as to why
the man did what he did?*

*Not at this point, Charlie. The matter is being handled
by the Metropolitan Police as a case of vandalism. You
will recall that three months ago there was a similar*

*incident at the National Gallery of Art. They are trying
to find out if the man had a medical history that might
account for his sudden death. Other than that, all they
will say is that it is under investigation.*

It was as if Joselyn were shell-shocked, sitting on the bed
hyperventilating, her brain running at warp speed.

"Oh, shit." She was talking to herself. "Oh, my God."

She got up from the bed and began pacing, looking at the
walls, frantic, trying to figure out what to do. The only calming
sound filtering through the strains of the television was the
constant force of the water hitting the bathtub in Gideon's
shower and the occasional sound of his voice as he sang.

She ran to the adjoining door, into his room, and straight
toward the bathroom. She didn't bother to knock but opened
the door. She crossed the steam-filled room in two strides and
pulled back the shower curtain.

Gideon stopped singing in mid-note, a bar of soap in his
hands, and his head covered with suds. He looked at her bug-
eyed, his Adam's apple still bobbing in place.

"Get out of the shower!"

"Excuse me?"

"Get out of the shower now!" She grabbed a towel from
the rod and threw it at him.

He caught it but didn't bother to cover himself. It was a
little late.

Joselyn walked out into his room and began pacing by the
end of the bed.

He opened the bathroom door. "Would you mind throwing
me some underwear."

She found a package of new jockey shorts on the bed and
carried them over, handing them through the sliver of an opening in the door.

"What's the matter?" said the Gideon.

"The man, that, that . . . guy. The one in the hallway outside of the room on Padget Island. I just saw him on television."

"Did they catch him?" said Gideon

"They did," said Joselyn. "Here in Washington."

Suddenly the door swung open, and Gideon looked at her.
He was standing in his underwear toweling himself.

"What are you talking about?"

"I just saw it on television. They arrested him someplace. The Air and Space Museum," she said.

"What was he doing there?"

"Throwing acid on a replica of an atomic bomb."

Gideon stopped toweling and looked at her intently. "Are you sure it was him?"

"Positive."

Gideon passed through the doorway and started pulling on his pants. He slipped his shoes on without socks. Rivulets of water were running out of his hairline at the temple and coursing down his neck into the sparse forest of chest hair.

"And there's something else," said Joselyn. "He's dead. They're saying it was a heart attack. Like hell," she told him. "Where is the Air and Space Museum?"

"On the Mall, near the Capitol . . ." Gideon didn't finish the sentence. They simply looked at each other for a split second before he dived for the phone. He picked up the receiver and looked at her. "Who do I call?"

"Nine-one-one. No. That's the police. It'll take an hour to explain it to them," said Joselyn. She looked at the clock on the table. They were less than forty minutes from the opening of the president's speech. "We don't have that much time."

They had been watching snippets all day on the news, every fifteen minutes, political teasers about the president's State of the Union address.

Joselyn raced to her room and ripped open one of the shopping bags. Inside was the FBI jumpsuit she'd put in the bag when she changed to street clothes at the store. She rummaged through one pocket and didn't find it. She tried the other and came up with a business card. It was Sy Hirshberg's. He had given it to her when she left the Situation Room, just in case she remembered anything else.

By now Gideon was standing in the doorway to her room with a polo shirt in one hand and a towel in the other.

She dialed Hirshberg's number at the White House. It rang twice. A woman answered: "NSC."

"Mr. Hirshberg, please."

"Who's calling?"

"This is Joselyn Cole. I was there yesterday meeting with the president and Mr. Hirshberg. This is an emergency."

"Just a moment, please."

The line went dead. She was put on hold. Joselyn looked at the clock.

"Is he there?" said Gideon.

"I don't know."

"Tell them the bomb is in Washington, D.C. Tell them we think it's at the Air and Space Museum."

The woman came back on the line. "I'm sorry, but Mr. Hirshberg has already left the office."

"I need to reach him immediately. This is an emergency," said Joselyn.

"What did you say your name was?"

"Joselyn Cole. Is there anybody else there that I can talk to?"

"Just a moment." The line went dead again.

"Shit," said Joselyn. She wanted to slam the receiver against the glass surface of the nightstand.

"Let me have it," said Gideon.

She handed him the phone and searched for her shoes, sat on the edge of the bed, and slipped them on.

When the voice came back on the other end, it was a man this time. "Hello."

"Who is this?" said Gideon.

"Who are you?"

"My name is Gideon van Ry. I am with the Institute Against Mass Destruction in California. I was in the White House Situation Room yesterday with Mr. Hirshberg and the president. I have information that there is a nuclear bomb in Washington, D.C., somewhere near the Capitol Building."

"Who is this?"

"Where is Mr. Hirshberg?" said Gideon.

"He's with the president. On his way to the Capitol."

It was too late. By the time Gideon and Joselyn got to someone in authority and explained what they knew, Washington, D.C., would be a flickering cinder.

"Listen to me. Do you have a pencil and a piece of paper?"

"Yes."

"Take a note," said Gideon. "I don't care how you do it, but get in touch with Mr. Hirshberg immediately. Do you understand?"

There was silence at the other end of the line.

"Tell him that Joselyn Cole and Gideon van Ry called."

"Give me those names again slowly," said the man.

Gideon spelled them for him.

"Tell him that we are on our way to the Air and Space Museum. Listen to me and get this right. He will know who we are. Tell him that the nuclear device is not in Seattle. Tell him that we believe it is at the Air and Space Museum, and that the president should not speak tonight. Do you understand?"

"I think so," said the man.

Joselyn was watching the television. The pregame show was already starting, political analysts were getting face time on the tube, and reporters were interviewing members of Congress under bright television lights. The coverage was live.

"Did you get all of that?" asked Gideon.

"Yes."

"Now do it," he told the man. He hung up the phone and grabbed Joselyn, nearly pulling her off her feet. He opened the door to her room just as the waiter was arriving with dinner on a rolling cart.

"Out of the way," said Gideon. He pushed the cart and the waiter against the wall.

"Just a minute," said the waiter.

They squeezed by the cart as the door to the room closed behind them.

"Leave it by the door," said Gideon.

"Hey. Who's gonna sign for this?"

"The government," said Joselyn. She looked over her shoulder as Gideon pulled her along down the hall.

Gideon got his hand, all the way up to the wrist, into an elevator door just as it was closing. The doors slowly opened. An older couple dressed to the nines looked at them wide-eyed, with more than a little disapproval. Gideon's hair looked like smoke in a windstorm, and Joselyn was winded with a wild expression in her eyes.

"That's a good way to lose a hand," said the man.

"If that is all I lose tonight I will consider myself fortunate," said Gideon.

There was nothing else he could do in the elevator but wait. Gideon ran the fingers of one hand through his hair in a losing effort to make himself more presentable. He reached in his pocket and found his wallet. He had thirty dollars in cash. Enough for a taxi.

When the door opened, they nearly ran over a man and woman standing outside. They hurtled across the hotel lobby, Gideon actually jumping over a small bench. A hundred sets of eyes were drawn to them like Doppler radar to a fast-moving object.

Receptions were forming up all over town tonight and the Hay-Adams was no exception. Gideon and Joselyn had to negotiate their way through a crowd at the door. When they got to the curb there was already a small mob waiting for cabs.

Gideon stepped in front.

"You'll have to wait your turn, sir." The doorman put his hand up and tried to push him back into line.

"We don't have time," said Gideon.

"What's your problem?"

Gideon thought for a second. "My wife. She is very ill." He put his arm around Joselyn and squeezed her shoulder. "I think she has food poisoning. Something from room service."

A look of some anguish came over the doorman's face. The crowd began staring at Joselyn. She began to look ill, holding her stomach.

The doorman wasn't in the mood to perform a diagnosis, not with a crowd watching. He blew his whistle and stepped out into the street. A second later a cab pulled up, and he ushered Joselyn and Gideon into the backseat and closed the door.

"The Air and Space Museum," said Gideon. "And there's an extra twenty in it for you if you get us there in under three minutes."

"Can't do that, but I can get you there in five," said the driver.

"Let's not negotiate. It's yours," said Joselyn.

The acceleration forced them back into the seat. It was a wild ride through the downtown streets of Washington, many of which were one-way. Gideon looked for his watch, which they had returned to him with his wallet. Unfortunately he'd left it behind in the hotel room.

"What time is it?"

She looked at her watch. "Eight-forty. Can we get there in time?"

"I don't know."

"What do we do when we get there?"

"We'll have to find some way to get into the building. If we have to, I'll throw something through a window."

"That should get the attention of the cops," said Joselyn.

"Let's hope we can get inside before they arrive. At least we can lead them to the device. Maybe if they see it, at least they'll call for help. If it's not too late," said Gideon.

The cab raced down H Street and took a left on Seventeenth, passed along the side of the Old Executive Office Building and the Ellipse, and headed for the Tidal Basin.

Joselyn could see the Washington Monument off to the left, its red beacon flashing in the night sky. They swung in a wide arc around the monument, past the Sylvan Theater and onto Independence Avenue. The cab shot by art galleries and museums, passed behind the back side of the Smithsonian Castle. It was approaching the Transportation Building on Seventh Street when they ran into thickening traffic, red brake lights as far as they could see.

"What is it?" said Gideon.

"I don't know, man. Something's going on."

Within a hundred feet, the cab was stopped dead in traffic. Joselyn could see stretch limos and large town cars, women walking on the sidewalk in evening gowns and furs, and men in tuxedos, all walking in the same direction.

"How far is the museum?" asked Gideon.

"It's only a block up."

Gideon looked at the meter. It showed eight dollars. He took the thirty out of his wallet and threw it over the front seat to the driver, opened the door, and got out. Joselyn followed him.

They hustled along the sidewalk, passing women in three-inch heels with their gloved hands through the arms of formally attired men. Some of them were wearing military dress uniforms. They were all headed to the broad terrace of stairs leading to the Air and Space Museum.

"At least we won't need to throw anything through the window," said Gideon.

"How are we going to get in?"

"I don't know."

The place was lit up like a church on Christmas Eve. There

was a vintage searchlight on the street out in front, its beam scanning the night sky. A sign on it read: RELIC OF THE LONDON BLITZ.

Docents were handing out programs with maps of the museum printed inside. Gideon saw a man get one and immediately drop it into a trash can. He went fishing in the can as the docent watched him with a sick expression.

"What are you doing?" asked Joselyn.

"Once we get inside there, we are not going to have time to go on a hunting expedition. The display that this man threw acid on. Do you remember the name?"

She looked up at the sky and thought. "I wasn't paying that much attention."

"Think," said Gideon.

"Boy. Boy. Something boy."

"Little Boy," said Gideon.

"That's it."

Like a magnet, Gideon's eyes found the words *Enola Gay* on the schematic of the museum floor plan. It was isolated in the northwest corner of the building, on the ground level. He oriented himself and the map to the front of the building as an army of formally attired guests climbed the stairs toward the gleaming glass facade.

"What do we do now?" said Gideon. "Go up to the man at the door and tell him there's a nuclear bomb inside?"

"Not unless you want to spend what is left of a brief life in the back of a paddy wagon," said Joselyn.

Suddenly she saw it. "Follow me." She grabbed Gideon by the hand and led him toward the stairs. They merged into the crowd, Gideon trying to be as inconspicuous as a man six-foot-five can be when he is improperly dressed and his hair is a mess.

Several people looked at them. Joselyn didn't pay any attention. Her focus was on the man in front of them in the wool topcoat, the one with the large square envelope holding up the flap on the pocket on his coat.

A woman in a flowing mink coat and wearing diamond earrings gave them a condescending look and continued to stare.

Gideon smiled. "I see you are a fan of animal rights."

The woman diverted her eyes and whispered to the man whose arm she was on.

They got to the terrace leading to the museum and the line stalled as the people piled up at the door trying to get in. They all seemed to have invitations in large envelopes, passing these to two staff members on either side of the door as a guard looked on.

Joselyn peeked around a shoulder and through an opening in the crowd. Slowly they inched their way forward. Ten feet from the door the man in front of them stopped dead in his tracks. He began frisking himself, slipping his hand into his inside coat pocket, then unbuttoning the coat. The woman with him looked at him.

"I swear I put them in my coat."

Joselyn neatly stepped around him and pulled Gideon after her. They reached the door ten seconds later, where the white-gloved attendant looked at them, then reached out and took the engraved invitation from Joselyn's hand.

"You know it is black-tie?" said the man.

"We'll sit in the back," said Joselyn.

Before he could say anything, they stepped through the door and into the lobby of the museum and kept walking.

Gideon took a brief sideways glance over his shoulder and saw the attendant talking to a guard, who was now looking at them with sufficient intensity to burn a hole through their backs.

"I'd ask you how you did that," he told her, "but we don't have time."

The man who had lost his invitation was at the door, still patting his pockets and now talking to the attendant.

At a near run, Gideon and Joselyn headed across the lobby, dodging around guests with champagne glasses in their hands. Gideon tried to make himself ten inches shorter so that he wouldn't be seen above the crowd.

With his long legs, he gobbled up the sixty feet of the lobby, passing the information booth, but not before a member of the staff behind the desk saw them. The woman picked up a phone and punched a button.

Joselyn tried to keep up with him. The leather soles on her new shoes slipped like ice on the smooth concrete floor. Now they were in full stride, left past the "Milestones of Flight" and down the main gallery past the escalators that led to the second level.

When Gideon looked over his shoulder, he saw them. Emerging from the crowd like destroyers under full steam were three armed guards. They were soon joined by a fourth, one of them with his hand already on the handle of his holstered revolver.

As they left the last cluster of wandering guests behind, Gideon and Joselyn stood out like two doughboys in no-man's-land.

Gideon broke into a full run. Joselyn followed him. They darted behind a temporary display in the center of the broad concourse and crossed over to the north side of the building.

For a second, Gideon lost sight of the guards. When they popped out from the other side of the escalator, one of them was talking with his chin pressed down into a microphone clipped to the lapel of his uniform shirt. Gideon saw the guard pop the safety snap of the leather holster from across the hammer of his gun and draw the pistol, holding the muzzle toward the floor with both hands as he ran.

He grabbed Joselyn and pushed her out in front of him, shielding her with his body, and propelling her down the concourse toward the *Enola Gay*. They ran between the last stairwell in the center of the building and past the final partition separating the displays.

There in the gallery to the right was the gleaming fuselage of the B-29. Without its wings, which could not be assembled in the confines of the building, it looked like a mammoth silver cigar. The giant nose wheel was turned just a little as if the plane had just taxied to a stop on the runway. The bright overhead lights of the display reflected off the Plexiglas bubble of the bombardier's station up front.

Under the body of the *Enola Gay*, halfway back toward the tail section, was the ominous green cylinder with its bulbous nose and square tail fin—the paradigm of the atomic age, the full-sized replica of "Little Boy."

For an instant Joselyn and Gideon stood transfixed, knowing that what they were looking at was no mere model. Unable to speak, they looked at the bomb for what it was: two kilotons of radioactive death capable of rising in a death-head mushroom more than nine miles into the stratosphere above the nation's capital.

The clatter of feet on concrete, approaching from the main hall, brought them back to the moment.

"What do we do?" said Joselyn.

Gideon turned toward the hall behind them, the footfalls closing. "Quick. Get inside the railing, under the plane," he told her.

They ran across the deserted gallery and jumped the railing, then moved under the belly of the plane, careful not to jostle the bomb or its rectangular steel dolly.

Gideon scanned the green metal casing, looking for a small covering panel with screws or an area of rivets, anything that would provide access to the device inside.

Even if he found one, he had no idea how he would pry it off. He had no tools.

The guards reached the corner of the partition leading into the gallery housing the *Enola Gay*. Joselyn saw one of them poking his head around the edge of the partition.

Another guard sprinted across the opening into the gallery and took up a position on the other side. Both had their guns drawn.

"Come out now, with your hands up," said one of the guards.

"We are not armed," said Gideon. He was breathing heavily, winded from their run down the concourse.

"Show your hands and come out," said the guard.

Gideon could hear movement in the shadows where the tail section of the huge bomber disappeared behind the walls of the exhibit. He knew that police or guards were moving in from that direction. In seconds, they would be on him. Anything he said would be lost in the din in a scuffle that would soon be over.

They could hear the sound of the giant television as suddenly it was piped into the speaker system of the museum.

Any moment now, the president will be announced by the sergeant at arms of the House. There we see Secretary of State Knowland coming in. He is followed by the attorney general . . .

"Listen to me," said Gideon. "The man who threw acid on the model of 'Little Boy' this morning. He was part of a terrorist group. This casing, the one under the plane, contains a nuclear device. It was substituted sometime during the day. Call Mr. Hirshberg, the president's national security adviser. Tell him that Gideon van Ry is here at the museum. He will vouch for me."

"Put your hands up where we can see them, and come out now."

There was more shuffling and movement and now whispering in the shadows where the tail of the plane disappeared into darkness.

You know, Tom, we do see the secretary of state. But you know who we don't see is Sy Hirshberg, the president's national security adviser. If he's not here tonight, that will indeed fuel rumors that perhaps Mr. Hirshberg is on the outs with the administration. There have been rumors . . .

Two uniformed guards rushed out of the shadows behind them. They flung the full force of their bodies into Gideon, one high and the other low. They sent him sprawling across the floor under the plane.

A third guard emerged from the darkness and grabbed Joselyn before she could move, throwing her to the floor and placing his knee with the full weight of his body in the center of her back. It felt as if the man broke her spine, the pain nearly causing her to black out.

As Gideon wrestled on the floor, the two guards rolled him so that he was facedown. As they held him, two more guards jumped the railing to help.

With his face pressed to the floor and turned to one side, Gideon saw it. There was a small panel, roughly four-by-ten inches on the underside of the casing. It was held in place by six small screws. Looking from the top of the bomb as it rested on the dolly, the panel was impossible to see.

He struggled to get free, but the guards only increased the pressure on his arms as they were forced up behind his back. Gideon was rangy and powerful. One of them applied a wristlock. Gideon closed his eyes in pain. They watered. He tried to focus on the metal panel under the bomb, as if by sheer force of mind he could will it open.

"Get off of them." It was a voice from out in the gallery, spoken with authority. "Did you hear me? Let them up now."

Gideon lifted his head and saw the lanky frame of Sy Hirshberg just beyond the railing. For an old man, Hirshberg was nothing if not agile. Balancing himself with a single hand on the railing he threw one leg over and then the other and within three seconds had his hand on the shoulder of one of the guards.

They didn't look at Hirshberg but at the man who was with him, tall, in formal attire.

The museum director nodded, and the guards released their hold. The one kneeling on Joselyn's back immediately got off of her. He reached for her arm and tried to help her up, but he had knocked the wind out of her.

Gideon got up off the floor, feeling his wrist to make sure it wasn't broken. He looked at Joselyn, but there was no time.

"I need a screwdriver." He scrambled over to the bomb and looked underneath. "Phillips head," he said. Then got on his back as if he were getting ready to crawl under a car.

The guards hesitated.

"What are you waiting for?" said Hirshberg. "Now."

Two of the guards scrambled into the darkness.

By now Joselyn had made it onto her knees. Holding her stomach with one hand and struggling to get air into her lungs, she crawled toward Gideon and the bomb casing.

Hirshberg moved in and got down on one knee next to them.

"How much time do we have?"

"Where is the president?" said Gideon.

"He's getting ready to speak," said Hirshberg.

"That's the key," said Gideon. "If I am correct, it will be detonated by radio signal as soon as the president appears on the floor of the Congress."

Hirshberg turned to an assistant who was behind the railing. "Can we reach the president's Secret Service detail on their radio frequency?"

"No," said the young man. "I don't think so."

By now some of the guests had wandered down, drawn to the commotion at the other end of the museum. They stood riveted as the tall slender man lay on his back looking up at the bomb.

"If we can't reach them by radio," said Hirshberg, "call the White House detail. Tell them to keep the president off the floor of the House. I don't care what they have to do. Hell. Tell them there's a bomb about to go off near the Capitol."

With those words a ripple of panic started to move through the crowd beyond the portal to the gallery.

"What did he say?"

"He said there's a bomb."

People started to move toward the lobby. The news traveled with them like a wave. Within less than a minute, it reached the front the doors and people started streaming out onto the street.

Hirshberg's assistant punched keys on a cell phone as Joselyn watched him.

One of the guards came out of the shadows with a small toolbox. Hirshberg and Joselyn fished in it until they found a Phillips screwdriver.

Considering the trauma to his wrist, Gideon worked with deft fingers to loosen the six screws on the metal cover. There was no time for finesse. He could only pray that Belden and his people had not taken the time to install a trip wire on the panel. Intuition and experience told him that this was unlikely. A trip wire trigger would make transport of the device more difficult, unless they had time to arm it after it was in place. In a public museum with staff watching, that was not likely.

He held his breath as he pulled the last screw from its hole, then slowly slipped a fingernail under the edge of the panel. The panel cover was heavier than it looked. Without the last screw, it fell off in his hands. Gideon flinched and squeezed his eyes shut tight. When he opened them, he was still there.

Joselyn could feel her heart thumping like a steam engine.

He dropped the metal panel cover onto the floor and looked inside. It was a maze of wires, different colors going in every direction.

Somebody handed him a small flashlight. He shot the beam inside and moved it around, looking for something.

"Damn."

"What's wrong?" said Joselyn.

"I don't see any receiver. There should be a small box. A

battery power pack." He traced the wires with his eyes. "There is no clock or timer switch that I can see." He was now breathless.

"It has to be remote detonation," he told them. "They would want to be far enough away not to be caught up in it. That would require a good-sized receiver." said Gideon. He was breathing hard, perspiration pouring down his forehead, as he flashed the light through the small opening in the casing, frantically searching for something that wasn't there.

He could see the spherical core of the nuclear device up near the nose of the bomb. It was only a fraction of the diameter of the bomb casing that disguised it, a twisted testament to the progress of man in the twenty years after the end of the war.

The core rested in what appeared to be a cradle of molded Styrofoam, designed to buffer the device and its multiple detonators during transit.

Something wasn't right. Around the core, fastened to the inside of the casing, were a number of small metal tubes, the size of a fire extinguisher, the kind you might carry on a small boat. Gideon counted nine of these.

Sweat was streaming down his forehead and into his eyes. He wiped them with the back of his hand and continued to flash the beam of light through the hole.

For a second, he thought the device was thermonuclear. Instead of two kilotons, Gideon wondered if he was looking at five megatons. If it was, it would take out the entire District, part of Maryland, and the northern reaches of Virginia.

Suddenly it settled on him as he looked at the wiring. It was not thermonuclear at all. The metal tubes were filled with radioactive cesium.

"Get everybody out of here," said Gideon.

"It's too late if it goes off now," said Hirshberg.

"It may be too late even if it doesn't go off," said Gideon. "Get them out now."

Hirshberg got to his feet. "Out. Everybody out," he said.

The guards began herding the few people who remained toward the main hallway and the exit.

"You, too," said Hirshberg.

"I'm not going anywhere," said Joselyn.

"Take her out of here," said Gideon.

Joselyn fought with the guards and wrestled with Hirshberg. They dragged her toward the railing, out from under the
Enola Gay, and finally Hirshberg managed to calm her. She
looked at Gideon lying on his back, his face nearly under the
bomb, shining the small flashlight inside.

"I won't go," she said.

"You must," he told her.

"No." Tears streamed down her face.

"Mr. Hirshberg." It was Hirshberg's assistant.

"I can't get through. The phone lines at the White House
are jammed."

"What do you mean, they're jammed?"

"They're all busy."

"There's two hundred lines over there," said Hirshberg.

"The circuits are jammed."

It settled on her like ether, looking at Gideon lying on the
floor. The cellular phone and the assistant. The jammed lines.

"It's not a radio receiver," said Joselyn. She called to him,
tried to run back to his side, but they stopped her. "It's a cell
phone." Two of the guards lifted her over the railing as she
fought them, struggled, using both hands.

Gideon on his back shot a glance in her direction. She was
hysterical, being carried away.

"It's a cellular phone," she told him. "That was Belden's
business. Voice identification. Look for a cellular phone." She
pounded on the guard's back but to no avail. He carried her
slung over his shoulder toward the main hall.

Almost as her lips said it, his eye caught it, not a phone,
but a single wire, gray in color and oval, heavier than the
others. It was ordinary telephone wire. It ran in one direction
and disappeared under the core of the device, where it rested
in the Styrofoam cradle. In the other direction, the wire passed
through what appeared to be a white cloth shield that sealed
off the tail of the bomb toward the square metal tail fin.

Gideon looked at the metal covering plate resting on the
floor. It was lined with lead. He flashed the light just inside
the hole and scratched the inside surface of the casing with
his fingernail. It was lead. The entire casing of Little Boy was
lined with lead to shield anyone handling it from the deadly
radiation of the cesium.

He was now alone under the still and looming body of the

B-29, the only sounds, the distant scream of Joselyn as they carried her toward the exit and the television feed from the giant screen.

Gideon took a deep breath, then stuck his hand and his bare arm into the opening in the case of "Little Boy." All the way to the shoulder. He felt the cloth shield that sealed off the tail section and the telephone cable that passed through. He pushed the shield with his fingers. There was resistance, but it was not solid. The shield was made of canvas surrounding a lead liner. He punched it with his clenched fist and the duct tape holding it to the inside of the case ripped. He hit it again harder, and the shield collapsed into the tail of the casing.

When he pulled his arm out and flashed the light back inside, he saw it. Fastened to the inside of "Little Boy" with black electrical tape was a small cellular phone. Completing the circuit, the phone cable plugged into the bottom of it. It had been necessary to get the cell phone outside of the lead shield in order to ensure a signal, reception to the phone.

Gideon guessed that at the other end of the phone cable, under the nuclear core, was a computer chip programmed with the verbal code. This would be attached to the principal detonator. From there, the current would fan out to multiple detonators planted in the high explosive surrounding the plutonium core.

He looked at the containers of cesium, then without hesitation he put his arm back into the casing of the bomb, all the way to the shoulder. He reached for the cell phone taped to the side of the casing, but he couldn't free it from the tape. He needed a knife.

He slid the toolbox closer and with his free hand he felt around inside. Something sharp. It was the flat blade of a screwdriver—not a knife, but it would have to do. Quickly he maneuvered it into the casing and tried to cut the tape with the metal end. Belden had secured it well.

Suddenly he heard footsteps running toward him. It was Joselyn. Somehow she'd gotten away from the guard. She jumped the railing and ran to him, slid on the floor on her knees until her head and upper body landed gently on his chest.

"You should be out of here. Please." He pleaded with her.

"I won't go. I won't leave you."

"You don't understand," said Gideon.

"I don't care. I'm not going," she told him.

They didn't have time to argue. Gideon struggled with the tape on the phone and finally got an edge loose.

He grabbed the phone as it dangled from the remnants of sticky tape and pulled until it came free.

"Please don't get close to me," he told her. "Move away to the other side of the bomb." If he couldn't convince her to leave, he could at least put the shield of the casing between Joselyn and himself. His body was now heavily contaminated by radiation, and Gideon knew it.

She looked at him with eyes that told him she would go that far, but no farther.

Carefully he withdrew his arm until his hand, with the phone in it, slipped through the opening of the casing. It was still trailing the telephone cable connected to the detonator. He considered cutting the wire but wasn't sure if this would set off the device. Even if Belden had used a verbal code to arm the device itself, Gideon couldn't be sure whether he'd wired the cesium with a separate explosive in the event that someone tried to sever a circuit.

Joselyn looked at the small phone, her gaze seeming mesmerized.

Ladies and gentlemen, the president of the United States.

The sound system in the museum erupted with applause, as the giant screen played to an empty room. The crowd of more than a thousand people, dressed in tuxedos and evening gowns, streamed out onto the street.

Women were falling down the stairs in their heels, others dropped their sequined bags, men stepping on them, running, visions of the carnage in Oklahoma City playing in their minds. They had no idea that the bomb was nuclear.

UNDER THE BELLY of the *Enola Gay*, the phone came to life in Gideon's hand. It rang, and the liquid crystal screen lit up.

Gideon didn't hesitate. There was no time. He reached up with his fingers and pressed the clip on each side of the wired fitting at the base of the cell phone. The end of the cable disconnected from the phone.

It rang again. As he looked at Joselyn, her eyes peering over the top of "Little Boy," the same question crossed their minds: with the phone locked away inside of the casing, who would have ever answered it?

The solution came with the third ring. Suddenly there was the hiss of an open line. They could hear someone breathing at the other end. Belden had programmed the phone with an answering chip.

He said only two words, but his voice carried crystalline and clear:

Critical Mass

Gideon looked at it for a moment, then held the mouthpiece of the phone to his lips.

"I'm sorry. You have the wrong number." Then he pressed the "end" button.

THIRTY-FOUR

BETHESDA, MD

The ward at Bethesda Naval Hospital was quiet, almost deserted. This section of the floor was now off-limits to all except a handful of doctors and specially trained nurses.

Joselyn had been coming by for three days, camping there most of the day. Still they wouldn't let her see him.

"Why not?" she said.

The doctor shook his head.

"Why can't I see him?"

"Because he's very ill," said Hirshberg.

It was the look that passed between the two men that told her it was much more serious than she had been led to believe. She had thought it was for security. That they were debriefing him.

"He's not going to die?"

Hirshberg and the doctor merely looked at each other, but neither of them spoke.

Then finally Hirshberg reached out and placed his hands on her shoulders. "He's absorbed a tremendous amount of radiation."

"We were all there," said Joselyn.

"His arms, inside of the casing, were exposed for too long," said the doctor.

"There must be something you can do." She looked at him with pleading eyes.

The doctor shook his head as Hirshberg released her and turned away.

"I want to see him now," she told them.

"That's not a good idea," said Hirshberg.

"I'm going in there."

She turned toward the room, and one of the guards started to move toward her.

"That's all right," Hirshberg shot him a look, and the guard backed off. He looked at the doctor.

"Only if we set up a shield. And then only for a couple of minutes," said the physician.

Joselyn waited outside the room in the hall while a device like a small dressing screen was rolled down the hall and into the room. A few seconds later the attendant, wearing a lead vest, came back out and nodded.

"You can only stay in there for two minutes," said the doctor.

"I will be watching you from the control booth. You have to stay behind the shield. And whatever you do. You are not to touch him."

The guard opened the door, and Joselyn looked inside. It was dark. There were no windows. It was a large X-ray room. She saw the doctor walk quickly into a booth from another entrance somewhere down the hall. She could see his shadow moving in the booth through a thick glass window the size of a postcard.

She entered the room, and the guard closed the door behind her. For a moment, she stood looking at the hospital bed rolled against the far wall, just beyond the X-ray table. She could hear his rasping breath and see his long form under the single white sheet that covered his body.

"Please get behind the screen." The doctor talked to her from beyond the shielded booth where he watched.

She walked over behind the shield that stood at the head of the bed. Tears began to well in her eyes. She could see his arms resting on top of the sheets as she approached, bleeding and blistered. They appeared to be covered with some kind of a gel.

Joselyn turned toward the booth and the doctor inside. "Can't you do anything for his arms?"

"We're making him as comfortable as possible."

With the sound of her voice close now, just beyond the shield, Gideon slowly rolled his head toward the side of the pillow and looked at her face through the specially shielded glass, a small window in the screen.

"Hello." Joselyn tried to smile.

"Hi." Gideon's face was marked with lesions and his lips were blistered and broken.

She wanted to reach out and grab him by the hand, pull him from this cave of a room out into the bright sunlight where life was fine and the world continued. Her hand hit the screen as she leaned forward.

Instead all she could do was look at him. "How are you feeling?"

"Oh." He was breathless, tried to smile, but started to cough. His respiration was ragged; his chest rose beneath the single sheet as he fought for breath. A trace of frothy blood formed at the corner of his lip.

Gideon's golden hair had turned to straw, and lesions had formed under the skin on his forehead.

She tried to keep herself from crying. She didn't want him to see her that way. Quickly she brought a hand up and rubbed her eyes with the back of it.

"I had to see you," she said.

He smiled. "You did the right thing," he told her. "If you had not told me about the phone, I would never have looked for it, and we would all be dead."

"Oh, God." Now she looked at the ceiling, tears streaming down her cheeks.

"It's not your fault," he told her. "There was nothing else we could do."

"We could have run," said Joselyn. "We could have left this place."

"No," he said. "No, we couldn't." He smiled at her, his soft blue eyes, the only part of him that seemed untouched, melting her soul.

"I love you," she said. Joselyn had no idea where the words came from, only that she could not control them.

All he could do was smile.

"Oh, God. I'm gonna lose it," she said. She turned away so that he couldn't see her face. She ached to touch his hand, to hold him in her arms and comfort him. She was two feet away and it was as if for all the world he was alone.

"No." He was breathing heavily. "Don't. Don't. Please." He was hyperventilating, struggling for breath as he spoke. He knew time was short.

"You must not feel this way," he said. "We did good."

As she turned back to him, his blistered face the picture of serene acceptance, Joselyn suddenly realized that it was not her actions or her words that night that brought him to this place, but what Gideon himself believed in. "Yes. We did good."

"You know," he said. "We never did get to exercise our constitutional rights."

She smiled, laughed, with tears running down her face.

It was the last thing she heard as the monitor above his bed began to scream, and the blip on the screen ran to a flat line.

Doctors and nurses in heavy lead vests streamed into the room, pulling a crash cart behind them.

Before they could hook up, the doctor in the booth stopped them. He shook his head, and slowly they filtered out of the room, leaving Joselyn alone, standing behind the screen, looking at Gideon's smile and his lifeless blue eyes.

THIRTY-FIVE

ANDREWS AIR FORCE BASE, MD

Sy Hirshberg made the arrangements to fly Gideon's body home to Amsterdam, aboard an Air Force jet with a full honor guard.

Joselyn was at Andrews Air Force Base when the hearse arrived.

The United States government paid for the special lead liner and coordinated with the Dutch government for burial. But the hearse itself bore a simple wooden coffin that had been requested by Gideon's parents.

Joselyn had never met them, but she wanted to. They spoke by phone the day after Gideon died and agreed that in the summer they would meet. She had much to tell them about how their son had lived his last days. They had a lifetime of stories to tell her.

Hirshberg had arranged for a separate plane to take Joselyn back home to Seattle. They met on the tarmac and watched as the coffin was carried from the hearse with military precision. The flags were folded, Dutch and American.

They offered the stars and stripes to Joselyn. She took it, but later handed it to Hirshberg with a request that it be given to Gideon's mother. The final tears made their way down her cheeks as the casket was slowly lifted and finally disappeared into the cargo hold of the big jet.

Hirshberg sighed. He choked. His voice cracked as he turned toward Joselyn. "I am sorry that this had to happen."

She looked up at him without missing a beat. "It didn't."

"I know. You're angry. You're bitter. You have every reason to be."

"No. He had every reason to be." She pointed to the open cargo door on jet. "Tell him that you're sorry."

Hirshberg didn't know what to say.

"You know, I read in the paper that there was an *incident* at the Air and Space Museum." She looked at him for a few seconds to allow the word to sink in.

"There was nothing on the news about a nuclear bomb. Nothing about Belden or Taggart. He died of a heart attack," said Joselyn.

"We know it was cyanide," said Hirshberg.

"Well, now, that's a start. Have you found Belden?"

"No."

Belden had called two more times to the cell phone at the museum, uttering the same message each time, before he realized what had happened. The NSC was able to trace the last call to a pay phone in Augusta, Georgia. By the time authorities got there, there was no sign of Belden.

"You don't understand," said Hirshberg. "There are important policy issues here. Matters of immense strategic concern."

"I would hope," said Joselyn. "The man tried to kill a few thousand people in your city. Hell. He tried to destroy the entire government. He managed to kill some good people on that island. And . . ." She looked at the Air Force plane with its cargo door still open.

"I don't understand how you can just let him go," she said.

"We are not letting him go," said Hirshberg. "He is as good as dead."

"Really." Joselyn looked at him, incredulous. "What's he going to die of, old age?"

A chill wind swept across the runway as jet engines screamed their high-pitched whine in the background.

"Why haven't I seen his name in the papers? A picture? You have one. Or has the president lost it?" said Joselyn.

Hirshberg took a deep breath and stared off in another direction. She was waiting for an answer.

"There once was a man named Dean Belden, or Thorn, or a dozen other names, none of which we're sure of. But he died in a plane crash near Seattle." Hirshberg found it impossible to look at her as he said it.

It was breathtaking. She stared up at the side of his face as he looked off into the distance at nothing in particular, then spoke the only words she could think of. "I don't believe it. You people are incredible."

"Joselyn, you have to understand what is happening here. The men on that island in the sound may have paid for Belden's services, but they didn't hire him."

Joselyn looked at him.

"There is no way they could have raised the money needed to pay for an intact nuclear device," said Hirshberg. "Maybe some fissile materials, a chemical bomb, but not a nuclear device. Not with the expertise needed to make sure that it would function as designed. Gideon knew that," he told her.

"Then who?"

"That's the question no one wants to answer," said Hirshberg.

"I don't understand."

"The United States government has a long-standing policy of maximum retaliation," said Hirshberg. "Any foreign nation that employs or attempts to employ a weapon of mass destruction on U.S. soil would face retaliation of a similar kind.

"Don't you see? We're not anxious to find Mr. Belden. At least not through any public channels of law enforcement. If we do, we run the risk of discovering the link between Belden and whoever sponsored his activities.

"If the government ever made a public acknowledgment that it knew who was behind that device, who paid for it and who hired the man you knew as Dean Belden, then national honor and credibility would require that we do something about it."

"What if the bomb had gone off?" said Joselyn. "Would you continue to stick your head in the sand?"

"If the bomb had gone off, it would have become someone else's problem," said Hirshberg.

"So we have a policy that we're afraid to carry out."

"The consequences for this nation and the world were that

to happen are too horrific to contemplate," said Hirshberg. "In such cases, ignorance is bliss."

"And in the meantime, Belden just walks away," said Joselyn.

"I would not wish to be in his shoes," said Hirshberg. "Whoever hired him, he took their money, and he failed. What's worse for Mr. Belden, he is now a very dangerous loose end in a game of nuclear brinkmanship. If he were to fall into the wrong hands, and if his story were to be made public in ways that it could not be denied . . ." With his furrowed brows, Hirshberg put an expression on the face of the obvious.

"His employers are not going to be anxious to have him wandering around. No," said Hirshberg. "If I were Lloyd's of London, I would not be writing any policy on Mr. Belden's life."

EPILOGUE

CHIAPAS, MEXICO

It was a small café with three tables in the sun out near the street. There were strains of mariachi music in the distance, signs that a wedding had just concluded at the Catholic church two short streets away.

The man had a growth of beard and straggly hair, an old Mexican blanket cut at the fold and worn so that his head went through the hole in the center and the blanket rested on his shoulders.

He had weathered three attacks on his life in the last month, killing one of his assailants with a knife and another with his hands. The third assassin planted a bomb that did not go off until he found it under the seat of his own car.

He carried a pistol tucked in his belt under the serape, and his gaze never rested in one place for long.

He had friends, but they no longer slept near him at night or rode with him in the same vehicles.

The Americans were relentless. They had eyes and ears everywhere. They may not have maintained diplomatic relations with some of the countries of the Middle East, but a note like this, detailing his whereabouts, they would willingly slip under a door.

He would have to leave Mexico soon, and he knew it. His funds were running out, and the local guerrillas were not going to hide him for much longer. The numbered accounts in Europe had been frozen. He saw the deft fingers of the American State Department visible in this.

By now he should have been lying on a private beach in Bali, sipping coconut milk and rum, earning 30 percent on his money. Instead they were hunting for him, his dreams of retirement, if not destroyed, certainly deferred.

He opened the U.S. newspaper. It was yellow with age, a copy of the *Santa Crista Herald*. It was three months old and spattered with oil from a hundred baked tortillas. Some of the pages were missing and others were torn, but he carried it like a relic.

He slapped it on the table as he ate and looked at the photo under the fold on page three. It was not much of a story, only four inches, along with a two-column photo of a group of people standing in front of a bronze plaque embedded in the wall of a Spanish Colonial bungalow.

It was a monument to a Dutchman named Gideon van Ry, awarded by an organization known as the Institute Against Mass Destruction.

He was not interested in the plaque, or the story that was sparse on details, but in the woman standing on the chair, lifting the cloth that had covered the bronze shield.

The image of her face was grainy and smaller than the nail of his small finger. The tips of her blond hair danced just off her shoulders in the wind as her eyes darted toward the lens, as if the photographer had caught her by surprise.

It wasn't much of a picture, but there was not a doubt in Thorn's mind that it was Joselyn Cole.

She had walked away from the house on Padget Island, how he would never know. Thorn had left her for dead on two occasions, and twice she had come back to haunt him.

His gaze burned a hole through the yellowing photograph on the table. She had cost him twenty million dollars and a life of ease. Now he would have to work again and watch his back while he did it.

He chewed with determination as he looked at the photograph and tried to imagine the expression on her face if she ever saw him again.